MY BEST FRIEND'S BRIDE

Ginny Baird

MY BEST FRIEND'S BRIDE

Published by
Winter Wedding Press

Edited by Martha Trachtenberg
Proofread by Sally Knapp
Cover by Dar Albert

About the Author

From the time she could talk, romance author Ginny Baird was making up stories, much to the delight—and consternation—of her family and friends. By grade school, she'd turned that inclination into a talent, whereby her teacher allowed her to write and produce plays rather than write boring book reports. Ginny continued writing throughout college, where she contributed articles to her literary campus weekly, then later pursued a career managing international projects with the U.S. State Department.

Ginny has held an assortment of jobs, including schoolteacher, freelance fashion model, and greeting card writer, and has published more than twenty works of fiction and optioned ten screenplays. She has also published short stories, nonfiction, and poetry, and admits to being a true romantic at heart.

Ginny is a *New York Times* and *USA Today* Bestselling Author of several books, including novellas in her Holiday Brides Series. She's a member of Romance Writers of America (RWA), the RWA Published Authors Network (PAN), and Virginia Romance Writers (VRW).

When she's not writing, Ginny enjoys cooking, biking, and spending time with her family in Tidewater, Virginia. She loves hearing from her readers and welcomes visitors to her website at http://www.ginnybairdromance.com.

Books by Ginny Baird

Holiday Brides Series
The Christmas Catch
The Holiday Bride
Mistletoe in Maine
Beach Blanket Santa
Baby, Be Mine

Summer Grooms Series
Must-Have Husband
My Lucky Groom
The Wedding Wish
The Getaway Groom

Paranormal Romance
The Ghost Next Door (A Love Story)
The Light at the End of the Road

Romantic Comedy
Real Romance
The Sometime Bride
Santa Fe Fortune
How to Marry a Matador
Counterfeit Cowboy
The Calendar Brides
My Best Friend's Bride

Bundles
The Holiday Brides Collection (Books 1–4)
A Summer Grooms Selection (Books 1–3)
Real Romance and The Sometime Bride (Gemini Edition)
Santa Fe Fortune and How to Marry a Matador (Gemini Edition)
Wedding Bells Bundle

Short Stories
The Right Medicine (Short Story and Novel Sampler)
Special Delivery (A Valentine's Short Story)

Ginny Baird's

MY BEST FRIEND'S BRIDE

Chapter One

Jillian Jamison strode off the tennis court feeling disconcerted. She'd bested Brad at singles, and normally would have relished her victory. The trouble was that Brad hadn't made it much of a match. Generally, his returns were hard and his serves were fierce. Today, he'd scarcely made an effort. Jill eyed him sideways, wondering what was up.

Brad dabbed his brow with the towel draped around his neck. "Nice job!"

"Hmm, yes." She bent to tuck her racket into its bag. "Almost amazing."

Brad shrugged, sweat glistening inside his open collar. He had a nice physique and a muscled chest. Too bad Jill wasn't drawn to it. That would make things *so much easier.* He grinned and dimples settled on either side of his mouth beneath a mop of sandy-colored hair. "What can I say? You're a natural."

Jill smirked. "And you're a natural-born liar. Okay, Brad. I'll bite. What are you hiding?"

His face fell in a wounded fashion, but Jill silently called his bluff. She'd known Brad Tate since the second grade, when his family had moved in across the street from hers. They'd gone to grade school together, and had taken swimming and tennis lessons together—right here at this very club. Later, he'd been shipped off to prep school but they'd kept in touch. And now, as fate would have it, they were getting married. *Well, no, not really. Fate's got nothing to do with it.*

"You're always so suspicious," he said. "You know I enjoy winning just as much as you do."

"Uh-huh."

"You've just really got your game on today."

"Right."

"I've never seen you in finer form."

Jill adjusted the headband that swept back her dark bangs and narrowed her eyes.

A grin tickled the edges of his mouth. "Come on, Jilly. Take a compliment."

"All right. If that's how you want to play it."

She was irritated with Brad for about a billion reasons, not the least of which was his throwing this game. Lately, he'd been acting funny. Reticent, almost. Like he was having doubts about going through with it. She started to walk away from him, but he stopped her, laying a hand on her arm. "Okay, all right. You've got me," he admitted. "You and I do need to talk, but not here."

She studied his eyes, questioning. They stared back at her with compassion and concern. "Let me buy you a drink at the grill."

Jill checked her watch. "It's ten in the morning."

"Bloody Mary?" he said, knowing she'd be tempted.

Jill twisted her lips, thinking this must be bad. Worse than bad.

When she didn't answer, Brad pressed, "Champagne mimosa?"

Jill heaved a sigh, deciding she needed to keep her wits about her. "I'll take coffee. Sounds like I might need a double shot."

Jill set her cup down so fast it clattered against the saucer. "You want me to *what*?"

Brad leaned forward to hush her. "Jilly, folks are gawking."

She blinked, spying heads swiveled in her direction. Everyone was dressed in tennis or golf attire. Some *were* already drinking Bloody Marys and mimosas. Now she wished she'd ordered one as well. Maybe one of each!

"I didn't say that you had to," he went on. "I'm just asking you to think about it."

She was certain she'd misheard him. "About marrying your best friend?"

To her astonishment, Brad nodded.

"But I thought—" Her voice cracked, rising a decibel. She caught herself and continued in a whisper. "I was marrying *you*."

"Of course, you're marrying me," he hissed back. "That's what we agreed."

Oh no, now she felt the *but* coming.

"But…"

Zing! There it was! Jill bit into her bottom lip.

"Yes, Brad?"

"Here's the thing." He grimaced, apology in his eyes. "It's Susan."

"What about her?"

"She's getting cold feet."

"She's not the one getting married."

"I guess that's kind of the point." He took her hand on the small tabletop. "Hey, you know that I love you."

Yeah, she loved him too. Just not *like that*. He knew it. She knew it, and both totally agreed. They were practically family, for goodness' sake. This was all about their deal. "Brad, what are you saying? That you're not going through with it?" She gasped, grasping the calamity of the situation. "The wedding's only six weeks away."

"That's the great part," he said. "The invitations haven't gone out yet."

"Deposits have been paid."

"For the caterer and reception, yes. But the date can be changed without losing that money."

Jill folded her face in her hands. They were in too deep to pull out now. She looked up, meeting Brad's eyes. "Did you explain it to her? About the circumstances, and how we'll have separate rooms?"

"Of course. But Jilly, it wasn't enough." He dropped his voice back into a whisper. "She freaked when she saw the dress."

"What dress?"

"*The* dress, and you in it. Made the society page of the paper."

Jill's mind flashed back over the arrangements they'd made with the wedding planner. She'd been so caught up with other preparations, she'd failed to check last Sunday's edition for the engagement announcement. As far as Jill knew, Brad had briefed his girlfriend, Susan, on their entire agreement. Up until now, she'd been fine with it. It was only for a year, after all, and there was so much at stake. Jill stared at Brad, agape.

"I can't believe you're backing out now, and letting me down this way."

"Don't you see? I'm trying to fix it!"

"By having me marry *Hunter Delaney*?" She said the name like it was some sort of disease.

"By offering a solution."

"The answer is a definite no."

"You haven't seen him in a long time."

"Thank goodness I haven't had to."

"Hunter's changed, Jilly."

"Sure he has. Next you'll be telling me leopards wear stripes."

"He's not the guy you remember."

"Mostly I recall he had a car. With a big backseat." She gritted her teeth, speaking through them. "He wanted me to get in it."

"We were seniors in high school!"

"Thanks a whole heck of a lot for the prom date."

"You were going to go solo."

"Maybe I should have."

"He never touched you, you said so."

She straightened and wrapped her fingers around her coffee cup. "Doesn't mean he didn't want to."

"Lots of boys wanted to," he told her honestly. "You were one of the hot girls, Jilly. The hot, brainy babes. No one could get next to you. You can't blame a teenage boy for trying."

She huffed. "And this is the man you think can live twelve months under the same roof with a formerly *hot and brainy babe*—in separate rooms?"

"I wouldn't say formerly."

"Flattery will get you nowhere. At this point, I'm ready to lift this tennis racket off the floor and clobber you." She grasped the neck of the bag with her right hand. "I trusted you, Brad!"

He flinched and sat back in his chair. "You know I'd do anything for you, Jilly." He lowered his voice.

"Anything but sacrifice my own happiness. When Susan was cool with everything, I thought, okay… But now?" he said, looking downcast. It was clear that Brad didn't want to disappoint her. Just as it was evident that he couldn't risk losing Susan. Brad was in a tough spot.

Jill suddenly felt like a heel. But this wasn't all about her. There was something in it for Brad too. "What about the money?" she asked him. "Your share?"

He slowly shook his head. "It's not going to mean anything to me without Susan. It was supposed to be for *us*—me and her. A way for us to get started on that dream we've always chased."

Jill sighed, then recited, "Starting a B and B in the San Juan Islands."

"Yeah, that. Only we can't on our teacher salaries, and it would take years to save up." Jill knew Brad came from money, but that he'd never ask his family for help. He still had access to this club only because it was one of his parents' membership perks. His parents had tried to discourage Brad from going into high-school teaching, hoping his expensive education would pay off in a more lucrative job. They'd never really approved of his decisions, including his romantic interest in Susan Miller, a fellow math teacher at Brad's school. The only time they'd gotten the tiniest bit excited about his choices was when he'd announced he was marrying bestselling writer and international personality Jillian Jamison. Their pride and admiration lasted as long as it took to explain the marriage was a sham. At that point they reverted to being *extremely disappointed in him.*

Maybe if she closed her eyes and counted to ten this would all go away. Just last week, things had been on track. "I don't get it," she said. "Susan no longer wants the money?"

"She says she no longer wants the *stupid San Juan Islands*—her words, not mine; between you and me, I still think they're great. It's just they're suddenly not so important anymore. Neither is that wad of cash, which Susan now calls tainted…foul. Ill-gotten gains. She's scared that if I go through with this, it will curse our relationship forever. No matter how far away we move, we'll never outrun its stench. Plus, she *was* visibly upset about seeing you in the dress. It made it all so real."

Ill-gotten gains? That sounded more like Susan's mother talking than Susan. Susan's mom was a retired English teacher. "Susan talked to her mom, didn't she?"

"Yeah, but that's the only person, I swear!"

This web of deceit was growing larger by the minute. Jill absolutely had to keep this under wraps or the whole thing would fall apart. Brad's parents knew the truth; so did Susan and her mom. Who would be next?

"Don't look now," Brad cautioned. "Here comes trouble."

Jill glanced at the door to see Cassandra Evans approaching, her short golf skirt swishing from side to side. "Well, well," she purred. "Look what the cat dragged in. Two little lovebirds."

Brad smiled tightly above the rim of his cup. "Morning, Cassandra."

She barely acknowledged him, turning her attention on Jill. "Saw the engagement announcement in the paper, so I guess it's official." She fanned manicured fingernails across the air in front of her with a dramatic sweep. "'The Lady Matchmaker Takes a

Groom.' *And*," she added bitingly, "*for more than six weeks!*"

"It never said—" Brad started before Jill cut him off.

"I'm sorry that it pains you." Jill frowned sympathetically at Cassandra. "That I'm marrying first."

Cassandra straightened on long, tanned legs. "That part doesn't worry me in the least," she lied. She folded her arms in front of her and cocked her blond head, her bob bouncing. "I'm much more interested in your next book." She homed in on Jill's eyes. "What's it about?"

Jill's words were clipped. "Probably not you, Cassandra."

"Oooh, being evasive, are we?" She scrutinized Brad up and down, and he squirmed in his chair, uncomfortable with her perusal. Jill waited expectantly for her next barb, trying to think up something witty to say. Anything to drive this woman away. Cassandra Evans, her nemesis. The one who'd picked on her since the ninth grade. And who'd lost to Jill as senior class president. And who'd come in a close second to Jill's valedictorian. Cassandra, who'd aspired to write great literature but now worked for a gossip magazine, the sort that spied on celebrities with long-lens cameras.

"Don't you have someone to interview, Cassandra?" Brad to the rescue!

She narrowed her eyes at Jill. "I'm much more interested in the discussion right here, and this sudden cacophony of wedding bells. How *sweet* that you've known each other forever—
almost like a brother and sister—and now you're getting hitched. Have you carried a torch all that time?"

"Brad and I were just leaving." Jill pushed back her chair, but Cassandra reached out and grabbed it, settling her claws on its high back.

"Don't think I don't know something's up with this little wedding deal." She cut a glance at Brad. "And, I'm going to find out *what.*"

Jill watched Cassandra stride away, her heart pounding.

"Don't let her get to you," Brad said. "She doesn't know anything."

"Yeah? And what will she think if I switch grooms?"

"That you've done better? Traded up?"

"Brad, *puh-leeze*... Don't let me down." She reached out and gripped both his hands in hers. "Pretty please, with jalapeños on top!"

"Stop trying to play to my weakness."

Jill fought back the heat in her eyes, thinking of her grandfather. "What about mine?"

He squeezed her hands in his. "I'm suggesting a solution, Jill. One that can work for all of us."

"Oh, great. And your *solution* has me play-marrying a guy I can't stand?"

"Play is the operative word there, as in pretend. Besides, how do know you still won't like him? You haven't seen Hunter in nearly twelve years."

Jill felt trapped, as if Brad had painted her into a corner. There was no way out that wouldn't leave messy tracks everywhere. If she didn't marry soon, she'd lose her book advance money. Without that, she couldn't help her grandpa. But this wasn't just anybody they were talking about as a replacement for Brad! Famed womanizer Hunter Delaney had recently moved to neighboring Parkland. He'd graduated from prep school with Brad, then had gone to an Ivy League college prior to accepting a job on Wall Street. Now, he was in business marketing of some sort and had taken a position at a prestigious advertising firm in the city abutting Sugar Hollow. It didn't matter if he'd improved himself professionally. Personally, Hunter was still a lout. Word was, he'd left a trail of broken hearts from Boston to Brooklyn. Who knew how many other women he'd crushed on his way here? No way was Jill sidling up next to him at the altar. Pretend or not. Not for any amount of money.

"Absolutely not," she stated firmly. "No way, no how."

Brad released her hands, then dropped his bombshell. "That's too bad. Hunter will be bummed."

Jill's jaw dropped so fast it nearly smacked the table. "You mean you've talked to him?"

Brad reached into his gym bag on the floor and pulled something from it. He nodded and extended an envelope in her direction. "Signed, sealed, delivered... He's yours."

Chapter Two

One week earlier, Hunter Delaney had set down the paperwork and looked up at his best friend. "No way, no how, buddy. No can do."

"I've already explained, it's for a good cause."

Hunter shrugged his broad shoulders. "Not my fault the girl's got career problems."

"You do recall who we're talking about, right? Jill Jamison? *The* Jillian Jamison."

"Hard to miss. She's in the media all the time." Hunter absently stared at the door through which two attractive women had just entered. They were obviously alone, and definitely prowling. Their eyes panned the sports bar in a predatory fashion, until the redhead found Hunter. He gave her a slow, sexy smile, then quipped sotto voce, "I'll take the redhead, you can have Goldilocks."

"I'm taken."

"Yeah, twice." He turned back to Brad and lightly shoved his shoulder. "Maybe you should ease up on that. Having a fiancée and a mistress doesn't look good. Not when one of them's a…" He spoke in a conspiratorial whisper. "…*relationship expert.*"

"I'm sorry," a woman's voice said. "Do I know you?"

Hunter turned to see the gorgeous redhead standing by their table. "I couldn't help but notice you," she continued. Pretty dark eyes sparkled, indicating interest. "You look *so* familiar."

Brad abruptly scraped back his chair and stood.

"That's because he's about to become a family man."

"Huh?"

Brad tugged at Hunter's arm, but Hunter pulled back. "Hey!"

Brad leveled a look at the redhead and spoke with conviction. "You know how some guys are. Just can't get enough."

She went pale.

Brad tried again, locking his grip on Hunter's bicep. "Come on, lover boy. A wedding rehearsal awaits!"

"Wedding?" Her voice was shrill. "Well, I never meant to…" She took a few hurried steps backward. "What I mean is… Gosh! Engaged? Are you, really?"

Hunter stood and straightened his trousers. "I…? No!"

The blonde, who'd been watching from nearby, rushed to her friend's defense. "Come on, Glenda," she said, hooking her by the elbow. "He's one of *those*."

Hunter exhaled audibly as the women walked away, occasionally turning to shoot disgusted looks at him over their shoulders. "Thanks, Brad. Thanks a lot."

"You'll be thanking me a heck of a lot more, once all of this is over."

"Oh?" He was totally unconvinced.

Brad scooped the paperwork off the table and shoved it at his chest.

"Just read the fine print."

It was Sunday, one of the days Jill customarily paid a visit to her grandfather. She also came on Wednesdays for lunch. When he'd been feeling better, she'd taken him out on little getaways from the retirement home in her car. Sometimes they ate at restaurants. Frequently, they picked up carry-out and went to the park. Gordon Jamison loved being outdoors. Now that his health had declined even further, their excursions had been reduced to visiting the interior courtyard of his building. She parked his wheelchair beside the butterfly garden, where a half dozen monarchs fluttered. "Beautiful, aren't they?"

He took her hand between his wrinkled palms and patted it. "Just about as pretty as you are."

"Thanks, Grandpa." She smiled softly. "You always did have kind words for the ladies."

"Yes," he replied wistfully. "Especially your grandmother." He glanced around expectantly past the shrubs and budding azaleas. "Where is she? Coming soon?"

Jill's heart ached as she fibbed. "Any minute."

She sat on a cool stone bench to watch a cardinal couple taking turns at a birdfeeder. She couldn't imagine how tough getting by without his wife must be for her grandfather. The two had stayed committed to each other through a long, loving marriage, and the delivery of one precious child: Jill's late mom. She hung her head, grateful for her memories, even the ones that pained her. At the age of twenty-seven, she'd lost both her parents within a year, her dad from heart failure and her mom from an incurable infection following a routine surgery. Neither death was anticipated and both had hit her hard. She was alone in the world now, except for her grandfather. Perhaps it was a blessing that, in his mind, he still had all of them.

"How are your parents doing?" he asked her. "They never come to see me anymore."

"They want to, and they will," she lied sweetly. "Just as soon as they get back from their trip."

"That's right," he said, but his expression was muddied. "I remember now. Alaska, was it?"

"Nebraska," she answered, referring to the last couples trip her parents had taken together. They were always doing things like that. Setting off on unusual adventures.

"Forget Paris, France!" her mom had chirped. *"We're hitting Rhome, Texas!"*

Jill's dad had chuckled his reply. *"Yee-haw, cowgirl!"*

Her parents' unabashed affection for one another had embarrassed her then. In retrospect, Jill was glad she had that type of exchange to remember them by. Though the time they'd shared together was cut short, they'd made the most of what they'd had. Besides that, they'd been mighty good parents. The only thing they hadn't prepared for was dying early and leaving their finances in a wreck. Her dad had planned to work for several more years, and enjoyed a lifestyle he figured his future earnings would support. When Jill's parents had passed, they'd been in debt up to their eyeballs. It had taken settling their entire estate to pay off the creditors, and there wasn't enough left over to provide for her grandfather for more than a few years. Jill had taken that upon herself, but gladly and with a whole heart. She loved her grandpa dearly.

"You're looking a little down today," he said keenly. "Is something wrong?"

"Just work worries," Jill replied, lifting a shoulder. "Those come and go."

"Well, you best tell your agent to make them scat! Have her tell that cranky publisher of yours that you're a world-famous author, ya hear? I've seen you on the television. All of us have." He was referring to himself and his fellow residents at the home. They had a large common area where they watched the evening news and the contemporary entertainment shows that followed. Jill's expertise as a relationship guru had been touted numerous times, thanks to the success of her bestselling first book, *Love Like You Mean It.* Her second book hadn't done as well. Now, if she didn't score big with this third one, she'd be out of a contract, and out of money—with no way to help her grandfather.

If she went back to her former job as a couples counselor, she'd only earn a fraction of what she did now in royalties, advances, and speaking engagement fees. Not nearly enough to pay the bills for this place. She glanced around at the gurgling fountains and pretty palmettos hedging the walkways. It was lovely and serene. Most important, her grandfather was settled here and had come to think of it as his home. "Don't you worry about it, Grandpa," she told him kindly. "Everything will work out fine. It always does."

They talked awhile longer about the weather, other residents who were his friends, how the food here was improving thanks to the new chef, and Jill's most recent book tour. Soon, the afternoon sun began to fade and Jill realized she should be pushing on. Though he always enjoyed their visits, and looked forward to them, it was clear that even her company became taxing after a point. As if on cue, a nurse arrived to tend to his personal care and wheel him to supper. "Will you be joining us in the dining room?" she inquired of Jill.

Sometimes Jill stayed, but tonight she had too much on her mind. She declined politely, saying she'd love to next time.

Jill stood and hugged her grandpa's shoulders, planting a kiss on his head. "You're such a good girl. So sweet to visit." He lightly patted her back. "Who did you say you are again? Friend of the family?"

She kept her voice steady and forced a smile. "A very close friend."

"Will you come back, then?"

"I'll be here on Wednesday."

His whole face brightened. "That's terrific! I'll introduce you to Rose," he said, naming his late wife. "I know she'd love to meet you."

Jill pursed her lips and gave a slight nod. When she spoke, the words scraped from her throat. "I'd like that." After bidding him so long, she turned and headed for the exit. As she did, the fat tears she'd been holding in broke free. Jill didn't dare lift a hand to dry them. She could feel her grandpa's eyes on her…watching her walk away. Sometimes life was harsh. Or as Morgan was fond of saying, *brutal*, Jill thought, recalling her last conversation with her agent.

Morgan Swift leaned across the small café table and frowned. She had light brown hair with frosted tips, and highlighted her petite figure with a jacket and matching slacks. She was approaching forty but looked ten years younger, except for when those worry lines surrounding her eyes deepened. Like they were doing now. "You're not going to like this, Jill, but I'm going to be brutal."

Jill slowly lowered her glass of Chablis. When Morgan had asked her to lunch, she should have expected an ambush. Instead, she'd hoped they'd be celebrating Jill's third book deal getting finalized.

"I hate to break the news," Morgan continued, "but your numbers on *Long-Term Love: Making It Last* weren't…encouraging. In fact, they kind of stunk."

Jill knew it hadn't performed as well as the first book, because it hadn't hit any major lists. Still, she'd thought it had done reasonably well. She'd been on talk shows, done interviews… "But I thought the presales were—"

"Mediocre at best." Morgan dropped her voice an octave. "That write-up in *Tempo Beat* sure didn't help."

Jill let the word slip out on an exasperated breath. "Cassandra."

"You can't entirely shoot the messenger," Morgan said. "A 'relationship expert' who can't keep a boyfriend of her own for more than six weeks *is* kind of news."

"That's not news! It's gossip!"

"Is what the article alleges true? Do you really start analyzing them by week five?"

Jill set her wine on the table and clasped her hands together in her lap. George Wesley; of course it had to have been him. Maybe Paul Thurston too. Who knew how many of her traitorous exes had spilled to Cassandra on the condition of anonymity? Could have been dozens! She cocked her chin to the side and asked evenly, "Are you with me or against me, Morgan?"

Morgan flinched, apparently affronted. "With you! Of course! It's just that…" She took a hurried sip of wine, then dabbed her lips with a napkin. "I need to know what we're dealing with here."

"I don't get what you're saying."

"I'm asking you if you can do it, Jill. Tackle a relationship for the long haul."

"You're asking me?" Jill staged a laugh. "I wrote the book on relationships, if you'll recall. A number one bestseller!"

"Hmm, yes. One on getting them started."

"What's that supposed to mean?"

"It was the second step, the part about keeping them going, that fizzled out." She shook her head sadly. "I'm going to be honest about this even if it pains you. Because your pain is my pain. We own it together."

Jill understood this was true. As her book agent, Morgan got fifteen percent. But fifteen percent of nothing was zero. Jill's stomach clenched, anticipating the next sock in the gut.

Morgan exhaled sharply. "It wasn't easy to pull this off, because Browning's none too happy," she said referring to Jill's publisher. "In fact, they didn't even *want* a third book, but I insisted. After all, we had a three-book deal.

"The thing is," she continued, "without their full backing, book three doesn't stand a chance. We need marketing support, a dynamite cover, advanced advertising, book tours!" Morgan's eyes shone with passion, and Jill recalled why she'd hired her. Morgan was not only good, she was driven. She was also as smart as a whip.

"So…?" Jill pressed. Morgan had obviously hatched a plan to make this work.

"So…" Her enthusiasm was growing so fast it was almost contagious. "I proposed we take this to the next level. Go all out!"

"Great!" Jill replied, not fully understanding what that meant. "Then they accepted my proposal?"

"Ye-es…" She drew out the word. "But not exactly as it stands."

"What do you mean, not exactly as it stands?"

"There were a few modifications." Morgan stared at her salad plate and started slowly spinning her wineglass by its stem. The goblet completed two revolutions before Morgan raised her eyes and spoke with a pasted-on grin. "Jill!" she said brightly. "You're getting married!"

Jill, who'd begun to take a sip of water, choked. She quickly lowered her glass and covered her mouth with one hand. "What did you say?"

"Married," Morgan stated matter-of-factly. "You really can't get much more long-term than that!"

Jill blinked; her whole world had gone fuzzy. Maybe she was dreaming and none of it was real? She pinched her leg through her skirt just to be sure. *Ow! That smarted!*

"Well, don't just sit there," Morgan complained. "Say something."

Jill set both elbows on the table and stared in disbelief. "That's the most ridiculous thing I've ever heard."

"It's a strategy for saving your career. Don't think I haven't studied this. Considered it from every angle. Jill, this *is* the only way. You've got to rebuild your trust with the public. Book buyers must *believe* you know whereof you speak."

"Yes, but…married?" Jill was still trying to wrap her head around it. "To whom? Did the publisher pick the groom?"

"Of course not. That's your job."

"Awesome."

"The title's been all worked out," Morgan informed her. "*Married Love: Keeping Those Home Fires Burning.* We're betting it will sell like hotcakes." She polished off her wine. "Provided you're actually married, that is."

"But I don't have to be married to write that kind of book. I've had plenty of experience, my background in counseling…case studies."

"No dice. This has to be the real deal. You with a ring on your finger. You've already duped the public once with *Long-Term Love: Making It Last.* They want to hear from *you.* You've got to make this book less clinical, more personal. Jillian Jamison practicing what she preaches!"

Jill's head throbbed. She needed this third book, she really did. She desperately needed the money. That's when a solution hit her. Nobody said she had to stay married forever—just long enough to pull off this project. All she had to do was find a guy to go along with it. That might prove a little tricky, but it certainly wasn't impossible. She already had a candidate in mind.

"How long does it have to last?" she asked. "The marriage?"

Morgan shrugged. "How long do most marriages last these days?"

"Some less than a year."

"That may be pushing it."

Pushing it a little, maybe, but the idea was starting to grow on her. Especially if she could contain it, control it, and make it her own. Jill's mental wheels turned quickly as the strategizing began in her brain. "Think about it, Morgan. I do the wedding, the big buildup…all that. It's agreed. Who can blame me if things go sour some time after? It wouldn't be my fault, or his either, as long as we tried. Just one of those things. Think of the public sympathy we could build. It might even lead to a fourth book, *Love after Love: Amor from the Ashes.*"

"Ew! Are you planning on cremating someone, or getting divorced?"

"Okay, maybe the title needs work."

"I don't know, Jill. That sounds risky. What about book sales?"

"The big push will be prerelease and during release week. I'll do the talk shows, tours—whatever it takes—to build up big numbers by then. By the time my marriage…unfortunately tanks, my book sales will be rocketing! Straight up to the stars." She sure hoped so, anyway. The book would have to earn back the advance and then some for her to cover her own obligations, as well as offer a financial enticement to a fake fiancé.

"And then?"

"With two bestsellers under my belt, I'll be a hot property, won't I? If Browning no longer wants me, I'll go to another publisher. I've got lots of great ideas. The proceeds from this book could tide me over in the meantime, if I'm prepared to give it my all."

Morgan surveyed her cautiously. Why was she acting skeptical? She was the one who'd devised this whole sordid plan. Jill was merely taking the lemons Morgan had thrust at her and making lemonade, using psychology and working things to her advantage. Jill felt her confidence surge. She was fully game-on. She could commit to marriage for a year, of course she could. It was just like accepting any job. All she had to do was hire an assistant…um, partner…in name only! That was clearly better than the alternative, rejecting this arrangement and seeing her grandfather moved to a lesser facility. She knew how her publisher worked. Browning didn't keep deals on the table indefinitely. If she was going to accept, she'd have to move quickly before someone in editorial changed their mind.

"Look, Morgan, I know how to do this. I've learned from the first book—and the second—what does and doesn't work."

"Precisely what the publisher is counting on." Morgan withdrew a contract from her purse and handed it over. "The advance I negotiated is hefty," she said. "You can't mess this up."

"I don't intend to." She unfolded the pages and flipped through them. "Wow, very cool. A much higher percentage on residuals."

Morgan preened like a peacock. "*And* merchandising. We really believe this can go big, Jill. Viral, even. Forget interviews, this could spawn an entire reality TV series!"

"*I'm* not going on television. Not in that way."

"Nobody said you had to. If a series comes out based on your book, it will profile other couples. Maybe couples having relationship troubles. Your words of wisdom will help them bring it all back together. They'll put the advice in your book to use, and the audience can watch as they heal and move forward."

Jill felt as if she'd been steamrollered. Like this idea had taken on a life of its own. Each time she thought she was totally on top of things, Morgan flattened her with something else. "I see."

"You won't have to do a thing about it, other than collect your share of the profits. That's what I'm trying to tell you. This deal is huge. All kinds of potential."

This snowballing arrangement was sounding more doable by the minute. *Potential* was code for big money. And if the sum were large enough, it could easily be shared. Okay, not half-and-half, but she could offer the groom a percentage. Jill knew just the guy in need of cash. He got bonus points for being someone she trusted.

"All I have to do is get married?"

"Yes, and you'd better make it snappy. Browning wants an engagement on the table when you receive your advance money."

"But it's okay if it's"—she hesitated on the word— "fake?"

Morgan lunged forward to grab her wrists. "Shut your mouth and seal those lips! That's the last time I ever want to hear you say that." She spoke in an urgent whisper. "For the rest of the world, it has to look real, all right? For the publisher too. Publicly? In the papers and on camera, you're a pair, all lovey-dovey. Whatever you and your new hubby-to-be do—or don't do—in the privacy of your own home is totally up to you."

Chapter Three

Hunter folded the contract and stuffed it back in its envelope, handing it to Brad. "There's nothing you can say to convince me." Brad sat back in his bucket seat behind the steering wheel. They'd left the bar and were supposedly on their way home. The only thing was that Brad had failed to start his car. "So—what? You're going to hold me hostage until I agree?"

"No. I'm just asking you to think about it," Brad said. "Like a rational person."

Hunter sputtered a laugh. "Nothing about this is rational!"

"Consider it a lease, a living arrangement."

"You're forgetting two very important points: A, I already own my condo and B, I like where I live."

Brad jangled his keys and cranked the ignition. "You think you know a man," he said, shaking his head.

"This is ludicrous, Brad. I can't believe you agreed to it in the first place."

"I already told you, she was desperate."

"Um-hum." Hunter pulled out his shoulder harness and clicked the seatbelt in place.

Brad sprang at him and latched onto his lapels. "Now *I'm* desperate. Can't you see?"

Yep, he could pretty much read that in Brad's eyes. He looked like a cross between a frightened rabbit and a chicken about to get its head lopped off. "I'm sorry, man. I feel for you, I really do. And Susan, but—"

Brad tightened his death grip on Hunter's jacket. If he didn't let go soon, he'd crease it and Hunter would have to get it dry cleaned. "You don't know what it's like. Loving someone like I do her."

"Jill?" Hunter couldn't help but say. He pressed his lips together to keep from smirking.

"No, jerk! Susan!" He released Hunter's suit coat and pushed away.

It was almost scary seeing Brad this way. He appeared borderline crazed, like he might do something unpredictable. It occurred to Hunter that perhaps he should be the one driving.

"I apologize," he said in a placating tone. "I didn't mean to make light of it."

"Yeah. Well, fine! You shouldn't have!" Sweat beaded Brad's forehead and he lifted the oil-checking rag on the console between them to dab it, leaving a black smear on his face. Maybe if Brad didn't drive such an old clunker he wouldn't have to check the oil twice a week. The sad truth was that Brad could use Jill's money far more than Hunter needed it. Financially, Hunter was doing fine.

In a last-ditch effort, Brad shot him a pleading look. "I told you about her grandfather?"

"Heartbreaking," Hunter deadpanned. "Though not my problem either."

"She's really under pressure, Hunter." Brad paused and pursed his lips in thought. "But you can't let on that you know that."

"Why not?"

"It's personal, might embarrass her."

"More personal than getting married?"

"You're not seeing the bigger picture!"

"Yes, I am, and it's a nightmare."

"Yeah, well, I'm living it."

"Maybe you should have thought that out before."

Brad glared at him angrily. "Jeez, guy, do you even have a soul?"

Hunter was fairly tough. Practically made of steel. But ouch, yeah, that pinched a little. Hunter stared at his best friend since the eighth grade. The guy whose skin he'd saved by not ratting Brad out to the headmaster after the two of them had shaving-creamed the chemistry lab. Brad was always coming up with mischievous plans and getting them into trouble. Correct that: Only Hunter got into trouble, because the administration routinely suspected him, the boisterous athlete. Timid Brad, with his keen focus on academics, had been beyond reproach. Hunter had not once squealed on Brad, and had always taken the heat. Even though every single lamebrain scheme had originally been Brad's idea.

In return, Brad had stood by Hunter, year after year, through one woman-disaster after the next. While Brad still didn't believe it, none of those breakups had been Hunter's fault. He hadn't left any of those women; they'd left *him*. The fact of the matter was that he did have a soul, and way down deep it was probably unlovable. It sure didn't know how to love back. Not that his parents had set much of an example in that department. They'd shipped him off to boarding school at fourteen and had never come to visit. Not even on family day. While he was gregarious and confident on the outside, emotionally, Hunter had donned a suit of armor that was impossible for anyone to penetrate. How many upset females had accused him of that before slamming their way out the door? Far more than Hunter cared to count or remember. "I'm not marriage material," he replied dryly. So many women had told Hunter that, and after a while he'd begun to believe it.

"That's what makes this ideal," Brad said. "You and Jill go in with your eyes open. Zero expectations." He shook the envelope in the air between them. "Other than what's written in here."

Hunter gave a weighty sigh and snatched back the envelope. He hated Brad for putting him in this position nearly as much as he disliked seeing Brad on the verge of a breakdown. Brad was the closest thing he had to a brother. A baby brother. The sort who repeatedly got himself into trouble, then required Hunter's help getting out of it. Jill Jamison, of all people. Of course it had to be her. "Okay, I'll think about it," he finally said. "But only for you."

A few days later, Hunter adjusted his red-and-yellow-striped tie in the washroom mirror. It made him look authoritative, not stuffy. In any case, that's what he hoped. He angled his head from side to side and set his jaw in a confident manner. "You've got this," he told his rugged reflection. A flicker of doubt flashed in his dark brown eyes. He cleared his throat and tried again, speaking more surely. His voice resonated in a deep baritone as he gave himself a steady thumbs-up. "You've got this."

A commode flushed and his coworker Fred Forester popped out of the bathroom stall behind him. "Got what? Catch something touching the toilet?"

Hunter startled, leaning forward to grip the edges of the basin. "Fred! Didn't know anyone was in here."

"Obviously." Fred stood at the sink beside him, washing his hands. He addressed Hunter's reflection in his mirror. "You're up for the big promotion, I hear."

"Word gets around."

"Sure does," Fred said smugly. Did Hunter imagine it, or was Fred appearing full of himself, like he knew something Hunter didn't? Then again, that was just Fred. Always one-upping everyone in the office. He was a few years younger than Hunter, but others viewed him as twice as ambitious. That's because Fred was very *obvious* in his aspirations, whereas Hunter tended to purposely underplay his.

"I wouldn't worry about it too much," Hunter told him. "I'm sure your turn's coming soon."

Fred dried his hands with a paper towel, then tossed it into the wastebasket, straightening on his reed-thin frame. "No doubt," he said flippantly. Then he turned and walked away, leaving Hunter with a sinking feeling. If Hunter was about to get good news, why did he sense the other shoe was about to drop?

Hunter's boss, Maxwell Abrams, crossed his ankle over one knee and started making small circular motions in the air with his expensive Italian loafer. Rather than remaining behind his desk, he'd joined Hunter in his office's sitting area. They now sat catty-corner in sleek leather chairs facing a low Lucite table. It held sketches of all kinds and mock-ups for new campaigns. Old man Abrams never stopped working, which was why he was rumored to need help. Word was that he sought an entrepreneurial partner to take under his wing and groom for taking over the business one day. Hunter hoped that man would be him. He'd worked hard and had landed some major accounts for the firm. Dollar for dollar, his efforts had certainly generated more revenue than Fred had brought in.

"You know I respect you as a worker," Abrams said, his silvery hair catching glimmers of sunlight through the window.

"Yes, sir. I appreciate that."

"You've got a keen eye where marketing is concerned, and that financial background of yours has only been a boon to the company."

"Thank you. It's a pleasure working here."

Abrams met his eyes. "I believe you'll go far someday."

Hunter's stomach clenched. *Someday? What about now?*

"But I'm sure you're aware," Abrams went on, "that a very big deal is at stake."

"Kaleidoscope Kids, yes, sir. I'm aware of it. Actually, I've been studying their prospectus, devising a plan—"

Abrams held up his hands. "I've got to explain this is a major account. Huge, Hunter. Landing it could completely change the financial face of this company, give us a whole new direction."

Hunter angled toward him and set his elbows on his knees. "That's why I'm determined to do everything I can to land it, sir. Just give me the word, and I'll bring that puppy home."

Abrams smiled wryly and shook his head. "That *puppy,* as you call it, is only interested in working with one kind of master."

"I'm sorry, sir?"

Abrams pressed his broad palms together. "Kaleidoscope is about kids, Hunter. *Family.* They want someone who understands that, inside out, to design the campaign. Now, I know Fred Forester is a little younger than you…"

Fred Forester? No way! He didn't have half the experience Hunter did. Plus, he was more than a little bit of a jerk. "Fred, sir?" Hunter was embarrassed to hear his voice squeak.

Abrams looked him straight in the eye. "Fred's married, and they like that. They want someone on their team who understands commitment…someone with the right frame of mind.

"Fred and Penny have been married five years. And now…" The loafer bobbed up and down. Yeah, here came the other shoe. "They're expecting a baby."

Hunter drew a breath. He had no idea Fred was about to become a dad. Hunter couldn't help but feel sympathy for the child. More than that, he felt sorry for himself. Fred Forester being positioned as his boss? That wouldn't just be uncomfortable for Hunter, it could prove disastrous for the whole office. While pretty much everyone got along with Hunter, nobody could stand Fred. What kind of supervisor would he make? Hunter couldn't believe there wasn't a way to turn this thing around. "Mr. Abrams, if you'll just give me a chance. Maybe let me talk to the Kaleidoscope people myself—"

"I'm sorry, Hunter." His look was sincere. "It's already been decided. I talked to Fred this morning and he accepted."

Of course he did, the snake! Hunter spoke frankly, because he didn't see any reason not to. "I'm really sorry to hear that, sir, because I honestly feel I'm the best man for the job. The best ad man for Kaleidoscope and the best manager for this company. I've got great leadership skills. You've seen them in action."

"Yes, and I admire that about you. Which is why I'm bringing you on board as Fred's right-hand man. He'll need someone with your talents to assist him."

The situation was going from bad to unbearable. Work directly under Fred? Hunter would have to leave the company first. The thing was, Hunter *liked* Abrams Advertising, and he'd given it his all. In the past year, he'd built relationships here, with his clients and with the staff. He couldn't just throw all that away. Nor could he stand the thought of Fred being in charge. He made one last desperate plea. "Is there nothing I can say to change your mind?"

Abrams gave a noncommittal laugh. "Only that you're getting married." He uncrossed his legs and stood. "But with a lone wolf like you, we both know that's not going to happen any time soon."

Hunter leapt to his feet, unable to stop the words that flew from his mouth. "Mr. Abrams!"

Max slowly turned his way.

"It already is!"

Abrams stared at Hunter agape. "Excuse me?"

Perspiration built at Hunter's hairline and slicked the back of his neck.

"I'm getting married," he reported evenly.

Max's brow shot up. "That so? When?"

"Soon, sir. Very soon."

Abrams sat back in his chair, apparently stunned by this turn of events. "And…who's the lucky girl?"

Hunter sucked in a breath, then spilled it. "Jillian Jamison."

"The relationship expert?" For some reason Abrams appeared amused. "But I thought she was marrying someone else. My wife, Diane, was just saying last Sunday she'd seen it in the—"

"*Was*, sir. As in, past tense. Let's just say it didn't work out."

Abrams was unable to mask the skepticism in his voice. "And Ms. Jamison decided to pencil you in? As a…replacement?"

"It's a tad more involved than that. Jill and I have known each other since high school," Hunter said. "This, um…attraction has been brewing under the surface for years."

Abrams studied him curiously. "I see. And you love this girl?"

"Almost as much as I love myself." Hunter called himself up short, realizing how awful that had sounded. "What I mean is—"

"I must say this comes as a surprise." Abrams brought a hand to his chin and sat still for a moment. When he met Hunter's eyes, he asked, "So you and your long-lost flame, Jillian Jamison, are determined to make this work? A full-fledged marriage?"

Hunter nodded numbly, not admitting he intended to make it work for just a year. Hey, many marriages only lasted that long. Why should his and Jill's be any different? By the time their agreement concluded, Hunter would be well on his way to proving himself a valuable asset at Abrams, and Fred would be caught up with baby duty.

"Well, in that case... It appears there's only one thing left for me to say." Abrams shot to his feet and held out his hand. "Welcome to my personal team, Hunter. I can't wait to see your ideas for Kaleidoscope Kids. If they're half as good as I've got a hunch they'll be, we'll lock down that account in no time. By this time next year, I might even be calling you *partner.*"

Hunter pumped Max's hand with a firm handshake. "Thank you, sir. You won't regret giving me this opportunity."

"I'm happy for the company, I really am. But mostly..." Abrams released his hand and slapped him on the shoulder. "I'm happy for you. Such wonderful news! Congratulations to you and Jill!"

Five minutes later, Hunter was back in the washroom and on his cell, furiously typing a text. He had to meet with Brad and get this deal sealed before something went wrong. He hit *send* just as someone walked into the room.

"Writing to Mommy with the bad news?"

Hunter looked up from where he leaned against the wall to see Fred standing before him. "In here again, Fred? Got some kind of condition?"

"Beats what you've got." Fred smirked. "Sore loser syndrome."

"Oh, I wouldn't be so quick to call a victory yet."

Fred paused midway into a stall, holding the door slightly ajar between them. "What's that supposed to mean?"

Hunter shrugged and shoved his cell into his pocket without giving Fred the satisfaction of a reply. It was up to Abrams to break the news, after all. All Hunter had to do now was confirm that Jill Jamison was fully on board. Of course, Brad had already assured him she would be.

Chapter Four

"You have got to be kidding me," Jill exclaimed, meeting Brad's eyes. They were still at the grill in their tennis clothes and Brad had just finished telling her how he'd explained her situation to Hunter roughly a week ago. Hunter had been so taken with Brad's story—and concerned by Jill's predicament with her publisher—that he'd naturally agreed to step right in. Hunter really had changed a lot, Brad assured her. No matter what she believed of him in the past, he was a true gentleman now. Jill stared down at the contract on the table, noting that Hunter had made several corrections with a bright red pen. If she didn't know better, she'd swear she was looking at some hapless high-school English student's first-term paper. Some of these changes were untenable. Hunter wanted *how much bigger* of a cut? "What's Hunter thinking?"

"That everything in life is negotiable?"

Jill answered combatively. "The things in my life aren't."

"Hey, don't shoot the messenger."

"Why does everybody keep saying that?" she asked, reliving her earlier conversation with Morgan, the one that had landed her in this crazy position. *Am I*

*actually perusing a contract between me and Hunter
Delaney? A marriage contract?*

"Look, Jill. It's all going to work out. Hunter really
wants it to. So he made a few minor tweaks to the—?"

Jill's brow rose with suspicion. "What do you
mean, 'He really wants it to'? What's in it for him?"
She didn't know why, but something in her gut said
things weren't exactly adding up, including Brad's
assertion that Hunter had suddenly morphed into a
gentleman.

Brad fidgeted with his coffee cup.

"Brad…?" she pressed.

"You can see for yourself! You're the one who
added the clauses! Ten percent of residuals, and…"
Brad blinked twice, like he always did when he was
lying. "Fifty percent of the advance money."

"The deal was twenty, Brad. Twenty percent. How
did that more than double?"

Brad sank back in his chair. "I'm afraid you'll have
to take that up with him."

"You can just bet I will. This is ridiculous."

She started to stand, but Brad stopped her. "Just
one more thing."

Jill took a breath, prepared for anything.

Brad spit it out quickly like he was afraid to say it.
"He wants you to move into his place, not the other way
around."

That was really crossing the line. From what she'd
heard, Hunter owned a cramped condo in the city. Jill
had a spacious country cottage with room for her pets to
roam. For all she knew, Hunter's condo didn't even
allow pets! Jill had so much on her mind already, she
couldn't tolerate one more complication. Her grandpa's
retirement home had called this morning. Their rates

were going up and they wanted to make sure Jill was renewing the assisted living agreement. There were several people on the waiting list, all of whom were prepared to make early deposits, if Jill found herself unable to. As her last bill was several weeks past due, the director found it necessary to press the point. Either she paid her balance soon—*and* a large deposit toward her grandpa's next year—or her grandfather was out. Jill didn't even know where she could move him at this stage. Most nice retirement places required residents to enter when they were still eligible for independent living.

"He says he'll keep covering utilities," Brad continued. Jill's blood pumped harder and her head ached. *There are more conditions? Seriously?* "But he wants you to pay your own parking."

This sent Jill straight over the edge. Here Hunter was offered a fair—no, make that *generous*—deal, and he'd thrown the whole thing back in her face. That was just like Hunter. Arrogant, self-serving, unbearable! A real gentleman now? Ha! Had she lost her mind even *toying with* the idea that this was doable? She'd sell off every last bit of her property first, starting with this stupid tennis racket. She reached for it again and her fingers tightened around its neck. That would save her from using it as a murder weapon. First against Hunter, then against Brad. Double homicide! No, wait. Since Brad was the one here, she'd probably have to kill him first.

Jill leapt to her feet and her racket slammed to the floor. Brad watched wide-eyed as she started shredding the contract, dropping it piece by piece on the table. One of the strips curled in Brad's coffee cup, absorbing the dregs of his latte.

"Wait!" he cried in panic before lowering his voice to a whisper. "What are you doing?"

"Showing you—and *him*—what I think of this little counteroffer."

"Jilly, you're not being rational."

"Read my lips." She set her hands on the table. "I…don't…care." And she didn't! Forget Brad, and especially forget Hunter. Surely there was another way to make things work. She didn't need Brad, nor did she require the help of his conniving best friend!

"Trouble in paradise?"

Jill spun on her heels to see Cassandra had reappeared like a lurking phantom. She was toting a carry-out bag from the grill. "Are you stalking us, Cassandra?" Jill asked, reaching a hand behind her to the table. Keeping her eyes fixed on Cassandra's, she grappled for the errant pieces of paper, balling them up in her fist. Brad helped by prying her fingers apart and shoving in a few extra strips.

"Hardly." Cassandra's eyes were cold blue crystals. Cassandra tried to peer around Jill to see behind her, but Jill shifted, blocking her view, and rammed the fistful of paper strips into her purse. "I just came back to pick up my lunch order. Headed back to the office." She flipped her hair in an indignant manner. "Some of us work, you know. Even on Saturdays."

"Yes, well…" Jill pressed her lips into a tight smile. "Don't let us keep you from it!"

Cassandra obviously wasn't ready to leave them in peace. "I could have sworn I heard you two arguing… Was that Hunter's name I heard mentioned? *The infamous Hunter Delaney?*" She cocked her head at Brad. "Don't tell me your sweet fiancée has a roving eye?"

Brad answered her stoically. "This is probably one of those times when it would be good for you to mind your own business, Cassandra."

"Oh, but this *is* my business. It could be very big business indeed. Salacious details about breakups and infidelities sells copy."

Instead of offering up a biting comeback, Jill held her tongue.

Cassandra gave Jill a slow once-over, then shrugged at Brad. "Fine. You two keep your little secret. But mark my words, I'll get to the bottom of it. Where there's smoke there's fire, as they say, and there are big puffy clouds going up everywhere." Her lips twisted in an evil grin. "My spidey senses are tingling."

Jill turned to Brad as Cassandra sashayed away, her short skirt swishing. "Spidey senses?"

"I know. The woman's touched."

"Worse than that, she's wicked," Jill said. "She'll do anything in her power to destroy me."

"Maybe you shouldn't have won that tenth-grade spelling bee," Brad teased.

She wanted to stay mad at Brad, she really did. But when he gave her those darned puppy dog eyes, he made it impossible. Susan was putting the screws to him, and he'd tried to find a solution. So what if it was an abysmal one? She should at least give Brad points for trying. "Shut up. That was years ago."

Brad reached toward the floor, then handed Jill her racket. "Don't want to forget this."

"You're being very trusting," she told him, taking the racket. "I was thinking about using it to kill you only minutes ago."

Jill stepped into the sunshine, recalling for the first time in an hour what a gorgeous June day it was. She'd been so caught up in those storm clouds of thinking about Hunter, she'd nearly forgotten. She addressed Brad, who walked beside her, hanging his head. None of this mess was his fault and she knew it. It would be good of her to let him off the hook, so he and Susan could move forward in repairing their relationship. "Don't worry about it, okay?" she told him. "I'll think of something else. I have to."

Brad raised his eyes to look at her. "Maybe if you just talk to Hunter?"

"Don't think so."

"It's still possible you could reach a compromise."

Across the parking lot Jill spied Cassandra setting her lunch bag on the backseat of her shiny sports car. Was it Jill's imagination or was Cassandra taking her sweet time getting away, just hoping to catch one more glimpse of them? "Truthfully, Brad? At this point in time, I'd rather die than see Hunter Delaney in person."

"Don't look now, then," Brad said under his breath. "Because here he comes."

Jill whipped her head around to spy a handsome, dark-haired man striding toward them and sporting a broad grin. He wore a blue polo shirt and khaki slacks, and was taller then she remembered, at least a good six inches taller than her. A heck of a lot buffer too. Muscles rippled beneath his shirt as he opened his arms wide. "Jill Jamison!" Hunter proclaimed effusively. "The woman of my dreams!"

Before Jill knew what was happening, he reached for her and clamped her against his chest in a big bear hug. His frame was rock solid and he smelled of musky cologne. Hunter's arms wound around her, securing her at the waist. "Sorry, bud," he whispered to Brad, "the press is watching."

Jill stared up at him, her mind whirling. "Hunter! Just what are you doing?" She didn't know why, but her knees felt weak and her mouth went dry. She was probably in a state of shock. It wasn't like she recalled that old longing she'd had when she'd hoped to be in Hunter's arms so many years ago. Then, she'd imagined him to be a different kind of guy…the sort who could really care for a girl, and sweep her off her feet with one kiss. Not that she'd let him try, especially after learning what sort of guy he *really* was. The type who was only in it for the moment, and wouldn't have given her a second thought once she'd completely given him her heart. His dark eyes caught the sunlight as he dipped his chin toward hers.

"Making us public," he said with a grin. At once, Jill felt transported in time and she was all of seventeen again, helplessly under Hunter's spell. The next thing she knew, his mouth was on hers, all hot and heavy, his tongue sweeping in to taste hers. Jill sagged in his arms and he tightened his embrace. This was wrong. *This is insane…* But Jill found herself kissing him back, just a little at first—and then a lot. He felt so good and smelled so fine, she nearly forgot they were standing at the edge of a parking lot. Jill's temperature spiked as her tennis racket crashed to the ground. Oh man, he was good. Better than good. Hunter's skill was top-notch. Excellent. Why oh why had she waited so long? Or perhaps it was good she'd waited, until the fruit of her desire had ripened to perfection. Was it Jill's imagination, or was Hunter just as ravenous for her? Somehow her arms were around him, her wrists overlapping at the back of his neck. It was almost like she was enjoying this, wanting more of him... *What? Hunter?* Jill called herself up short and broke away, stepping back with a gasp. At least she hoped she was gasping and not panting. *Whoa.*

Hunter saucily cocked an eyebrow and spoke with a husky rasp.

"Can I take that to mean you missed me too?"

Jill cupped a hand to her mouth, her cheeks flaming. And it wasn't just her face; her whole body felt on fire, particularly the parts of her that had touched him—flesh pressing flesh. For a moment she felt faint. Brad handed Jill her racket and she used it like a cane to steady herself against the ground. "That was a little over the top for *hi, how've you been.*"

Hunter screwed up his face with mock confusion. "I thought we were engaged?" His eyes darted to a parking spot not fifty feet away, and Jill glanced in that direction to find Cassandra watching them, her jaw unhinged. She stood by her open driver's door, not bothering to hide her rapt interest. In fact, she appeared to be hastily packing away a camera. Brad had obviously spotted Cassandra too, because he leapt right in with a shrill cry. *"Engaged?"*

"Sorry, Brad," Hunter said loudly. "But all's fair in love and—"

Brad spewed his retort, immediately picking up on Hunter's cue. "You think you know a man." He motioned between Hunter and Jill. "All this time...? My girl and my very best friend? You and she...?" It was like he couldn't force himself to say it. "Unbelievable!" he finally yelped with a moan.

Jill stared at Brad in a panic before catching a glimpse of Cassandra rapidly fastening her seatbelt and zooming away. She'd gotten a scoop all right: a big one. Who knew how soon this story would be rushed to print? Yet none of the details had been ironed out. Jill didn't even know whether she and Hunter could make this charade work! And there he'd gone and spilled the whole can of beans to the entire world. Things couldn't go any more global than *Tempo Beat*. Surely, Hunter knew that. "Well, I hope you're proud of yourself," she said in a scolding tone.

Rather than appearing admonished, Hunter smiled, one side of his mouth rising higher than the other. "I thought we put on a pretty good show."

Brad nodded in agreement and shook his fingers as if fighting off flames. "Hot, hot."

Jill flushed in spite of herself.

"You did all right too," Hunter said, giving Brad's shoulder a nudge. "Really convincing."

Jill's mind was still spinning from the rapid turn of events. "When you two boys are done congratulating yourselves," she hissed at them, "maybe you can explain how bringing Cassandra in on this makes things any better?"

"Far better that she works for us, than against us," Brad explained.

"My thinking exactly," Hunter said. "You know, Jill," he told her, apparently seriously, "you've held up pretty well over the years. I don't think I'll have any trouble at all fitting the bill." He stepped toward her, playacting like he wanted to scoop her back into his arms.

"Oh, no you don't, big boy." She reached out a hand to stop him, placing her palm to his chest. His heart thumped beneath it. "You and I have some talking to do." Before this fake fiancé number could proceed any further, Jill needed a couple of answers. Like about why Hunter had agreed to it in the first place? Brad's story about Hunter suddenly morphing into a gentleman seemed to be holding less and less water. Particularly in light of that flaming hot kiss. The current rumors about Hunter were obviously true. No man could kiss like that who hadn't been around the block a time or two. Jill was just mortified that she'd given in to it. She clung to the hope that Hunter hadn't noticed and had taken her response in the vein it was supposedly given, as an outward sign to Cassandra of her new involvement with Hunter.

Brad gave a slight bow. "This is where the jilted ex excuses himself."

Jill grabbed for his arm as he turned back toward the clubhouse. "Brad! Don't go!"

"Three's a crowd, haven't you heard?" After walking a few paces, he peered over his shoulder to give Jill and Hunter an evaluating look. "You two really do make a great couple, by the way. Utterly charming." Jill seethed as he added, "Don't neglect to send me an invite!"

Jill massaged her forehead for a beat, then caught Hunter watching her. "You want to talk?" he said. "I'll talk. Shall we find a spot in the shade?"

That's when Jill looked past him to spy Cassandra's car slowly trolling back through the parking lot, her driver's side window lowered and a smart phone angled outside it.

"Film at eleven," Hunter quipped.

Chapter Five

Hunter sat with Jill at an outdoor table spanned by a large umbrella. They were by the adults-only pool. This club had five: a competition pool for lane swimming, a diving pool, a kiddie pool with a spewing fountain in the middle, a smaller kidney-shaped pool with broad steps leading into it and a gradual slope with an underwater ramp for the senior citizen crowd, and this one. Hunter lowered his sunglasses to survey a nearby pair of bathing beauties in small bikinis stretched out on lounge chairs. Nice, but neither was much competition for the woman at hand. Even in her tennis shorts and simple T-shirt she outshone them. Jill actually looked kind of cute, nervously adjusting her ponytail as their server set down their lunches beside their lemonades. She reached for the tab, thanking their server.

"I've got it," Hunter said, deftly snatching the slim leather folder from the waiter before Jill could take it. They'd asked for the bill to be brought with their food as both were in a hurry. Jill had a meeting with her agent later, and Hunter had to get back to the office. She'd been disinclined to lunch with him at all, until he'd insisted she'd have to eat sometime. This way they could discuss the contract, and arrange damage control for Cassandra's media revelations.

He'd ordered a burger and fries, which smelled delicious. Jill had gotten a small Caesar salad, claiming she couldn't eat anything hot in this weather. Secretly, Hunter wondered if she was watching her figure, though she clearly didn't need to. Jill packed a dynamite form into that austere athletic outfit. He flipped open the bill holder and reached for a pen, his eye snagging on Jill's legs. She sat with the toes of her sneakers pointed downward beneath her chair, one ankle crossed behind the other, her divine calves pressed together. Her legs were a sculpture in and of themselves, sleek and finely formed, practically inviting his touch. For a second, Hunter forgot he was supposed to be signing the tab. He cleared his throat and took care of business, adding a gratuity.

The server left them with a polite nod, saying he'd check on them in a bit.

"You didn't have to do that," Jill said. Her eyes were just as pretty as he remembered, warm brown with hints of honey around the irises. He'd spent a lot of time considering their color back in high school. Probably more time than he should have, considering her apparent disinterest in him. If he'd understood that better ahead of the prom, as opposed to afterward, he might have saved himself a heap of trouble. "I'm perfectly capable of paying for myself."

Hunter's lips twisted in a smile. Either she was still bent out of shape about that kiss, or she was steaming over the changes he'd made to the contract. "A *thank-you* would have been nice."

"Thank you," she said without the slightest hint of gratitude. "But that was unnecessary."

Hunter lifted the ketchup bottle from the table and liberally doused his fries. He'd ordered his burger with the works, so that didn't need fixing. "That's right. I've heard. You're pretty famous now."

She primly laid her napkin in her lap. "I do all right."

"A *relationship expert,*" he said, emphasizing the words. He re-capped the ketchup bottle and returned it to the table. "How's that working out for you?"

Jill pressed her lips together, her cheeks firing red. After a beat, she spoke in an annoyed tone. "Really well."

Hunter lifted his burger and mumbled, "Hmm…"

Jill looked at him askance. "Hmm?"

He sank his teeth into the burger, savoring a bite. "Mmm, this is good!" He dove in again, before nabbing a French fry. "Want one?" he asked, holding it toward her.

She somehow managed to contain herself. "No, thanks."

Hunter shrugged and shoved the steaming piece of potato in his mouth, thinking it tasted like heaven. He hadn't realized how hungry he was. It must have been Jill that got his metabolism going, and boy had she ever. He used to privately think of her as an ice princess. She'd obviously experienced a deep thaw since high school. Maybe that was her problem with men now. Too eager. A lot of men couldn't handle that. Hunter prided himself on not being one of them. Eager women were easy enough to deal with. It was the serious-minded ones that gave him headaches. The ones who wanted to talk things out, again and again, and never understood why he wasn't being "honest" with them. He would be, if he could only understand what they wanted him to be honest about. Each time he shared his confusion, it sparked a fight, and fights led to even greater frustration. Yep, he'd take eager over serious-minded any day. At least eager helped his metabolism. Hunter set down his food and took a sip of lemonade, watching the prongs of Jill's fork dance around her salad. Either she was a very picky eater or had somehow lost her appetite. "Not hungry?" he asked.

She loaded up her fork and brought it to her mouth. "Starved."

"That's what a good physical workout will do for you."

Her cheeks flamed again. "Hunter! About that—"

"I was talking about the tennis," he lied. "You and Brad did play earlier?" He raised his brow, feigning an innocent expression. "What were you thinking about?"

She shook her head and chewed vigorously. After a few more rabid assaults on her salad, she said, "This is never going to work."

"Jilly."

"Please don't call me that."

"But I thought everybody—?"

"That was years ago."

"Brad still—"

"Brad is different. He's my friend."

"I can see how that puts him in a different category than me. I'm just the man you're going to marry."

She set down her fork and stared straight at him. "Yes, and why is that, Hunter? What would make you even want to agree to it?"

"I have a very good heart," he said sincerely. "The doctor says my other parts are in working order too."

To her credit, she didn't react to this other than to say, "What's working of yours—and what *isn't*—is actually of very little concern to me."

Now, this was a turn Hunter didn't expect. Jill clearly liked kissing men and didn't mind running her hands all over them—even in broad daylight! That's when another idea occurred. Jill was playing Hunter and had someone else on the side. Another guy she was involved with, maybe even someone she cared for deeply. Then why wasn't Jill marrying *him*? Could it be that the other man was somehow unavailable? Possibly already married? Or maybe her publisher was vetting the candidates and mystery dude hadn't passed muster? Which would mean that Hunter himself would have to. Hunter felt an irrational flash of jealousy over the entire imagined situation. He'd never come in second to anyone in his life and didn't intend to start now. He most certainly wasn't going to put his reputation on the line by getting cuckolded in public. "There's someone else, isn't there?" he asked, hoping he'd masked the tinge of insecurity in his voice.

"What?" she asked in shock.

"You're involved. Not with Brad, with someone else."

"No! It's not that. Is that what you think? Just because I don't want to…?" She fumbled with the words until his meaning dawned. Jill tilted her head to the side, looking slightly amused.
"Oh…my…goodness. You're not actually—?"

"Of course not," he said gruffly. "Don't be ridiculous."

"Then why would you care?"

He gathered his wits about him. "Because, Jilly… I'm sorry, Jill. If we're even going to discuss this arrangement as a real possibility, I believe we need to be up front with each other. Totally frank. No holds barred."

"I couldn't agree more."

"And I'd rather not have a wife, even a pretend one, seen as catting around on me. It wouldn't look right. It probably wouldn't help your position with your publisher either."

She smiled and clucked her tongue. "You are."

"Am what?"

"Wow!" She tried to stifle a giggle with her napkin, but failed. "Wow…wow…wow. I wouldn't have believed it, if I hadn't seen it. World-class womanizer Hunter Delaney is actually jeal—"

"Hunter, my boy, I thought that was you." A slim, silver-haired man appeared at their table dressed in golf attire. "I thought I spotted you out here from inside the grill."

Hunter blanched and stood to greet him. "Mr. Abrams! I didn't realize you were golfing this afternoon."

"Hate to waste a beautiful day." He shot Jill an admiring look. "I can see you're not wasting it either."

"I'd planned to go right back to the office after—"

"You know you're not expected to work on a Saturday. Although I do admire your gumption. Getting a jump on those mock-ups, are you?"

The man stepped toward Jill and extended his hand. "Max Abrams. I don't believe we've had the pleasure."

"Sorry, sir!" Hunter raced in. "This is—"

Max's blue eyes twinkled. "The lovely Jillian Jamison, in person, yes. Impossible to miss her." He smiled at Jill. "I'd like to be among the first to offer my congratulations."

She firmly shook his hand. "Congratulations?"

"Don't be coy, darling," Hunter told her. "I've already filled my boss in."

"Have you now?" Jill asked forcing a grin. "How...wonderful."

"It is, isn't it?" the older gentleman said. "And the timing couldn't have been better."

"Oh?" Jill asked.

"We don't need to burden Jill with business details," Hunter told Abrams.

"No, please," Jill said, smiling at Max. "Burden me. I'm keenly interested in all that Hunter does."

Hunter stared at her and murmured, "Such a loving and supportive fiancée."

"That's so nice to see these days," Max said warmly. "Not always the case with dual-career couples."

Jill pulled her gaze from Hunter to address Abrams. "Sad but true. There can be petty..." Her lips puckered in a frown. "...jealousies."

Hunter coughed loudly. "Don't let us keep you, Mr. Abrams."

"Please, have a seat, Hunter. I didn't mean to disturb you. And what's with this Mr. Abrams nonsense? We're practically partners now, you know. Don't you think it's about time you called me *Max*?"

Hunter sat unsteadily as Jill gasped with surprise. "My goodness! It seems more congratulations are in order." She raised her lemonade glass toward Hunter. "*Partners.* I had no idea."

"Well, of course, I may be jumping the gun just a little bit," Abrams said with a wink. "Though I'm sure my prognostication will come true before too long. Once Hunter lands that Kaleidoscope Kids account, and now he's well positioned to..." His words suddenly fell off and worry lines wrinkled his brow. "Oh, dear. I hope I haven't let any cats out of the bag. Perhaps Hunter was keeping this as a surprise?"

"A big one!" Hunter reached out and took Jill's hand on the table. She squirmed and tried to pull away, but he held on. "The very best! For my new bride!"

"Of course. Dear me. My apologies for talking out of turn."

Jill blinked and smiled politely at Abrams. "I'm speechless."

I've got a really big heart, Hunter had said. That lout! He was nothing but one gigantic phony. Hunter wasn't interested in her fake marriage deal due to any form of altruism, not toward her—or his best friend, Brad. He was merely out to benefit his career. Jill didn't know exactly how Kaleidoscope Kids figured in, but Max's intimation about the timing of Hunter's engagement being perfect had to mean something. Once again, it was all about Hunter! Nothing about him had changed since high school. Okay, apart from the smoking way he looked. Certain physical qualities had definitely improved with age, like the definition of his chest and the musculature of his arms. *Ow!* Why did he have to hold on so fiercely? She tried to tug away again, but his grasp clamped down on her.

"No worries," Hunter said kindly to Max. "She was bound to learn the truth sooner or later." Then he turned to Jill and said cheerfully, "It was a wedding gift, darling. My long-hoped-for promotion is right on the horizon! I just didn't want you to know until everything was one hundred percent sure."

"Yes, well…" Abrams nodded and backed away. "I suppose I'll leave you two alone to discuss this new revelation."

Hunter put on his most professional tone. "I'll have my preliminary sketches ready for you by Monday morning at eight."

"That's terrific, son," Abrams replied. "I'll look forward to seeing them. Jillian," he said, slightly bowing his head. "It's been a pleasure."

"Equally, Mr. Abra—"

"Please…"

She grinned in understanding. "Max."

Abrams smiled and added, "Diane and I will have to have you over to the house sometime soon. So we all can celebrate."

"We would be delighted." Hunter pinched her hand harder. "Wouldn't we, darling?"

"Ye-es!" Jill practically shrieked, wincing in pain.

Abrams sighed. "It's so refreshing to see young people in love."

The second he'd gone, Jill jerked away her hand and started massaging it furiously with her other one. "What on earth were you doing" she hissed in low tones. "Trying to crush me into compliance?"

"Crush…?" His mouth fell open. "Oh gosh, Jilly… Um, Jill. I'm so sorry. Did I hurt you?"

"I'll live." She shoved both fists into her lap. "Not so sure about you."

"What's that supposed to mean?"

"I smell a rat here, and my nose has always been very good. A lot better, evidently, than your *heart.*"

"Ah." He inhaled deeply. "I get what's going on. Your feelings are hurt."

"What? No!" She was still whispering so as not to call attention to them. "Are you insane?"

"You were actually kind of flattered I'd deign to help you. Now that you see there's something in it for me, you're bent out of shape."

"I never said that. There's been something in it for you all along. Just not as much as you're asking for. Fifty percent of the advance money, Hunter? Don't you think that's a little aggressive?"

"Not really," he said calmly. "I look at it as insurance."

"Insurance?"

"I don't plan to keep that money. The truth is, I don't need any of it. I'll need it even less once I make partner at the firm. I plan to give it back at the end of the year."

"Then what—?"

"I want a lock on this, Jill. A guarantee that you won't walk after six weeks."

"You read that article too?" she asked with dismay.

"Brad filled me in."

"Remind me to thank him."

"To my way of thinking, there's no point in even staging this charade if we're not going to make it stick."

"For one year," she reinforced.

"Twelve months, yes," he said. "That's a lot longer than six—"

"I can count, you know. Believe or not, I'm pretty good at math."

"As I recall, you were pretty great at everything. Everything I was privileged to know about, that is." He gave her a sideways glance and added playfully, "You obviously have some skills you were keeping under wraps."

Jill cheeks burned. "If you're alluding to that kiss, that was strictly for Cassandra's benefit."

"In that case, I hope she swings by more often."

Jill huffed.

Hunter casually lifted his lemonade. "I don't see why you care so much that I'm getting a promotion out of it. It's pretty clear that you are too."

There wasn't a lot she could say to that, because—darn it—he was right, though she was loath to admit it. Her success as a credible writer hinged on this fake marriage deal. So who was she to cast stones at Hunter's motivation? In the grand scheme, did it really matter?

"Why don't you get out that contract," he offered reasonably, "and let us have a look at it?"

Jill voice constricted in her throat. "Contract?"

"You know, that two-page deal-with-the-devil you crafted?"

Deal with the devil, indeed. Just look at him sitting there smugly like he's the one in charge. How in the world had Hunter managed to turn things around?

"I… I'm not sure I have it."

"I thought Brad told me he was bringing my copy over to review with you this morning?"

"He did, but…" She thought of the shredded document strips in her bag. "He took it back!"

"What?"

"He took the contract back!"

"But why would he do that when he knew I was coming here to discuss it with you?"

"Brad knew…?" And yet he'd let her be blindsided. It was tough to mask her irritation. "Wonderful."

"Don't be mad at Brad for not telling you I was coming here. I asked him not to because I was worried that if he did, you might bolt." There was something that looked like sincerity in his eyes, but it was impossible for Jill to know if it was real. "I thought it would be good for us to talk things over. You know, face-to-face. I didn't count on the Cassandra complication any more than you did.

"I actually look at it as a stroke of luck," he added, surprising her. "We needed a way to explain your dropping Brad and moving on to me. Thanks to Cassandra, we're going to have some very public help with that."

"Speaking of public," Jill admonished sternly. "We've got to get one thing straight. There will be no more PDA of that kind. Period."

"Then how will we look convincing?"

She thought this over. "Okay, so maybe we could hold hands."

"Nice."

"Occasionally, share a peck on the lips."

"Sweet."

"Closed-mouthed, Hunter."

He assessed her wryly and Jill felt heat sweep up her neck. She pushed ahead, needing to make it clear. "There will be no hanky-panky in private either."

"Now you're bursting my bubble."

"Look, Hunter. I know the kind of guy you are."

"Do you?" he challenged, dark brown eyes on hers.

She hesitated just a fraction of a second too long. "Yes. Someone used to getting your way—with women. What I'm trying to tell you is, that won't be happening with me."

"So, then, it's okay if I date other people?"

"What?"

"If you're saying there's going to be nothing physical between—"

"I can't have my husband playing around on me!" Jill stared at him aghast. "That will defeat the whole purpose of the staged marriage!"

"I see. So, you expect me to…" Hunter coughed loudly. "Remain celibate the entire time?"

She leaned forward with a whisper. "You don't think you can do it, do you?"

"I can do anything I put my mind to."

"Right. Well, I'm glad we got that clear."

Hunter lazily dragged a hand through his hair. "The truth is, I've been considering this for some time. Taking a break from women. They can be so much trouble, you know?"

Jill took to finishing her salad. "The point I'm making is—*if* we find a way to make this work—it will be a business deal. Pure and simple."

"With a contract," he surmised.

"Yes."

"The one you don't have."

"Not at the moment." Jill dabbed her mouth with her napkin and continued eating. "Which maybe doesn't matter, as I'll need to draw a new one up."

"For what purpose?"

"Including these other things we've just agreed to. Like, no sleeping together."

"I never said I agreed." Jill looked up to find a smile teasing his lips.

"Then there's no deal," she said flatly.

"You drive a hard bargain."

Jill flushed with pride. "I can hold my own."

"So can I," Hunter told her. "Which is why I'm not budging on the condo."

Jill's fork clanked to her plate. "You can't possibly expect me and Fifi and Mimi to—"

"Fifi and Mimi?" He grimaced unabashedly. "You must be joking."

"No, I am not," she said with an indignant snort. "Fifi is my yellow Lab and Mimi is—"

"Wait a minute. You named a *Lab* Fifi? Fifi's not a Lab name. Think poodle. Pomeranian…"

Her mouth hung open. "Now you're an animal savant?"

"I know dog names and Fifi's not one of them I approve of."

"Nobody asked you to!"

"Sorry, no Fifi's living at my place."

Jill fumed.

"Probably not Mimi either. If that's a cat, I'm allergic."

She glared at him until she realized he was sporting a grin. "You made that up!"

"You're right," he admitted, before pausing and then asking, "Which part?"

"Probably all of it!"

"No, I was serious about dog names."

"We are not moving into your place."

"Then we're not getting married."

"Why are you being so stubborn about this?"

"Me?" He sputtered a laugh. "My place is better, plus it has a bigger TV."

"How do you know that? About the television?"

"I'm a guy."

"Now you're being sexist."

"No, practical."

"Come on."

"Okay," he baited. "Then answer. How many inches?"

"What?"

"How big is your screen?"

"I honestly have no idea."

"That kind of proves it."

Jill blew out an exasperated breath. "If it's such a big deal, we can move your television into my place."

"I don't like living in the country. It makes me sneeze."

"Now you're lying again."

He watched her for an extended beat, then his dark brown eyes sparkled. "You know, this is kind of fun."

Fun? Jill felt positively winded. It was all she could do to keep up with him, and Jill was generally pretty good at thinking on her feet.

"Just listen to us," he said with a grin. "Arguing like an old married couple." He pushed back his chair and stood.

"You're leaving?" she asked, caught off guard.

"The fact is, I really do want this promotion, and, believe it or not, my being married won't be enough for me to nail it. I'll actually have to work for it too."

Jill swallowed hard, her head muddled. It still seemed to her they hadn't settled anything. "What about our contract?"

"Print a new one out, and we'll go over it. Oh, and Jill…" He leaned into the back of his chair, bracing himself on his arms. "You might want to think about being a little more conciliatory next time."

She was about to spout out a pithy reply when she caught a glimpse of her watch and saw that she was ten minutes late for her meeting with Morgan.

Chapter Six

"I've got to say I'm impressed, Jill. Here I questioned your ability to come up with a groom under such short notice, and somehow you've managed to find two!" Morgan sat in her chic modern office surrounded by potted ferns. A small bonsai tree stood on the corner of her desk.

"I've only got one left at the moment," Jill replied. "And he's not my first choice."

"Whyever not? I've seen Hunter Delaney, and the man is *very* good-looking."

"Maybe," Jill conceded. "But impossible just the same. Fifty percent of the advance money?"

"Less my fifteen percent," Morgan interjected.

"You know what I'm saying."

"Yes, but I don't quite agree that he's being greedy. The fact that he's willing to give the money back at the end of the year sounds more than reasonable to me."

"He's only in it for himself."

"Bingo! So are you. Sounds like a match made in heaven."

"I'm not moving to the city."

"Then negotiate."

"He won't budge."

"Everything's negotiable."

"Now you're sounding like Brad."

"What?"

"Never mind." Jill shook her head. "Maybe this is a loony idea."

"Actually, I think the arrangement's ideal. No false hopes, no worries. You and Hunter go in with all expectations clear."

"What am I supposed to tell my grandfather?" Jill desperately wished she could share the truth with her grandpa, but given his memory issues she couldn't trust him not to reveal it to the wrong people.

"The same thing you're going to tell the rest of the world. That you're *in love*."

"I already told him I was marrying Brad."

"And that women are fickle."

"Morgan!"

"Hey, I don't know. Tell your grandpa you've had a change of heart. That you've had a thing for Hunter all these years, and it was mutual. Reciprocated."

Jill recalled the heat of Hunter's mouth on hers and felt her temperature spike. She hastily turned away, hoping her face hadn't colored. "Nobody would believe that."

"Everybody *has to*. That's the only way to make this work." Morgan thumped her pen against a stack of papers on her desk, apparently mulling something over. "Okay, here's an idea," she offered. "Let's say you haven't seen Hunter in ten years—"

"Twelve."

"Whatever. Let's ballpark it."

Jill sat back in her chair, prepared to listen. "Fine."

"Anyway, here's what I'm thinking," Morgan went on. "Hunter's been out of the picture because you and he had no reason to interact. *Then,* you became engaged to his best friend, Brad. Naturally, you and Brad celebrated your happy news among friends, and logically—"

"Hunter attended some of those celebrations," Jill surmised.

Morgan's expression brightened as her notion picked up steam, and she continued dreamily, "When you and Hunter saw each other again—I mean from the very first time—it was like...*bada-boom*...chemistry! Fireworks! Maybe he even swept you into his arms and kissed you!"

"What?"

"Okay," Morgan conceded. "Perhaps that's carrying things too far. Nobody's that irresistible." She studied Jill sympathetically. "Sorry, hon, not even you.

"My point is," Morgan continued. "Sometimes these things happen. It's not your fault or his. You didn't even know you'd be desperately attracted. But...maybe... There had been some kind of never-forgotten fling in high school?" She tried to read Jill's eyes. "Yes?"

"No!"

"Then why are you fanning yourself with my proof copy of *Fated Flames: Long-Lost Lust*?"

Jill looked down to find the paperback edition waving furiously back and forth in her hand. She quickly stopped the motion and put the book down. "I just think you're blowing things up a bit, that's all."

"Nonsense! They have to be big. Bigger than big. Enormous! And..." She set her elbows on her desk and leaned forward, raising her eyebrows. "Dramatic, romantic…glorious! Don't you see? Your affair will capture the world's imagination!"

Jill nodded with understanding, once again sensing Morgan's genius. "And this will help me sell books."

"Of course. Every woman on earth knows there's nothing more challenging than transitioning from insta-lust into a real relationship. That's what book three is about! *Married Love: Keeping Those Home Fires Burning. Naturellement!*"

"Naturellement," Jill repeated, the entire scheme taking root in her mind. Morgan was right; this was perfect. Even if Hunter Delaney proved himself to be a perfect pain in the neck, no one would fault a girl for having the hots for him. He was successful and gorgeous…with the worst sort of reputation any guy could have! "What about Hunter's well-known standing as a womanizer?"

"You'll be the beauty that tamed the savage beast. Women everywhere will stand up and applaud you!"

Jill glanced at her doubtfully. "You're mighty sure of this."

"Look, Jill. I don't know much, but I do know two things: I know books, and I know the public. Between those two I can create a package that sells. If the numbers on this book break where I think they will, you'll never have to worry about your grandpa's comfort again. He'll be well taken care of, and you'll be set for the long haul too."

"Even after my…" Jill stumbled on the word. "…divorce?"

"Now, hush your mouth, and let's not go there! For heaven's sake, we haven't even gotten you married yet."

Brad sat next to Hunter at the sports bar. Both were positioned on stools, strategically close to the televised ball game. "I'm not saying I don't believe you," Brad said. "I'm just a little stunned she didn't put up more of a fight."

"Oh, she fought, all right." Hunter chuckled into his beer. "Seems like she's pretty used to winning too."

Brad eyed his friend. "I'm guessing, so are you."

"I'd be lying if I said it's all ironed out, because it isn't. There are still a few things to get straight, like where we're going to live."

"I thought you were dead set on staying in the condo?"

An evil smile creased Hunter's lips. "That's what I told Jill."

"You mean, you honestly don't care?"

Hunter shrugged. "Why would I? As long as I can bring my stuff with me, I'm cool."

"That's not what you told Jill, is it?"

Hunter nursed another sip of his brew. "Nope."

"Why not?"

Hunter met his buddy's eyes. "She needs to want this as badly as I do. If Jill wins the battle over our living situation, she'll feel invested. Stay committed and won't slip up. Max was at the club today, and—"

"He saw the two of you together? No way!"

"Yep, it's true. And, you know the interesting thing? I think he totally bought it. Me and Jill, the loving couple."

"Well, I guess that part's good."

"It's a start, anyway," Hunter said.

They watched another batter hit a home run, then contemplated their mugs during the commercial break.

"So, you're moving to the country!" Brad proclaimed with a laugh. "Never thought I'd see the day."

"Let's wait and see how long I can stand it."

"According to that contract, it's going to be a year."

"She wants separate bedrooms, did you know that?"

"Of course. I mean, in my case, it was no problem. Susan would have insisted… I mean, I would have too… Hang on. Hold the bacon."

He slowly met Hunter's eyes.

"Are you saying you *wish* you were sleeping together?"

"Haven't you heard the term conjugal rights?"

"Sure, when applied to a real marriage."

Hunter dropped his voice. "She wants me, man, I'm telling you."

Brad's voice squeaked. "Jilly? Nah-uh."

Hunter elaborated in a raspy whisper. "The woman was all over me with that kiss. Swear to goodness, nearly ate me alive."

"Jilly?" Brad asked again, apparently not believing it.

"Yes, *her*." Hunter leaned toward him. "Jillian Jamison, relationship expert extraordinaire. It's like she was starved for affection. Couldn't get en—"

Brad cut him off. "Don't let your ego get the best of you. And don't you dare go taking advantage of—"

"Advantage?" He stared at Brad agape. "What are you talking about? She's going to be my wife."

"In name only," Brad hissed back. "I'm sure she made that clear."

"Crystal, yeah. But that doesn't mean I can't read between the lines."

"She was faking it with that kiss," Brad said, "and you know it."

"Trust me, I know *faking it* and I know the real deal. That kiss was not pretend."

"I was an eyewitness."

"You'll forgive me for saying my perspective was a bit more personal than yours."

Brad looked him up and down and narrowed his eyes.

"Come on, man. Stop looking at me like that. You know I'd never *take advantage* of any woman, married to her or not. I'm just saying I wouldn't be opposed if she initiated."

"Don't hold your breath, pal."

"No worries. I won't." He downed the last of his beer, then winked at his friend. "But I don't intend to lock my bedroom door, either."

Jill wheeled her grandfather into the great room rather than the courtyard because it was raining outside. The stormy weather matched her mood. While Jill didn't like lying to her grandpa, the thought of his being abruptly uprooted held even less appeal.

A gracious nurse brought them two cardboard cups of hot tea and Jill thanked her as she went away. Her grandpa took a sip of his, then balanced the cup on his knee. "A little hot," he said. "I'll wait a bit."

"Here, let me set that down." Jill offered to take it from him, but he politely declined.

"This way I'll have it when I need it."

That was so like him. Determined to remain as independent as possible. Jill's heart broke over his current condition. If there wasn't someone there to dress him each morning, he'd likely spend all day in his pajamas. Her grandpa had been a proud man who took care with his appearance. Jill was grateful the good staff here were helping preserve his dignity. He looked dapper in his chinos and button-down shirt, which was covered with a lightweight pullover sweater. Even in summer, he tended to feel cold. That was another good reason to have hot tea to warm him up. He blew into the hot liquid in his cup, then tried again with a tiny sip.

"So?" he asked her. "How did things go with your agent? All straightened out?"

Jill was amazed at how he sometimes remembered things so clearly. "Yes," she said with a sigh. "Thankfully."

"The publisher too, then, I take it?"

"I shouldn't have troubled you with my work."

"Poppycock! If you can't tell me, who can you tell?"

He had her there. Despite her job, which involved a flurry of tours and professional interaction with people, Jill didn't have many true friends. She'd spent far more time giving relationship advice to others than focusing on building relationships of her own.

She took a sip of her own tea, finding it weak. Kind of like the lame storyline she'd prepared. "Grandpa?" she asked tentatively, looking up.

"Yes, dear?"

"You remember me saying I was getting married?"

"To Brad, yes. That chap you knew in grade school. When are you going to bring him by to see me, by the way? Seems if he were half a gentleman he'd have asked my permission."

"Not too many people do that anymore."

"Why not? Unless they're hiding something. Why, in my day—"

"I know." She reached out and lightly patted his free hand. "But times have changed."

"That's why there are so many bust-ups," he retorted surely.

"Bust-ups?"

"Divorces. Couples not staying together. Nobody goes in it for the long haul anymore. They might as well write a short-term contract."

Jill swallowed hard. "I don't think that's because of the groom failing to ask permission."

"That's where it all starts, can't you see?" he said, light blue eyes glistening. "When someone has honorable intentions, he presents those to the family. Right now, I'm the only family you've got."

"Yes, but—"

"Why don't you bring Brad by so we can get this over with? It's a little after the fact, but better late than never."

Jill drew a breath, speaking softly. "There is no Brad."

Her grandpa's hand grabbed hers. "My dear, I'm so sorry." She opened her eyes to find him angling toward her in his wheelchair. "What happened?"

"He... I..." She hedged and looked away. "It's complicated."

"Love is always complicated." He squeezed her hand and let it go, sitting back with his tea. "You work it out."

"Grandpa, I don't think there's any way."

"Of course there's a way! *Where there's a will, there's a way.* When you love someone, you..." He stopped and studied her stance. Jill hung her head.

"You don't love him, do you?" her grandpa asked quietly.

Tears stung her eyes. "I'd hate for you to judge me."

"I'm not your judge," he said soothingly. "I'm your advocate, and someone who loves you very much."

Jill sniffed and set her chin, still avoiding his eyes. "What if I were to tell you there's someone else?"

He barely paused at all. "Well, now, my! That *is* a complication." To her surprise, he chuckled warmly. "How did this all come about?"

She gritted her teeth before speaking. "It's… Hunter Delaney. The man I've fallen in love with. He's Brad's best friend."

Her grandfather studied her thoughtfully for a moment.

"I have to give you credit, Jill. When you said complicated, you meant it. You clearly know your vocabulary." This made her smile.

"Oh Grandpa… You're not mad?"

"Why would this upset me? I'm not the jilted party." He took one last sip of tea and placed his cup on a side table. "So, how is Brad taking it? I assume he knows?"

Jill nodded. "Surprisingly well. If I didn't know better, I'd almost say he was hoping this would happen."

"See what I mean about presenting your intentions?" her grandpa interjected. "I'm guessing the boy got cold feet."

"But I told you I—"

"Naturally, you turned to someone else. Brad wasn't *all in,* and you could sense it, couldn't you, dear?"

"You're the sharpest tack in the box, Grandpa."

"Well, it doesn't take a rocket scientist to see it. You're a wonderful catch, Jill. Talented, intelligent, beautiful. Not to mention very accomplished in your work. What man wouldn't knock himself out trying to impress you?"

Jill could name a long list, but decided against it. "You're being very sweet."

"The truth is, if Hunter's the better fit for you, then I'm glad you and Brad fell out. More than glad. I'm elated. Because, you know… I only want the best for my girl." He met her eyes with a tender smile and Jill almost feared she'd cry again. Her grandpa was having such a good day, and there seemed to be fewer and fewer of those. She'd give anything if his mind was always this clear. She loved him so.

"So, what are you doing about the wedding?" he asked her. "Still planning on a big affair?"

"I… We're not sure. This has all happened sort of suddenly."

"Well, while you're figuring it out, don't waste time in my department. Bring that new man of yours around to see me posthaste."

"But Grandpa—"

"No *but*s about it, sweetheart. I'm not inclined to see you go through the same heartbreak twice. If this Hunter Delaney is man enough to marry my granddaughter, then he's man enough to come see me and ask for her hand."

Chapter Seven

Hunter waited for Jill at a downtown coffee shop. It was pretty convenient, only a few blocks from where he worked. It was equally handy that he had Jill's number. She'd apparently gotten his cell information from Brad. Now that she'd texted Hunter, he also had a way to reach her—something he decided was really necessary, since she was about to become his wife. Apparently, she'd mulled over his counteroffer and had come to her senses. *I'm ready to deal and sign*, she'd said by text, meaning she was agreeing to make concessions. It would likely be a surprise to her that he was too.

Hunter couldn't wait to see the expression on Jill's face when he shared that he was willing to move to the country. She'd probably jump all over him with hugs and squeals. If he got lucky, she might even kiss him again. Right here, in this café… Bumping into their table with her shapely hips and upsetting their coffees as she sprang to her feet. She'd wrap him in her arms above their teetering cups, strawberry-red lips closing in. Hunter sighed deeply, absorbing the fantasy along with the aroma of freshly ground Guatemalan Breakfast Blend.

The truth was that he liked surprising women, in a good way. When he caught them off guard in an unhappy manner, things didn't work out so well for him. Like that time he'd forgotten Sabrina had arranged for him to meet her parents for dinner. He'd been working overtime on a project and the occasion had entirely slipped his mind. She'd been so furious when he'd walked in the door, she'd thrown one of her high-heeled shoes at him.

Her parents apparently had held a table at a restaurant for an hour and fifteen minutes before finally giving up. Hunter had been unreachable because he'd neglected to charge his cell. He'd never let the darn thing go dead since. But that still didn't save things with Sabrina, not that they'd merited saving anyway. If it hadn't been for that dinner disaster, she would have discovered another reason to become annoyed with him. Most women eventually did, though Hunter couldn't fathom why. At heart, he was a very nice guy. Just look at the extraordinary lengths he was going to out of compassion for his best friend, and to help Jill. Okay, yeah, so he was helping himself a tiny bit too.

The café door whooshed open, letting in a wave of summer heat. Though nothing was as hot as the woman walking toward him. Jill was astonishingly polished in a teal silk blouse and an ivory jacket. The matching white skirt hit a few inches above her knees, revealing the long, lovely legs he recalled from the tennis outfit. His eyes snagged on her three-inch heels and his heart beat double-time. Those appeared even more dangerous than the ones Sabrina used to wear. Thank goodness he wasn't late.

"Have you ordered yet?" She spoke casually, like they were business acquaintances out for a coffee. Well, in a way, he supposed they were.

Hunter stood and pulled out her chair. "I was waiting on you." She seemed a bit perplexed by the gesture, but sat anyway, smoothing her skirt over the tops of her legs.

"That was nice. You didn't need to."

"What can I get you?" he offered. "This one's on me."

"Oh, no you don't." She tugged a wallet from a purse that matched her outfit and shoes. Jill opened the billfold and pulled out some cash. "This one's on *me*," she said, handing it to him.

Hunter accepted the bills, noting her eyes on the large chalkboard behind the register that enumerated the café's various offerings. Her hair fell just past her shoulders with a section on top pulled back in a barrette. "The Guatemalan Breakfast Blend's pretty good, if you're still deciding," he offered.

She turned back to him with a smile, and his heart did that weird little two-step again. He'd thought before it was out of primal fear. Now he wasn't sure what it was. Perhaps it was the pressure of the situation. A man didn't sign a marriage contract every day. "I'll take a double-whipped Jamaican latte," she said. "That sounds really good."

He nodded, then glanced at the cash in his hand. "Are you sure about this? I don't mind paying."

She alarmed him by stifling a giggle. "You really are old-fashioned, aren't you?"

Hunter kind of resented that. Coming from her, it hadn't sounded like a compliment. "I'm just trying to do the gentlemanly thing."

"This isn't a date, Hunter," she reminded him.

"Never said that it was."

"Then why were you trying to pay?"

"That's what guys do."

"Not when it's not a date, they don't."

"Did you just use a double-negative on me?"

She cracked a grin. "Just go on and order the coffees, okay? I promise to let you pay next time."

The shop was real art deco, with colorful modern art adorning the walls and small hand-blown glass lamps hanging from beams in the ceiling. In her upscale business attire, Jill seemed to fit right in. When Hunter had seen her at the club in tennis shorts and a ponytail, she'd appeared athletic and youthful. It was hard to imagine her being an international celebrity in that guise. But here, with this funky upbeat shop serving as a backdrop, Hunter could more easily envision Jill in a professional environment, lecturing at a podium or signing book copies.

She was poised and meticulously put together, like many of the women he worked with. Only Jill was one hundred and ten percent better-looking. No wonder he'd had a crush on her in high school. She outshone all the other girls then too. The thing was, all the other girls had wanted Hunter—and Jill hadn't. My, how times had changed. Even if it was for outward appearances only, Hunter still took satisfaction in knowing Jill's graduating class would see she'd wound up with him. Sure, she'd say that it was just pretend. But it wasn't easy to forget the reality of that kiss. "Better hurry," she whispered, motioning toward the counter with her chin. "A line is forming."

Hunter went to place their orders and Jill watched him walk away, thinking what a fine form he cut in his suit. It was well tailored and the hang of it was just right. It looked expensive and European. Hunter was clearly used to having the best, just as he was accustomed to getting his way. She hoped Brad was right when he'd hinted Hunter might actually move into her place. She was willing to concede on the money if he would make that concession on living arrangements. She gulped in some air, recalling she also had to mention that minor detail concerning her grandfather. Though perhaps she shouldn't worry. Wasn't Hunter already proving himself a somewhat traditional guy? Buying her lunch, and now offering to pay for coffee? Asking for a girl's hand in marriage couldn't be that much more of a leap. The only things missing were dozens of dates, a bouquet of roses, and a real proposal.

Hunter returned and set their cups on the table before taking his seat. "I'm glad you've thought this over," he said. His eyes were just as enticing as she remembered, and he still had that cocky way of smiling that caused butterflies in her stomach. Not that she was about to let him know it. If she was strong enough to forestall his advances in high school, she could certainly accomplish that now…that little matter of their setting up house together aside. "There are bound to be benefits for the two of us."

Jill ignored any hint at innuendo. "For me, professionally, yes. Maybe you should explain about Kaleidoscope Kids?"

"It's a big account Max has been courting. They distribute kids' clothing and toys."

Jill nodded, thinking she'd heard of them.

"Their network is enormous, domestic and international. They want an advertising campaign designed across all platforms."

"Something that will work cross-culturally?" she guessed. Actually, that sounded pretty exciting, and she said so.

"Yeah, I'm amped about it. I've got lots of ideas already. The thing is…" He looked straight at her. "The company CEO only wants to work with a married man."

"That sounds so retro!" Jill cried with a gasp. "Is that even legal?"

"The customer's always right." He took a sip from his cup and shot her a smile. "Kind of like your readers."

"That's why Max was so happy to see us together."

"In many ways, the timing couldn't have been more perfect. Both in seeing Max at the club, and in that account coming along, right after Brad presented your offer."

"Speaking of which…" She withdrew some folded papers from her purse and flattened them on the table. "I went back through and made a few changes."

He studied the numbers in the top paragraph. "You're conceding on the fifty percent?"

"Sounds to me like I'll be coming out ahead. You've promised to give it all back in the end. See? I added that clause in here." She pointed to a sentence set in italics.

"That's awesome, Jill. I can't thank you enough for being so…magnanimous."

She gave him a steely look, but any ire was just for show. "You already told me you're doing it to lock down the deal. So I don't decide to bolt. Trust me, I won't. I need all of that advance money for…" She stopped herself, deciding it was none of his business. The more professional she kept this arrangement between them, the better.

"For what?" He laid his hand on top of hers and her pulse thumped beneath it. Only a few days ago his mouth had claimed hers and she'd gone weak at the knees…and the world had tilt-a-whirled around her…sort of like it was doing now. Jill pulled back her hand.

"I'm building a new addition," she fibbed.

"To your house?" he asked, incredulous. He thought of her grandfather's predicament, wondering why she wasn't telling the truth. "Do Fifi and Mimi need their own rooms?"

"No, thankfully, they have one. Except now…" She paused, then continued quickly. "They'll have to move out. I mean, I guess we'll have to make do. Don't worry, I'll clean it up! Use a chemical spray if I have to. No, not chemical. Organic. That's what I meant." She stopped talking to catch her breath. Hunter's eyes were as big as saucers.

"Are you telling me you want me to move into the room where your pets stay?"

She grinned tightly, realizing that didn't sound very inviting. "Just joking! Ha-ha!" Jill took a quick sip of java. "The truth is the pets *do* have their own space, but they stay in the laundry room."

"The laundry room?"

"Of course!"

Hunter eyed her suspiciously "What makes you so certain I'm moving to your house in the first place?"

Oh yeah, she wasn't supposed to let that part slip. "Brad told me."

"So much for a surprise," he said, confounding her.

"Huh?"

"Doesn't matter." His lips were a hard line, but she couldn't read his expression.

Jill felt a little nervous and on edge. She couldn't have Hunter bail on her now. According to Brad, Cassandra's story had hit the pages of *Tempo Beat* magazine. Plus, she'd already talked to Morgan and her grandfather. Not only that, Hunter's boss, Max, knew!

"Don't say you're backing out on me?"

He looked at her seriously. "I *am* bringing my TV, Jill. That part's settled."

Jill leapt to her feet, banging into their table and sending coffee sloshing out of their cups. "Thank you!" She threw her arms around his neck and pulled him close—until she realized what she was doing. His mouth hovered inches above her own.

A sly smile tilted up his lips. "You were saying?" he asked sexily.

Jill collected herself in time to redirect and plant a peck on his cheek. Then she stepped back and primly straightened her skirt before sitting. "I was going to say, that's very kind. Generous of you to make that concession. Fifi and Mimi will be relieved."

"No doubt they've been suffering from bouts of anxiety."

"Animals have feelings, you know."

"That's not what you told me in high school," he quipped.

Jill's cheeks flamed as she recalled the conversation that had occurred the night of her high-school senior prom. She didn't have a date, so her childhood friend Brad, who was home from boarding school, had arranged for her to go with his best friend, while Brad went with her classmate and his long-term flame, Susan. Jill had been instantly attracted to handsome and outgoing Hunter, and there was apparently a mutual spark. Everything had gone reasonably well until the two couples had taken separate cars to go to the after parties. What Hunter had in mind was obviously a very private party of his own. They'd been talking amicably when Hunter had leaned in to kiss her. When Jill withdrew in surprise, he'd suggested they might be more comfortable in the backseat of his car. She'd called him an animal and then some, and had asked him to take her home. He'd replied with one word uttered in total disbelief: *Seriously?* Then, without speaking again, he'd cranked the ignition and driven Jill home. That was the last she'd seen of Hunter Delaney until Saturday at the club.

"That was a long time ago," she finally said.

"Sure was," he answered. "A lot has changed since then."

"Sure has," Jill agreed.

They sat there a moment, staring each other down as if each was daring the other to blink.

At last, Hunter pulled a pen from his pocket and handed it to her. "So," he said, his voice husky. "Are we going to do this thing?"

Jill took the pen and gathered her courage. "There's just one more request."

Hunter pursed his lips and waited.

"It's about my grandpa," she said in a sheepish tone. "He wants you to meet him."

"I suspect I'll have to, eventually. Just like you'll need to meet Max's wife, Diane."

"No, what I mean is…" She gripped the corner of the contract between her thumb and index finger. "He wants you to ask for my hand."

Hunter didn't just laugh, he *howled*. So loudly that people stared. "He what?"

"Can you please not make a spectacle?" she said, attempting to hush him.

"Okay, yes. Fine, I'm sorry." He adjusted the lapels of his jacket. "And you say I'm the old-fashioned one."

"It's not me!" Jill sputtered. "It's—"

"No worries," he told her calmly. "I'll do it. Just tell me where and when."

"As soon as possible would be good. Before the wedding for sure."

His gaze lingered on hers. "When *is* the happy day? We'll need to discuss that."

"My date with Brad was July eighteenth."

"Wow, that's close!"

"It's okay. I've already canceled the caterers."

"The other arrangements too?"

She nodded. "I had to give six weeks' notice in order to preserve a transfer option."

"What's that mean?"

"I can apply my deposits—for the caterer and the reception hall—to another event taking place at any time during the course of the next twelve months."

"So you can't get the money back?"

"It was too late for that."

"I don't want us spending a lot of money on a fancy reception, Jill."

"Then we don't have to. If my book goes well, maybe Morgan can talk the publisher into hosting a book party."

"Then they'd pick up the tab?" he asked.

Jill nodded.

"So you'd get back your money, after all."

"I know it all sounds really crazy," she said.

"Both of us should probably have our heads examined."

"But you think we can make this work, yeah?"

He spoke with assurance. "Yeah."

Hunter took the contract and scanned it briefly before adding his signature. When it was Jill's turn, she asked, "How about if we elope?"

It didn't take Hunter long to mull this over. "That sounds like a good plan," he agreed. "The right plan. We've already garnered some media attention. Perhaps it would be good if we were to be seen as laying low. You know, out of deference to poor Brad's feelings."

"That's very sensitive of you, Hunter." She scratched out her signature and eyed him thoughtfully. "I'm sorry about what I said in high school. I was just very…" She searched for the word. "…conservative, and you were so—"

"It's all right," he said, stopping her. "I'm sure I deserved it. Now, here's my question for you." He pulled a glossy magazine from his interior coat pocket. It had been doubled over, but he opened it for her, revealing its sensational cover. "Do you think we deserved this?"

Jill's mouth dropped open and her face flushed fiercely as she read the enormous caption: *Red Hot Heartbreak!* What was even worse was the couple on the cover, engaged in a heated embrace. The man held the woman in his arms, but she was practically climbing up him! It was like she was the cat and he was the tree, as she attempted to scale his broad torso…winding arms and legs around his muscular frame. And heaven knew what she was doing with her mouth! It was shoved so far up into his you couldn't even see her lips! "Goodness!"

"Yeah." Hunter shared a saucy grin, not looking the least bit embarrassed. "That's what I said."

Chapter Eight

Morgan flipped the magazine around after examining its explicit cover. "Now, that's what I call convincing," she said, thumping the photo of the couple with a manicured fingertip. She lowered the magazine in front of her lips to mask a giggle. "You didn't say it had gotten physical."

Jill snorted with irritation. "Are you here to help or offer commentary?"

Morgan pressed back the red bandanna she'd knotted around her hair like a headband and surveyed their surroundings. She wore jeans and an untucked button-down shirt with flat, sensible loafers. She'd supposedly arrived to help Jill clean out her guestroom, but had spent the past ten minutes drooling over the salacious details printed in the magazine. "I'm just saying you've done well. It will be obvious to the public that you and Hunter are quite combustible when we publish *Married Love: Keep—*"

Jill stopped her abruptly. "FYI, the kiss was a fake."

Morgan arched an eyebrow.

"One hundred percent pretend."

"O…kay."

Heat swept up Jill's neck. "I mean it. Brad was there. Cassandra was watching."

Morgan shrugged, clearly sensing Jill was not ready to give her the whole story. She glanced around and tossed the magazine onto a bedside table, the one housing a photo of Jill's fluffy gray cat, Mimi. "I can't believe your cat has his own bed," she said changing the subject. "Does he share with the dog, or what?"

"Of course not." Jill caught herself, realizing she sounded a tad indignant. "Fifi sleeps on the futon."

Morgan turned to the large wooden structure with a southwestern-patterned cover, noting its fine patina of tiny yellow hairs. The low table beside it held a reading lamp and a framed photo of Jill's yellow Lab, Fifi. "Hunter's going to love it in here."

Jill paused from loading pet toys into a laundry basket and shoved the basket in Morgan's direction. "Maybe you can help by putting the rest of them away?" she said, eying the multitude of items scattered about the floor. Morgan was probably thinking most children didn't have this many playthings, and perhaps she'd have a point. "I'll go grab the vacuum."

"Better bring the attachments!" Morgan shouted after her as she left the room.

When Jill reached the kitchen closet, she caught a glimpse through the window of Fifi and Mimi romping together in the yard. Mostly the cat was terrorizing the dog by claiming a bright yellow tennis ball as his own. He rolled lazily onto his back, then flipped over again, centering his claws on the toy as he swatted it slowly around. Fifi's big block head bobbed up and down and back and forth, her tail pointed high and her front legs hunched low, as she tried to keep track of the ball. The dog periodically leaned forward in an open-mouthed attempted to nab the prize. But Mimi would tap the dog's nose with a paw, sending the dog bolting backward every time. Fifi had been on the receiving end of Mimi's claws once when she was a little pup, and had learned to steer clear of them since.

Maybe the pair *did* have as many toys as some kids, but at the moment Mimi and Fifi were the only children Jill had. She'd rescued Mimi from a shelter six years ago, and had received Fifi as a Christmas gift from her short-term boyfriend at the time a few years afterward. Isaac had actually broken up with Jill the day he'd brought the puppy home. He'd already had it on order from the breeder, he'd said, and put down a deposit, so he figured going through with the gift was reasonable, even if he could no longer stand dating Jill. That had smarted, particularly given the fact that it was, you know, *Christmas*—and Jill had just been required to move her grandpa into assisted living the week before.

Sure, she'd cried a little, but mostly out of disappointment and frustration. While she hadn't been convinced she truly loved Isaac, she'd at least been determined to give it a go. He was handsome and intelligent, well-spoken and well employed. All the things she typically looked for. Yet, Isaac had been her third relationship disaster in less than a year. The only thing that helped ease the sting of his departure was that pudgy bundle of joy that leapt into her lap—that very first night—to lick up her tears with a heavy wet tongue.

In retrospect, Jill understood that she and Isaac were never right for each other. Isaac was uptight and exacting. Plus, he was exceptionally withdrawn, typically keeping his emotions to himself, while Jill was open and expressive. Much better that Isaac wound up with the conservative and tight-lipped Felicity—or whatever the new woman's name was—someone equally contained and perfunctory. Jill was provided with far more spontaneity and affection by Fifi than she'd ever gotten from Isaac. The dog had been a bit of a rascal in the beginning, but had turned out to be a wonderful pet once she'd settled in. *Just look at how well Fifi and Mimi get along,* she thought, as Mimi swatted at Fifi again and Fifi bounded backward.

Jill hauled the heavy vacuum cleaner out the closet and grabbed a nearby bucket of cleaning supplies. The guestroom would need a thorough scrubbing down before it would be habitable by any human, much less one who initially didn't want to live here. Jill was grateful to Hunter for conceding on this point, and intended to see that her pets made the best of it. She'd set up a nice sleeping station for the two of them in the corner of the laundry room, complete with a new climbing tower for Mimi and an overstuffed dog bed for Fifi. She planned to place extra toys and treats in there for them as well, until they got the hang of staying in their new digs. Jill seriously hoped Hunter had been joking when he claimed an allergy to cats. She intended to run all the guest room linens through the laundry an extra time in hot water, just in case.

Three hours later, they were almost done with their task. Morgan turned from wiping the last windowpane with cleaner and a paper towel. "It's hard to believe it's the same place!" Jill had to give her credit. She really could get down and dirty when the occasion called for it. Morgan was not only a dynamite agent, but also a great friend.

Jill sighed with satisfaction and set her hand on her hip, gazing around the room. Everything was neatly in place, and not a speck of pet hair remained. The bedspread and futon cover had each been through the wash and dry cycle twice, and looked immaculate. "I can't thank you enough for your help," she told Morgan. "It really does look terrific."

Morgan chucked her paper towel into the brimming garbage bag they planned to haul from the room. "So?" she asked eagerly. "You going to tell Mr. Hot Stuff he's moving into pet central?"

Jill shoved a few last things into the trash bag and knotted it. "Of course not. As far as I can see, there's no reason for Hunter to know."

"No," Morgan agreed. "As long as he's not allergic or anything."

A lump caught in Jill's throat. Surely, Hunter wasn't. "I...don't think so," she said, uncertainly. "Besides, we cleaned up very well! Laundered everything twice!"

"You're right," Morgan agreed. "That should do it. But even if Hunter *loves* pets, he might feel...awkward knowing he's displaced them."

"But, how would—?"

Morgan scooped the framed pet photos off the tables that held them and handed them to Jill. "Oh."

"It might be best to put these somewhere else," Morgan suggested. "Like...in the laundry room?"

Brad picked up some packing tape and used it to seal another moving box. "I've got to say I'm pretty surprised you let her talk you into it." He glanced around the glitzy contemporary apartment, admiring the huge leather sofa with comfy side chairs and the enormous sliding glass door that opened onto a balcony overlooking the city. "I thought you loved this place."

"I do," Hunter answered, "but I love certain other things more."

"Like?"

"Like…the sound of…" Hunter smiled wistfully. "Abrams and Delaney Advertising."

"It does have kind of a ring to it," Brad agreed.

"A *ca-ching, ca-ching* ring," Hunter responded. "When I make partner, my income goes up."

"I like the way you said *when* and not *if*."

"I've always been an optimistic guy."

Hunter sorted through some CDs and placed them back in their slots on a shelf. He had most of the music he liked downloaded to his laptop and personal devices anyway. No need to take these. "It's not just about the money, you know," he said turning to Brad. "I really want this promotion."

"You're the best one for it. I can't believe Max actually considered tapping that weasel Fred."

"I'm not convinced that's the way he wanted it. Max was under pressure from Kaleidoscope Kids."

"How do you know you and Jill won't start feeling some of that *pressure* to produce a few kids of your own? Isn't that part of the expectation?" Brad teased. "That you'll be in a *family way*?"

"Married means family," Hunter stated reasonably. He hefted an old football trophy into his hands, examining it in the natural light of the windows. "You can't get much more related than that."

"Don't tell me you're taking your old sports trophies with you?"

Hunter studied the lettering on the plaque: *Most Valuable Player* of his graduating class year. It had been the first time Hunter had truly felt successful at something, and he'd accomplished it all on his own by rising early for extra workouts before the seven a.m. start of his prep school classes. He'd become determined to be the best goal kicker in the history of the elite institution, and, after driving himself hard— through snow, mud, and rain—he'd accomplished that objective. It wasn't just about football; it was about what Hunter could achieve when he put his mind to it. It didn't matter that his parents never attended a single game, while the other boys routinely had their families in the stands. It was the lesson Hunter had learned that counted. And that lesson was, Hunter could get anything if he wanted it badly enough. He'd gotten into an excellent college, interned for various companies, worked hard to keep his grades high—and secured a super job immediately upon graduation. Hunter knew how to play just about any game that life could toss at him. But basically, it had all started with football.

Feeling a sentimental tug in his chest, Hunter dusted off the trophy and set it in a packing box. "I'm only taking this one," he said, answering Brad. Then, to mask any hint of emotion, he added, "Might use it as a paperweight or something." He sealed up a few cartons of his own and turned to his friend, who was piling up other boxes in the corner beside a well-padded large-screen television. "And what's all this talk about family, anyway? Weren't you the one giving me the hands-off speech when it came to Jill?"

"Yeah, but that's before I saw that magazine cover. Honestly, man, I had no clue she was that into you."

"You were standing right there!"

"Cassandra's camera caught the kiss at a better angle."

"Cassandra's gifted, I'll give her that. I didn't even see a long-lens camera, but she managed to get that close-up somehow."

"Maybe she enhanced it in Photoshop?" Brad suggested.

Hunter recalled every inch of Jill's body torridly pressed to his, her lips and mouth on fire. But he wasn't sharing those details with Brad. He'd probably already shared enough. The truth was, Hunter kind of liked Jill. And when he liked a woman, he tended to keep amorous details concerning the lady to himself. Perhaps he'd dished a little to Brad before, but things seemed different now that Jill was really becoming his wife. They'd both signed a contract. It was happening. Plus, she'd looked awfully sweet when she'd petitioned Hunter about speaking with her grandfather. For some reason Hunter hadn't been able to get that look in her eyes out of his mind. That, and the vision of her long, lovely legs tapering toward those menacing heels… Jill Jamison was a woman he'd have to treat right. It occurred to Hunter that buying a backup phone charger might not be a bad idea. "Maybe."

Brad set his last box on top of the heap by a collection of hanging bags and suitcases. "You guys sure have fast-tracked your elopement."

"Jill says the sooner we start our year of wedded bliss, the sooner we can end it. I've got to admit she has a point."

"Everything's happening next Friday?"

"The ceremony's Friday. That's when we could get the judge. My movers come Saturday morning."

"Who's standing up for you guys? Don't you need witnesses or something?" Brad asked. He tried to sound casual about it, but Hunter could tell Brad feared for a moment that Hunter might not extend the offer to him.

"Jill's already asked Morgan." He strode toward his buddy and patted his shoulder. "And I wouldn't undergo a fake marriage with anyone else at my side." He eyed Brad uncertainly. "That is, if you can get the morning off?"

"No worries. I'll put in a sub plan." Brad paused reflectively, then stunned Hunter by wrapping his arms around him. "I can't believe this!" he cried, gripping Hunter in a tight bear hug. "You're getting hitched!" Holy cow, Brad was practically squeezing the wind out of him.

"And you never thought I'd bite the bullet." Hunter wheezed, struggling out of Brad's hold.

"But here you go!" For some odd reason, Brad was beaming brightly.

"What are you so happy about?"

"You and Jill together. It somehow just hit me. Hunter, I know that this sounds nuts, but what if by some incredible miracle you and she—?"

"Bite your tongue," Hunter said. "Jill Jamison and I have cut a deal, a deal that involves *separate bedrooms,* as you'll recall. Not too long ago, you worried over protecting the woman's virtue."

"I still care about Jill!" Brad protested hotly. "The truth is I care about both of you!"

"Then it would be good of you to keep our secret, and not try to complicate things by implying they might develop into something more than they are. Jill didn't want me twelve years ago, like she doesn't want me now, not in any sort of serious romantic way. That's what makes this charade easy. Jill and I are both very clear on where we stand." Hunter's conscience winced as he recalled his response to Jill's kiss. Okay, so maybe he couldn't fault himself for that. He was only human, after all, and male. A physical reaction didn't mean anything. How many times had he experienced that with other women, only to have the prospect of any real relationship fizzle?

"But what about that kiss? I thought you said in the bar that—?"

"I know what I said, but I could have been mistaken. Who knows? Maybe Jill just reacted to me like she would have to any available guy? The way I reacted to her as an attractive woman? Perhaps she had a brief lapse…experienced a moment of carnal weakness, but that's all that it was, a simple mistake. Fortunately, I'm the forgiving sort. One kiss means nothing in the scheme of things, my friend. Absolutely nothing. Nothing at all."

Brad twisted his lips in a frown. "It's a good thing Cassandra can't hear you talking, because your cover would be blown."

"That reminds me!" Hunter snapped his fingers. "Since you know her, would you mind calling Cassandra and inviting her to the wedding?"

"You're joking."

"Dead serious. Please let her know it's next Friday morning at ten o'clock. Sugar Hollow courthouse. No other press is allowed. Jill and I are offering her an exclusive."

Brad stared at him. "You really mean that?"

"You betcha. The whole thing was Jill's idea. And, honest to goodness?" Hunter grinned. "I think it's brilliant."

Chapter Nine

Hunter and Jill entered the lobby of the assisted living building at Green Meadows Retirement Village. It was called a *cottage,* but seemed much more expansive than that, with inviting common areas, a large resident dining room, and a landscaped central courtyard. Jill had explained to Hunter on the way over that the building's design allowed for each resident's private bedroom to overlook a flowering green area. It was easy to see why Jill felt so good about having her grandpa here. A uniformed woman with a pleasant face and a name tag that read "Hilda" looked up from her seat behind the reception desk. A large vase of Asiatic lilies perched beside the sign-in book, giving off a sweet scent that perfumed the air. "Good afternoon, Miss Jamison," Hilda said, recognizing her at once. She checked the calendar on the wall, scanning the list of activities for Thursday. "Your grandfather's just finishing up his morning exercise. You can find him in the gym."

Jill thanked the woman and led Hunter through a common area where a foursome sat by a window playing cards. They all looked up with happy smiles when they saw Jill approaching. As she passed, she greeted them each by name. "You're quite a regular here, I take it?" Hunter asked as they traversed a broad hallway with built-in handrails on either side.

"I come by every Wednesday and Sunday," she told him. "Whether or not my grandpa's expecting me. Most days, he still does."

Hunter nodded, knowing Jill was referring to her granddad's memory problems. She'd told him that they were getting worse, though she was hoping today would be a good day. Hunter found it admirable that Jill cared for her grandfather as she did. She was apparently the only family the old man had and vice versa, and she took her responsibility toward him seriously. The fact that she visited regularly showed a sense of commitment. Hunter wondered vaguely what that was like, feeling committed toward someone in that way. So far in his life, Hunter had been responsible for no one but himself.

Apart from providing early financial support, his parents had never apparently felt much obligation toward him. That was one reason Hunter had decided to become financially independent as soon as possible. Though his dad would have been happy to stroke a check for college, Hunter felt more comfortable tackling his academic bills on his own. He'd won some scholarships and had waited tables on weekends and in the evenings after classes in order to get by. That was far better in his mind than accepting further charity from his parents. He'd never really wanted their money anyway. Perhaps in a manner he resented it, as it was the only thing they'd appeared willing to provide.

The double doors to the gym were propped open. Just as they entered, a uniformed nurse pushing a wheelchair approached them. She exchanged a greeting with Jill while the face of the elderly man in the chair lit up. "Well, look who's here!" Mr. Jamison warmly extended his arms toward his granddaughter and she rushed into a hug, wrapping her arms around his neck. "Hi, Grandpa," she said, planting a kiss on his cheek. "You're looking snappy today!"

Gordon Jamison beamed, his eyes settling on Hunter. "You've brought a friend to see me?"

"I have!" she proclaimed sweetly. "Shall we take you to visit in the great room, or would you prefer the courtyard?"

"Let's go outdoors," the old man said. "I'd like to get some sunshine."

Jill thanked the nurse who'd been assisting him, then commandeered the wheelchair, steering it back down the hall she and Hunter had just walked through. "This is that fellow, isn't it?" her grandpa asked in a loud whisper. "The one that you were telling me about?"

Hunter repressed a grin, thinking Mr. Jamison seemed like a little boy, practically bursting from a very big secret. He hoped his and Jill's news would make Mr. Jamison's day, as opposed to causing him concern. They were cutting things fairly close. Their ceremony was tomorrow. Hunter held open the door to the patio, letting Jill and the man in the wheelchair pass through before him. He couldn't help but marvel at the obvious affection between Jill and her grandfather. It made him think more of Jill somehow, like she had to be a pretty fine person to treat a relative so well. Back in high school, Hunter had thought of Jill as stuck up. During lunch at the club and then later over coffee, some of that earlier impression had lingered. But here, with her grandfather, Jill's character seemed different. She appeared warm and genuine, caring even. This put Jill in such sharp contrast with any of the women Hunter had dated that he didn't know quite what to make of it.

Jill parked the wheelchair near a fountain and gestured to a semicircular bench for Hunter to take a seat beside her. "Mr. Jamison," Hunter said, seizing the opportunity. "It's so great to finally meet you." He held out his hand and the old man took it. "I'm—"

"I know exactly who you are," the old man said with a perfunctory grin. His pale blue eyes surveyed Hunter coolly. Hunter shook and released Mr. Jamison's hand, feeling very much as if he'd just been sized up. "You're the one who's planning to marry my granddaughter."

"Yes, sir. That's right." Hunter wasn't certain what the protocol was here. Surely, he wasn't expected to get down on one knee? That part was generally reserved for the groom proposing to the bride. Whatever he was supposed to do, he apparently wasn't doing it well enough. Mr. Jamison's eyes narrowed, and Hunter could have sworn they glimmered with disapproval. Hunter glanced at Jill, who was biting into her bottom lip, before barreling ahead. "That is, if I can have your permission?"

Mr. Jamison spoke in an icy tone. "I must say this is a pretty big turnaround from last Christmas."

"Christmas?" Jill asked weakly.

"Yes, sweetheart," her grandpa answered. "And don't think I can't recall what this young man put you through."

Jill gasped with understanding. "Grandpa, no. This isn't—"

"I know what you're thinking." He studied his granddaughter kindly. "That this isn't any of my business. But to my mind, anything that concerns you certainly is." He briefly glanced at Hunter before focusing back on Jill. "I'd like to have a word or two alone with Isaac. Why don't you go and see if you can rustle us up a few cups of tea?"

Hunter stared at Jill, seeing her eyes had pooled with tears. She was working hard to contain them, pressing her lips firmly together. He couldn't imagine how hard this must be for her, seeing her grandfather become confused this way. He'd obviously mistaken Hunter for someone else. But who the heck was Isaac? "I think tea sounds very nice." Hunter cocked his head toward Jill. "If you don't mind?"

"But…" Her chin trembled slightly, and a painful lump rose unexpectedly in Hunter's throat. It was as if Hunter could sense Jill's pain, but that was impossible, wasn't it? He barely knew her. "I don't think I should—"

"We'll be fine," Hunter said, in the most soothing tone he could offer. "Really." He met her eyes and she blinked quickly, turning away.

"Bring mine with lemon, please!" her grandpa called as she scurried across the patio. Hunter couldn't help but notice that as Jill had left she'd drawn a hand up toward her face. Had it been to muffle a sob, or dry a tear? He had an overwhelming urge to go after her and try to find out, and to lend her some comfort. But Hunter understood he had important business here.

"Mr. Jamison," Hunter began. "I'm sorry to see that you appear disappointed in me."

"No doubt your parents were heartbroken too."

"Sir?" This turn in the conversation caught Hunter completely off guard. Jill had warned Hunter that her grandpa's mind might wander. If it did, she'd suggested the best course of action was to follow along, and let Gordon take the lead. Arguing with him or attempting to correct him only made him agitated and confused.

"Your parents, I said. Although I never met them, I understand they met Jilly. And if they met her, they were bound to have loved her. How could they not have?"

"How could they not have…?" Hunter echoed softly, sensing the veracity of the words.

"How could *you* not have?" Mr. Jamison asked combatively. He angled forward in his chair, and for a moment Hunter feared he might spill out of it. He scooted to the edge of his seat and readied himself to spring forward and catch the older man if necessary.

"I'm not sure what you're—?"

"I'm talking about that darned dog, Isaac."

Dog?

"The one with the ridiculous name!"

"Fifi?" Hunter asked huskily.

"That's the one." Jamison sat back in his wheelchair. "As if that could make up for what you did to her."

"For what I did to…Jill?" Hunter queried, putting the pieces together.

"Yes, I'm talking about when you left her, but said she could keep the dog because you'd already bought it for her anyway. And on Christmas Day too. Now tell me," the old man said with a glare. "Don't you think that was slightly uncharitable?"

"What a jerk!" Hunter's mouth hung open, then he closed it. "I mean, what a jerk I was to do such a thing. That was highly unforgivable."

"And yet, by some miracle of nature, my granddaughter has apparently chosen to forgive you."

Jamison perused him slowly from top to bottom. "You're getting married, she said."

Hunter swallowed hard. He'd been prepared to ask for Jill's hand on behalf of himself. He wasn't sure if he could do it pretending to be some obvious cad who'd dumped Jill during the holidays. Wow, talk about a very un-merry Christmas. Some people had all the nerve. Others just clearly didn't think. "Um," Hunter hedged. "We've been talking about it."

"Oh?" said Jill, returning. "What have we been talking about?" She carried a small cardboard carrying tray that held three paper cups of tea. An assortment of sugars and creamers nestled in the middle of the box. Hunter noticed that her eyes were dry but bloodshot, and her face was pink, as if she'd splashed cool water on it.

"Our...upcoming wedding." Hunter tried to conceal his perplexed expression by reaching for some tea. He offered a cup to Mr. Jamison, then took one for himself as Jill set down the tray between them on the bench.

"Here, Grandpa," Jill said reaching for his cup. "Let me fix that up for you."

"All right," Jamison said, handing it over.

"I'm sorry," Hunter said, realizing belatedly Jill meant to add lemon to her grandpa's tea for him first.

"It's okay." She smiled wanly, but her eyes looked sad. "You couldn't be expected to know how he takes it."

After the teas were readied and everyone held his or her own cup, they each took a few sips and contemplated one another in silence. Birds chirped in the courtyard and butterflies hovered over stands of flowers. There was even a hummingbird nearby drinking happily from a tall hibiscus plant. Mr. Jamison surveyed his lovely surroundings, then let out a long sigh.

"So then," he said, turning his attention on Hunter. "When's the wedding?"

"We…um…" Hunter worried if admitting the ceremony was so soon would be too much. Jill apparently thought otherwise because she quickly said, "Tomorrow."

Jamison's eyebrows rose. "What's the rush?"

"When it's right, it's right." Hunter reached out and took Jill's hand. She started with surprise, but let him hold it.

"Yes," Jill added. "We thought it best not to prolong things."

Mr. Jamison analyzed Hunter for a moment and said, "I only have one question for you."

Hunter held his breath. "Yes, sir?"

"Do you love Jill?"

Now, that was a loaded question, and one Hunter had better become practiced at answering. Only twenty-four hours from now, he'd be proclaiming his true love for Jill before a judge. Particularly as Cassandra would be attending the ceremony, Hunter understood it would behoove him to sound convincing. He could begin by sharing a bit of that conviction here and now.

"With my whole heart," Hunter said.

"And he has a *very good heart,*" Jill added sweetly. She batted her eyelashes at Hunter, and for a fraction of a second he wondered if she was flirting with him. Then he realized with a flash of disappointment that she was probably only teasing. But why should Hunter feel disappointed about that? He didn't actually want Jill flirting with him, did he? Although she just might do so for the benefit of others, from time to time, during the course of their fake marriage. Hunter supposed he'd better resign himself to receiving mixed messages and get used to it. Or maybe that's how a lot of real marriages were, with the husband never quite understanding where he stood with his wife. Being kept constantly on his toes.

Hunter lightly squeezed Jill's hand and smiled at Jamison. "So, sir. Do I have your blessing?"

Jamison shrugged and said brusquely, "If Jilly wants you, who am I to stop her? Nobody's ever been able to stop that child from getting what she wanted since she was two years old."

Chapter Ten

Jill was pretty quiet during the drive. It reminded Hunter of another time he'd driven her home, but that instance was very different. She'd been in high school and living with her parents. Now, she was an adult woman living on her own. *In a house that I've never seen but am moving into on Saturday,* Hunter reminded himself. When they'd set the date for going to Green Meadows, they'd agreed to meet up at the coffee shop near Hunter's office. Jill had been strategizing with Morgan earlier, discussing book tours and marketing details. Morgan had picked Jill up at her house and they'd gone to lunch. Afterward, Jill had connected with Hunter in town. The plan was for him to meet her grandpa at Green Meadows and then drive Jill back to Sugar Hollow so he could catch a glimpse of where he'd be hanging his hat for the next twelve months. Hunter hoped Jill's house was passable.

She was staring at her feet, apparently contemplating the bright red polish on her toenails. They were visible in strappy sandals and she wore a pretty sundress splashed with bright yellow sunflowers. Hunter had never known one woman to have so many varied looks. There was the spunky and sporty Jill, like he'd seen at the club. Then, the highly polished and professional Jill who had arrived at the coffee shop to sign their contract. And now, this soft, feminine rendition, a tender-hearted granddaughter with warm, expressive eyes. "I want to thank you," she said quietly. "Thank you for being so kind to my grandfather."

"I liked your grandfather," Hunter offered honestly. "I liked him a lot. I enjoy a man who speaks his mind."

"I know…" Her words trailed off. "It's just hard to see his mind wander sometimes."

"That can come with age, Jill."

"Doesn't make it any easier."

"I'm sure that it doesn't."

She let that thought linger a moment before asking, "What did he want to talk to you about? I mean, when he thought you were Isaac?"

"Not much really that I recall."

"You don't have to hide it from me. I know my grandpa sometimes says things. He doesn't mean to. I apologize if he was rude to you."

"No apologies necessary," Hunter said. "The truth is he was a perfect gentleman." Hunter was sure Mr. Jamison would have been, if he'd had his wits about him. Besides, Hunter didn't take it personally that Jill's granddad was angry with Isaac. Hunter had never even met the guy, and he instantly disliked him. He and Mr. Jamison evidently had that in common: a distaste for anyone who would mistreat Jill. Though Hunter had experienced his ups and downs with women, he'd never hurt any of them intentionally. He'd clearly never done anything as callous as breaking up with someone on a holiday. Come to think of it, he'd never broken up with anyone at all. It was always the other way around. Hunter released a deep breath.

"You all right?" she asked him.

"Just thinking."

"About what?"

"About how crazy it is that we're getting married."

"It is kind of crazy, isn't it?" She surprised him by cracking a grin and his heart cartwheeled slightly. Not all the way around. Maybe a seventy-degree turn. Hunter couldn't believe he was analyzing it.

Hunter answered past the lump in his throat. "Yeah."

"You know what I think?" Her tone was almost playful. "I think it's good to be crazy once in a while." She caught his attention before he turned it back on the road. "Don't you?"

Hunter shook his head, wondering what his teenage self would have said if someone had told him he'd be marrying Jill Jamison someday. Probably that he was nuts, certifiable, dreaming the impossible dream. But here they were in the light of day, about to embark on the adventure of a lifetime: a blessed union that was patently false. "You can't get any crazier than us, Jill."

Hunter parked in Jill's gravel driveway and she climbed from his SUV. "Let me just run in for a minute and shut up the pets."

Hunter closed his driver's door behind him and followed Jill up the steps to the front porch of her cozy country cottage. It was pale yellow and its shutters and front door were freshly painted black. With its bucolic setting on five wooded acres, it almost looked like a house out of a child's fairy tale. Azalea bushes hugged its perimeter, and stands of pansies and daffodils danced in front of them. "If it's Fifi and Mimi you're talking about, you might as well let us get acquainted. We're going to be spending some time together, it seems."

Color stained Jill's cheeks as she unlocked the door. "Well, if you're sure…"

Hunter studied the covered porch, which was broad enough to host several cushioned wicker chairs and a large love seat with a matching table. On the opposite end from the drive, a dangling porch swing for two rocked gently in the afternoon breeze. "This is nice, Jill. Very sweet," he said. "I didn't quite expect it." His nose twitched a tiny bit, but he figured that would improve once they got inside and away from so many flowering things.

"Thanks," she said with a smile. "It's home."

Yep, Hunter guessed that it would be his home too, for the next twelve months. No matter. He'd just look at it as a vacation from the city. He'd kept the condo, of course, as he'd be needing it later. Besides, if things got too crazy here, he could always head back to his place for a night or two. He supposed he and Jill could work something out that gave Hunter a degree of flexibility.

Jill had barely pushed back the door when a big golden-colored dog came bounding in their direction. It had huge dark eyes and a stuffed toy of some kind in its mouth. "Hunter!" Jill exclaimed proudly. "Meet Fifi."

The back end of the animal wiggled furiously until Jill commanded it to *sit*. It did so immediately, dropping the toy from its mouth at Hunter's feet. Fifi stared up at Hunter with big dopey eyes and a panting grin, and Hunter heard himself chuckle. "Well, hey there, you poor abused animal," he said, stooping to scratch the dog behind the ears.

"Abused?" Jill countered contentiously.

Hunter ignored her and continued addressing the dog. "Your mom couldn't come up with a proper name for you, huh? No worries. I'm here to help in that department."

Fifi licked the back of his hand, then craned her neck to run her tongue along the side of his face when Hunter leaned forward. He laughed out loud again. "Very friendly dog you've got here."

"Yes," Jill said, "and she's very well treated, thank you very much."

Hunter's nose twitched again and he hoped he wasn't about to start sneezing. Perhaps he should have taken an allergy pill, but he hadn't even considered it. They were just dropping by for a bit. Besides, he hadn't had trouble with his allergies in years. Hunter gave Fifi one last pat on the head and stood. "So? Am I going to get the rest of the tour?"

"Sure!" Jill glanced around the small living room, which was well-appointed with quaint décor and something Hunter hadn't seen in a very long time: a real wood-burning fireplace. "Just let me check something first," she said, darting from the room into another that was obviously the kitchen. Hunter couldn't understand why, but she looked mildly panicked. It wasn't like he was the kind to be disturbed by a few dirty dishes in the sink.

Jill raced through the kitchen to the open laundry room door. She'd known something was amiss the moment Hunter's SUV had approached the house and she'd spied Fifi's big block head observing them through the living room window. When she'd left to have lunch with Morgan, she'd secured Fifi and Mimi in the laundry room with treats and toys. She'd worked so hard to clean the house, she hadn't wanted them to make a mess of things before she brought Hunter by. She also didn't want them assaulting him the moment he walked in the door. Most especially though, Jill didn't want the pair sneaking back into the guestroom, as they had repeatedly done after she and Morgan had so thoroughly cleaned it. She quickly scanned the laundry room, finding Mimi nowhere in sight. He hadn't been in the living room or the large eat-in kitchen either. This only left three more rooms: Jill's bedroom, her office, and… "Excuse me!" she told Hunter, scampering through the living room and toward the other part of the house. He stared at her with a curious expression as she whizzed by.

"Jill, you really don't need to worry about—"

"No worry!" she cried, scooting past him.

"I'm really not that picky!" he called down the hall as she stepped into her office. Mimi sometimes slept in here, grabbing a spot in the sun by the window. No cat. Uh-oh.

"It's fine!" she yelled back to Hunter. "Just checking something!"

Jill didn't expect to find Mimi in her room. The pets had been trained since they were little to sleep elsewhere, so they rarely came into her sanctuary. Why would they, when everyone was accustomed to occupying his or her own territory? She peered into the empty master bedroom, then spun toward the guestroom, finding that door slightly ajar. She'd been quite certain she'd closed it, but the latch didn't always engage completely and something had apparently nudged it open. "Mimi!" she hissed softly, flipping back the bedding. Sure enough, he'd broken in and had made himself a cozy nest between the sheets and comforter. Jill scooped the cat into her arms with a scolding look. "You sneak! Now I'll have to launder everything again!" Mimi blinked in the natural light streaming in from the window. He'd apparently been enjoying himself quite a bit in his dark little cave.

"Is this where...? *Aaaachoo*!"

Jill stared in horror at Hunter standing on the threshold, covering his mouth and nose with both hands. He sneezed violently a second time, and then a third. Jill nabbed a few tissues from a box on the nightstand, carrying them to him. When he spied the approaching cat, Hunter only sneezed again. "I'm sorry." His eyes were watery and beet red. He accepted the tissues and loudly blew his nose while Jill waited, her heart thumping hard.

"You weren't kidding?" Her gaze flitted to Mimi, then back to Hunter. "About pets?"

Hunter grabbed for the tissue box and sneezed again. "Just cats." He glanced around the sunny space. "This is not where I'm staying, is it?"

Jill backed away and put down the cat, shooing him out the door. "Mimi hardly ever comes in here," she fibbed. "He generally stays outdoors."

Hunter's brow shot up. "He? With a name like Mimi, I thought—"

"Oh, that!" Jill gave a nervous laugh. "The shelter said he was female when I adopted him. Somebody must have gotten it wrong on the paperwork, or he was too young to tell."

"And you never thought to check?" he asked, teary eyed.

Jill flushed brightly. "I... Well, no. Not until I took him to be spayed, and the vet informed he'd need a different kind of…" Her voice fell off when she noticed Hunter viewing the rumpled bed. "Don't worry about the linens! I'll wash them extra well between now and Saturday."

Hunter nodded, looking miserable. "I think I'd better step outside," he said sniffling.

"Right!" Jill replied quickly. "Should I bring us some lemonade to have on the porch?"

"I'll probably just go back now." Hunter inched toward the hall. "I've still got work to do at the office this afternoon."

Jill felt terrible, hoping Hunter could manage to work in that condition. He looked a wreck. "Can I...get you anything for the drive?" she offered lamely. "An antihistamine maybe?"

"I'll take one if you have it," he said.

A slight panic seized her. What if Hunter's allergies were too much and he couldn't tolerate living here? Would she have to move to the city? What about Fifi and Mimi? Who would take them? Neither Brad nor Susan lived in places that allowed pets, and she doubted Hunter's condo allowed them either. "I'm so sorry. I didn't think your condo would allow pets."

"They don't, and it's okay." He took a deep breath, then wiped his eyes and nose with more tissues. "I think I'll take a few extras for the drive if you don't mind."

Five minutes later Jill stood at Hunter's driver-side window, passing him a chilled water bottle and an antihistamine tablet. "Are you sure you should take this and drive?"

"Town isn't far away," he said. "By the time this kicks in, I'll be at the office and drinking coffee."

Jill felt horrible and at a loss, but she wasn't sure exactly what else she could do. "I feel really awful, Hunter. I hope we can still work things out?"

"It's fine. I'm fine. I've got some stronger meds at home. I'll pack them."

Tears streamed down his cheeks and suddenly Jill had an image of what Hunter must have looked like as a little boy, one who'd just gotten some bad news or misplaced his favorite toy. It occurred to Jill that Hunter must have been an adorable child. He'd no doubt produce one just as attractive, with gorgeous dark eyes…like the ones that were now gushing like waterfalls!

"Mimi's like my baby," she said pleadingly. "If I didn't feel that way about him, I—"

"Nobody's asking you to get rid of your baby, Jill." He blew his nose and started his engine. "Just make me a promise."

"Name it."

"Keep the cat out of my room."

Jill nodded numbly, unable to believe what a good sport he was being. What other man would have put up with this…and her…and this totally wack situation? Was this really happening, in spite of it all? Were she and Hunter really getting married tomorrow? "We're still on, then?" she asked a tad sheepishly. "For the wedding?"

He looked at her, his eyes bleary. "You may not know much about me, but I can tell you this: I'm not a guy who goes back on his word." He grabbed a few more tissues from the box in her hand, then she shoved the entire box toward him.

"Better take the whole thing," she said sympathetically. "For the road."

Chapter Eleven

Morgan sniffed into a tissue. "I just love weddings, don't you?" She and Jill had arrived at the courthouse twenty minutes early and had taken refuge in the restroom to make last-minute preparations. Jill didn't know why she should worry when it was all a stage show anyway. Still, she found herself wanting to look nice for the day. Plus, she was well aware the press would be watching and taking photos. Cassandra had eagerly accepted Brad's invitation and had promised to be there.

"Sure," answered Jill. "But I tend to enjoy them more when they're not my own." She adjusted the bodice of her dress in the restroom mirror. It was a simple design with spaghetti straps and an Empire waistline. The satin charmeuse fabric was silky to the touch and a rich cream color. Its A-line skirt was tea-length, just grazing her calves. She wore brushed ivory pumps to match. The outfit was simple but tasteful, and she'd decided to forgo the fussiness of a train or a veil. That had seemed the right decision when she'd purchased the dress for marrying Brad. Now that Jill was wedding Hunter, she was even more thankful her getup wasn't over the top. "What do you think?" she asked, turning to Morgan, "are the earrings too much?"

Morgan studied the pretty pearl drop earrings and smiled. "They're perfect."

"Even for the morning?"

"They look just right with the dress," Morgan answered. She primped in the other mirror, applying a swath of pomegranate lipstick. Her crisp linen suit was a pale lemon yellow. Her heels and purse were a vibrant red. Morgan tended to spice things up by adding a splash of color. She extracted a mascara wand from its tube and began touching up her eyelashes. "So?" she asked. "What did you and Hunter decide to do about the rings?"

Jill sucked in a gasp. "Oh my gosh! The rings!" She stared down at her ring finger and the pretty antique ring that had belonged to her late Grandmother Rose. She'd used it as a placeholder during her fake engagement to Brad. She'd gotten so used to wearing it, most days she didn't recall it was there. But there it was! And she and Hunter hadn't even discussed exchanging wedding bands. Not even inexpensive ones with a good return policy. She and Brad had thought they'd buy a basic set, then return the rings or sell them back later on. With Brad out of the picture as the groom and her nuptials getting bumped up, Jill had completely forgotten about that plan.

"It's all right," Morgan added hastily. "This elopement came on very quickly. I'm sure the judge has married other people in your position."

Jill eyed her doubtfully. "I'll have to say something to Hunter."

"He probably hasn't thought of it either."

"No. It never came up. Between seeing my grandpa and—"

"How did that go, by the way?" Morgan asked her.

Jill angled her head thoughtfully. "You know, actually pretty well."

"Your granddad and Hunter got along?"

Jill exuded pleased surprise. "Yeah."

"Hunter was nice to play along with that."

"I know. And Morgan…" She latched onto Morgan's arm. "You'll never believe this next part. Hunter *is* allergic, to Mimi."

"Oh, no!"

"Oh, yes."

"What are you going to do?"

"He says he'll suffer through."

"Good man," Morgan said with a smile. "And there you thought this was going to be difficult!"

Jill self-consciously adjusted her skirt. "It is going to be difficult. Just maybe…" She tried to keep the smile from her lips, but one crept up anyway. "Not as much as I thought."

"Holy tamale!" Morgan exclaimed in a whisper. "You *like* him, don't you?"

Jill protested, keeping her voice low. "I didn't say that."

"You didn't have to." Morgan spoke with a gleam in her eye. "It's written all over your pretty pink cheeks."

Jill cupped her hands to her face. "Morgan!" she hissed, "Shhh!"

"It's okay to actually like the guy you're going to marry, you know," Morgan stated reasonably. She tucked her makeup back in her purse and starting helping Jill pack away her accessories in the small carry-on bag that now contained the jeans and T-shirt Jill had arrived in. Morgan had carefully carted in the hanging bag with the dress.

"It's not that I *like* like him," Jill countered. "It's just that I'm discovering there's more to Hunter than meets the eye."

"And what meets the eye is really pleasing," Morgan said with a wink.

"Okay, yes." Jill blushed. "He's hot. Even better-looking now than he was in high school. But back then I thought of him as a total jerk."

"Only last week you thought of him as a total jerk."

"That's what makes this so weird," Jill whispered. "I'm beginning to wonder if he's not."

"Well, wouldn't that be lucky for you?"

"It would certainly make the next year more tolerable." Jill draped the strap of her bag over her shoulder.

"Here, let me have that," said Morgan, taking it from her. "We wouldn't want to wrinkle that pretty dress!"

"Morgan," Jill asked seriously. "Do you think I'm doing the right thing? This bogus marriage and all?"

"In truth, Jill? Even I think it's a little crazy, but no crazier than complete strangers getting hitched in Vegas, and apparently that happens all the time."

"Yeah." Jill sighed.

"Besides," Morgan reminded her, "you've got the book deal to think of."

"And my grandpa," Jill said. She felt a certain melancholy that he couldn't be there. Then again, did she really want him present when the whole thing was a sham?

"Yes, especially him."

"Maybe it won't be so bad?" Jill raised her brow hopefully. "Cohabiting with Hunter?"

Morgan pulled Jill into her arms in a hug. "Oh, darling, I hope not. After all, it's only for twelve months. How bad could it be?"

"By this time next year I'll be a free man." Hunter adjusted the cuffs on his tuxedo as he and Brad stood outside the courthouse. It was a warm spring day and the sun was shining, beaming down on them through the drooping branches of a large willow tree.

"That was really cool of you to rent a tux," Brad said. "You didn't have to."

"I didn't," Hunter answered. "I own it."

Brad looked at him in surprise.

"I don't know if I told you about Veronica in Boston?"

"The name vaguely rings a bell."

"She was into society parties. Her job was in fund-raising for the arts, so there were lots of them."

"How long did that last?" Brad asked.

"Likely longer than it should have."

"You know what I'm thinking?" Brad dragged a hand down his face. "I'm thinking that this thing with Jill will be good for you. Teach you a thing or two about longevity."

"If you're talking about long-term commitments, I've found they're overrated."

"That's because you've never experienced any."

Hunter patted Brad's shoulder. "Sad but true."

"I want to thank you, Hunter. Say thanks again for taking this on."

Hunter met his eyes. "You know I wouldn't be doing it unless I'd thought it through. Besides..." He quirked a grin. "I'm finding Jilly kind of sweet. I believe I'll handle being domesticated by her just fine."

Brad chuckled. "Domesticated, you? Right." He paused a beat, then goggled at Hunter in surprise. "Hang on, are you saying that you've started to like—?"

"Not in the least."

"Not even a little?"

"No, sir."

"Your pants are smoking."

"What?" Getting it, Hunter shook his head with a laugh. "Now you're being juvenile."

"I tend to think of it as astute."

"My, my, aren't you two fellows a handsome pair!" Hunter turned toward the walkway to catch Cassandra approaching, a camera bag dangling from the crook of her arm. She wore a form-fitting pantsuit with strappy high-heeled sandals.

"Good afternoon, Cassandra," Hunter said with a nod.

Brad adjusted the tie beneath his tweed jacket, the only sports coat that he owned. "Thanks for coming. Really glad you could make it."

She glanced up at the sky, then shot them each a megawatt grin. "Looks like the perfect day for a wedding!"

Cassandra latched on to an arm of either man as she headed up the courthouse steps between them. "I must say, this is cozy. The new groom-to-be and the jilted best friend. However on earth did the two of you work that out?"

"Let's just say we had certain goals in common." Hunter smiled mildly. "Like Jill's happiness, for example."

Cassandra glanced at Brad for confirmation and he nodded. "I'm a big enough man to know when I need to step aside."

"My goodness." Cassandra's voice was saccharine. "Aren't we being grown-up today?"

"Perhaps you ought to try it," Brad said. "Might suit you."

Cassandra scowled as Hunter held back the door. "Don't mind Brad," he whispered. "Despite his outward bravado, it's bound to burn some."

"I'm sure you're right." Cassandra sashayed in the door ahead of them. "Just like a tiny dagger to the heart."

As she passed them, Brad and Hunter exchanged glances, each stifling a chuckle. "Ah, Cassandra," Hunter said gallantly. "We're so glad that you could join us. Frankly, I couldn't imagine this day without you."

She paused to study him, as if trying to discern whether he was being sincere. "I'm glad to be here," she finally said. "Thanks for inviting me." She pulled a small recorder from her purse. "I hope you don't mind if I take notes?"

"Record all you'd like," Hunter answered before flashing her a brilliant smile. "Please, take photos too."

Cassandra twisted up her lips like she was puzzling something out. "No worries. Mr. Delaney. I intend to document every little thing for posterity."

They passed through a security checkpoint where Cassandra's purse and camera bag had to go through a scanner. Hunter approached a woman sitting at an information desk on the other side and asked her a few questions. "If you'll excuse me," he said returning to Brad and Cassandra. "It seems my presence is required in Court Records. I've got some document signing to do."

Morgan pulled Jill back over the threshold as she attempted to exit the restroom. "Don't go out there," she whispered. "Hunter's in the hall."

"Hunter?" Jill cautiously poked out her head to spy around the corner. It was him all right. In a tuxedo!

"He must have gotten the memo it's a black-tie affair," Morgan said quietly.

"He cleans up well," Jill couldn't help but say. It was the truth. Hunter looked absolutely dreamy all decked out in formal attire. She recalled the last time she'd seen Hunter in a tux and her heart skipped a beat. Of course, that outfit had been a rental; this one looked as if it had been tailor-made for him.

Morgan's eye caught Cassandra turning in their direction and staring down the hall. "Guess who's headed our way?"

"Don't tell me she's going to powder her nose?" Jill said.

"Her nosy nose, yeah."

"Oops! Here she comes" The women darted into the bathroom and were at separate mirrors pretending to primp when Cassandra waltzed in.

"Well, if it isn't the other half of the wedding party!" Cassandra proclaimed brightly. Her smile was broad yet her stare was cool. "I was just speaking with Brad and Hunter. Hunter's signing the paperwork as we speak. I presume you've already taken care of your portion?" she asked Jill. Cassandra had covered enough courthouse weddings to know it was customary in Sugar Hollow for the bride and groom to apply for their marriage license separately, so as to preserve that magical moment when they first laid eyes on each other in the small adjoining chapel.

Not every courthouse in every town had access to a chapel to use for private ceremonies. Then again, not every town was Sugar Hollow. The quirky throwback nature of the rural locale was just one of the many things Jill loved about it. Once again she felt grateful to Hunter for agreeing to spend their year of marriage here, rather than in Parkland, the neighboring city that housed a bustling downtown area with a funky selection of restaurants and shops. Sugar Hollow had exactly one grocery store, one pharmacy, and one family-owned Italian restaurant. The courthouse sat on the central roundabout beside the one post office, one church, and a perpetually blooming park that held flower gardens and birchwood benches.

Jill pivoted in Cassandra's direction and forced a pleasant smile. "It's so nice you could join us, Cassandra. I honestly couldn't think of anyone I'd rather have cover my wedding." She motioned toward Morgan. "Do you remember my good friend Morgan?"

"Of course." Morgan shook her hand and issued a polite greeting, which Cassandra returned.

A few seconds later, Morgan peeked at her watch. "I'm going to check and see if the coast is clear," she said to Jill. "If it is, we might want to sneak on over to the chapel while Hunter's occupied here."

"Good idea," Jill agreed.

Cassandra popped open her purse and strode toward the mirror, withdrawing a lipstick. "I'll catch up with you ladies in a minute."

But as Jill headed for the door with Morgan, she could have sworn she felt Cassandra's eyes watching her in the mirror. When Jill had initially thought to invite Cassandra to the wedding, Hunter had assured her it was a stroke of genius. Now, Jill wasn't so sure. It was hard enough to pull off an authentic wedding with the press present. Getting through this fake one with Hunter, while Cassandra looked on, would take finesse. Jill shut her eyes tightly and thought of her grandfather. Then suddenly an image of Hunter flashed through her mind.

The handsome, buff guy stared up at her with weepy eyes that were running like faucets. Sympathy and relief flooded through her. She'd been worried that Hunter was some ogre she'd have to live with. But he was apparently a very human man with real vulnerabilities. Plus, he'd been caring and kind to her grandfather. Surely, she and Hunter could find a way to get along over the course of these next twelve months? Particularly as they each had a vested interested in the outcome.

Morgan walked through the door ahead of her, then quickly darted back into the bathroom, picking up Jill's carry-on bag. "Okay," she whispered hoarsely. "They're gone. It's time to skedaddle."

Chapter Twelve

Jill stood in the miniature narthex and stared into the chapel. It was very small, with only ten rows of pews and a simple altar in front. "Look," Morgan whispered from beside her, "here they come."

Jill watched as an ornately carved door to the vestibule swung open as three men stepped into the sanctuary. The official-looking man in robes was clearly the judge. Brad followed in a coat and tie, trailed by Hunter in his tuxedo. Jill's heart rose in her throat. *Am I really about to do this? Marry Hunter Delaney?*

"I'm going to slip around and take a seat up front," Morgan whispered to her. Jill nodded numbly as Morgan hastened down the side aisle of the chapel. She took a seat in the first pew and Brad patted Hunter's shoulder before withdrawing from the altar to sit beside Morgan. The lady in Court Records had detailed the procedure in advance. Brad and Morgan would be present as witnesses, but didn't need to stand at the altar during the actual exchanging of vows. It was presumed that both the bride and groom were of age and therefore perfectly capable of acting and speaking for themselves. Jill questioned that now as her tongue felt plastered to the roof of her mouth. Was she actually going to be able to talk and say *I do* to the handsome heartbreaker?

Jill tried to put her previous negative notions of Hunter aside, attempting to replace them with thoughts of the more recent version she'd come to know. The one who'd changed her initial terms from twenty to fifty percent… The one who'd strung her along mercilessly over living arrangements…hinting that he wouldn't move to the country, when he knew he'd planned to all along. Jill's blood started to boil as she recalled the smug way Hunter had ridiculed her pets' names, and the way he'd challenged her standing as a "relationship expert." *How's that working out for you?* No matter how nice he'd been to her grandfather, there was still a side of Hunter that made her see…

He turned her way and Jill caught her breath. She feebly smiled back, her pulse racing. His dark eyes caught the light from the stained-glass windows and twinkled as he held her gaze. All Jill could think of when he looked at her like that was being in his arms— and on the receiving end of his kiss. A kiss that had totally undone her and swept her away. A kiss that had made her forget everything else in the world… *Every other man in the world.* The nosegay that Morgan had shoved into her hands slid in her grasp. Somewhere in the background, music began to play. That's when Jill became aware that the receptionist had taken a seat at the baby grand piano and was pounding out a hit-and-miss rendition of "Here Comes the Bride."

A bright light flashed and Hunter realized he'd been caught on camera. Cassandra had positioned herself to the left of the second pew with her full regalia of equipment, including a video recorder on a tripod, which she'd just swung around to focus on the incoming bride. Hunter looked into Jill's eyes and his heart thudded. She was stunning in an unadorned white dress, dark hair coiled in a loose knot at the nape of her neck. The truth was that Hunter had never seen a woman look more exquisite, not even at any of those ritzy soirees he used to attend. Color dusted Jill's cheeks as the music picked up, kicking into a second chorus with gusto. The judge beside Hunter held up a hand, motioning Jill forward. She appeared to glide toward them with measured steps, the fabric of her gown brushing lightly against her calves. Delicate fingers curved around a pretty collection of flowers. Lilacs, lilies, and daffodils. Not stuffy like a stiff rose bouquet, but beautiful and natural...like Jill.

Hunter swallowed hard, wondering for a split second what he was doing. He had a strong urge to run and get out of this quagmire his best friend, Brad, had landed him in. Hunter glanced at Brad, who beamed broadly, evidently pleased with the situation. Morgan, beside him, was weeping already. And the ceremony hadn't even begun! The music came to a shrill crescendo and mercifully stopped. That's when the judge cleared his throat and parted the book in his hands to a bookmarked page. "Dearly beloved, we are gathered here today," he began, "in the presence of God and these witnesses..."

For some reason, Jill was nudging Hunter, trying to get his attention by lightly knocking her elbow into his. He stared down at her and she dropped her eyes to the lovely engagement ring that had belonged to her grandmother. Hunter didn't quite get her meaning, so he raised his brow. In response, Jill lifted one finger holding her nosegay to tap another—the same one wearing the ring. When Hunter leaned toward her, she whispered, "I don't..."

"Excuse me," the judge interrupted loudly. "Do we have a problem here?"

Hunter stared at Jill.

"It's just that he and I didn't have time to... What I mean is..." She drew a breath. "I forgot to tell Hunter about the r—"

The judge's bushy eyebrows shot up.

"No worries, darling," Hunter said smoothly. His dark brown eyes crinkled at the corners when he smiled. "All taken care of." Hunter patted his jacket pocket and Jill blanched.

Who did she think Hunter was? He simply couldn't show up for a wedding ceremony—even for a bogus marriage—without wedding bands. Hunter might be accused of being many things, but being unprepared wasn't one of them. Hunter always did his homework, which was why he'd learned from Brad that Jill's ring size was six, same as her dress and shoe size. Hunter was actually kind of impressed Brad had remembered that, but had chalked it up to Brad having a memory for numbers. Plus, it was easy when they were all the same.

Jill gaped at him in surprise. To Hunter's delight, it was in a pleasantly surprised way. "You mean?"

"I've got your number," he said. "Six!"

"Okay, then!" the judge boomed loudly. "Now that that's settled... I hope."

"Yes, sir," Jill replied a bit breathlessly. Hunter squared his broad shoulders, perfectly delighted he'd stunned her that much. *Well, turnabout's fair play, isn't it? Jill positively took my breath away when she entered the chapel. Now we're even.*

Hunter wondered how he was going to handle being married to such a beautiful woman. Her grandfather hadn't been mistaken in his assessment of Jill as a catch. She wasn't only great-looking, she was genuinely sweet and professionally accomplished. A rare combination that Hunter hadn't even realized was possible in a wife. Well, he supposed if he had to have a spouse it was nice he'd gotten a good one for this next little while. Jill's poise and easy conversational skills would serve Hunter well in the business arena, just as Hunter was prepared to pull off his role as the perfect husband. He grinned at Cassandra and a bright flash bloomed as he took both of Jill's hands in his. "To have and to hold from this day forward," he repeated after the judge. "As long as we both shall live."

The judge turned to Jill, leading her to follow, "I, Jill…"

She shot a quick glance at Hunter and flushed madly. "I, Jill…"

"Do hereby take Hunter…"

The words went on, but were lost in a blur as Hunter held on to Jill's hands. Was it his imagination, or were her fingers trembling slightly? He tightened his grasp to steady them just in case. He also hoped to indicate to Jill that he was there: with her and for her. For as long as this charade lasted, which would be until precisely this time next year.

Jill sucked in a breath to steady herself, but her knees still shook wildly. After years of helping so many other couples find their way to the altar, she was finally here herself. With Hunter. She repeated every word of her vows, not even sure she heard them as she spoke them out loud. Perhaps that's because she was barely speaking at all, each meager phrase coming out in a whisper. Hunter tightened his hold on her hands, and at once she didn't feel alone. She and Hunter were in this together. She finished her responses and the judge asked for the rings. Hunter gently released her and slipped a hand into his jacket pocket. When he opened his hand, she saw two matching bands nestled together in his palm.

The judge took the rings then handed the smaller one to Hunter to slide onto Jill's finger. The cool rim of the plain gold band touched her top knuckle and Jill's heart leapt. She'd never imagined Hunter would arrive for the ceremony carrying rings. There were so many things about him that were still a mystery. Like how he could simultaneously prove so infuriating yet endearing. Hunter's voice cracked slightly as he slid the ring onto her finger. "With this ring," he said hoarsely, "I thee wed."

Butterflies flitted about in Jill's stomach and her face burned hot. She questioned whether this was what it felt like to marry for real. Pretend or not, Jill was giddy with the moment. She could only imagine how a woman must feel when she was marrying a man she actually cared for. Someone she loved desperately.

"In token and in pledge…" Hunter paused, and for a second there was an instant connection between them. Somewhere far away Jill heard a clock ticking. Or perhaps it was the sound of a fan spinning. Jill didn't know and didn't care. All that mattered was the look in Hunter's eyes. They held an unexpected tenderness that spoke volumes. "Of my constant faith…and abiding love."

A tear escaped the corner of Jill's eye and she pressed her lips together. This had to be what it felt like: being loved. She'd known love from her parents, and her grandfather. But this feeling was a world apart. Plus, she reminded herself harshly, *it's one hundred percent fake.* She peered over at Morgan, who was fanning herself rapidly with the envelope holding their paperwork. Tears were streaming down her cheeks, and Brad appeared a bit weepy himself.

When it was her turn to place the other ring on Hunter's finger, Jill wasn't sure she could carry through with it as masterfully as Hunter had. But she soldiered ahead, putting as much deep-seated emotion into it as she could muster. She sure hoped Cassandra was getting every bit of this on camera, because from her perspective Jill believed she and Hunter should be awarded Oscars. Finally, the short ceremony ended and the judge pronounced Hunter and Jill husband and wife. Without preamble or warning, Hunter swept Jill into his arms. "Darling," he said bringing his mouth down on hers. Then he surprised her with the sweetest, yet most immaculate kiss—closed-mouthed, just as she'd insisted. Jill's knees buckled anyhow, and Hunter clasped her at the waist to hold her as he spoke in a rough whisper. "There will be more of *that* on the honeymoon."

"Honeymoon?" Jill asked weakly, still swooning.

"Yes!" Cassandra called brightly from the aisle. "Where are you going?"

Jill noted Cassandra was smiling, but her cheeks were damp as she sniffed into a tissue.

Hunter reached under his coat and pulled a pair of airline tickets from his inside pocket. He handed them to Jill with gallant flair and a dashing grin. "Niagara Falls."

Jill's head felt light. For the first time since this whole thing started with Hunter, she wondered if she'd gotten in way over her head.

"What a lovely wedding surprise," the judge said. Even he appeared on the verge of tears. There was scarcely a dry eye in the house. Now Jill's eyes were watering too, darn it. What on earth was Hunter Delaney trying to do to her? She intended to ask him just that. But first, she and Hunter had a press release kit to pose for.

Chapter Thirteen

Jill pulled a pair of summer shorts from her suitcase and replaced them with a knee-length skirt. She was still in her wedding gown and flustered. After the photo op with Cassandra, Hunter had given her one hour to go home and pack. Their plane for Niagara Falls left later this afternoon. They would stop by Green Meadows to fill her grandfather in on their plans on the way to the airport. "I can't believe he did this!" Jill cried, searching frantically through her dresser drawers. She tossed a few undergarments onto the bed beside her packing pile. Morgan lifted a single item with a frown. "Big white panties won't do."

Jill gasped.

"You *are* going on a honeymoon."

"A fake one."

"Maybe, but the marriage was real."

"That was pretend too."

"Tell that to the judge." Morgan quirked a smile and pulled something lacy and lilac from Jill's dresser drawer. "Now that's more like it."

Jill snatched the thong away and threw it in her bag. "Fine, I'll take it, but don't count on me to wear it."

Morgan arched an eyebrow. "I think it's terribly sweet he surprised you with a honeymoon."

Jill grabbed a pair of jeans and a couple of shirts from her closet. As an afterthought, she decided to grab a sundress, the one with pretty sunflowers that Hunter had seemed to admire. Not that she really cared whether he liked her clothes or not. "How did he know I'd have a passport anyway?"

"You travel all the time, Jill. Besides…" She giggled lightly. "It seems Hunter covered his bases."

Jill had to admit Hunter had thought of everything. He'd booked hotels both in New York and on the Canada side of the falls. Their flight was to New York and he'd arranged to rent a car there. If they couldn't cross the border, they'd stay on the U.S. side, although Morgan assured Jill she'd like being in Canada better. Jill sat on the side of the bed, feeling winded. Everything was happening so fast. "He did think of everything," she conceded. Jill stared down at the pretty wedding band on her finger resting beside her Grandma Rose's engagement ring. "Even this."

"I know." Morgan brought a hand to her heart. "Almost took my breath away."

"Hunter's definitely full of surprises," Jill said.

"I wouldn't mind having a man surprise me with a getaway!"

"Yeah, but…" Jill bit into her bottom lip. "I just hope he booked separate rooms."

"After all he's done, you're still insisting on that?"

"Morgan! I barely know him!"

"Some blushing bride you turned out to be."

"Very funny."

"Okay, all right. I know you're concerned about it, but you probably needn't be. Hunter agreed to the terms of the contract, after all."

"Yes," Jill said, remembering his chaste wedding kiss. "He seems to be keeping the bargain."

"From all that I've seen, he is," Morgan agreed. "So, go on and run off to Canada! Have a fine time. When's the last time you had a vacation?"

"I was in Vancouver in—"

"Not a business trip, Jill. One for pleasure."

Jill tried not to think about the many kinds of pleasure a man like Hunter could provide, and focused instead on the fact that he and she had cut a business deal. An arrangement. Purely platonic. Yeah, that.

"Can't remember, can you?" Morgan asked after Jill's pause. "Exactly my point."

Jill stared at her friend, panic taking hold. "Five days, Morgan. *Five days.* What am I supposed to do with Hunter all that time?"

"Ride the *Maid of the Mist*?" Morgan suggested.

"What's that?"

"Oh, that's right, you get seasick. Never mind." Morgan stood and began to help by neatly folding garments and carefully tucking them inside the suitcase. "Don't worry. I'm sure there will be plenty to do. And, by the time you return, your advance money will be here."

"That's something, at least." Jill heaved a sigh. "Then I'll need to start writing."

"In earnest, yes. That little proposal we threw together for them won't hold Browning's interest for long. They'll want an outline by August. The first three chapters by—"

"October," Jill filled in for her.

"And polished," Morgan reminded her with a firm smile. "They want the final draft by Christmas."

"That shouldn't be a problem," Jill said. "I'm a fast writer."

"Yeah. But this time what you write quickly has to be good. Better than good—outstanding."

"Nothing like putting the pressure on," Jill quipped.

Morgan pulled her into a hug, then replied with a grin, "You work better under pressure. I've seen you."

Well, Jill certainly couldn't be in a bigger pressure cooker than this. "Thanks, Morgan," she said, hugging her back. "You're a peach."

"Do you want to take the boxers with the kiwis on them or what?"

Hunter snatched the shorts out of Brad's hands with a frown. "Will you please stay out of my knickers?"

Brad relented with a snicker. "Only trying to help."

"Don't you have to go teach or something?"

"I took the whole day off, put in a sub plan, remember?"

"Oh yeah, thanks!"

"I actually think the ceremony went very well. Cassandra bought it hook, line, and sinker. And that move with the rings, man…" Brad stroked his chin. "That was classic."

"Do you think that Jill liked it?"

"Liked it? For a second, she looked like she would have married you for real. I mean, if you weren't already… You know what I'm saying."

Hunter studied him thoughtfully. "Just as long as you don't think it was too much."

"Listen, Hunter, now's not the time for Monday morning quarterbacking. You did an awesome job with everything—including those airline tickets. You keep these gentlemanly tactics up, you might even have Jill liking *you* by the time this whole deal is over."

"Thanks for the vote of confidence, pal."

"I meant that as a compliment. A real one. Just three weeks ago, Jill Jamison hated your guts. Now she's your wife! Not many other men could have pulled that off."

"She might still hate me—slightly."

"Way down under the surface, you mean?" Brad stared at the ceiling and contemplated this a moment. "Yeah," he said, addressing Hunter. "You're probably right. But…" he added optimistically, "you'll have plenty of time to work on that!"

"That's fine, because I intend to," Hunter stated reasonably. "I've lived with women who didn't like me, and trust me on this, it was not a joyful experience."

"That's because those girls *loved you*, man. Or at least thought they were 'in love' with you. That's what made them hate you so much."

"Now you're making perfect sense."

"Love unrequited, Hunter," Brad replied. "No one enjoys being on the downside of that."

"Spoken like a true philosopher. Hey—I thought you taught math."

Brad swatted him with a tie he was holding, then eyed it carefully, holding it up to the window. "This one's sharp," he said. "Swimming dolphins."

"Not taking that one." Hunter nabbed it out of his grasp and tossed it onto a chair. "That was from Sabrina."

"The one with the heels?" Brad asked.

"That's the one."

Brad shuddered. "Maybe you should start a pile for charity?"

Hunter grinned broadly. "Excellent idea. Great time for spring cleaning."

"But it's, um…June."

"First day of summer's not here yet," Hunter reminded him. He strode to the kitchen and returned with some empty grocery bags. "I've already packed for the move, and my honeymoon gear goes in there," he said indicating the duffle bag on the bed. "Everything else is going out!"

"Everything?"

Hunter walked to the hall closet and pulled a couple of squash rackets from a high shelf, tossing them in a bag. "There's a reason I didn't pack lots of these items," he said with a wink. "And most of those reasons are female."

Brad checked his watch. "Better hurry, then, you don't have much time."

"It won't take long to shed the 'unwanted,'" Hunter answered. "Say, would you mind dropping a few bags off for me at the shelter?"

"I'd be glad to." Brad glanced around the Spartan apartment, which now had a bare-bones appearance. "I guess it's good you're keeping this place for the year."

"Doesn't make sense to rent it," Hunter said. "Might as well have it for when I need to return. Besides, you never know when married life might get too tough, and I might need a little getaway."

"Just be sure any 'getaways' you plan don't happen on Cassandra's watch."

"I know to be careful."

Hunter went through a few more items in the hall closet, then pulled the old rowing machine from under the bed.

"Whose was that?" Brad asked him.

"It was Patti's."

"The one who used to crew in college?"

"Your memory seems to be better than mine." The truth was, images of those old girlfriends were kind of fading. It was hard to remember any of their faces clearly. Even Sabrina's parting scowl was a fuzzy blur. Maybe that's because they'd all been replaced by the look in Jill's eyes as she'd taken his hands and pledged to be his. She'd been so convincing, at one moment in time Hunter had almost believed her affection for him was real. But that was impossible, wasn't it? Jill was no more capable of authentically caring for him than he was of loving her back. Hunter's grades in the relationship department weren't A-plus. In fact, he probably needed remedial training. But where did you go for that when there was no raw material to work with?

Something burned in his chest, and Hunter chided himself for his self-pity. Better to move forward and pretend to be the man Jill acted like she wanted him to be. Hunter could do anything when he set his mind to it, even living purely platonically with Jill Jamison. She'd declined changing her surname, because—after all—changing it back after a year would be extra trouble. No one would question a professional woman keeping her name in today's society. Though Hunter couldn't help thinking Jill Delaney had a better ring to it, he'd never say so to Jill, nor to Brad. Some cards were better played close to the vest, and this was a very long hand Hunter was in for. The better practiced he became at maintaining his poker face, the better off he'd be in the end. No point in letting his guard down and admitting to Jill he was actually starting to like her. It was only a little bit, anyway. Nothing serious at all. He had a reasonable respect for her, which was a great way to start off a marriage. Ideal, actually.

"Can you fit it in your car?" Hunter asked Brad, indicating the rowing machine.

"I've got a hatchback."

Hunter hoisted the bulky piece of equipment off the floor and carted it to the front door, while Brad lifted a few bulging paper bags into his arms and followed him. "It's good to see you making a fresh start."

"Brad, my friend," Hunter said sagely. "There's no better time for a man to reassess his future than on his wedding day."

Chapter Fourteen

Jill took a sip of her Bloody Mary and stared out the airplane window. She and Hunter were in business class seats and the economy passengers were still boarding. Hunter hadn't spared any expense in planning this trip. "You really didn't have to pay for the upgrade," she said turning to face him. "In fact, you didn't have to plan a honeymoon at all."

"I know. I considered that. Only, I thought it might prove a bit of a letdown." His attractive mouth puckered in a frown, and Jill tried not to recall the feel of his lips pressed to hers. Hunter spoke with a whisper. "After such a fabulous wedding."

Jill caught the glint of a wedding band on Hunter's hand. He was obviously going through with it, keeping up appearances completely. "Besides," he added good-humoredly, "it was my turn."

"What do you mean?"

"I bought the lunch, you got the coffee…" He gestured casually like it was the most natural thing in the world.

"You bought two first-class tickets to Niagara Falls," she completed for him.

"Business class," he corrected with a smile.

"It's all the same these—"

"We'll be taking off in a few minutes," a polished flight attendant interrupted. "Would either of you like another drink?"

Hunter stared down at his bourbon on the rocks and quipped to Jill, "We probably should have ordered champagne."

"Oh?" the flight attendant said with interest, balancing on high-heeled boots. "Are we celebrating anything in particular?"

"Only our wedding." Hunter beamed at her brightly and latched onto Jill's hand. "Isn't that right, darling?"

Jill squirmed and grimaced imperceptibly, she hoped, belatedly smiling at the flight attendant, who now eyed them both in a dreamy fashion. "Newlyweds!" she proclaimed. "Congratulations! This does call for bubbly! Absolutely!" She cleared their cups, which weren't quite empty, and scurried back to the cabin as other passengers pivoted in their direction. Soon people were offering heartfelt congratulations and men were leaning over airline seats and across the narrow aisle to shake Hunter's hand. Once the commotion subsided, the hostess returned with two plastic cups and a split of champagne. "On the captain," she said, smiling prettily. "He's a newlywed himself!"

Jill caught an enormous diamond sparkling on the flight attendant's finger and accidentally wondered aloud, "Are you…? Oh my goodness, I'm sorry. That's really none of my business."

"That's all right, hon." The flight attendant's cheeks colored brightly. "Nothing wrong with guessing the truth."

"Well, congratulations to you!" Hunter said pleasantly, toasting her with his glass in the air.

"Yes! Congrats!" Jill added quickly.

The flight attendant nodded and backed away, preparing to deliver her predeparture demonstration. "You two enjoy your flight now, and—please—let me know if there's anything that you need."

As they taxied to the runway, Jill pulled back her hand. "You can let go now," she said under her breath. "Nobody's watching."

Hunter glanced at her innocently. "I'd nearly forgotten I was holding on."

"Comes that naturally to you, does it?" she couldn't help but say.

"What?"

Jill looked him in the eye. "Getting what you want."

"Probably about as naturally as it does to you," he retorted.

"Touché." Jill sat back in her seat and closed her eyes, thinking this was going to be a long trip. What was she going to do with Hunter during all that time? Clearly not go ballroom dancing or to cabaret shows as her grandpa suggested. Or gambling either. Jill wasn't even sure if they had gambling in Niagara Falls. Perhaps her grandfather was mixing up Niagara Falls with Las Vegas.

Jill kept her eyes shut as the plane took off, lifting weightily into the air with roaring engines. She never had liked takeoffs or landings, though the flying part in between was all right. When Jill opened her eyes again, she found Hunter observing her.

"Oh," he said suddenly, pretending to read the airline magazine in his hand. "I thought you were sleeping."

"No," she answered. "Just thinking, that's all."

"I was thinking too," he told her, "about what good friends we have. It was really nice of Morgan to stay at your house and look after the pets, and really super of Brad to agree to meet and supervise the movers."

"Especially so last-minute," Jill reinforced.

"Yes."

"I wish Morgan would meet someone," Jill said with a sigh. "She's such a nice person. Very talented at her job as well."

"There aren't a lot of literary types in Sugar Hollow." He considered this a moment. "Or in Parkland either, come to think of it. I guess you and Morgan kind of stand out."

"That's because we both got good enough at our jobs to work from anywhere."

"I can see why you'd want to be in Sugar Hollow. You grew up and have family there. But what about Morgan?"

"She wanted to move some place far from men."

"Really?" Hunter asked with interest. He closed the magazine and tucked it in the pocket of the seat in front on him. "Then it seems she moved to the right place. I don't think there are more than ten single guys in Sugar Hollow—over the age of eighteen and under the age of eighty."

Jill laughed because she knew it was true. That was one of the things she liked about the small town: its quaintness. That, and the fact that everybody seemed to know everybody else.

"I guess she got burned pretty badly?" Hunter ventured.

"You might say that," Jill answered. Then she shrugged. "But, you know, it's really her business, so I'd rather not talk too much about it."

"Of course." Hunter reached for the champagne bottle between them and offered to refill their cups. Jill didn't see any harm in accepting. Neither of them was driving anywhere for a while, and two cups of sparkling wine weren't enough to do her in. "At least I don't have to worry about Brad," Hunter said, handing Jill her cup.

"No," Jill agreed. "He's spoken for."

"I'm sure Susan is relieved by how everything worked out."

"No doubt."

Hunter raised his glass in the air. "I think we should have a toast."

"What should we drink to?"

"How about we drink to new beginnings?" Hunter grinned and—darn it—Jill's pulse fluttered. "Not too long ago, you hated me."

"I never hated you, Hunter."

"Okay. Disapproved of me, then."

She dropped her chin to hide her blush. "Was it that obvious?"

"Oh, yeah." Then, to her surprise, he chuckled. "Starting with when you tossed that corsage back in my face."

"That was years ago."

"I guess you took some time to get over it." He met her eyes and Jill's heart stilled. "Are you, Jill?" he asked hoarsely. "Over it? I was only a kid, you know."

"You were a grown man when you kissed me at the club."

His warm laugh rumbled. "So, we're on to that now?" He perused her cautiously. "Was it…that you didn't like it?"

Jill's face fired hot. "I…no! I mean, I don't know. It's not that I—"

He leaned toward her and she felt the brush of his breath against her cheek. "Because to tell you the truth, it sure seemed like you were into it to me."

Jill set her jaw. "You're a good kisser, okay? Fabulous!" A few heads swiveled her way and Jill realized with horror she'd spoken too loudly.

"It's okay," Hunter assured her with a whisper. "They all think we're married."

Jill daintily cleared her throat. "The point I'm making is this…"

Hunter's rugged face hovered another inch closer and Jill lost her train of thought. He sexily cocked an eyebrow, his mouth just a hairsbreadth away. "Yes?"

She withdrew against her seat and took a swallow of champagne. "I've forgotten."

"Splendid," Hunter said, tapping his cup to hers. "Then that's what we'll drink to, letting bygones be bygones. *And* to new beginnings."

"Okay," she said evenly. It had taken everything she had to get her wits about her. What had gone on with Hunter just then? She'd totally lost her bearings. "Under one condition."

"What's that?"

She lowered her voice so the other passengers wouldn't hear. "That you tell me you booked us separate rooms in Niagara Falls."

"Why, Jilly!" He drew a hand to his heart and spoke with an exaggerated edge. "You've cut me to the quick. Of course, I did, darling. What kind of beast do you think I am?"

Jill lifted her cup toward his. "To letting bygones be bygones," she said reluctantly.

"And?" he prompted with a too-easy grin.

"To new beginnings," Jill said crisply before downing her champagne. But the real thing she looked forward to was getting to her very own room in the hotel and having some downtime. Maybe taking long soak in the bath. What a day this had been. What a rare mood she was in, and no, it wasn't exactly like being in love.

Chapter Fifteen

Cassandra perched behind a camellia bush with the camera that was outfitted with a telephoto lens. According to her mole at the moving company, the movers were supposed to arrive at Hunter's at eight. Apparently, they'd gotten there an hour early, because the truck was already loaded up and preparing to go. As lovely as the impromptu wedding had been, something about it had seemed a little…staged. Cassandra didn't know why she felt that in her gut, but she did, and her gut was seldom wrong. Except for that time she thought it wanted that double-jalapeño carnitas taco from the food truck. That had been a colossal mistake and had cost her two days of work. There was movement in the brush ahead of her and Cassandra thought she spied plaid. What a horrific pattern! Who on earth would wear that assortment of colors, and in summer of all seasons? It was practically summer, anyway, but the burnt oranges, browns, and reds spelled fall.

Suddenly, a figure turned in her direction and she found herself facing broad lapels. "Excuse me?" a gruff voice queried. "Just what are you doing?" Cassandra raised her chin to find bulging blue eyes peering down at her through the foliage.

He was wearing tan corduroys—again, wrong for the season—and a strange tweed cap and horn-rimmed glasses. In his hands, he held a digital camera. "I might ask you the same thing!" Cassandra cried, taken aback. "Who on earth are you?"

"Mauve Peterson," he said mildly. *Mauve?* People actually named their children Mauve? No wonder the guy had fashion issues. He was named after a color that couldn't decide if it wanted to be gray or purple. "And you are?"

Cassandra pulled down a couple of branches between them to view his face more fully. It actually wasn't a bad face, given his name and all. While it was thin, he had square cheekbones and a relatively firm jaw. "I am none of your business," she answered smartly.

He studied her a moment, then recognition sparked in eyes. "Cassandra Evans. Yes, of course."

She gave him a suspicious perusal. "How do you know who I am?"

"You're with *Tempo Beat* magazine. You've got your own column and I read it." Cassandra stared at him in surprise. "I've got to say, it's quite good. What's the new piece you're working on, I wonder?"

"I'm afraid I can't discuss it."

"Can't or won't?"

The movers closed the back of their truck with a loud bang and Mauve glanced over his shoulder, surreptitiously raising his camera and snapping a shot. Cassandra narrowed her eyes at him. "What are you doing here, exactly? Don't tell me you're a naturalist?"

He laughed roughly, almost like someone on the verge of bronchitis. "Hardly that. I'm much more comfortable indoors."

"My question stands." Cassandra inched closer, trying to get a better view of him through the leaves and branches, but all she came up with was a poorly dressed man with a camera and bland brown hair. Then the obvious answer occurred to her. "You're trying to scoop me, aren't you?"

A puzzled look passed over his face. "Scoop you?"

"You're a writer. All right. Come on, spill. Who do you work for?"

"Now it's my turn to say, none of your business."

Cassandra fumed. "I'll report you, you know."

"For what offense?"

"Spying on Hunter's apartment."

"Then I'll report you back." This guy was highly annoying. Cassandra could practically feel the steam blowing out of her ears. She couldn't afford to have anyone scoop her on this story. At the moment, it was the biggest thing she had. They were making cutbacks at *Tempo Beat* and even the regular columnists no longer felt their jobs were secure. Many had already been let go and had been reduced to becoming freelancers, having to eke out a living piecemeal by taking work here and there and patching assignments together.

The moving van pulled away and Mauve tucked his camera in his pocket. "If you're not trying to scoop me," Cassandra asked, "then why not share what your interest is in Hunter Delaney?"

Mauve shrugged mildly, apparently deciding telling Cassandra this much didn't make any difference. "Let's just say someone at Abrams Advertising has an interest in knowing how this marriage is going."

Cassandra sucked in a gasp. "You're a private investigator?"

"One of Sugar Hollow's finest." Well, that didn't say a lot, but Cassandra decided not to mention it, thinking it best not to offend this guy. You never knew when someone like him might prove useful.

Cassandra tucked a strand of hair behind her ear and batted her big eyes at Mauve. "Where are you headed next?"

He flushed brightly and took a step back, removing himself from the shelter of the foliage. In the full morning light, he cut a slightly better form that he had while shrouded in leaves. He wasn't great-looking, but then again he wasn't terrible-looking either. Perhaps he had a good personality. "I…" Mauve glanced around uncertainly before continuing. "I was headed to the moving destination, of course."

"What a *co-ink-ee-dink*!" Cassandra grinned brightly. "I'm headed to Jill's house too. The only thing is…" She paused to set her teeth against her crimson-colored thumbnail. "My car's running very low on gas."

Mauve stared at her and blinked. "Well, um… That's really too bad. I wish I could—"

"Why, thank you!" Cassandra yelped, startling him. "I'd love to ride with you!"

"But I didn't say—"

"No need to look at it as a date or anything!"

"A da…date?" Mauve's Adam's apple rose and fell. The poor guy probably hadn't had one in a decade.

"No worries, Mauve. I'm sure you wouldn't try anything improper." Cassandra sashayed out from behind the bushes, revealing her full, feminine figure. Thank goodness she'd dressed well today in a miniskirt and flats with a cute matching T-shirt. *I mean, seriously. What guy could resist me?* She linked her arm through his, steering him in the direction of what was apparently his car: an old-model clunker. Oh well, one couldn't have everything. Mauve ambled along beside her as if in a daze.

"I'm not so sure this is a good idea," he said.

"Sure it is!" she replied with confidence. "You and I go and see what's up at Jill's, then I'll ask you out for coffee."

His chin quivered. "But not on a da—?"

Cassandra swatted his arm with her hand. "Of course not, you silly man. But we could call it a little get-together." She shot him a saucy wink. "An opportunity to compare notes?"

Mauve nodded and said something barely intelligible like, "I g…guess that would be all right," his face hot pink. Oh, this was going to be easy, Cassandra thought. Way too easy. Like taking candy from a baby.

Morgan rolled off the floor and positioned herself on all fours when she heard the moving van pull into the drive. "You've been a good girl," she said patting Fifi on the head. She reached for Mimi, but the cat had scampered away the moment he'd heard tires crunch on gravel. Morgan had been playing with the pets by pretending to be one of them, lying belly down on the carpet and swatting a tennis ball around with the dog and the cat. *If the folks in New York could see me now.* Morgan got to her feet and dusted off her sweats just as the doorbell rang. She opened the door, expecting to see the movers. Instead, Brad and some other man stood on the stoop. Another man who was—whoa!—*very good-looking.* He stood just under six feet with a nicely toned frame outlined by a T-shirt and jeans. His face was suntanned and his hair was tawny. He studied her curiously with gorgeous green eyes, and for a split second Morgan felt faint.

"Morgan," Brad said in a friendly tone. "This is Susan's older brother, Owen. I don't believe the two of you've met?"

Morgan self-consciously adjusted her bandanna headband. "No." She quickly extended her hand, noticing that the sleeve of her sweatshirt was coated in dog hair. "Not yet!"

Owen shook her hand firmly. "Nice to meet you, Morgan."

"Same," she somehow managed to say. Susan had a brother? Since when? Morgan was sure she'd managed to avoid every man in this town. Every man that Jill said lived here.

"Owen offered to lend a hand, in case there's anything here that needs rearranging once Hunter's stuff gets moved in."

"That's very nice of you, Owen."

Owen smiled and Morgan had to steady herself against the back of the couch. "Anything for a friend."

Brad thumbed out the door toward the moving van. The movers had climbed out of the cab and were opening the back of the truck. Was it Morgan's imagination, or had a clunky old car just pulled into the drive of the house next door? Jill's house was set back from the road and the neighbor's house was quite a ways over, so it wasn't too easy to see. Still, Morgan thought that was strange. Jill had told her the neighbors used that house as a country home and were rarely there, except for during the months of July and August. "They've got quite a lot to bring inside," Brad told her. "Where should we tell them to put the stuff?"

Morgan glanced around, unsure of the answer. "Why not say to put it all in here initially. With you and Owen around to help…" She paused to smile sweetly at Owen before realizing with humiliation she was acting like a giddy teenager. "Um… We can divide everything up among the appropriate rooms once they've gone."

"Sounds like a plan," Brad said. "We're only dealing with boxes anyway."

"That and a few suitcases," Owen added.

"Yep," Brad agreed mysteriously. "There are a few of those."

Forty-five minutes later, Morgan stared aghast at the jam-packed living room with boxes stacked floor to ceiling. "What was Hunter thinking?" she pondered aloud.

Brad shrugged. "I guess that he was moving in. Just be glad he didn't bring any furniture."

"Then what do you call that?" Morgan asked, pointing to the enormous wide-screen TV that practically dwarfed the room.

"An appliance?" Brad ventured.

Owen rumbled a laugh. "Why don't we haul some of these suitcases into the room where Hunter's staying? That should clear up some space in here."

That was another thing, Morgan thought, grabbing two separate hanging bags and leading the way. Why in the world did Hunter have so many clothes? Poor Jill had no idea what she'd be coming home to.

"Don't worry," Owen said, trying to reassure her. "The boxes on the porch aren't nearly as large."

"On the porch?" Morgan's voice rose in a shriek. "You mean there's *more*?" Fifi trailed eagerly behind her, hugging her heels every step of the way. The cat hadn't been seen for a while. Presumably, he was hiding.

Brad passed her in the hall as he headed back to the living room for more luggage. "And they say women have baggage," he said in a teasing tone.

"Hey!" Morgan shouted over her shoulder.

Owen set down his load, then took the hanging bags from Morgan's hands. "Should I hang these in the closet?"

"If you can find room."

Owen pulled back the pint-size door and surveyed the very tight space. "I see what you mean." He hung one bag easily, then had to jimmy the second one in to wedge it in place.

"Do you have that many clothes?" Morgan asked him blithely.

"Most days I don't wear much at all."

A picture of that flashed through Morgan's mind and her face burned hot.

"What I mean is…" he said in a rush, "I'm fairly casual." He motioned to his T-shirt and jeans. "What you see is what you get."

"You're not a teacher like Susan and Brad?"

"Actually, I'm in publishing."

"Publishing?" Morgan echoed in a whisper, that odd sensation of vertigo overtaking her again. Perhaps skipping breakfast had been a bad idea. "In Sugar Hollow?"

"Manhattan," he said with a grin. "I'm just here visiting family."

Morgan collected herself enough to say just as casually as she could, "My, isn't it a small world?"

His green eyes twinkled. "How small?"

"You guys just about done in—?" Brad fell silent when he saw Morgan and Owen staring at each other. "Oh!" Then he studied the situation more carefully and repeated, but with a different, knowing intonation, "*Oh...*"

Owen attempted to sound casual. "We were just discussing publishing."

"Yeah," Brad said, his eyes lighting with mischief. "How interesting is that? Both you and Morgan being in the same profession?"

"What?" Owen asked. He viewed Morgan with renewed admiration, apparently pleased. "Is that a fact?

"I'm an agent," Morgan said. "Jill's agent. That's how we met. Now, we're also very good friends."

"You live in Sugar Hollow?" Owen asked, evidently surprised. "What made you leave New York?"

Morgan waved her hand in the air. "Oh, this and that. Nothing terribly important."

"Perhaps she wanted a more bucolic lifestyle?" Brad offered. "A pace a little less hurried?"

"Yes, exactly!" Morgan said, latching on to Brad's brilliant summation.

Owen grinned in her direction. "I never imagined meeting anyone in my field here. We probably have some contacts in common."

Brad nodded, liking the sound of this. "I think that's a brilliant idea, Owen."

"What is?" he asked, turning to Brad in surprise.

"Having Morgan join us and Susan for lunch. We were going to that new Mexican cantina," he told Morgan. "You do like Mexican?"

"Love it, but…" She glanced at her clothes with an embarrassed flush. "What time were you thinking of going?"

"We were going to give Susan a call when we finished up here. Once we leave, why don't you take a moment to clean up and join us when you're ready?"

"If you're sure…" She peeked uncertainly at Owen. "I mean, I don't want to intrude on Owen's time with his sister."

"Honestly, Morgan," Owen told her. "It would be a relief to have your company. It can get pretty overwhelming being with those lovebirds sometimes." When he said the word *lovebirds*, Owen rolled his eyes at Brad and Morgan giggled.

"Well, all right," Morgan said cheerily. "If you gentlemen insist."

Mauve called to Cassandra as they scampered toward his car. "Hurry! The van is about to pull away."

They scrambled back into their seats and fastened their seatbelts. Both were panting and slightly out of breath. A heady sense of euphoria overtook Cassandra. Somehow the hunt seemed a tad more thrilling with a companion along. Cassandra had always worked solo and had never had a partner. Not that Mauve was her partner or anything like that. He was merely an acquaintance, a private eye investigating none other than Hunter Delaney. Once they'd hunkered down in the hedges together, recording the unloading of Hunter's things, Mauve had been all-too-happy to spill. Perhaps his line of work got a little lonely too. "So, are you satisfied?" he asked her.

"Satisfied that Hunter moved quite a bit of stuff into Jill's house, yes."

"Then why do you still look unconvinced about their union?"

"It came up very quickly," Cassandra said.

"There was another man in place before," Mauve answered.

"Jill's childhood friend Brad. I always wondered about that one. Somehow it didn't seem right." Cassandra pulled a tissue from her purse to dab her neck and hairline, hoping she was perspiring lightly rather than sweating profusely. Not that Mauve seemed the type to mind. His brow was soaked completely. He was viewing her in a funny way, but Cassandra couldn't quite read it.

"I say we forget the coffee," Mauve said, "and go for something cooler."

"Smoothies?" she suggested.

Mauve surprised her with a quirky grin. "I was thinking more like margaritas."

For some reason his sudden invitation pleased her. "Why, Mauve!" she fake protested. "In the middle of the day?"

"We can talk more about Hunter Delaney," he said, clearly trying to tempt her. "I can tell you what I know and vice versa."

Now that was an invitation hard to resist.

Chapter Sixteen

Jill woke up in her hotel room, at first unsure of where she was. Albuquerque? San Francisco? No... Niagara Falls! She sat up suddenly and the bed sheets rumpled around her. Heavy curtains were drawn, but a piercingly bright light shone through the miniscule crack between them. Jill's eyes flitted to the nightstand and hotel-issued digital clock. Goodness, it was way past noon! Nearly one o'clock!

She scrambled to her feet, getting her bearings. Yesterday had been such a long day, she must have slept like a ton of bricks. First, there'd been the airport delay in landing due to fog. Their plane had circled around and around the runway until their full split of champagne was empty and Hunter had fallen asleep against her shoulder. When they'd finally landed, the hold-up at the rental car agency had been even worse. They'd lost Hunter's reservation and only finally provided a car after Hunter demanded to talk to a supervisor. Then there was a line to cross the border. By the time Jill and Hunter got to their hotel in Canada, it was well past nine and she was beat. Hunter had appeared fatigued too. He'd tried to insist they grab something to eat, but Jill couldn't even think of it. All she wanted was a hot shower and a soft mattress. Now that she was awake and rested, Jill realized how famished she was.

She decided to dress quickly and try to find Hunter. But when she knocked on his door across the hall a few minutes later she got no response. She pulled her cell from her purse and tried calling.

"Where are you?" she asked when he answered.

"Good morning, Sleeping Beauty. You rested well, I take it?"

"I slept like a log, an entire felled forest really."

Hunter laughed warmly. "I'm sure you needed it."

"What about you?"

"I got some shut-eye, after ordering room service pizza. You didn't eat anything, though, did you?"

"No," Jill admitted, hearing her stomach rumble.

"Then why don't you meet me down here, and we'll have some lunch before touring the town?"

"Where's *here*?" Jill asked him.

"I'm in the lobby," Hunter replied pleasantly before clicking off.

Jill found Hunter sitting in a roomy chair beside a high wooden table that held his drink. He appeared to be having a cocktail already. He lowered the newspaper he was reading when he saw her approaching. Jill almost missed a step when his eyes settled on hers, and they crinkled at the corners. "You look nice this morning." He rose and gave her a very formal peck on the cheek. When his mouth was close to her ear he whispered, "Darling…" A tingle raced down Jill's spine and heat rose in her cheeks.

"You don't need to call me that," she said. "Cassandra's not around with her camera."

Hunter nonchalantly folded his paper. "I didn't even realize I'd said it," he lied. "I guess it's becoming a habit."

"Have you spoken to Brad?" she asked him. "To see how the move went?"

"Not yet," Hunter answered. "Now that you mention it, maybe we should call."

"I'll call Morgan," Jill offered, extracting her cell. But when Morgan answered, there was such a commotion in the background, Jill could barely hear her.

"You'll have to talk louder!" Morgan instructed. "I can't hear you over the mariachi band!"

Mariachi band? "Where are you?" Jill shouted into the mouthpiece.

When Hunter shot her a curious look, Jill said, "She's with Brad, Susan, and somebody at Maria's Cantina."

Hunter nodded. "I've heard that's very good."

"You what?" Jill spouted loudly. "Did what?" She covered the mouthpiece, then spoke to Hunter. "She said something about margaritas."

"They must be celebrating a successful move."

"I suppose," Jill replied, peering up at him. He looked really good this morning. Very attractive in a polo shirt and jeans. Jill noticed he hadn't bothered to shave, but the light smattering of stubble only made him look... What? Oh, no. Not that. Was she about to think *sexy*? "Sounds like I better call you back!" Jill said to Morgan.

"Good plan!" Morgan answered before chirping brightly, "Olé! Olé!"

"Oh, dear," Jill told Hunter. "Sounds like Morgan's maybe had one too many margarita."

Back at Maria's Cantina, Cassandra and Mauve slowly lowered their menus to peer across the room. "It *is* them," Cassandra said. "And look, Brad's with Susan."

"Who's Susan?"

"Only the girl Brad dated in high school," Cassandra responded. "And the one that he works with. *And...*" She turned to Mauve with a telling look. "The one everyone always thought Brad was going to marry."

"Then along came Jill," Mauve said.

"Yes..." Cassandra drummed the tabletop with her manicured fingernails. "Then along came Jill."

"Now that Jill has thrown Brad over for Hunter, Brad is back with Susan?"

"It would appear so," Cassandra said, watching Brad wrap an arm around Susan's shoulders.

"Who's that man with Jill's friend Morgan?" Mauve asked her.

"I have no idea, but they seem to be having quite a bit of fun." She and Mauve observed the others in silence while Morgan guffawed loudly, caressing his shoulder. "Oh, Owen! You're just too much!"

"Owen," Mauve whispered. "His name is Owen."

"Hmm, yes," Cassandra whispered back. "I caught that part. I wonder if he's one of Susan's brothers? She's got two, but they grew up with their dad in New York."

"Are we interested in Owen?"

"I don't think so. All I want to know is if Jill and Hunter's marriage is for real, or whether it's an elaborate setup."

"I'm interested in knowing that too."

Their margaritas arrived and they each took a sip. After their server departed, Cassandra turned to Mauve. "Why do you want to know that, really?"

"Well, if you must know… I'll tell you." He lowered his voice and leaned toward her. "Fred Forester is very keen on making partner at Abrams Advertising."

"He was passed over for Hunter?" Cassandra asked, guessing.

"Only because Hunter's sudden marriage came about."

"Uh-huh," Cassandra said. "Um-hum, um-hum, um-hum."

"You know what I'm thinking?" Mauve asked her. "I'm thinking if we put our heads together, we can crack this thing."

Cassandra stared across the room at Morgan. "It would sure help to know about that new book Jill is writing. Somehow I've got a feeling that's got something to do with this."

"How about you and I work together on that?"

"I thought you were only interested in Hunter?"

"No, I think you're right. This is bigger than Hunter and his ambition. Something else seems to be going on."

Cassandra tapped her fingers against the side of her glass. "Yeah, but what?"

Mauve playfully nudged her shoulder with his. "Isn't that what we're going to find out?"

Cassandra shot him an appreciative glance, then narrowed her eyes. "Yes," she said slowly. Cassandra raised her glass to Mauve's with a wicked smile. "It is."

Chapter Seventeen

Jill could hear the cacophony of the falls even before they reached them. It was the first official day of summer and the weather was spectacular. The sun was shining, the sky was blue, and birds were singing merrily as she and Hunter traversed the large green park that led to the water. They'd enjoyed club sandwiches and iced tea in the hotel restaurant and taken a brief walk down one of the town's main streets, which was replete with kitschy shops selling souvenirs and "Believe It or Not" museums stocked with wax figures holding court in their dark doorways. When she'd seen that, Jill had questioned the wisdom of anyone—much less honeymooners—wanting to vacation in Niagara Falls.

But the moment she and Hunter approached the walkway hemming the falls with its high metal railing, Jill completely changed her mind. She stood stock-still as winds ripped off the waters, dotting her nose, cheeks, and forehead with their fine spray. And the view was absolutely outstanding. One set of falls was shaped like a horseshoe, glorious rapids cascading over its edges, while the other across the way was a tumultuous band of raucous waves taking a steep downward dive.

"Fabulous, aren't they?" Hunter reached out and took her hand and she let him. This was one of those breathtaking moments that was meant to be shared.

Jill tightened her grip on Hunter's hand. "I didn't realize there were two falls."

Hunter nodded in front of them with his chin. "Those over there are on the New York side of the Niagara River. The Horseshoe Falls are in Canada."

"It's beautiful, Hunter." She swallowed hard and met his eyes. "Thank you for bringing me here."

He perused her warmly. "I'm glad you're having a good time."

Hunter's heart beat double-time as he stared down at the gorgeous woman who'd become his bride. While his head urged caution, stating none of this was real, he couldn't help the way his throat swelled slightly when he beheld her. What a picture she made. That gave him an idea. Hunter pulled out his phone and selected the camera feature. "Would you mind? I mean, would it be all right if I took your picture?"

Jill's face was damp and her hair looked wind-whipped, but she was probably prettier than Hunter had ever seen her. "No," she said shyly. "That would be fine. Might even give us ammo for Cassandra."

"Cassandra?"

"We'll have a way to prove we were really here."

"Don't you think she'll let it drop now?" he asked her. "Her whole pursuit of you?"

"Cassandra's not the kind to let things drop. She'll probably be dogging us for the whole year."

Hunter sighed and shook his head. "Good old Cassandra. Maybe what she needs is a boyfriend. You know, someone to occupy her time?"

Jill laughed, her expression sunny. "You thinking of fixing her up?"

"I wouldn't dare do that to a friend of mine." He stepped back from the railing to frame Jill in the viewfinder with the Horseshoe Falls behind her.

"Would you like me to fit in the two of you?"

Hunter turned to find a kindly Australian gentleman standing beside him. He was dressed like a tourist and his wife was with him. Both wore T-shirts from the Niagara Falls Hard Rock Café.

"That would be really nice, thanks!" He handed over his phone and went to stand beside Jill, wrapping an arm around her shoulder. "This will be a good one for the papers," he told her.

"A lot better than the last one," she said with a blush.

The next few days flew by in a swirl of activity. They got a better feel for the town, toured some funny museums, and took in an IMAX theater presentation on Niagara. As hard as it was to believe, Jill and Hunter were actually having fun together. Plus, he'd played the perfect gentleman. Apart from taking her hand at the falls that first day, he hadn't touched her again. A few times when they'd parted for their separate rooms and said good night, Jill had wondered if Hunter might try to kiss her, but he never had. She was probably being silly about it anyway. Isn't this exactly what she wanted? The bargain she'd struck?

On the final full day of their trip, Hunter surprised Jill at breakfast. "I hope you don't mind," he told her over coffee and scones, "but I went ahead and made some arrangements. It's our last day here and there are still some landmark things we haven't done."

She beamed at him, thinking what a nice guy he was, and about how different he was from how she'd imagined him. "That sounds great, Hunter. Thank you. What are our plans?"

He took a sip of coffee before detailing their itinerary. "I thought we might take some time to do some souvenir shopping this morning, in case there's anything you'd like to bring back for your grandfather and Morgan. Then, after lunch, I have us booked on the *Maid of the Mist.*"

"Maid of the Mist?" Jill echoed, thinking that sounded vaguely familiar. Then she recalled Morgan saying something about it. "That's not a boat, is it?"

His eyes danced. "A great big ferry boat, goes right under the—"

Jill's stomach filled with lead and her head felt light. "Hunter, I can't... I'm sorry, but—"

"It's a once-in-a-lifetime experience, Jill. If you're worried about getting wet, they provide raincoats."

Jill felt herself blanch. "Super."

Hunter leaned toward her with concern. "What's wrong?"

"Hunter," she admitted sheepishly. "I get seasick."

He stunned her by bellowing a laugh. "Is that all?" For the second time in Niagara Falls, he reached out and took her hand. "There's no need to worry. I'll be right there with you."

Later that afternoon, Jill sucked in a breath as tourists were herded onto the ferry boat like hapless animals. She could see another boat on the water far away, already approaching the base of the Horseshoe Falls. Good gracious! What if there was a tidal wave, or a sudden swell? A whirlpool, even, that would spin the ferry around and around like a tiny toy boat, then swallow it deep into the Niagara River? Jill suddenly felt dizzy and leaned against Hunter. He propped her up by the elbow and gave her arm a reassuring pat. "You're going to be so glad you did this."

"Yeah," she said. "When it's over."

People crowded onto the bow of the boat, all of them wearing the disposable plastic raincoats the ferry boat service had provided. Jill shot Hunter a sideways glance as a family of four scooted by them to get a closer position near the railing. "Are you sure about this?"

He smiled down at her and his smile warmed her through and through. "Extra sure."

Jill steeled her nerves, determined she could do this. Hey, perhaps she could even incorporate the experience in her book? A vague idea began to form in her brain, something about couples taking shared adventures. Before she could think things out further, the big boat began to move and Jill's stomach roiled. "Oooh, oh Hunter!" She latched onto his arm with a death grip.

He steadied her shoulders in his hands and stared down at her. "You've got this, darling. And don't forget that I'm with you."

Jill nodded numbly, hoping the antinausea medicine Hunter had purchased for her earlier would kick in. Then they were off and chugging toward the falls.

People around them chattered excitedly and snapped photos as they approached the enormous semicircle of cascading waters. Jill had to concede the view was stunning close up, even more spectacular than it had been from above. Hunter wrapped his arms around her from behind, holding her against his broad chest, and she didn't protest or make an effort to pull away. She found his presence calming and reassuring in a way she'd never anticipated. Plus, she felt all snuggly and warm, drawn up in his embrace, even as the dashing spray doused her.

"So what do you think?" he bent down and whispered in her ear.

She peered back over her shoulder and into his eyes. "I think it's fantastic, Hunter. I really do."

He raised his brow. "You're not afraid?"

"Not with you here with me."

"Jill, I know this is out of place. But we may never be here again. Never have this opportunity."

"For what?"

There was heat and longing in his eyes. "To kiss under a waterfall."

For a moment her heart stopped beating. Then it whipped into overdrive because she knew exactly what she wanted to do. What her entire spirit was calling her to do. She pivoted gradually in his arms until they were chest to chest, cheap rain slickers crinkling between them. "I know I said I didn't want this."

He dipped his chin toward hers. "We both agreed."

She spoke in a breathy whisper. "Tomorrow we go back to the contract."

Hunter cradled her cheek in his hand. "If that's what you think is best."

Jill didn't know what she thought was best anymore. She really didn't. Tomorrow would be different. They'd be back in Sugar Hollow and Jill would be writing her book while Hunter went to work. Jill didn't need to become involved with Hunter Delaney for real. She'd gone to extraordinary lengths to avoid it, right down to having them each sign on the dotted line. The original plan was the right one and she knew it. Despite the outward expertise she displayed to the world, Jill was actually an expert at *messing up* relationships. She'd never even had *one* last for more than six weeks. If she was going to last an entire year living with Hunter, she couldn't risk them becoming involved and then having a falling out so soon into their contract. What if he became upset as all those other men had and walked out on her? Where would that leave her book deal, and her grandpa? "I don't know what I think," she finally answered.

Hunter's voice was raspy as his mouth closed in. "I think you're thinking too much about it." Then he brought his lips to hers, sweetly at first, and then with a ravenous hunger that wasn't at all chaste, and which competed with the vigor and the thunder of the falls.

A little while later, they exited the boat holding hands. Hunter sensed that something had changed between them. Then again, Jill was sometimes hard to read, so he wasn't sure. Perhaps he should just ask her and get this out in the open. "Jill," he said as they wadded up their wet raincoats and stuffed them in a recycle box. "About what happened on the water...?"

"It's okay, Hunter." She drew a deep breath. "It was a moment. We were swept away."

Hunter certainly had been. He'd never had a woman kiss him like Jill had. Perhaps that was because he'd never hungered for any other woman's kiss as much as he had hers. Hunter thought back to his earlier conversation with Brad, when he'd said he wasn't going to press Jill. If she wanted him, he was going to let her come to him. Of course, then, he'd been talking about wanting Jill physically. Now that his emotions were getting tangled up in this, Hunter wasn't entirely sure how he felt. He looked to Jill for guidance because he was committed to letting this remain her call. "If that's the way you want to leave things, we will."

"I think that's how we ought to leave things." She met his eyes and quickly turned away.

"Well!" Hunter said cheerily. "At least you didn't get seasick!"

"Thanks to you," she said with a smile, relieved he'd changed the subject. "And the medication."

"I hope you're going to be hungry tonight."

She arched her delicate eyebrows. "Did you have something planned?"

Hunter pointed to a tall tower in the distance with a revolving restaurant on top. "I thought we'd eat up there," he said. "It will give us just one more perspective on Niagara Falls."

"Sounds ideal, but Hunter…"

He looked at her.

"This time I'm paying."

The food was delicious and the view was superb. It was amazing to see the falls from this high up at night, particularly as they radiated with rainbow colors from the lights that had been installed around them. "I hope you've had a good honeymoon," Hunter said as he poured their wine.

"I've had an awesome honeymoon," Jill said. "I don't think I could ever have another one to compete."

"But you will have another someday, don't you think?"

Jill shrugged shyly. "I don't exactly have the best track record."

Hunter took a sip of his wine. "I guess that's something we have in common."

They paused a long moment to stare out at the falls. When she turned to him, she sighed. "That was some kiss, Hunter."

"Which one?"

Jill giggled lightly. "There have been three, haven't there?"

"You're counting?" he asked, appearing pleased.

She smiled, but a bit of melancholy tinged her voice. "I guess all of them. All of them were pretty nice, including the one in the chapel." She lifted her wine, deciding to tease him. "If I'd had any idea what good kisser you were, I might have even let you kiss me in high school."

"That's all I wanted to do, you know. Not anything more, like you assumed."

Jill's cheeks warmed. "Are you telling the truth?"

"I may have been a big football star, Jill, and I might have attracted my share of interest. But between you and me, I wasn't into girls who seemed to be after that."

For some reason, this stunned her. Hunter had surprised her, yet again. A new idea bloomed in Jill's head for her book. *Surprises, yes*. What was a successful relationship without a few surprises thrown in? The unexpected turn could revitalize things, keep them fresh! "You're full of surprises, Hunter," she told him.

"Good ones, I hope?"

She didn't have to stop to think about that. "The very best."

He reflected on this, then asked her, "So what's happening between us? Are we becoming friends, do you think?"

"I've certainly had a great time with you these past few days."

"And yet you…" He swallowed hard, appraising her. "You're not interested in anything more than those three kisses. The kisses you admitted yourself were pretty darn good ones."

"Oh, Hunter, I wish that I could explain."

"Why don't you try?"

"It's very important to me that we make it. That this deal between us lasts a year."

"It's important to me too."

"That's why we can't risk fouling it up. Can't you see? If we legitimately become involved and it doesn't work out, how will we manage to stay together and keep up appearances for the entire year?"

Hunter hung his head, because—darn it—in a convoluted way Jill was making sense. Had Hunter ever managed a long-term relationship? The answer was no. Had he and any of his former girlfriends ever stayed together for a year? No, again. And did they all hate his guts with a passion by the time the relationship ended? Easy reply. An emphatic *yes.* Hunter heaved a breath and studied Jill sadly. "I guess I see what you mean."

"So, here's the deal." She sipped her wine. "I've had a wonderful vacation. Thank you. I can't tell you how long it's been since I've taken a break, and apparently I really needed one. Now, it's time to go home and focus on work. You on your job, and me on mine. I'm glad we're getting along because that makes things easier." But even as she said that, it sounded like she was questioning whether it really did. "When you need me to attend your work functions as your loving wife, I will. When I need your support as my husband before the media's prying eye, I know you'll be there for me."

Hunter nodded his assent and sounded resigned. "Meanwhile, separate rooms and everything on the straight and narrow."

"I can't chance getting hurt, Hunter, and neither can you. What's more, neither of us can do anything that might jeopardize our deal."

"You really want the renovation that badly?" he asked, hoping the moment might be ripe to talk about Jill's grandfather. Jill still hadn't admitted to Hunter the pressure she was under concerning her grandfather's financial affairs. Maybe if she opened up to him and they talked about it, they could discuss ways to address that problem.

Jill looked blank. "What?"

"Your advance money. You said you needed it for—"

"That's right, I did," she said quickly. "But it's not all about that. It's about getting my career back on track too. Long-term security."

"Of course," Hunter said, understanding that was all Jill was prepared to reveal at the moment.

They finished the rest of their meal in silence, each mulling over the difficult conversation they'd just had. In his head, Hunter understood Jill had lots of good reasons for sticking with their plan, yet his heart was already starting to grow uncomfortable with it. But Hunter wasn't a quitter; he stuck with the commitments he made. He'd committed to living platonically with Jill for the year, so that's what he intended to do. At the end of their contract, if he still felt the way he was starting to feel about her now, they could have a different conversation. Maybe after he moved out, they could try dating for real? Hunter took a swallow of wine thinking what a crazy, backward situation he'd gotten himself into. Here he was already married to Jill, but plotting out ways to court her after their divorce!

The bill arrived and Jill reached for it, intending to pay. This time Hunter didn't stop her.

"You do understand?" she said, raising her eyes to his.

"In a crazy way, I suppose it makes sense."

She laid her hand on his on the table. "Thank you, Hunter. This means...more to me than you'll ever know." She blinked, and for an instant Hunter suspected she was fighting back tears.

"It's not a problem," Hunter croaked hoarsely. "We signed a contract, Jill, and a deal's a deal. I intend to keep it."

Chapter Eighteen

Morgan pressed her palms against Owen's broad chest as he stood on her doorstep. "It's time to go home now, lover boy, or I'll never get anything done!"

Owen pulled her up against him and attempted to nuzzle her neck. "I thought you asked me over for pancakes?"

She pushed back with a laugh. "That was more than twelve hours ago!"

Owen stared up at the night sky and the stars that twinkled above. "It has gotten late, hasn't it?"

"Very," she purred, planting a kiss on his lips. What a whirlwind romance this had been! For the past three days, Morgan and Owen had been nearly inseparable. Apart from the brief few hours when he'd gone back to sleep at Susan's place, he'd spent every waking hour here. Including this morning, when he'd come over for a big country breakfast. Morgan had even made cheese grits! She was so darned proud of herself. "But if you don't leave," she continued, "I'll never be ready for Jill coming home tomorrow."

"Jill and Hunter."

"Yes, them."

Fifi sat at Morgan's feet, contentedly thumping her tail against the floorboards. The dog looked up at the embracing couple with a big, dopey grin. "You know," Owen said. "I think Fifi kind of likes us. Dogs have a sense about people being together that way."

"Shut up."

"I'm serious. We published a book on animal instincts only last year."

Morgan wrapped her fingers around his sturdy biceps. "Yes, well… My animal instincts are telling me not to let you go."

"Then don't."

"I must. I still have some picking up to do."

He jostled her in his arms. "You *will* come to New York? You promised."

"Yes, you impossibly insistent man. I've already marked the Fourth of July weekend on my calendar."

"Good." Owen pulled his gaze from hers to glance around the porch and then survey the yard. "That's a bit odd, isn't it?"

"What's odd?"

"The cat. The gray one. I haven't seen him since we moved Hunter's stuff in."

"Mimi?" Morgan asked in a haze. Then suddenly it dawned on her and she shrieked. "*Mimi!* Oh, no!" she cried with a gasp. "You're right! I haven't seen him in days!"

"I thought you were feeding him?"

"I was! I filled up his bowl in the laundry room twice a day. The next time I looked, the bowl was always empty." She stared down at the dog, whose tongue was lolling out sideways. "Fifi! You scamp!" Morgan could have sworn that Fifi grinned.

"We have to find him," Owen said.

Morgan gaped at him in horror. "I thought he was hiding all this time!"

"Maybe he still is. Where was he the last place you saw him?"

After a thorough search of the other rooms in the house, they approached the one door that Morgan had kept shut since Saturday. Morgan laid her hand on the doorknob to the guestroom and grimaced apologetically. "Jill didn't want the pets getting in Hunter's room."

The moment they stepped near the bed they heard the scratching, and the whining… A soft pitiful mewing coming from…Morgan gulped as her eyes grew big…the closet!

Owen was braver than she, so he opened the door. Mimi leapt out of its hollow with a *reee-oow!* and streaked across the room, bolting into the hall. Morgan clasped a hand to her mouth as a horrific odor overtook her. "Oh, no."

"Oh, yes," Owen said, pulling two heavily stained and obnoxiously scented garment bags off the hanging bar. "I don't suppose Sugar Hollow has twenty-four-hour dry cleaning?"

"This isn't Manhattan. I'll have to drive to Parkland."

"Then I'm coming with you."

"You…what?" Morgan didn't know why Owen appeared to like her so much, but he obviously did and it absolutely thrilled her. Morgan hadn't been this excited by interest from a man since…since she didn't know when!

"I said, I'm coming with you," Owen repeated. "This is too big a job for one person." Perhaps he felt guilty that he had distracted Morgan from her pet-sitting duties, but Morgan didn't care what Owen's motivation was for helping her. At the moment, she needed all the help she could get. This was a disaster! Jill and Hunter were returning tomorrow!

"All right," Morgan said. "But I should probably feed the cat and disinfect the closet first."

Owen held the garment bags at arm's length, his nose crinkling. "Where should I put these?"

Morgan quickly scanned the room. "Definitely not on the bed! Or on that chair! Wait..." she told him. "Just stand here while I grab a couple of black garbage bags to wrap around them. Then, we'll put them in the trunk of my car."

When Jill walked into her living room, the first thing she saw was the television. A gargantuan flat-screen television that took up nearly the whole expanse of a wall. It blocked her bookshelves and access to the more normal-size TV settled on the entertainment center behind it. "Oh, my."

To her dismay, Hunter grinned. "Looks great! Doesn't it?"

"I, uh... Well..."

Morgan strode in from the kitchen wearing a happy grin. Fifi was leaping and bounding in front of her. "I thought I heard the front door open," she said as Fifi practically tackled Jill, pouncing up on her with eager pants and licks.

"Fifi, down!" Jill commanded. When the dog dropped onto her haunches, she knelt to hug her pudgy neck. "I guess she missed me," Jill said, giving the top of Fifi's head a kiss.

Mimi padded out of the kitchen and beelined toward her with a sulky whine. "Sounds like Mimi missed you too," Hunter said, covering his nose as it twitched.

Jill shot him a look. "You did take your medicine?"

"I'll be fine," he replied, his eyes already turning red.

Morgan studied them one at a time, then together as a couple. "How was your trip?"

"Fine…good…uh-huh," the two of them said, their words overlapping each other's.

Morgan lifted an eyebrow. "Well! Isn't that great news!"

"How did things go here?" Jill asked her.

Mimi wound himself around Jill's legs, protesting loudly. For some reason, the color drained from Morgan's face. "Great! Just super! We all got along like peas in a pod."

The doorbell rang and Hunter answered it to find a deliveryman from a laundry service. "Your suits, sir?" he said, handing several items over.

Hunter turned to Morgan with surprise. "You had my suits dry cleaned?"

Her face turned bright red. "There was a minor incident with the movers."

"Oh?" Hunter responded. "Did something happen in the truck?"

The cat meowed forcefully.

"Uh, not in the truck," Morgan spewed. "It just happened!"

Jill and Hunter exchanged looks.

"That's all right," Hunter said mildly. "Whatever the problem, I appreciate your taking care of it,

Morgan." Then he addressed the deliveryman, asking him how much he owed.

"No worries," the guy said with a parting smile. "All taken care of!"

After Morgan departed, Jill and Hunter retired to their separate rooms to unpack and settle in. Hunter was relieved for the respite. That cat dander was driving him wild. Thankfully, Jill had assured him that she'd cleaned out his room and the pets hadn't been allowed in there in weeks. Yet the moment he walked through the door, Hunter sneezed vehemently. Wow, he thought, nabbing a tissue to wipe his nose. *Worse than I thought.* He pulled a medicine pack from his duffle bag and took another allergy tablet, but knew two was the limit. Perhaps he just needed time to adjust to his new environment.

Hunter carted the freshly laundered clothes he'd temporarily laid on the bed to the small closet. When he opened it, a wave of some unpleasant scent wafted in his direction. *Whoa!* He stuck his head in the door and sniffed around, but upon closer examination all he smelled was heavy-duty disinfectant. Hunter's eyes traveled from the empty closet to the pressed suits and shirts on the bed and back again. Then, after some thought, he decided to knock on Jill's door.

She'd already changed into more comfortable clothes and was in the process of taking things out of her suitcase and piling them on the bed. "Everything all right?" she asked him.

Hunter lifted the collection of clothing in his hands. "I was wondering if there was any extra room in your closet?"

"My closet? What's wrong with yours?"

"To tell you the truth, I'm not sure."

Jill indicated for him to drop his clothes on her bed, then followed him into the guest room. All it took was one whiff for Jill to understand. "Eww! Oh my gosh, Hunter! I'm so sorry. I didn't realize it smelled that stale."

"Given that they've been dry cleaned and all—" he began.

"No, you're right," she agreed. "Absolutely." Jill led him back into her room, which was much better appointed than his and twice as large. "You can put them in that second closet."

"So nice to see you have two."

Jill shrugged. "This is the master bedroom."

"I don't want to have to trouble you," Hunter said, "every morning when I'm getting ready for work."

"Then don't," she said reasonably. "Just pick out what you're going to wear the night before."

"That sounds a whole lot like fashion planning."

Jill loudly cleared her throat. "This from the clotheshorse who can't fit his stash in his own room."

"It's the closet!"

"Even if it wasn't. Everything you've got would barely fit."

"Since when has dressing well been a crime?"

"Not ever," she told him. "I'm just saying that you're different from the other men I've known."

"Seeing that I'm going to be here a year, and not six weeks, that seems a huge advantage."

"That was mean."

"So were you."

Jill twisted her lips in thought. "You know, Hunter. I think we're both tired. It's been a long day. We probably both need some rest."

"Oh, that will be easy," he said, "given my room's stacked floor-to-ceiling with boxes."

Jill wheeled on him. "Yeah? And whose fault is that?"

"Yours!"

"Mine?"

Hunter looked around. "Why can't I stay in this room?"

Jill huffed.

"It's bigger," he continued. "Plus, the animals apparently don't come in here."

"You can't blame me because you overpacked!"

"Overpacked? Jill, I moved in!"

"You're raising your voice."

"Well, so are you."

"I think I'm going to bed."

Hunter's face was a sea storm of emotion. "Great. Then I am too."

He walked out the door and Jill shut it behind him, catching her breath. This wasn't going to be nearly as easy as she'd hoped. In fact, it might not be easy at all. Two seconds after he'd left, Hunter knocked at the door. Jill cautiously cracked it open.

"My clothes for tomorrow," he said in a flat tone. Jill stepped aside with a sweep of her hand and Hunter ambled toward the closet. After selecting a few items coated in clear laundry sacks, he strode out, not bothering to give Jill a second glance. *Well, fine! Pleasant dreams to you too.*

The next morning, Jill awoke feeling bad about her and Hunter's little spat. They'd both been weary from travel, and each had a lot to adjust to. Jill also understood Hunter wasn't putting on his discomfort due to pet dander. She'd barely slept a wink hearing him sneeze all night, which meant Hunter likely hadn't gotten much rest either. She quietly padded to the kitchen in her slippers, deciding to make coffee as a peace offering. Fifi and Mimi had been sitting outside her door in the hall and waiting for her to wake up. They followed her eagerly now, occasionally leaping in front of her and nearly causing her to trip over them as they all made their way to the kitchen. "I know you're hungry too," she told them. Anything concerning the words *food* or *hunger* made Fifi start to drool. Mimi meowed pitifully, as if he hadn't eaten all week. Was it her imagination, or had the fluffy gray cat lost weight?

Jill started the coffee, then fed the animals. When she went to take Fifi outside, she caught the dog naughtily trying to eat the cat food. The yellow Lab had already gobbled down her kibbles in record time and now was after Mimi's crunchies. "Why, Fifi!" Jill said, setting a hand on her hip. "I'm surprised at you!" The dog stared up at her with a big happy grin, not the least bit embarrassed. Now that Jill thought of it, it actually appeared as if Fifi had been *gaining* weight, particularly around the middle. "Hmm," Jill said, giving the dog a new perusal. "It seems someone I know has been double-dipping." She scooped up the cat dishes, deciding to put them on the laundry folding table. She hefted Mimi off the floor and placed him there as well, and he leaned over his bowl eating ravenously. Jill cocked an eyebrow at the dog, thinking she'd never had this problem before. Then again, Fifi was an opportunist. Perhaps the Lab had used the opportunity when Jill was away to start a brand new culinary routine for herself? One that benefited her own tummy more than the cat's.

The coffee beeped that it was ready and Jill let the pets out into the yard before pouring herself and Hunter a cup. She knew Hunter was feeling grumpy last night, but perhaps he'd be in a better frame of mind this morning? She carried his cup down the hall, stopping right outside his door. Jill knocked lightly at first and then a little harder. When she got no response, she gently turned the knob. The door creaked open, revealing an immaculate bedroom with a couple of unpacked boxes still stacked in the corner. Sunlight poured through the window, shimmering in between the slats of the open blinds. But the bed was made and Hunter was gone.

Chapter Nineteen

Brad set his mug down on the bar beside Hunter's and surveyed his best friend. "I've got to say, pal. You look rough."

Hunter knew his eyes were bloodshot and there were bags under his eyes. He'd had to face his reflection in the mirror each morning when he'd shaved at dawn, then had gotten out of Jill's house just as quickly as possible. Hunter lifted his beer with a groan. "It hasn't been easy."

"I thought you had a great time on your honeymoon?"

"We did. You might even stretch it so far as to say we had fun."

"Platonic fun, you mean." Hunter was quiet a moment too long and Brad's brow shot up. "Is there something you're not telling me?"

"Not anything you need to know."

"But you did have separate rooms?"

"Hey," Hunter said defensively. "Do I ask you details about your relationship with Susan?"

"No, but that's because I *have* a relationship with Susan, an authentic one."

"Well, maybe Jill and I have a relationship too."

Brad angled toward him with a whisper. "Seriously?"

"Not like that. Get your mind out of the gutter."

"Okay. Like what, then?"

"Like…" Hunter put down his beer to snag a fistful of bar peanuts and chew on them contemplatively. "It was almost like we were friends. In Niagara Falls, I mean. I can't really speak to much of a relationship since we've returned."

"Why not?"

"I barely see her."

"But you're living together!"

"I work late at the office and have dinner there. Take-out or delivery, something easy. In the morning, I'm up and out of her place before she's even awake."

"What about keeping up the appearance of a happy marriage? Doesn't Abrams wonder—"

"Abrams commends me for my dedication to the new account. We landed Kaleidoscope Kids, did I tell you?"

"No, that's fantastic. Congratulations."

"Anyway," Hunter continued, "my work success aside, my personal life is killing me. I mean, look at me. That guestroom is murdering my sinuses. I don't know how long Jill's pets have slept in there, but whatever cleaning she did wasn't enough to prevent me from having problems. Truthfully, I'm thinking of moving back to my place."

Brad latched on to his arm. "You can't do that. That would ruin everything."

"I'm falling apart, Brad. Not sleeping, no downtime to speak of. I can't keep living like this."

"So talk to her."

"And say what?"

"That you want to switch rooms?"

"I already did and she said no."

Brad sadly shook his head. "I'm sorry, man. When I asked you to do this, to step in for me, I had no clue things would be this tough."

"Me either."

They both studied the game on the bar television a few minutes before Brad asked him again, "So, the honeymoon was good, huh?"

"Shut up."

"Did I tell you about Morgan and Owen?"

"Who's Owen?"

"Susan's big brother."

"Oh, that's right. What about them?"

Mirth danced in Brad's eyes. "They're an item."

"No way."

"I mean it. The two of them got together when you and Jill were out of town."

"How sweet. I bet Jill's happy about that."

When Brad shot him a puzzled look, he continued. "Everyone wants their best friend to be happy. You know what I'm saying?"

Brad gave him a compassionate sigh. "Yeah."

"I think that's fantastic about you and Owen," Jill said, refilling Morgan's mug. Morgan sat at Jill's kitchen table and had been reviewing Jill's draft of an outline for her new book. Jill poured herself more coffee as well, then went to join Morgan at the table.

"Yes," Morgan replied. "I guess you could say it caught both of us by surprise." Morgan sat up a little straighter, appearing pleased with herself. "He said that I'm the first woman who's turned his head in months."

"And you haven't looked at anyone since—"

"Zip your lips and let's not go there, all right? Who wants to think about dreary things when I've got a New York vacation to look forward to?"

"It's fun you'll be there for the Fourth."

"What are you and Hunter going to do?"

"Hard to say since I haven't talked to him."

"Jill," Morgan said seriously. "You have to stop this. Go ahead and break down, release some of your pride, and talk to the man."

"I would, but he gets up early."

"Then set your alarm and get up earlier." She shuffled some pages in front of her. "Isn't that one of the chapters in your new book? Compromise?"

"How is it compromising if I'm giving in?"

"Giving in to what, exactly?"

"Making an effort at reconciliation." She frowned into her coffee. "I already made one effort, you know."

"If you're talking about making Hunter coffee, he doesn't even know that you did that."

"I don't think things are really so terrible," Jill lied. "The way things are, Hunter stays out of my hair and I get my work done."

"Aren't you worried someone will notice he's never here? Like someone in the press?"

"If you're speaking of Cassandra, she hasn't come around at all. In fact, I think she's moved on to greener pastures."

Morgan gave a weighty sigh and handed Jill's outline to her. "This still needs work."

"What do you mean by that?"

"I'm not feeling it, Jill. There's no heart in it."

"It's just an outline!"

"Well, go back and outline it again. Come up with an angle. That more personal thing the publisher is looking for. We can meet again when I get back from my trip."

Cassandra approached Mauve wearing a trench coat and dark glasses. He was dressed just the same even though it was July. They were meeting at an out-of-the-way restaurant to plan their next move. Cassandra didn't know why she'd let Mauve talk her into the Dick Tracy getup, but it was kind of exciting pretending to be amateur sleuths. Mauve was so full of fun ideas.

The hostess eyed them curiously as she led them both to their table. They'd requested one in the back in a dark corner. "So," Cassandra asked in hushed tones once both of them were seated. "What have you got?"

"No one at Browning is squawking. Jill's new project is strictly hush-hush." He lifted his menu and spoke behind it. "What came of your recon?"

"Hunter's hardly at home," she told him. "Out early and back late."

"Marital woes?"

"Either that, or he's under job demands."

"Kaleidoscope Kids," Mauve told her. "That's the big account he just landed. The one he snagged from Fred."

"So it could be he's working late?"

Mauve met her eyes. "How many newlywed guys do you know who'd rather spend their nights at the office?"

Chapter Twenty

Max Abrams appeared on the threshold of Hunter's new office. It was big and roomy with two corner windows and a large drafting table. Hunter angled forward on a tall stool, redrafting a sketch. "You've been working awfully hard," Max said, causing Hunter to look up.

"Now that we've got Kaleidoscope Kids, I figured it would be good of us to keep them. Plus I'm working on ideas for the Metro Mart pitch."

Abrams pointedly checked his watch. "All of that can wait until morning."

"But, sir—"

Max's face wrinkled in a frown.

"I know the Edwards team is going after Metro too," Hunter explained. "The early bird catches the worm."

"The early bird also requires some sleep." Max studied him thoughtfully and leaned into the doorjamb. "When's the last time you got any?"

"Well, I—"

"Hunter, my boy, you're a newly married man, and your new bride is gorgeous. It seems you ought to be spending a little more time there, and less of it here. Especially after hours."

Hunter started to speak but Max held up his hand. "From now on I want you leaving by six."

"But, Max—"

"Okay, fine. Seven o'clock at the latest. I don't want you making the same mistakes that I made when I was your age." For a moment he appeared distant, then he solemnly met Hunter's eyes. "I was just like you, driven and ambitious. Also, like you, I had a lovely, caring wife at home. Unfortunately, I put more time into the job than I did my marriage. I've admitted this to very few people, Hunter. But in those early years, Diane and I almost didn't make it."

Hunter swallowed hard and the back of his neck felt hot.

"I'm not saying I don't appreciate what you're doing for the company, because the truth is I do and your work is outstanding. I just don't want to be responsible for one more troubled relationship."

"But, you and Diane?" Hunter said, surprised. "I thought you seemed so happy."

"We are happy together. Ecstatic, most days. But that's only because I was called up short and told what a numbskull I was being."

"Did Diane...?"

"She gave me an ultimatum, son. Either I got my priorities straight or she was walking. Fortunately, I had the good sense to listen. Now, I'm sharing a bit of advice with you. You married Jill, so she must be the one. Nobody stands up and says 'I do' without meaning it. Even couples whose marriages fail go into them with good faith in the beginning. This is your good faith window, Hunter. The time for you to show Jill what

you're made of, and make her glad every single day
that when you asked her to marry you, she said yes."

Hunter felt as if he were drowning, with high-
peaked waves crashing in on him from all sides.
Everything Max was saying made sense, and would
certainly hold water in a regular marriage.

"There's another thing," Max said, interrupting
Hunter's train of thought. "Diane and I are hosting a
barbecue this Fourth of July and we were hoping you
and Jill could attend. I'm sorry if this is last-minute, but
we'd originally planned to be out of town. Then our
daughter, Marina, surprised us saying she was coming
home with her husband, Dave, and the baby. It will just
be family and a few of the neighbors. I hope you and
Jill will join us."

Hunter caught his breath and forced a smile. "I
can't think of any better way to spend the holiday, Max.
Thank you. I'm sure Jill will agree."

Max grinned broadly, seemingly satisfied. "I fire
up the grill at five o'clock and could probably use your
assistance. My son-in-law, Dave, is often too busy with
the baby."

"Anything I can do to help."

An hour later, Hunter shoved his hands into his
pockets and stood on the front porch. It was his home
for now, so he could go on inside, and yet he hesitated,
unsure of what he'd do or say. He hadn't spoken to Jill
in nearly two weeks, which must have been fine with
her because she hadn't made any efforts to contact him.
She had his cell number. Plus, she knew where he slept,
for crying out loud. If she'd wanted to talk to him badly
enough she could have. Hunter's conversation with
Max had left him feeling out of sorts and confused. If

Hunter abided by the terms of his contract with Jill and ended the marriage after a year, would Max view him as a failure? Particularly after he'd taken time to share some fatherly, and truly personal, advice?

Rather than going inside, Hunter opted to sit on one of the wicker chairs on the porch and sort through his thoughts instead. He inhaled deeply, taking in a breath of summer evening air. Now that spring had passed, his hay fever had pretty much ended. The only thing he appeared to have continued trouble with was that darned cat. Fifi seemed okay, but he hadn't spent much time with her. Of course, Hunter had barely been around. As if on cue, the dog loped out of the bushes and galloped through the grassy front yard. Spying Hunter on the porch, Fifi raced toward a tennis ball on the lawn and scooped it into her mouth. Before Hunter knew what was happening, Fifi was on the porch, resting her chin on his knee. Big puppy eyes stared up at him as Fifi clenched the ball in her teeth, her tail whipping furiously back and forth behind her. "What is it, Fifi?" Hunter cringed when he said the name. What had Jill been thinking?

The dog nuzzled in closer, pressing the front of her body against Hunter's legs. She shook the ball side to side in her mouth, then again met his eyes with a hopeful expression. "Is that it?" Hunter asked with a chuckle. "You want to play ball?"

The dog excitedly lowered the front of her torso, crouching on the porch. Then she dropped the ball at Hunter's feet. "Okay, but here's the deal." Hunter leaned forward with a whisper. "I'll play with you, if I can give you a new name. Something we'll just use between us." Hunter picked up the tennis ball and pondered the dog's face. "How do you like the name Sport?"

Fifi immediately sat on her haunches and smiled. Hunter laughed out loud and held up his hand. "High five, Sport!"

Fifi immediately raised her paw to slap his palm. "Well, what do you know?" Hunter said, getting to his feet. "Maybe you and I can be friends after all."

Jill didn't know if her eyes were playing tricks on her, but when she looked through the kitchen window, she thought she saw Fifi running across the yard. Not only was Fifi running, she was retrieving a ball! For— wait a minute—Hunter? Jill hadn't heard Hunter's SUV pull in the drive. He must have arrived while she was washing dishes at the sink and had the water running. She'd just made up a large batch of chicken pasta salad that she planned to munch on this week. Jill often made a casserole or pot of soup that could stretch into several meals. This proved convenient when she was caught up with writing and didn't want to stop to prepare food. It was always nice to have something ready-made on hand.

Jill watched as Hunter pulled back his arm and threw the ball again. He was dressed in shirt sleeves and his nice slacks. Jill presumed he must have removed his jacket and tie and left them on the front porch. But why hadn't he come into the house or told her he was home? Jill's cheeks heated when she suspected the reason. Hunter felt uncomfortable facing her. They'd both been avoiding each other forever, it seemed. But Morgan was right: This silliness had to stop. If she and Hunter had been a couple Jill was advising, she would have insisted they talk with each other long before now. The main difference was that none of the couples who'd come to her for counseling had married by contract. At least as far as Jill knew. Who else on earth would be crazy enough to do that? And here Jill was a relationship expert. She sighed weightily, deciding what to do. She'd been about to pour herself a glass of Chablis. Perhaps she should offer one to Hunter too? He hadn't been here when she'd made him coffee, but he was clearly present now.

Jill walked out the front door a few minutes later holding a couple of glasses of chilled wine in her hands. Hunter stood up to greet her and hold back the door. He'd apparently finished playing ball with Fifi, who now rested, panting, at the base of his chair. "You're home!" she said, acting as if she didn't know. *Yeah, right. Then why am I holding two glasses of wine?*

Hunter stepped aside, then closed the front door behind her. "Hard day?" he asked, his eyes on both full goblets.

"Oh, no." Jill felt herself flush. "These aren't both for me." She quickly handed one to him. "The other's for you!"

A slow grin replaced his perplexed expression. "Thanks, don't mind if I do." He accepted the wine and sat back in his chair beside Fifi, who laid her head on his shoe.

Jill sat in the chair beside him. "I saw you playing ball with Fifi," she began, looking for something to say.

"She's a good dog." Hunter reached down and patted Fifi's head. "The two of us have come to an understanding."

"Well, good. That's good." Jill took a small sip of wine, trying to come up with something else to say.

Eventually she braved it. "You're home early today. I mean, earlier than you have been."

"Yeah, I'm sorry about that." He pursed his lips for a beat. "It's been crazy at the office."

"I know what you mean. Here too."

They both sat staring at the sunset as its gentle glow faded behind the trees. "It's nice out here," Hunter said, referring to the porch. "Now that spring is over, my allergies aren't bothering me half as much."

"How are you sleeping?" Jill asked softly.

He met her eyes and she saw his were ringed with dark circles. "Not well."

"Oh Hunter, I'm so sorry. Maybe we can make some changes?"

"Yeah? What kind?"

"I'll call a cleaning service tomorrow, some place specialized. There's allergy-proof bedding we can buy."

He viewed her doubtfully. She continued, "You won't have to do a thing. I'll research it all, put it all in place."

"If you think that will help, then I'm all for it."

Jill nodded, realizing she was getting hungry. She guessed Hunter might be too. "If you want something to eat, I've made some pasta salad."

"That sounds delicious, Jill. Have you eaten?"

"No, I was thinking maybe we could eat together? Out here on the porch?"

"I like that plan," he said with a grin.

So they ate and they talked about nothing too sensitive or particular, all the while Fifi keeping them company and Mimi dozing contentedly nearby. At this point, Jill felt it better not to bring up their previous disagreement. It was so small, and she could barely even remember what it was about. She and Hunter appeared to be getting along and that's what mattered. They weren't getting along as well as they'd done in Niagara Falls, but they were at least being civil to each other and "civil" was better than not talking.

Hunter thanked her for the dinner, which he said was delicious, then broached a new topic. His boss, Max, and Max's wife, Diane, had invited them both to a Fourth of July cookout. That sounded like fun, but it was only a few days away. "Is there anything we're supposed to bring?" Jill asked him.

"I didn't think to ask, but it sounded like Max has things covered."

"How about I make some brownies and you bring some wine?"

"I'm sure both would be appreciated," he told her.

Cassandra lowered her binoculars in front of her. "Well, darn."

"Looks like domestic bliss to me," Mauve said from beside her.

"It sure does."

"A man, his wife, and his dog."

"I think the dog belongs to Jill."

"Seems like it belongs to both of them now," Mauve said, observing Hunter giving the animal's head a pat.

"That's just like them," Cassandra said in a snarly tone. "To go and get cozy, and just when we thought we were beginning to figure things out."

They watched as Jill and Hunter both got to their feet and cleared their plates from the outside table. Then they disappeared through the front door, the large yellow Lab leading the way.

"Guess there's not much left to do here," Mauve said.

Cassandra frowned at him. "Is it possible I was wrong about them? What if their marriage is for real?"

"There are worse things that can happen, you know. People jump into hasty marriages all the time. Sometimes they work out, at others they don't." He stared back at Jill's house. "From the looks of things tonight, this one seems pretty successful to me."

Cassandra packed her binoculars away. "Well, I'm not giving up on it yet. Not until I know what Jill's next book is about."

"After tonight," Mauve said, "I'm afraid Fred might stop paying me. If there's nothing to make this marriage look suspicious, it seems that Hunter is in like Flynn with Mr. Abrams, and there's not a lot Fred can do to stop that."

"He's pretty sneaky, isn't he?" Cassandra asked. "This Fred guy?"

"We're pretty sneaky, Cassandra."

"Oh yes, I know it's true." She preened, then said in hushed whisper, "But it's kind of fun being sneaky together."

Mauve's neckline colored. "Yeah, it is."

Cassandra trailed a hand down his arm. "So... Even when you go off Fred's payroll, you'll continue to help me?"

Mauve shot her a grin and it alarmed her, because it was almost...saucy. "Are you saying you can't get by without me?"

Cassandra blinked. "I... No! It's just that, I thought you might want to, that's all. I mean, aren't you the least bit curious to see how all this ends?"

"I'm curious on a couple of counts." To her amazement his lips drew near, and she wasn't totally repulsed by them. "I'd like to see how a lot of things end, to tell you the truth."

Cassandra licked her own lips, her mouth feeling dry. "Well, then, perhaps we should continue our collaboration?"

Hunter hesitated a moment when he and Jill reached their separate bedroom doors. He'd help her clean up the dishes, then both had decided to turn in early. Hunter was glad they were speaking again because it relieved some of the tension in the air. Even when he hadn't been seeing her in person, it had seemed a thick and weighty presence in the house each morning when he'd arisen and every late night he'd come home. "I'm glad that we talked," he told her, the words scraping from his throat.

"Me too." Her pretty brown eyes peered up at him through dark lashes. "It sure beats not talking."

"I'll be coming home earlier, now that the Kaleidoscope Kids account is nailed down. I hope that's all right?"

"You landed it? Why, Hunter, that's terrific!" Her cheeks colored and Hunter had to resist the urge to reach out and hold her the way he had in Niagara Falls. "And of course it's all right that you'll be getting home sooner. I look forward to it. Maybe we can eat together again?"

"I'd like that."

Her mood perked up. "What shall I fix us for dinner?"

"I don't want you cooking for me."

"I'll be cooking for myself anyway."

"Then I'll have whatever you're having, just make more."

She wrinkled her nose at him. "You'll eat tofu and bean sprouts salad?"

"Maybe I'll pick up Chinese."

To Hunter's delight, she laughed. "All right, but just this once. Over dinner tomorrow we'll work out a plan. We never really talked about that, you know. How we'd handle the food part."

"I usually do carry-out."

"But Hunter," Jill protested. "That's not healthy, not on a regular basis."

Hunter grinned, surprising her. "Spoken like a real wife."

Jill set a hand on her hip. "Well, maybe so. You can count that as one of your perks. After living here with me, your health will improve."

Hunter turned and stifled a sneeze. "That's another thing." She looked up at him, a serious expression on her face. "I meant what I said about getting in a service. Carpet and upholstery steamers, whatever it takes. I want you to feel comfortable, Hunter. Comfortable in your own home, because this is your home, at least for the next little while."

Chapter Twenty-One

Hunter awoke the morning of the Fourth of July feeling phenomenally good. For the past few nights, he'd slept like a dream. Jill had stayed true to her word and had completely revamped the house. When that woman was determined, she was on fire. She'd brought in cleaning specialists and pet allergy experts. Yesterday evening he'd even been able to sit in the living room and enjoy the playoffs on his widescreen television without his sinuses making him miserable. Each evening when Hunter came home from work, the house looked in better order. Soft jazz music played from Hunter's high-end stereo system and decorative candles burned on the mantle. What's more, there was always something delicious cooking in the kitchen, and the heavenly smells greeted him the moment he stepped in the door—right after Sport had raced toward him and given the back of his hand a lick. Mimi was a little more standoffish, but that seemed to be working well for the two of them. Hunter didn't dislike cats, but their dander sure didn't agree with him.

Hunter lay there in bed with his eyes closed, reveling in the quiet of the morning. He could hear birds chirping outdoors and a few rattling noises in the kitchen. Jill was likely making coffee and would have it ready by the time Hunter was dressed. Ah, yes, this was a lifestyle a man could get used to. The only thing that would make it better would be having a real relationship with his wife and waking up each morning with her snuggled up against his chest.

That's when Hunter realized there *was* something resting there: a warm heavy thing that was rumbling like a motor and spiking tiny needles through the threads of his T-shirt. Hunter's nose twitched and his eyes sprang open. Big yellow cat eyes stared down at him, nearly frightening Hunter out of his wits. "Jill!" he cried at the top of his lungs. Hunter sat up abruptly, wiping the coating of cat hair from his shirt. It swirled all about in the air. Mimi yowled and bolted off the bed. Hunter sneezed violently and grabbed for some tissues, breaking into a sneezing fit all over again.

Jill tore down the hall and stopped in his open doorway, surveying the scene. "What happened?"

"It's Mimi!" he cried, breaking into another sneeze. His eyes were running and his throat burned, feeling scratchy and dry.

"Not after everything we've done!" Jill wailed. She frantically scanned the room, finding Mimi crouching behind a chair. "You bad boy," she told him. "I can't believe you're such a sneak!"

She hauled the cat from the room as Hunter hacked and *achoo*ed. "I don't know how he got in here."

Hunter spoke between fitful attacks. "I don't think…the latch…always sticks on the door."

Jill turned to face him, the cat in her arms. "You don't lock it?"

"Why would I?"

Jill colored from head to toe. "You're right and I'm sorry. Terribly sorry about this, Hunter. Let me just go and put Mimi outside."

"I think I'd better shower," Hunter said, "and launder these linens and clothes."

Jill fumed at the cat as she carted him down the hall. "Now look what you've done, Mimi! You've left your cat fur all over Hunter's room!" The cat looked at her sadly and a pang of guilt stabbed Jill's heart. "You're right," she acknowledged hoarsely. "It was really your room first."

By the time Hunter arrived at the breakfast table Jill had made up her mind. They would have to trade rooms. She couldn't put Hunter through another night of this, and her animals clearly weren't cooperating. At least, one of them wasn't.

After her honeymoon trip, Jill had resumed her biweekly visits with her grandfather and each time she'd seen him his spirits had seemed brighter. He was so glad that Jill had found someone special. Her new marriage to Hunter recalled her grandpa to several happier times involving his late wife, Rose. Suddenly he was replete with stories about his newlywed years and the trials and joys he and Rose had lived through. Jill loved hearing these tales, especially as her grandfather had never thought to share them before. The thing that interested Jill was that each of her grandpa's vignettes seemed to hold a common theme: one of sacrifice. There were things he and Rose had done for each other and other things they'd forgone merely out of love for one another. That's what real love was, her grandpa said. It wasn't all about the easy stuff like attraction; it was about sticking together through the hard times, and putting the other person first when you knew it meant their happiness.

Jill fought back her tears, thinking of her grandparents' beautiful union. Her parents had been in love too, but in a more fun-loving, contemporary way, whereas her grandparents had been very traditional. Jill supposed this was part of the marvelous equation that made some relationships work. If you had common values, you had a way to understand each other. And when you truly cared, as any good-hearted person should, you learned to sacrifice. Jill understood with certain clarity that this also needed to be a chapter of her new book. But first she had to start by putting that theory into practice here.

Hunter didn't typically eat much for breakfast, but she at least had him eating hard-boiled eggs. If she had them ready and in the fridge, he'd often have one with his coffee, which was better than his eating nothing. He peeled one now as Jill dug into her low-fat yogurt. She could hear the washer whirring in the next room, indicating he'd already started his laundry. "I've made a decision," she told him. Hunter paused with the pepper shaker in midair. "I want you to move into the master bedroom."

His neck and the tops of his ears colored slightly. "With—?"

"I mean, I think we should switch," Jill rushed in, suddenly realizing what she'd implied. "Swap rooms!"

"But you've always had the master."

"That doesn't mean that things can't change."

"That's really nice of you, Jill, but I don't want to put you out of your own bed."

"You're not. I'm putting myself out."

"But why?"

"Because it's the right thing to do, and it's a way we can both live here peaceably over these next several months. Together, with Fifi and...Mimi."

He took a bite of his hard-boiled egg, considering her proposition. "Are you sure you can live with that?"

"Yes, and I want to. We can move things around when we get home from Max's cookout."

Hunter grinned. "Why, thanks, Jill. That's really nice of you. And, to tell you the truth, it would probably help things."

"Good, then that's settled," she said, standing to refill their coffees. "What time are we expected at Max and Diane's?"

Hunter parked his SUV in front of Max's house, then he and Jill followed the sound of happy chatter along the side path that led to the backyard patio. A sprightly middle-aged woman with springy golden curls hurried toward them, her arms spread wide to wrap Hunter in a hug. "Congratulations on landing Kaleidoscope Kids! You know I was pulling for you."

She released Hunter to graciously appraise Jill. "And you must be the lovely new wife I've been hearing so much about. Welcome, Jill. My name is Diane." She gave Jill a warm hug and a lump rose in Jill's throat. Diane was the kind of woman who made everyone feel at home. Unexpectedly, that made Jill miss her mother.

"You and Max were so sweet to include us," Jill said. "We brought a few things for the party." She handed Diane her plate of brownies and Hunter presented his bottle of wine.

"How nice of you, Jill and Hunter. Please follow me. Let me introduce you around." Diane presented them to an assortment of neighbors and her daughter, Marina, who cradled an infant. Max stood beside the grill with a younger man Jill took to be his son-in-law. The patio abutted a big swimming pool that appeared to be brimming with happy neighborhood kids doing cannonballs off the diving board and frolicking in the water.

"You didn't tell me it was a pool party," Jill said, once the introductions were done and Diane had disappeared to get them some drinks.

"I didn't know myself," Hunter said. "Though it looks like only the kids are swimming."

Max caught Jill's eye and strode toward her with a cheery laugh. "My dear, we're so glad you could make it. This old man of yours has been working too hard," he said nudging Hunter. "It's good to see him taking a breather."

"Thanks for sending him home in time for supper," Jill said good-naturedly. "Hunter told me you insisted he stop working late."

"That's true," Max said, motioning them both toward the grill. "Why don't you come on over and meet Dave? Hunter, he'll be relieving Marina of the baby in a moment so she can help Diane in the kitchen. Would you mind assisting with the burgers?"

Hunter glanced uncertainly at Jill and she could tell he was a tad worried about leaving her by herself. That just showed how little Hunter knew her still. Jill could hold her own in any crowd. "I think that's a fine idea," she encouraged. "Why don't you do that and I'll see if Diane needs more help in the kitchen?"

Twenty minutes later, when Hunter carried in the plate of cooked hamburgers and hot dogs, he was greeted by uproarious laughter in the kitchen. A crowd of women and a couple of men were gathered around Jill as she stood at the center island, tossing a salad and holding court. "And that's only the *second* thing you need to know about starting relationships." The group cheered and applauded, someone even calling out, *"Brava!"*

Diane sidled up next to Hunter, who stood there stunned. "You never told us that Jill was so charming, nor so full of funny stories! The things she's heard about in her line of work! You'd never imagine. It seems she gives some pretty sound advice." Diane lowered her voice in a confidential manner. "Some couples can be so crazy."

"They sure can be," Hunter agreed. "But, you know, Diane?" he said, thinking of the conversation he'd had with Jill the day she'd first shown him her house. "Sometimes being a little crazy can be a good thing."

The rest of the afternoon passed pleasantly, but everyone was so eager to speak with international celebrity Jill, Hunter barely spent any time with her. Instead he talked with the guys, commiserating over recent game scores and team trades, while he kept a casual eye on Jill. She really seemed in her element and everyone appeared to love her. Not just because she was a famous personality, but because she was famously entertaining. Yet another side of the multifaceted Jill, Hunter thought to himself.

When there was a pause in the action around her, Jill walked up to Hunter, smiling brightly. "Are you doing all right?"

"I'm having a great time. How about you?"

"Me too. Everyone here is so nice to talk to. It reminds me of being on the road on book tour."

"I suppose it must get a little lonely for you during the day at home."

"Fifi and Mimi are loyal," she stated. "But they don't offer much in the way of conversation."

"No, I'm guessing they don't."

"There you two are!" Diane shot each a sunny smile. "The rest of us are taking the kids to see the fireworks in the park later on, and we were wondering if you'd like to come along?"

Hunter and Jill exchanged glances. "Oh, that's so sweet of you," Jill said.

"But Jill and I have other plans," Hunter finished for her.

Diane eyed them both and giggled. "Of course you do. What was I thinking?"

Hunter wrapped his arm around Jill's shoulder. "Perhaps another time?"

"There's always next year. Today has been so much fun, Max and I have decided to make it an annual event. I hope you know you'll be regularly included." She paused a beat to study them, drawing a hand to her chin. "What an absolutely gorgeous couple you make. You two are going to have beautiful kids."

Jill blinked and Hunter coughed loudly. "Yes, well, on that note. I guess we'd better get home and get to it!"

"Making babies?" Diane asked with a sly tilt to her mouth.

Jill turned fire-engine red. "We've…decided to wait a while," she stammered. "You know, adjust to the marriage first."

"Excellent idea," Diane said, smiling broadly. "You two run along now and do all the *adjusting* that you need to."

"Ha-ha!" Hunter said, pivoting Jill in the opposite direction. "Thanks so much for having us!" Then he whispered to Jill, "We'd better go make our excuses to Max too, before any more innuendo gets served around here."

Jill eyed him with amusement. "You're embarrassed, aren't you?"

"No, I was thinking of you. Not wanting you to be uncomfortable."

Jill giggled into her hand. "Diane's a trip, but very sweet."

"Yeah, I'd say Max has his hands full with her."

"But in a good way."

"Definitely in a good way."

Four hours later, Jill dragged the last of Hunter's boxes across the hall and into the master bedroom. "I think that about does it."

"Thank you for doing this," Hunter told her sincerely. "It really is a big sacrifice."

"That's part of what marriage is about."

"Real marriages."

"Of course, and sometimes friendships too."

"I owe you a double thank-you then, because you also were a very good sport at Max's today. Everybody loved you."

"I had fun, Hunter. Really, I did. It was such a nice crowd of people. I especially loved Diane and Max."

"Yeah, they're a pair."

"I'd call them an inspiration."

Hunter considered this. "You know, I would too."

"I'm probably going to shower and get ready for bed," Jill said. She felt hot and sweaty from all the moving they'd done and was exhausted from the activities of the day.

"Okay," Hunter said, standing in front of the master bedroom doorway. "Then I guess I'll see you in the morning." Hunter had the impulse to hug her, but knew that wouldn't be right. And a kiss was definitely off limits, so instead he held out his hand. "We made a good team today, I thought."

She grinned as she shook it. "An excellent team, yeah." Jill looked up into his eyes and time froze. It was like they were in Niagara Falls all over again, together on that boat. Jill quickly released his hand and backed away. "Yes, well. Good night, Hunter! Sleep well!"

But he barely slept a wink. There were fireworks booming outdoors, but the louder noise was the thudding of his heart in his chest when Hunter realized what he really wanted. He didn't want Jill across the hall in the guestroom. He wanted her right there in his bed with him.

Chapter Twenty-Two

Jill sat up under the covers feeling disoriented. At first she thought she was in a hotel, then she remembered she was at home. It was the Fourth of July, wasn't it? She was groggy with sleep when she realized why she'd awakened. She needed to use the restroom. She stumbled out of bed and reached for the bathroom door, but instead she encountered a closet. Slowly it dawned she was in the guestroom, and that the bathroom was in the hall. That's right, the hall. She'd just head down there, then come right back to bed.

A few hours later, Hunter opened his eyes with a jolt to find a woman's arm draped across his chest. He stared down the arm to the sleeve of a T-shirt. Then his eyes snagged on the top of her head. *Jill!* Her face was turned to the side, one of her cheeks pressing his pillow. He could feel her light breath against the side of his neck. Hunter lay there paralyzed, unsure of what to do. Then she woke up and started screaming. "Hunter! What are you doing in my bed?"

He stared at her in a panic. "I was actually about to ask you!"

"Me?" Jill appeared to gather her wits, then she cupped her hand to her mouth with obvious embarrassment. "Oh my gosh, Hunter!" She sat up and clutched the comforter to her chest. "I must have walked in here last night by mistake. I got up to…"

Hunter pressed his lips together to repress a smile, but he wound up chuckling anyway.

"What's so funny?"

"You are, *darling*," Hunter said, emphasizing the endearment. "And all this time I thought you didn't care."

Jill lifted a pillow to swat him, but he held it back. "Play nice, now. I'm not the one who started this."

Jill's cheeks flamed. What in the world was happening here? And how on earth had she wound up in bed with Hunter? It wasn't like she wanted to subconsciously, was it? Jill was always preaching to others about their subconscious desires. Their inner yearnings for closeness. "It was an accident, and you know it. I must have come back through the wrong door after I went to use the restroom. Why, in heaven's name, didn't you lock yours?"

"I never lock my door," Hunter told her. "It's not like I'm living with anyone dangerous." He playfully raised his brow. "Am I?"

Jill snatched the pillow out of his hands and bopped him on the head. "Hey!"

In one deft move, he'd yanked the pillow from her grasp and maneuvered on top of her. Jill could feel the beating of his heart against her chest. She stopped breathing for a moment, caught up in Hunter's eyes. Dark brown eyes that seemed to be looking right through her, and way down into her soul. He lowered his face to hers and spoke in a husky murmur. "You never know who could prove the dangerous one in this relationship if you're not careful."

Jill pulse pounded harder. His mouth was just inches away and she found herself desperate for his kiss. His sexy, marvelous kiss, like the one that had poured all over her at Niagara Falls. "I won't kiss you if you don't want me to," he said.

Jill's head was spinning and her breath felt ragged. But she couldn't give in, she just couldn't. That would risk ruining everything. "Then don't," she managed to say.

Hunter released her and pulled away. He sat up on the edge of the bed, his back to her. "Then let's get up and do something."

"What?" she asked weakly, the room still spinning around her.

He stepped into the khaki shorts that were on the floor and as he did Jill caught a glimpse of his boxers, which were covered with kiwi fruit. He spoke, still facing the window. "I said, if we're not going to stay in bed all day, then we should go out and do something."

Jill clutched the pillow to her chest and asked primly, "What did you have in mind?"

After they'd each had coffee, Hunter took off on an errand. Without telling Jill where he was going, he'd recommended she wear something comfortable.

She didn't feel much like arguing since she'd already lost the battle over taking the day off. Jill had tried to say she needed to stay home and work on her new outline. Morgan was expecting to review it when she returned on Monday from New York. Hunter had countered that if Max could instruct him to take some time off, then he as Jill's faux husband at least had the right to suggest she spend one day with him without working. It was a holiday weekend after all.

Jill slipped into her sundress, studying her reflection in the mirror, and what she saw there gave her pause. It was hard to believe she was the same woman she'd been a few weeks ago. Then she'd been competent, confident…someone with her eye on the ball, a person who was used to setting and obtaining goals. Now she looked surprisingly like—Jill's heart beat faster as heat rose in her cheeks—a woman in love. No, this couldn't be happening. This wasn't the way things were supposed to go at all. Every time she'd fallen for a man before, things had ended in disaster. In retrospect she understood she'd played a role in that by constantly questioning her partners.

With Hunter, things were different. She didn't have to question his commitment, because it was written down on paper. Jill didn't need to ask about his goals, because he'd told her precisely what those were. He wanted to land a good account and become promoted to partner within his company. By all appearances, Hunter was solidly on his way. He had no reason to like her personally. Theirs was a business deal and its terms were clearly delineated. There were only two explanations for why he'd looked at her the way he had when his body had been pressed to hers on that bed. One, he was the animal she'd always imagined him to be and he was merely after a roll in the hay. Or two, he was falling for her.

Jill sank onto the bed as the realization hit her. Hunter was not only falling for her, she was falling for him as well. What else could explain the way her pulse had picked up these past few evenings when she'd heard his SUV pulling into the drive, or the way she'd looked forward to making his coffee in the morning? This wasn't about hormones or lust, or the surface type of attraction she'd doubted her previous boyfriends over. This was something deeper. And how inconvenient was that! Jill couldn't let herself fall for the man she had married. She didn't know the first thing about running a real relationship herself. She understood them much better in the abstract. The clinical training she'd had made her analytical, and she'd typically been able to analyze everything away, including her boyfriends. Everything but her feelings for Hunter.

Jill leapt to her feet when she heard his vehicle returning. He was back and apparently prepared to take her on an adventure, and Jill had resigned herself to going along. It was only for today; she'd get back to work tomorrow. She had real writing to do, and Morgan would be expecting to review the results soon.

Morgan stood on the curb by the taxi, passionately kissing Owen good-bye. "You make it awfully hard to leave New York," she told him.

"You made it awfully hard to leave my apartment," he replied. "I'm sorry we missed the fireworks."

She lifted an eyebrow and smiled. "I'd say we made some fireworks of our own."

He kissed her firmly on the lips. "Stay one more day," he begged. "What would it hurt?"

Morgan's gaze flitted to the taxi, then back to Owen's gorgeous green eyes. "I've already booked my flight."

"I'll buy you another."

Morgan flushed with pleased surprise. "You'd do that?"

"You betcha," he said, his eyes twinkling.

Morgan felt weak in the knees and leaned into the handle of her rolling bag. "Owen, you're impossible."

"Tell me impossible means yes?"

He grinned and Morgan's heart fluttered.

"I'll pay the taxi," Owen offered. "I'm sure it's no difference to him if I cover the fare."

Morgan looked at him in wonder. "Where have you been all my life?"

Owen passed the driver a couple of large bills and took her in his arms. "Waiting for you, I guess."

Chapter Twenty-Three

Cassandra followed Mauve down the narrow trail through the forest. She felt like such a nature girl. Who knew? When Mauve had suggested this little outing, she'd put on short shorts with tennis shoes and baby-oiled her legs. She didn't know why she cared how she looked, but she did. And she looked *good.* Mauve came to a clearing and halted, holding out his arm to stop her. "Wait!" he said quietly. "Is that who I think it is?"

Cassandra peered across the flowering field to spy none other than—oh, yes it was—Jill and Hunter! They were having a picnic beneath a shady tree. Hunter leaned back on his elbows laughing easily, while Jill prettily pulled provisions from a picnic basket. She was dressed in a flowing sundress that was tucked around her knees, and on the blanket between them there appeared to be a bucket of chilling wine. "Well, I'll be," Cassandra said.

"Looks like a very romantic picnic," Mauve observed.

"It does look romantic, darn it." Cassandra backed into the woods, feeling weak. Everywhere she turned, Jill and Hunter seemed to be paired up in some cozy couple's act. Hadn't she and Mauve just spotted them the day before driving through town together in Hunter's SUV? They'd both been dressed casually, but nicely, like they were going somewhere. Probably some Fourth of July deal, the sort Cassandra never got invited to. And now here they were again! It was like Cassandra couldn't escape their lovey-doveyness! Cassandra suddenly felt the need to sit down. She backed into a boulder lining the path and plunked down on it. "I don't know what's happening to me," she said, bringing a palm to her forehead. "I'm totally losing my touch!"

Mauve sympathetically laid a hand on her shoulder. "No, you're not."

"I *am,*" Cassandra whined pitifully. "Can't you see? All this time I've been on a wild goose chase, believing there was something more than meets the eye to their hasty union."

Mauve shot her a placating look. "There still could be."

Cassandra vehemently shook her head. "No, I hate to admit it, but Mauve…" She stared at him blankly. "I think I may have been wrong." She doubled forward and buried her face in her hands. "What am I going to do?"

Mauve patted her head to soothe her. "Maybe you could try your hand at something else?"

"Something else?" she cried, teary-eyed. "But writing for *Tempo Beat* is all I know!"

"Come on." He took both her hands in his and pulled her to her feet. "Look at me." When she did, Mauve said, "You're a brilliant, beautiful woman. I'm sure you have many talents, some of which you haven't explored."

She gasped hopefully. "You really think so?"

Mauve nodded. "Now, tell me. Isn't there anything else you've ever wanted to do? I mean, apart from working at *Tempo Beat*?"

She studied her shoes, then glanced at him shyly. "Once upon a time I wanted to write."

"You do write."

"Not like that, not for a gossip magazine. I mean fiction."

Mauve's mouth drew up in a smile. "Cassandra, I think that's splendid. Then that's what you should do!"

"What? Now?"

"Why not now?"

"Because," Cassandra said, "I wouldn't even know where to begin."

"Then start small. With short stories, maybe. Those are probably about the length of your articles anyway."

The dark clouds hovering above her began to lift as she pondered this aloud. "Yeah, short stories." Then she grabbed him by the shoulders. "But what will I write about?"

"Well…" Mauve said, drawing out the word. "You do like investigating, don't you?"

"Love it."

"Then how about a detective piece?"

Cassandra's whole face warmed. "You mean like Dick Tracy?" she asked excitedly.

"Why, yes, I supp—"

Before he could finish, Cassandra pulled him violently against her and planted a big one on his lips. Mauve stared at her aghast and fell back a few paces, his knees wobbling. "Wh…what was that for?"

"For inspiring me!" She stepped toward him and this time, he didn't back away. He let her scoop him into an embrace. "And Mauve," she said gazing at him dreamily. "Nobody's ever inspired me before."

His voice quavered. "Not ever?"

"Not even once," she purred, tightening her arms around him.

Mauve made some little animal sound and held her close. "Oh, Cassandra," he said. "You're amazing. In fact, you're the most amazing woman I've ever met."

Cassandra tilted up her chin to take him in. This wonderful, weird, quirky man that she was actually starting to like. "I'm glad that you think so," she said, kissing him again.

Hunter lifted the bottle from its chilling bucket and poured Jill more wine. "No more after this," she told him. "It's still the middle of the day, and I've got writing to do tomorrow."

His dark eyes sparkled in the sunlight. "All work and no play?"

Jill giggled into her plastic cup. "I'd say I've played quite a bit with you these past few days."

"Yeah, and it's been good, hasn't it? Almost like Niagara Falls."

"That was a truly memorable trip," she told him.

"I'll never forget it," he answered. "That's for sure."

Hunter had packed them marvelous sandwiches made from gourmet cheeses and deli meats and fresh French bread. They'd gone well with the white wine, and it was a beautiful July day out. Sunny and clear, but not too warm. Jill was happy Hunter had gotten her to come out and play. Maybe she needed to play more often. Perhaps when the pressure of this book project was done, she would. "Thanks for the picnic, Hunter. It's been fun and a really nice break."

"You've been working pretty hard on that new outline of yours."

"That's because Morgan wasn't thrilled with the first one."

"What was wrong with it?"

Jill lifted a shoulder. "Not personal enough."

"I see." Hunter stared up at the sunlight streaming down through the branches of the tree they were under. "What have you got so far?"

"You know the title of the book?"

"*Married Love: Keeping Those Home Fires Burning.*" He quirked a grin in her direction. "Who thought that up? Morgan?"

"Yep."

Hunter chuckled warmly. "Thought so."

"Anyway," Jill continued. "It's supposed to be about what makes marriages work. You know, the building blocks of a solid relationship."

"Like a recipe, you mean?"

"A recipe?" Jill took a moment to consider this, then smiled broadly. "Hunter, that's brilliant!"

His expression was murky. "What is?"

"A recipe! Yes! The recipe for a lasting marriage! That gives me a way to frame the information in the book! I already have several 'ingredients' in mind: shared adventures, the element of surprise, sacrifice…"

"Sacrifice?" he asked with interest. "That sounds a little old-world, doesn't it? Kind of Aztec?"

"Hunter!" She swatted a hand at him. "You know what I mean."

"Yeah, but maybe you ought to call it 'compromise'? Something a little less bloodthirsty?"

"How do you know I don't already have a chapter on compromise?" she asked, flirting.

"Do you?"

Jill rolled her eyes, but she was laughing. "What are you now, my project consultant?"

He shrugged. "I suppose I could be. I'm just saying that 'sacrifice' sounds a little one-sided. With compromise, the sacrificing goes both ways."

"And you know so much about married love, because…?"

"I know as much as you do."

Jill laughed again, realizing what a good time she was having. "You've got me there."

"A recipe for love…" he pondered aloud. "I like it."

"I like it too," Jill said surely.

Her pretty face was aglow and Hunter was pleased by how excited she looked. He was even happier he'd had a part in that. Hunter didn't fully understand what was happening between them, but he knew he felt happy in Jill's company. She'd been a star at Max's cookout, and this morning when she'd woken up in his bed he would have given anything if she'd looked pleased rather than petrified. While Hunter understood that Jill's walking into his bedroom in the middle of the night had been a mistake, inwardly he knew he wouldn't be opposed if she made that mistake again. He'd like it even better if she came in there on purpose. Hunter sighed, imagining what that would be like, waking up each morning with Jill in his arms.

"When do you have to finish the book?" he asked her.

"Morgan wants to see the new outline when she gets back from New York. We have plans to meet on

Monday. Assuming she approves, I'll write the first three chapters based on that. Those will be due to the publisher for review by October."

"And the final draft?"

"Browning wants it by Christmas."

"Christmas? That seems fast."

"They want to rush it into print for their spring catalog."

"Isn't that pushing things? I thought the process generally took longer."

"Browning wants the big push before summer, so they can get me on the talk show circuit. Otherwise, they'll have to plan for a fall release. And speaking engagements and conferences are harder to book around the holidays. Everyone has other things going on."

"Sounds like you're really going to be under the gun."

"I'll be working pretty hard these next few months, yeah."

"Then I'm going to help you."

Her expression was grateful. "What do you mean?"

"I mean, I want to support you, Jill. With this endeavor. Isn't it the whole reason you got into the fake marriage in the first place?"

"Yes."

Hunter regarded her kindly. "I know it means a lot. So, just for now, let's put everything else aside. You've got your room and I've got mine. What's more, we seem to be getting along."

Color dusted her cheeks. "Isn't that amazing?"

"It's not something I expected, I can tell you that."

"I like getting along with you, Hunter. It feels so much better than…"

"Not talking," he finished for her. "I agree."

"So, you're okay with this?" she asked him. "Prepared to continue our arrangement?"

"I'm in it for the long haul just like you are."

Her face fell almost imperceptibly. "The long haul meaning a year?"

"Now's not the time to talk about the future, Jill. Next June is a long ways off. In the meantime, you and I have some goals to reach. You've got to finish your book and I want to make partner at Abrams. After all that's done, maybe we can reassess?"

She bit into her bottom lip and waited a few seconds before answering. "I'd like that," she said at last in a whisper. "I really would."

"You know, Jill, I'd like that too."

Chapter Twenty-Four

Morgan set her reading glasses down on the coffee shop table. "This is fantastic, Jill. Such an improvement! Love it. Love it."

"It really feels like it's working," Jill said. "The whole concept is totally gelling for me."

"I can see that in the outline." Morgan thumped her glasses case against the papers. "It shows."

"It's awesome that you approve. So we're set to move ahead?"

"You make those first three chapters as good as it sounds like they could be, we're golden."

Morgan took her time toying with her coffee cup, then asked, "So, how are things going at home?"

"Actually," Jill told her brightly, "very well."

Morgan studied her. "Care to elaborate?"

"Not really."

"My, my. It's going that great, huh?"

Jill cupped a hand to her mouth with a blush. "Oh, Morgan," she whispered. "He's wonderful."

"Hunter?"

"There's so much more to him than I thought. And he's patient, you know? And not pushy. Plus, he's promised to be supportive and—"

"Has he kissed you again?" Morgan pressed. "Since the wedding?"

"Maybe just once, on our honeymoon."

"You don't remember?"

Jill recalled it quite clearly and the memory took her breath away. "My point is, we had a little difficulty in the beginning…settling in. Now, we seem to have arrived at an understanding between us due to our common goals."

"His promotion and your book," Morgan stated.

"Exactly."

"Well, good. That's good, Jill. I'm glad that it's working out for you. In the beginning you were so concerned about living with Hunter."

"I know, but he was a different man then."

"Was he? Or could it be you didn't know him?"

"Why don't you tell me about your time in New York?" Jill said, changing the topic. Morgan smiled wistfully at the thought of it.

"Owen's pretty wonderful too. He convinced me to stay an extra day, did you know that? Even paid for the replacement flight."

"Wow."

"I know! And for me, right? Who could have imagined?"

Jill leaned forward and sweetly squeezed her hand. "I could have, Morgan. I could have imagined it in a heartbeat. I'm just so glad you've met someone who recognizes your specialness too."

Hunter let himself into his darkened condo and flipped on the lights. Even with all of them shining, it still seemed dismal somehow. He'd come back to check on the place and pick up any mail that had missed getting forwarded to Jill's. Walking around here now, it was difficult to believe he'd once considered it home. Where were the decorative candles and the vases filled with fresh flowers? And what about that big, dopey dog that always came rushing to the door to greet him, and that crazy gray feline with whom he'd struck a secret deal? In his new lifestyle with Jill, Hunter had developed two regular habits. When he got home in the evening, he did two things right away. One, he opened a small pull-tab can of tuna fish for the cat and set it on the porch. This had somehow given Mimi the idea that when Hunter was around, he got rewarded for being outside. Two, he removed his suit jacket and tie and played a few rounds of fetch with Sport.

Not that Hunter would ever suggest Jill make Mimi an outdoor pet only, especially in wintertime. The cat seemed to enjoy lazing about in the sunshine on the porch just as much as he did sleeping by the windowsill inside. And the more Mimi stayed outside, the less Hunter's allergies bothered him, even when he was sitting in the living room watching TV. Hunter stared at the empty space in his condo that had once held the large television. It looked a little bare without it, and the rest of the room appeared forlorn too. Hunter had never imagined a home could have a personality, but Jill's house did. It was cheerful and warm and inviting, in a friendly and open-hearted way…just like Jill.

Hunter strode into the bedroom and sat on his king-size bed. At one time he couldn't have imagined sleeping anywhere more comfortable. Now, the prospect of returning to slumber here seemed almost unbearable. The room was lonely and depressing, without too many personal touches. Hunter acknowledged that that was because he'd packed most of his personal things and taken them to Jill's. Like that silly football trophy, which was still in a box. When he'd decided to take it over there, he'd had his rational reasons. Now Hunter felt foolishly sentimental for clinging to the relic from his past. That may have been the first time he'd tested his mettle, but it certainly wouldn't be the last. His relationship with Jill challenged him constantly.

Hunter opened his bedside table drawer and pulled out the contract. Who could have guessed a month ago he'd have such a different perspective on things today? Hunter smiled, recalling Jill's combative stance as they'd lunched together at the country club, and the way she'd been so horribly embarrassed over surrendering to—no, make that *commandeering*—his kiss. Hunter thought briefly of Cassandra, realizing he and Jill hadn't heard from her in a while, which was likely a good thing. The memories swirled through Hunter's mind: Brad's early insane proposition that Hunter take over Brad's role as Jill's groom; his and Jill's rushed yet fantastic wedding day; that unforgettable honeymoon in Niagara Falls… Hunter swallowed hard, reliving their kiss on the boat. Jill had seemed all his then, and for an instant he'd wondered… No, he'd dared to hope…that maybe she wanted to be. But that was ridiculous at the time. Or was it?

Hunter questioned whether he and Jill had already started falling for each other then, or whether that had transpired later, after they'd started living together as pretend husband and wife. The way it had snuck up on him had been so subtle, he hadn't noticed the transition as it happened. It was like one day he and Jill were engaged in this elaborate charade, and the next day he couldn't imagine living without her. Hunter considered how different things were with Jill than they'd been with any other woman. His experience with her had caused Hunter to take stock of himself and learn things, like what it meant to have a relationship with a woman that went beyond the physical. With each of his previous girlfriends, the physical aspect had come first. In some strange way, it had dominated. Perhaps that was because he didn't understand how to give more of himself than that, and that was what his exes ultimately found infuriating. They wanted a deeper relationship and a commitment, but how could Hunter commit to something he couldn't recognize or understand?

Hunter felt a raw tear in his chest as he realized what was happening. It was the feeling of his heart opening up. For his entire life, Hunter had believed himself incapable of profound emotion, perhaps because he'd never been able to receive it. Now, with Jill, things were different. He cared for Jill, more deeply than he had for any other woman. And he liked living with her—a lot. The contract trembled in his fingers as Hunter imagined there could be more. That he and Jill might actually get together and be able to love each other completely, as husband and wife. A yearning overtook him that was painful and primitive. Hunter had a burning desire to make Jill his wife in every sense of the word. Yet he knew in his heart that he couldn't push her. The best course of action was to support her as he'd promised, and then hopefully let destiny take its course. And, if it didn't? Well, then, Hunter would have learned something still: that he wasn't the empty shell of a man he'd always believed himself to be. Hunter was finally beginning to believe he possessed a human heart, one fully capable of loving someone else.

Chapter Twenty-Five

Three weeks later, Hunter met Brad on the golf course. Brad selected a five iron from his bag and addressed Hunter. "I've got to say, you're looking better rested. Married life must be agreeing with you."

"Married life is keeping me busy," Hunter laughed. He firmly gripped his club and swung his arms forward in perfect alignment. The ball arched through the air, bounced twice, then glided along the green, stopping a few inches shy of the pin.

"Nice," Brad remarked, lining up his shot. He took his turn, his ball landing about a foot behind Hunter's. "So what about it is keeping you so busy?"

They strode toward the flag, carrying their clubs. "This and that," Hunter said. "I'm working, she's working… I'm burning a lot of pizza."

Brad stared at him in shock. "You're cooking?"

"I promised to help out. Jill's got a big deadline coming up."

"For that book?"

Hunter nodded. "In October. Then the whole thing is due by Christmas."

"That's right," Brad said, as if remembering. "I'd forgotten the particulars."

"Anyhow," Hunter said. "At least I'm sleeping better now that I moved into the master."

Brad grabbed his shoulder. "No way."

"Not like that," Hunter chided, brushing him off. "We switched rooms. Mimi and Sport were used to staying in the other bedroom."

"Wait a minute, who's Sport?"

"The dog."

"I thought her name was Fifi?"

Hunter adjusted his cap to keep the sun out of his eyes as he tapped the ball in. "Long story."

"Well, at least you're all on a first-name basis," Brad teased. "Sounds like you've set up a regular household there. Almost like a real marriage, but without the…"

Hunter cut Brad a steely look that silenced him. "Lots of marriages don't have that. Maybe it's overrated."

Brad made a mock effort to clean out his ears. "I know I didn't hear that coming from you."

"Speaking of marriage," Hunter said in an effort to change the subject. "When are you planning to make an honest woman of Susan?"

"Don't you think one engagement per year is enough?"

"For you? I don't know."

Brad sank his putt, then they both retrieved their balls. "To tell you the truth, Hunter, that close call with Jill called me up short. Really got me thinking—and wondering what I'm ready for."

Hunter met his buddy's eyes. "How does Susan feel about this?"

"Oh, she's ready all right. That's what scares me half to death."

"Then don't rush into anything. Take your time."

"Susan says twelve years is plenty of time. Plus…and this part is a little scary…she thinks her biological clock is ticking."

"That would scare the devil out of me too," Hunter said. "Why don't you just try doing one thing at a time?"

"That's what I'm thinking, nice and easy." They returned to the golf cart and climbed aboard. "But Susan is all rush, rush, rush. She can't understand why I'd fake marry Jill, but not *real* marry her. I tried to explain the meaning of 'fake,' but that only made her steamed."

Hunter chuckled sympathetically. "I'm sorry, man. It sounds like you're between a rock and a hard place."

"Yeah?" Brad said. "And how about you?"

"The truth?" Hunter replied with a grin. "I like the place where I'm at. I think I'll stay there awhile."

When Jill wheeled her grandpa into the courtyard a few days later, autumn leaves were already turning and there was a light nip in the air. "I'm sorry I've missed seeing you these past few weeks," she said. "I've been working really hard on a special project."

"I know," her grandfather said, catching her off guard. "Hunter told me."

"Hunter?"

"He comes by Tuesdays and Thursdays. Plays canasta with me and the boys."

"He *what*?" Jill asked, thinking she couldn't have heard her grandfather correctly.

"Of course he can only stay for one hand, given that he has to get back to the office. Takes him twenty minutes to drive here."

Jill stared at her grandpa in shock. "We're talking about Hunter Delaney?"

"Your husband, yes." Her grandpa shot her a questioning look. "Sweetheart, why won't you take the man's name?"

Jill felt the whole world spinning around her and the ground shifting beneath her feet. She quickly sat on a bench beside her grandpa's parked wheelchair. "You mean why didn't I change mine to Jill Delaney?"

"Yes, granddaughter."

"I... Well, I... I'm a professional woman, Grandpa. I've built a reputation and a readership as Jill Jamison."

"Poppycock! Haven't you ever heard of a pen name?"

Jill blinked. Not only was his mind sharp today, his tongue was too!

"You could still write and present as whoever you want to, but in your private life, you should be a proper wife."

"Grandpa—"

"Now, don't 'Grandpa' me because I've got more mileage on me than you do, which means I happen to know a little more, particularly in the marriage department."

Jill heaved a breath, understanding there was no point in arguing with him.

"You've got a career and that's fine. We're all very proud of you. But sometimes in a marriage you've got to let a man know he's the man by showing him you're a woman. That's including in the bedroom."

Jill sucked in a gasp. She'd never heard her grandfather speak this directly, and certainly not about her personal life. She softened her tone and broached the topic lightly. "Did Hunter say something to you? Something to make you concerned?"

He met her eyes square on. "Like what?"

"Like…maybe I'm not being a good wife?"

"Heavens! All the opposite. The boy does nothing but sing your praises, to everyone and anyone who'll pay attention. *Jill's so kind and so smart. Have you heard she's working on a new book? Her first one was a bestseller!* Hunter loves you, Jill. It's as plain as day. I just want to make sure you're giving him all the good loving he needs back."

Jill gulped and her mouth felt dry. For someone as verbose as she normally was, Jill couldn't think of a word to say. So instead, she just sat there and listened.

Her grandpa fondly patted her hand. "I know you're a good girl with a big heart, but I also understand how absorbed in your work you can get. Don't let that stand in the way, sweetheart. Not of the best thing that's ever happened to you."

After Jill returned home, she'd attempted to write, but the words were a jumble. All she could think of was her grandfather's rumbling voice and his stern admonishments concerning her taking care of her marriage. Jill wondered if Hunter had somehow let something slip, or whether her grandfather simply had uncanny insight. In any case, Jill's eyes had been opened to a brand new fact: Hunter was regularly visiting her grandfather! Not only that, it appeared they were now bosom buddies. Gracious. Jill didn't know whether she should be grateful to Hunter for taking an interest in her grandpa or furious at him for not letting her know what he was doing. If it was a genuine gesture on Hunter's part, which she suspected it was, then why the big secret?

Jill gave up on her office and walked to the kitchen to brew a pot of coffee. But just as she did, she heard Hunter's SUV in the drive. She checked the kitchen clock and saw that it was only a little past four. It was unusual for Hunter to come home early. In fact, she couldn't recall a single other time when he had. Hunter barreled in the door and made straight for Jill's office, calling her name. Not finding her, he headed back toward the kitchen, encountering her in the living room. Hunter's face was flushed and it appeared he was about to burst with news. Fifi must have sensed this too, because she was hurriedly scampering around him and Mimi was meowing frantically at the front door. "Hunter, what is it?" Jill asked worriedly. "What's wrong?"

He proudly raised a bottle of champagne in his hand that Jill had neglected to notice earlier. "I have news!" he cried, wearing a proud mug. "I made partner!" Jill instinctively rushed into his arms and he pulled her up against him with a happy laugh, lifting her feet off the floor. Jill kicked them freely in the air behind her as she squealed. "You did it? Oh, baby!"

He set her down slowly, the front of her body sliding seductively down his. "Did you just call me baby?" he asked with a pleased grin.

Jill couldn't contain her enthusiasm, nor her affection. It was oozing out of her, seeping through her pores. She was so proud of him, and he'd worked so hard. Nobody deserved this promotion more than he did. Jill's face burned hot as she stared into his eyes. "Yeah, I guess that I did. Oh, Hunter, I'm so proud of you." Fifi barked loudly and Jill laughed. "I think Fifi is saying she's proud of you too."

Hunter glanced at the dog, who'd nabbed a tennis ball off the carpet and now held it between her teeth. "I think she's saying she wants to play ball."

Jill laughed again, hugging Hunter to her. She didn't know when her heart had felt this light. "Is that why you came home early? To tell me?"

His gaze poured down and into her. "You're the first person I thought of to tell."

"What about Brad?"

"I'll let him know tomorrow. But for now..." He tightened his arms around her. "I wanted to share the news with my very best friend."

"But I thought—"

"You're special, Jill," he replied huskily. "A very special kind of best friend. Maybe the best friend I've ever had...in a wifely way."

Jill felt herself swoon. "I think that's the nicest thing anyone has ever said to me."

"What do you say?" he asked, displaying the bottle between them. "Shall we open this?"

"Yes!"

A little while later, Jill sat on the porch sipping bubbly and watching Hunter play fetch with Fifi. She'd noticed some time ago he'd started calling her Sport, but had decided to leave that between Hunter and the dog. Fifi obviously loved him, and amazingly, Mimi had taken to Hunter as well. The moment Hunter arrived home each evening, Mimi eagerly followed him out the door. Jill knew Hunter was sneaking the cat tuna fish, but she didn't mind. She'd adjusted the portions of his cat food to compensate so he wouldn't grow a big round tummy.

When Fifi started to wind down, Hunter led her back to the porch and poured himself a glass of champagne from the bucket on the table. "You're really great with them," Jill said, indicating the pets.

"They're good kids." He smiled over the rim of his glass. "Most of the time."

"So when does it become official?" she asked.

"Max gave me a bigger office when I landed the Kaleidoscope account. Now, it's just a question of changing the company name on our logo and marketing materials."

"Oh, how exciting," she said, meaning it absolutely.

"Abrams and Delaney," Hunter said happily. "The day I've worked for, the one I've waited on, is finally here."

"I know."

Hunter reached out and took Jill's hand and she held his firmly. How could she not at a moment like this?

"This will mean a lot more money for us, you know."

"For us?"

"Why, sure…" He stopped talking and a silence burned between them. "I mean I could cover more of our expenses, help you pay your mortgage."

Jill released his hand and turned to look at him. "I've never asked you to pay my mortgage. I'm handling that just fine; besides, you've still got your own on the condo. And the utilities here are shared—at your insistence. As it stands you're buying more than half of all the groceries—"

"That's because I eat more than half of them."

She studied him kindly. "My point is, you're already doing enough. Maybe even too much."

"But that's silly when I could do more."

"Hunter, I don't want you to do more. That might only make things more complicated."

"For establishing a clean break, you mean?" Hunter looked away.

"Look," Jill said calmly. "I don't want this conversation to get out of hand between us. Not tonight, okay? I'm so proud of you, Hunter. I truly am. I think it's good for us to celebrate without worrying too much about the future."

Hunter released a weighty breath. "Jill…"

"Just let me finish, please. I appreciate the gesture, I really do. It's very sweet. I just don't feel right about it."

"Because you're an independent woman?"

"Is there anything wrong with that?"

"Not at all, Jill. That's one of the reasons I…care for you so much."

"I care for you too, and don't want you to think I don't appreciate all you've done for me. Hunter, I went to Green Meadows today and saw my grandfather."

"That's wonderful. How is he doing?"

"Perhaps I should ask you? It appears you've been seeing him more than I have."

Hunter was unabashed. "Yeah, that's true. He and I have been building a relationship. Plus we're a deadly duo at canasta."

"But why didn't you tell me?"

"Oh, Jill. Can't you see?" His face fell in a frown. "You've been working so hard, knocking yourself out. I know you've been feeling guilty about missing your regular visits to Green Meadows, but I've also seen you sweating bullets trying to get your manuscript done. That's why I thought it might be a good idea if I, you know, stepped in. I didn't tell you because I didn't want to stress you out, make you feel bad for not being there yourself. Not when I understood the pressure you're under."

Emotion flooded her and Jill felt overwhelmed, not just by Hunter's thoughtfulness, but also by his compassion. Of all the men she'd been involved with, none of them would have been selfless enough to do something like this. Not a one would have sacrificed two lunch hours a week to ensure the grandparent she loved was looked after. She decided this was the time to tell Hunter what she'd held back, the truth about her grandfather. "Hunter," she said, "it's not all about the manuscript. I mean, yes, there is pressure to get it done, but when I said it was for professional reasons that was only half the truth. And when I told you I was building an addition…" Her lips quivered. "I'm afraid that part was a lie."

Hunter took her hand. There was acceptance in his eyes. "You didn't have to lie to me, Jill. You could have told me the whole truth from the beginning."

"Maybe then, I thought it was too personal. Now that you've gotten to know my grandpa and see how special he is, perhaps you'll understand. Green Meadows is a great place."

"Top-notch, from what I've seen," Hunter answered.

"Yes, but all that excellent care comes at a price. A very high one, Hunter. And without this book deal…" Her voice fell off and she was unable to finish, there was so much hurt in her heart. If Jill couldn't continue to help her grandpa, she didn't know what she'd do.

"I know how much you love your grandfather, so I do understand what this project means to you, and how the fake marriage figures in. You probably felt like you had nowhere else to turn. That you were alone in this." Hunter squeezed her hand. "But Jill, you aren't any longer."

Jill's throat felt raw as tears leaked from her eyes. She'd never had a man be this kind to her, this caring. And there was no pretense in this moment. Every word that Hunter said came from his heart. "Would you mind?" she asked with sniff. "If we sat on the swing?"

Worry marred his features. "Of course not. What's wrong?"

"If it's not too much to ask…" Her chin trembled as a tumult of emotion closed in. "Could you hold me? Just for a while?"

Hunter calmly set aside Jill's champagne, still holding her hand. Then he led her to the porch swing, where they snuggled in together. Warm breezes blew as Hunter wrapped her in his embrace, securing her in his arms. "It's going to be all right," he told her. "Everything's going to work out."

"I know." Her voice warbled. "But, my grandpa, he's so old and…"

Hunter stroked her hair, holding her close. "He's in a good place, Jill. And you and I are going to keep him there, okay? Together we'll find a way."

She nodded through a blur of tears and Hunter placed a tender kiss on her forehead. "You're a wonderful person, and the world's best wife. Don't think I won't stand by you." He steadied her against him and sent the swing into a gentle rocking motion, while she listened to the slow, rhythmic beating of his heart. Then they stayed there together for a long while, until well after the sun went down.

Jill and Hunter made a quiet supper together, pulling leftovers from the fridge and dining by candlelight. The feelings between them were too powerful to be contained by mere words, so they barely spoke. Instead they went about the business of putting a meal together and eating and cleaning up, as if all their motions were choreographed in a graceful dance. They weren't awkward together in this silence. Rather, it was beautiful and telling. They held hands walking down the hall until they reached the doors to their bedrooms.

"Hunter," Jill told him. "I don't want to be alone."

His voice was gravelly. "Are you sure?"

She nodded and Hunter cupped her cheek in his hand. "You don't know how long I've waited for you."

"I think I do." Jill tilted up her chin and brushed her lips against his, before speaking in a whisper. "I've waited for you too."

Hunter bent to grab her behind the knees and lifted her into his arms. "Well, darling," he said with a sexy growl, "your waiting is over."

Then he kicked back the master bedroom door and carried her to the bed.

Chapter Twenty-Six

Jill rolled over under the comforter and reached for Hunter, but he was gone. She opened her eyes, fearing for a moment she'd dreamed it. Then her nose caught the fine aroma of brewed coffee. She slipped into her robe and headed to the kitchen, hoping to find Hunter there. But as she passed the living room window she saw his SUV was gone. When her eyes snagged on the clock over the stove, she saw why. It was nearly ten o'clock! No wonder she'd overslept. Hunter had tenderly made love to her, taking all the care in the world, then he'd cradled her in his arms all night long. She'd slept with her back pressed to his beating heart. Jill had never known such comfort or serenity, and had never fully understood the meaning of becoming one. But she was united with Hunter. She understood that now, body and soul.

She strolled to the coffeepot, her spirits soaring. There, she found a note from Hunter saying he'd fed the pets before leaving and would miss her the whole day through. She lifted the notepaper to her face and caught a whiff of him. The masculine scent of his heady cologne. Oh, how she wanted him home already, but Jill understood Hunter had work to do. He'd made partner! What a glorious and well-earned achievement for such a hardworking man.

Jill couldn't help but recall how he'd sweetly held her on the porch swing and the way he'd later brought his body to hers, gently but with passion and skill. Jill flushed from head to toe thinking of him, knowing she'd miss him all day through as well. But just like Hunter, she had a job to attend to. And today, Jill sensed, the writing would go a whole lot easier. From this day forward, in fact, it was bound to be a breeze. She was no longer just writing abstractly about married love: Jill was living it. At this moment in time, Jill couldn't imagine her life being any more perfect.

Mauve strode out of Cassandra's contemporary kitchen wearing baggy pajama pants, a droopy shirt, and his horn-rimmed glasses. He held a coffee mug and the morning newspaper. "You'll never believe what I found in today's edition."

Cassandra looked up from the sofa, where she was busily typing on her laptop. She'd been so intent on her story she'd missed some of what he'd said, and by his expression it was urgent. "Did you say something?"

"Jill's new book!" His eyes grew big. "There's a press release announcement."

"Press release?" Cassandra asked, confused. "It's come out already?"

"No, not until late spring, but the publisher, Browning, has set up preorders."

Cassandra flipped her laptop shut. "Let me see that," she said, reaching for the paper when Mauve came and sat beside her. She quickly scanned the text on the page, her mouth hanging open. She shut it long enough to swallow a mouthful of saliva. "Well, well, well… What do you know?"

"*Married Love: Keeping Those Home Fires Burning,*" Mauve recited with a knowing air. He turned his eyes on hers. "Are you thinking what I'm thinking?"

"You know I am!" Cassandra stared at him in disbelief. "All this time I was right, Mauve. I just *knew* something was up with Jill's marriage! First she's engaged to Brad, then the next thing you know, she's hooked up with Hunter? They marry two weeks later?"

"We did see them, Cassandra," Mauve reminded her. "We watched them for a while and both came to the conclusion their relationship was legit."

"Yeah, a legitimate pack of lies."

"How are you going to prove it?"

"I don't know, but there must be a way." She drummed her fingernails against her laptop, thinking. "There was clearly something in this for the two of them. We already knew Hunter wanted that promotion, because Fred Forester paid you to try to debunk Hunter's marriage."

"And Jill's career was on the brink," Mauve said.

"The brink of disaster, yes. Her second book was a stinker, and for good reason. Nobody believes an 'expert' giving advice who can't keep a man of her own." Cassandra folded her arms across her chest. "Isn't it *convenient* how this sweet little marriage between Hunter and Jill suddenly evolved—right out of the clear blue sky?"

"A little too convenient, if you ask me," Mauve said.

"Precisely."

"What are you going to do?"

Cassandra flipped her laptop back open to study the story she'd been writing. "Detective work, hmm."

"Cassandra, what are you thinking behind those crazy blue eyes?"

"You know," she said, looking at Mauve. "I just might have a plan."

Later that evening Cassandra and Mauve huddled by Hunter's unit door in his condominium building. They were dressed as pizza delivery people and each carried a steaming box. They'd been lucky to sneak in with another tenant while the doorman was away. "We probably could have gotten in without the pizza," Mauve said.

"Sometimes it's better not to take chances," whispered Cassandra. She scanned the narrow hallway, checking the angle of the ceiling at either end, but thankfully found no security cameras installed. "Here, take this," she said, sliding her pizza box on top of the one Mauve held.

When he did, Cassandra withdrew a thin plastic card from her jeans pocket. "What's that?" Mauve queried.

"Library card," she hissed back. "It's more pliable than a credit card."

Mauve stared at her with a combination of fear and awe.

In a matter of seconds, Cassandra had jimmied the card between the door latch and frame and popped the door ajar. It swung open just a crack.

"Remind me to stay on your good side," Mauve quipped.

"Shut up and come on," she said, urging him inside. Cassandra looked around the darkened space and Mauve reached for a light switch. "No, don't!" she warned him. "We don't want to call attention." Mauve scanned the efficiency-style room that melded a living area with a kitchen and set the pizza boxes on the counter between them, while Cassandra slipped into a pair of latex gloves and pulled a penlight from her hip pocket.

"Can I at least have a piece of pizza?" he asked, whining like a baby. "I'm hungry."

"Oh, all right," Cassandra replied testily. "Just don't drop anything on the floor and don't make a mess." He followed her around the room, sending the scent of pepperonis wafting through the condo, as Cassandra opened and closed drawers and peered under objects.

"What are we searching for?" he asked between swallows.

"I'll know it when I find it." Mauve was so close on her heels he was driving her insane. Plus he was chewing loudly. "Why don't you just wait in here?" She shot his food a derisive look. "With your pizza?"

Mauve shrugged and walked back to the counter while Cassandra crept into the next room. Her eyes stealthily took stock of the king-size bed and Scandinavian dresser. There was a matching nightstand to one side of the bed. She decided to start with that. Cassandra pulled out the single drawer, finding a legal-seeming document inside. It looked suspiciously like some kind of contract. She raised her penlight to examine it more closely, her heart pounding fiercely. *Bingo, you little lovebirds. Gotcha!*

Mauve came searching for her a few minutes later to see what was taking so long. He found Cassandra hunched over papers laid out on the bed with her cell phone camera, snapping shot after shot. "You found something?" he asked with unmasked glee.

Cassandra shared a sneaky grin. "Mauve," she crowed quietly. "We've hit pay dirt." When she finished taking her pictures, Cassandra placed everything back in the drawer, just as she'd found it. Then she instructed Mauve to wipe down the counter where he'd set the pizza boxes with one of the sanitary wipes she'd made him bring in his fanny pack. Seconds later, the two of them backed out the door and shut it. Mauve nervously glanced around, then cleaned the knob with another sanitary wipe.

As they passed the doorman in the lobby, he eyed the two pizza boxes and asked with a puzzled expression, "Nobody home?"

"Wrong address," Cassandra said in a businesslike tone before leading Mauve out the door.

Chapter Twenty-Seven

Hunter had never seen anybody as excited about Thanksgiving as Jill. She flitted about the kitchen, checking on this and testing the temperature of that, and peering under tinfoil tents that emitted incredible aromas. "When do you think they'll get here?" she asked, speaking of Brad and Susan.

"Any minute. I'm sure they're just running a little late." They'd also extended an invitation to Morgan, but she'd declined, saying she was going to be in New York with Owen and his brother's family.

Hunter admired the golden brown turkey as Jill pulled it from the oven. It was hard to imagine there were only four of them for dinner. Jill had prepared a veritable feast. She was certainly a domestic goddess, and this fall of living with her couldn't be described as anything less than marital bliss. Since joining Hunter in her old bedroom, Jill hadn't returned to the guestroom once. The pets had gleefully taken up their former quarters in the guestroom, and Hunter had grown accustomed to waking with Jill in his arms. Neither one had said "I love you," but perhaps at this juncture that wasn't necessary. It was evidenced by the way they spent their time together and lived harmoniously in caring consideration of one another's needs.

Jill's first three chapters were received enthusiastically at Browning, and the publisher quickly put out an announcement about the upcoming book. They were lining up speaking engagements and promo tours for her already, and Jill was making steady progress in completing her manuscript. She claimed it was so much easier now that her advice quite literally came from the heart, and Hunter was pleased to have played a role in her professional success. More than that, though, he was ecstatic over the relationship that had developed between them. It was rich and multi-textured, unlike any he had known.

The doorbell rang and Hunter offered to answer it. "I'll get that, darling."

She laughed, obviously loving the endearment. Once she'd bristled at its very uttering. Now, it had become a code word between them. One that always made Jill laugh and Hunter sigh, because she was his *darling* and always would be. There was absolutely no one more precious in his life.

Brad and Susan entered and removed their jackets as the pets scampered indoors after them from the yard. "Happy Thanksgiving, you two," Hunter said congenially. "We're glad you could make it."

Brad shook Hunter's hand, slapping the back of it with his other palm. "Happy Thanksgiving, bro. Thanks for including us."

Susan smiled softly, her auburn hair pulled up in a ponytail. "Sure beats spending the holiday at Mom's house. She's *always* correcting our grammar."

Hunter chuckled as Jill appeared in the doorway, dusting her hands on an apron. "Welcome! Both of you!" She hugged each of them briefly, then motioned them into the kitchen. "We've got wine or beer, whatever you'd like."

"I think beer goes best with turkey," Brad said. Susan rolled her eyes and smiled, accepting a glass of wine. They visited for a short time in the kitchen while Jill whipped up the gravy, then everyone pitched in, setting things on the table in the nook.

After they'd all settled into their seats, Susan said, "I think this is kind of cool. The four of us having Thanksgiving together. Thank you, Hunter and Jill, for inviting us."

"Well, Hunter doesn't have any family in the area," Jill began. "And my grandpa's at the stage where he can't leave the home."

"How is he?" Brad asked with compassion.

"We went over there this afternoon," Hunter answered. "Green Meadows held a Thanksgiving dinner for the residents and their families at noon."

"How nice," Susan said, taking a sip of wine.

Hunter held out his hands to Susan and Brad, who were seated on either side of him, and Jill took their hands from where she sat at the other end of the table. "Shall we bless the food and begin?"

An hour later, everyone was laughing lightly and moaning heavily as they patted their stretched bellies. "Amazing dinner, Jill," Brad said. "Thanks."

Hunter eyed Jill with affection. "Yes, it was. The very best."

Color rose in her cheeks. "Thanks, darling," she said with a lilt.

Susan glanced at them both, then stood, offering to help clear the table. "Yes, delicious, all of it. I especially loved the pecan pie."

When they were away from the men, Susan asked Jill, "So how's it going with Hunter? Pretty well, huh? The two of you seem, well…like you're really together."

"We are together, Susan," Jill said mildly. "We're married."

Susan leaned toward her. "Like I don't know all about that."

"How are things going between you and Brad?" Jill asked, turning things around.

Susan's mouth puckered in a frown. "I don't know. I mean, sometimes I think I know, but at others it's hard to say."

"Why don't you talk to him?"

"Don't think that I haven't."

"Hey, ladies," Hunter said as he and Brad carted their dishes to the sink. "What do you think about a game of Scrabble, or maybe watching a movie?"

The votes centered on a movie, but to the guys' dismay a chick flick was soundly lobbied for. So Hunter and Brad gave in and retreated to the living room to set up the video streaming while the girls finished packing away the leftovers in the kitchen. "So everything's really good here?" Brad asked Hunter when it was just the two of them.

"Everything is perfect."

"Good, but I want you to be careful."

"Careful of what?"

"Remember last week when you asked me to drop by your condo just to check on it?"

"Sure," Hunter answered. "You said everything looked fine."

"It did, but…"

"But what?"

"I don't know man. I got a funny feeling."

"Funny, how?"

"I know this is going to sound crazy…" Brad wrinkled up his nose. "But the place smelled a lot like pizza."

"Pizza?"

"Pepperoni, to be exact."

"That's impossible."

"That's what I thought, and why I didn't say anything earlier."

"What made you change your mind?"

"I saw Cassandra yesterday and she was acting a little strange."

"Stranger than usual?" Hunter queried skeptically.

"Yeah. Plus, she was with this weird guy, Mauve."

"Who's Mauve?"

"I think he works for a pizza delivery service, because he was wearing that kind of shirt. You know, one with a logo and slogan with a big slice of pie on the front?"

"Yeah, so?"

"So, I was at the coffee shop downtown and Cassandra was apparently meeting Mauve there. When he showed up wearing that T-shirt, it was like she totally flipped out. Really lit into him."

"For wearing a pizza shirt?"

"She was shouting, yeah. *You don't do that, Mauve! Are you some kind of idiot? Don't you think someone might put two and two together?* Then she suddenly lowered her voice and peered around the room, like she was worried she'd been overhead."

"I still don't get what this had to do with me and Jill," Hunter said.

"I don't know exactly either. I'm just saying with Cassandra, you never know. It probably pays to watch your back."

The girls appeared and the two couples settled in for a movie, but all the while Brad's scary warning kept echoing in Hunter's brain. What in the world could Cassandra know, or have put together? She clearly didn't have any proof... Unless she'd been in Hunter's place.

Hunter rose early the next morning and went back to the condo. He scoured it completely but didn't find anything amiss. If Brad had smelled pizza earlier, the scent hadn't lingered, because Hunter couldn't smell it now. He decided not to mention Brad's speculation about Cassandra to Jill, because he didn't want to worry her unnecessarily. She'd had such a great time at Thanksgiving and had played the perfect hostess. It had been the first time they'd entertained as a married couple and both were proud of their accomplishment. They'd dozed off snuggled in each other's arms, reliving the happy memories of the day. When Jill asked Hunter where he'd been the following morning, he said he'd stopped back by his old place to pick up a few DVDs. The next time they had company, he wanted more equal say in what they'd be watching. Jill had lifted an eyebrow and stared at him like she didn't quite buy his story. Then again, she probably assumed he didn't really have anything to hide. And, hopefully, Hunter didn't.

Chapter Twenty-Eight

When Hunter arrived at work that cold December day, the last thing he expected to find was Max standing in his office. "Hunter, my boy, you don't know how much it pains me to say this." To Hunter's astonishment, Max was holding a copy of *Tempo Beat*. "It couldn't hurt me more if you were my own son. In fact, in some ways..." Max paused and drew his lips into a thin line, his eyes never leaving Hunter's.

"Sir, I'm sorry. I haven't even seen the issue. I don't know what's in—"

Max's voice cracked with incredulity. "A fake marriage, Hunter? How could you? Do you really take the truth that cavalierly? Does honesty mean nothing to you?"

He flipped the magazine around and Hunter stared in horror at his own signature line at the base of his contract with Jill.

"Max, I—"

"I beg your pardon," the old man said gruffly. "It's Mr. Abrams to you." He slapped the magazine down onto Hunter's drafting table. "Marriage by contract? How contemporary!"

"Max…sir…Mr. Abrams." Hunter felt he was standing in quicksand and it was rapidly sucking him under. "If you'd only let me explain."

"Save your breath for the unemployment office. You'll probably need it."

"Unemployment?"

Max pointed an accusing finger. "I trusted you, Hunter! Brought you into my company and into my home! And this is how you repay me?"

"But everything I've done for Abrams Advertising has been for real. I've worked hard, sir. Spent countless hours…"

"Of course you have. Now I understand it. Your desire to spend time away from home."

"No! It's not that! Jill and I… Things are different now. You have to believe me." Hunter was desperate, grasping at straws, but they were all slipping away.

Max's eyes were a steely gray. "That's where I'm afraid you're wrong. I no longer have to believe anything you say. You have exactly two hours, Hunter. Then I want all of your things out of this office."

"Two *hours*? Not even two weeks?" Hunter's head reeled.

"You're just lucky I didn't have the custodian dump your gear on the street."

Then Max turned abruptly and was gone.

Hunter stood there stunned, wondering if this was some kind of nightmare. Then Fred waltzed in, carting a big office box stuffed with his belongings. "Out with the old and in with the new," he said in a singsong voice.

In the old days, Hunter might have throttled him, but now all he could do was stare. This couldn't be happening to him, it just couldn't. He'd become a laughingstock in all of advertising, and would never in a million years recover.

Jill was surprised to hear Fifi's excited barking before noon. Perhaps it was a delivery truck, or something arriving by certified mail? Jill fell back a step when she saw it was Hunter. He passed through the front door appearing ashen, a box full of office supplies in his grasp.

"Hunter?" Jill asked with concern. "What's happened?"

He stared at her with red-rimmed eyes. "I've been fired, Jill."

She turned white in shock.

"I'm sorry, but it's true."

"I don't understand." Her voice trembled. "You were doing so well. Just got promoted!"

Hunter pursed his lips. "Fred has taken that position now."

"Fred Forester?" she asked like she couldn't believe it. "But why? How?"

Hunter set down his box and pulled out the latest issue of *Tempo Beat*. "Cassandra nailed us, Jill. She nailed us good."

Before Jill could respond to Hunter's horrific revelations her cell buzzed. It was a text from Morgan, saying she needed to meet with Jill *now*. "I'd better go," Jill told Hunter, still aghast. "And see what she has to say."

Hunter hung his head and sank down on the sofa, Fifi immediately taking up her position beside him. "Sure," he replied without looking up. "You go ahead."

"I'm sorry," Morgan told Jill at the coffee shop. "But this is bad, worse than bad actually. Browning's rescinded your contract."

"What? Can they do that?"

"They're the publisher. They can do anything they want."

"But the advance money? My grandfather?"

"Nobody cares about the advance money. You can keep it. What Browning wants is to keep its nose clean. They're divorcing you, Jill. The second book tanking was bad enough, but this recent fiasco—"

"The whole thing was your idea, Morgan! From the get-go! You suggested it!"

"I've got plausible deniability and you know that."

"Oh," Jill said, feeling the hurt spike to her core. "And all this time I'd thought we were friends."

"We *are* friends, which is why I'm willing to help you. Owen has contacts in New York. I can get him to ask around."

"Thank you for your charity, Morgan." Jill stood from the table and snatched up her purse. "But I don't think I'll take it."

Jill cried all the way home. At one point, she pulled over because she doubted her ability to see the road. This was a horrible mess, but surely she and Hunter could fix things somehow? While their marriage might have started as pretend, it definitely felt real now. She and Hunter were a team. She was his wife and he was her... A sob caught in Jill's throat as she pulled into the drive, and she couldn't believe her eyes. Hunter was loading up his SUV.

Jill raced out of her car and through the cold. Snow had been predicted and the air was frigid. It couldn't be any chillier than the ice in her veins. Was Hunter really packing—and leaving her?

"Hunter!" she cried, racing toward him. "Where are you going?"

"This whole thing is a disaster, Jill. Professionally, I'm ruined."

"Professionally?" Her voice squeaked. "Yeah, well, professionally I've got my worries too."

He squared his shoulders and stared at her. "I'm very sorry about that. It looks like this is a disaster for both of us."

"But no!" Her chin trembled. "You and I… It's different now!" When he didn't reply, she whimpered, "Isn't it?"

"The truth, Jill? I don't know what it *is* and *isn't* anymore. Despite its reputation as a city, in many ways Parkland is a small town. Don't you realize I'll never be able to work there again?"

"That's not true!"

"Who's going to hire me, huh? A *man of no scruples*, as Cassandra wrote?"

"That's not who you are. I know the real you."

"Do you?" he challenged. "Or did you only see the 'me' you were hoping for?"

Jill huddled her arms around herself as icy winds blasted and tears streamed down her cheeks. She'd known from the start that this marriage wasn't real, so why did she feel her heart breaking? It was because things between her and Hunter had changed. He hadn't said he loved her, but he'd made love to her, as her husband. She'd felt so sure—and had believed in her soul—that their relationship went beyond that stupid contract. How could she have been so wrong?

"You love me, Hunter. I know you do."

"Yeah? Well, do you love me? Will you take me as I am, now that I'm unemployed and no longer successful? Could you really love a man who would sell his soul on paper, even to you?"

Jill stared at him, because at this moment, she didn't know what to think. This was a side of Hunter she hadn't seen. An angry side. He was so out of sorts and seemed to be laying it all on her. The air hung heavy between them as icy winds ripped at their clothing and lashed at their skin. At long last, Jill whispered, "What happened with *Tempo Beat* wasn't my fault."

"Perhaps not, but we're both to blame for signing that contract. How could we believe it would never blow up on us? That such a ludicrous plan could work? Or did you maybe hope we'd *really* fall in love and then live happily ever after?"

When she didn't answer immediately, he said, "Here's a little advice for your new book: Sometimes love isn't enough."

"Is that really how you feel?" she asked, her voice shaking. "That everything was a mistake?"

"Things sure haven't worked out stellar for us, have they?" He raked a hand through his hair, then abruptly asked, "What did Morgan have to say?"

"Browning's rescinded the book deal."

"And your advance?"

"The publisher said I can keep that."

"Well then, that's something. The marriage wasn't a total loss."

Jill reached for him as he stepped into his SUV, but Hunter pulled back. "I told you I didn't want half the money and I still don't. I'll mail you the check returning my fifty percent tomorrow."

Snow lightly drifted around her as Jill watched Hunter's SUV pull away and her heart shattered into a billion pieces. Fifi dejectedly sat by her side and whimpered. "I know, Sport," Jill said with a sob. "I know."

Chapter Twenty-Nine

Brad helped Hunter unpack the last box. Hunter had returned to his condo and everything was settling into place. The moving truck had brought Hunter's things back from Jill's this morning. "I'm sorry that you let someone like Cassandra wield this power over you."

"It wasn't Cassandra, it was Jill," Hunter said. "And you, Brad. Don't think I can't remember the two people who dragged me into this."

"I've already apologized a dozen times."

"You know I'm not really mad at you. I'm mostly angry with myself."

Brad sadly shook his head. "I never imagined it would end this way."

"That's what we all get for being stupid."

"Hunter," Brad told him. "I can't believe you'd just walk. At Thanksgiving, things between you and Jill seemed to be—"

"It was nothing, okay? Nothing without that gosh-darned contract. Maybe I'd fooled myself into believing there was more, but that just shows how gullible I was. You should have seen the way Jill looked at me. It was like I was someone she didn't even know. Honestly? I think Jill was pretty relieved when I left. Particularly when I said I'd send back the money."

Brad sighed. "What do you plan to do?"

"I don't know. Maybe relocate."

"Have you heard from your parents?"

"Oh yeah."

"What did they say?"

"How I'd embarrassed them terribly in front of their friends. *Hunter, how could you?* Trust me on this, I won't be relocating there."

"That's rough."

"What's even rougher was the humiliation I experienced in front of people I'd viewed as my friends, the ones I'd supervised and been good to at Abrams. You should have seen them lining up to watch me clean out my desk with their sad and disappointed faces."

"What's Jill going to do?"

"I have no idea. I didn't ask her."

"Hunter, just take a moment."

Hunter glared at him.

"Okay, fine. Take a few days, a week. But then think about what you're losing. Maybe Jill was meant for you."

"I gave her a chance to tell me, Brad. Say that she still wanted me anyway, even after I'd lost my job— and my reputation. And you know what she said?" Brad stared at him blankly as he continued, "Absolutely nothing."

Jill finished singing a Christmas carol with her grandpa, then went to grab them some eggnog from the festive table the staff of Green Meadows had prepared. When she returned, he asked her, "Why isn't Hunter here with you? Since today is a Sunday, he can't have work?"

"No, he doesn't." Jill pulled up a chair and sat beside him as a pianist with blue-gray hair began a new holiday tune and the other residents and their families joined in singing. Jill hesitated a moment, gathering her courage. "Grandpa," she finally said. "I've got something to tell you."

Her grandfather turned his eyes on hers. "If it concerns that *Tempo Beat* article, I know all about it."

Jill gasped. "You what?"

"It made the evening news."

"I'm so sorry." She hung her head. "That must have been very embarrassing for you."

"I'm old enough to know it's not all about me, Jill," he answered solemnly. "How are you and Hunter holding up?"

Jill turned the eggnog cup in her hands. "We're not."

"I'm afraid I don't understand." Her grandfather's expression was puzzled. "Did you not listen to anything I told you—about love and sacrifice?"

"This is different, Grandpa. The marriage…it wasn't…" She sniffed and dabbed the corner of her eye with a napkin. "It wasn't real."

"Poppycock!" her grandpa declared. "I saw the two of you together and I saw you apart. What you had with Hunter was as real as most marriages I've witnessed, maybe more."

"None of that matters much now," she told him sadly.

His brow wrinkled with concern. "Has something else happened?"

"Hunter's moved out."

Her grandpa heaved a sigh. "Oh, dear."

They sat there listening to another song proceed through several stanzas and a chorus. When it ended, her grandpa asked, "Will you come over for Christmas dinner?"

Jill gave a wan smile. "Of course I will."

"Superb. Because if anyone can help straighten out this problem between you and your husband, it's my Rose. She'll be here, did I tell you?"

Jill bit into her lip and paused before replying softly, "No, I don't think so."

Her grandpa looked distant a moment, smiling at the twinkling lights on the artificial Christmas tree. "You'll love meeting her, my Rose. She's a real angel, you know."

Cassandra knocked at Mauve's front door, then rapped loudly once more. She pushed in the doorbell a couple of times, thinking he had to have heard her by now. Finally, the door swung open and Mauve stood there in ratty sweatpants and that darned pizza delivery shirt. "Mauve!" she cried in horror. "What are you doing? We'll be late for the party!" *Tempo Beat* was throwing a big celebration and Cassandra was their new star. Her recent exposé had rocked the gossip rag world, and she'd been promoted to managing editor of the magazine. Tonight was technically *Tempo Beat*'s annual Christmas party, but her boss had let her know there'd be a presentation in her honor. Accordingly, Cassandra had dressed to the nines in a bright red, figure-hugging sweater dress and chic black boots. And just look at what Mauve was wearing!

"I'm not going, Cassandra."

Her mouth hung open. "What?"

Mauve adjusted the glasses on his beak-like nose. "I said, I'm not going to your stupid office party. I'm staying here."

She gaped at him. "What on earth is going on?"

"It's you, Cassandra," he told her coldly. "When we first got into our detective work, it was sort of like a game, almost fun. Now, we've ruined two people's lives—and just look at you, you're glowing!"

Cassandra blinked, flustered. "Well, of course I am, Mauve. This was a big achievement, a huge score."

"And here's another thing," he said, pulling himself up and standing straighter. Cassandra noticed his fists were clenched at his sides. "I didn't really appreciate the way you talked to me at the coffee shop downtown. The way you *yelled* at me in front of other people. Nobody deserves that from you, Cassandra, not even Mauve."

Cassandra was speechless—and somehow desperately attracted. She'd never seen Mauve exhibit such chutzpa! "Okay, all right," she said quickly. "I'm really sorry about that, but Mauve, it's getting late. Please run along and change now."

He stuck out his bottom lip like an impudent child. "No."

"No?" Cassandra set her hands on her hips in utter disbelief, then grated between clenched teeth, "Nobody says 'no' to me, Mauve."

"I'm afraid I just did," he said, and then he slammed the door shut.

Chapter Thirty

Morgan excused herself from the dining room table, where she was having Christmas dinner with Owen's family. His brother and his brother's wife were hosting and they had two reasonably well-behaved little kids. Owen's brother had also included some couple friends from his office, and everyone was chatting amiably. Snowed streaked outside the enormous living room windows, and in the distance Morgan caught a glimpse of the Manhattan skyline. She was supposedly on the way to powder her nose, but she'd secretly planned to text Jill. Morgan absolutely couldn't stand this anymore. She and Jill had been work colleagues and friends for more than five years. Morgan was an only child and Jill was the closest thing to a sister she had. But since their conversation in that café, Morgan had felt she'd been abandoned by Jill. She'd tried calling her before coming to New York and had texted repeatedly from the airport. It was obvious that Jill didn't want to talk to her. But, come on, today was Christmas.

Morgan had made a huge mistake and she was prepared to admit that. She'd talked the whole thing over with Owen and he'd been nothing but supportive.

She couldn't believe Owen still cared for her after knowing all she'd done, but somehow he did. Perhaps because he understood the pressures of the business too. It was he who'd urged her to continue trying and to not give up on Jill. *She'll come around, you'll see*, he'd told her with a kiss under the mistletoe. He also promised to help place the book, should Jill decide she still wanted to release it. The manuscript was already completed, and Owen believed the concept was sound. Perhaps there was a way to spin all this publicity around to the positive?

Morgan stepped into the tastefully appointed half-bath and quietly shut the door. "Come on, Jill. Come on…" she begged, extracting her cell from her purse and starting to type.

Jill was just leaving dinner with her grandpa at Green Meadows when she heard her cell buzz. She looked down at the screen, seeing it was yet another text from Morgan. It hadn't been a good day with her grandfather. He'd appeared more confused than ever. Jill's heart was breaking on so many counts, she wasn't sure she could deal with Morgan on top of that. Then again, in her heart and in her soul, Jill desperately missed her best friend. Her best woman friend. Her *husband* best friend was no longer in the picture. Tears welled in her eyes and Jill sat there paralyzed, unable to start her car. The sky was a gloomy gray and she felt just as miserable inside as it was outdoors.

Her cell buzzed again and Jill decided she might as well call Morgan back and get this over with. Otherwise, Morgan was just going to keep texting and calling for goodness knows how long. She lifted her cell and speed-dialed Morgan's number. Morgan immediately took the call. "I'm so glad that you answered," Morgan breathed. For some reason it sounded like she was whispering.

"I saw you've been trying to reach me." There was emotion in Jill's voice, but she tried to mask it.

"Oh, Jill. Hon, listen to me. I'm so sorry about that last conversation we had. I was an ass to say that thing about plausible deniability. I hope you'll forgive me."

Jill's pulse pounded as she held the phone to her ear.

"You don't have to say anything yet," Morgan went on. "Just please hear me out. Maybe the fake marriage was a mistake, but the book that came out of it wasn't. Jill, it's absolutely perfect. Owen agrees."

"Owen?"

"He read the manuscript and believes the project still has potential."

"But how can it?"

"By changing the title," Morgan said. "To *Married Love: Lessons Learned.*"

Jill mulled this over as tears burned down her cheeks.

"We can clean it up a little, make it about more than just your relationship with Hunter. I know that you have notes from many other consultations with couples."

"Yeah, so?"

"So we weave those in, mix in other vignettes. Make things more general, less personal."

Jill didn't see how a book like that could remain anything but personal to her, not after what she'd been through with Hunter. "And you…and Owen think that would work?"

"The recipe formula is still good, and the ingredients are excellent. Apart from a few minor tweaks, all the manuscript might need is an epilogue."

"An epilogue," Jill repeated thoughtfully. "What about?"

"I'll leave that up to you," Morgan said. "You're the writer."

Over at Susan's mother's house, Brad anxiously rose from the sofa where he was sitting beside Susan and dropped down on one knee. Susan stared at him in surprise. "Brad, what are you doing?" They'd had Christmas dinner with her mom, who was now brewing them a pot of tea. Susan's two older brothers had stayed in New York for the holiday, so it was just the three of them.

Brad took her hand. "Susan, I know you think I didn't get you anything for Christmas…"

"Nonsense. You told me we'd exchange gifts later."

"Right, that's right. But now I've changed my mind."

She screwed up her face, like he was acting funny. Which he was, ha-ha! What a fool. He'd better hurry up and get this done before he mucked it up. Brad took his free hand and reached into his pocket, his fingers shaking. "What I mean is… I couldn't wait! Here, this is for you!" He fumbled with the small box and popped it open, exposing a nicely cut diamond ring. At least, he hoped it was high quality. He'd paid a small fortune for it. He'd thought she might thank him, or jump up and down on her feet with a weepy look saying *yay*! Instead, Susan just blinked and said, "Oh."

Sweat beaded Brad's hairline. "Oh?"

A subtle smile crept onto her lips and Brad realized she wasn't mad at him. She was growing misty-eyed! In that womanly, "I'm so in love with you" way. Susan leaned toward him with a whisper. "Isn't there something you're supposed to ask me, Brad?"

Oh! Yeah! *That.* Brad swallowed hard, then swallowed again. Gosh, he hoped he could get the words out before Susan's mom walked into the room and started correcting his diction. "Susan," he rasped. "Will you marry me?"

"I thought you wanted to wait?"

That wasn't the answer he expected, so Brad croaked, "Haven't we waited long enough?"

Susan's whole face beamed as she leapt into his arms. "Yes, we have, you crazy man!"

He tried to catch her, but the force of her enthusiasm was too strong, sending them both tumbling backward onto the carpet, with Susan landing on top of him while Brad giddily slid the ring on her finger.

Her mom strode briskly into the room and eyed them both with disapproval. "What on earth is going on?"

Brad grabbed Susan's hand with its newly planted ring and happily waved it in the air. "Susan and me are getting married!"

"I," her mother said sternly. Then, to Brad and Susan's amazement, she clapped her hands together and broke into a grin. "But what's grammar at a time like this? How about we have some champagne!"

Chapter Thirty-One

Cassandra stood on Mauve's doorstep, holding a big, ridiculous card and a bouquet of roses. It was Valentine's Day and, up until eight weeks ago, she thought she'd finally have someone to spend it with. She rang the bell once and waited until Mauve arrived at the door. "Cassandra!" The color drained from his face. "I'm stunned to see you." She peered past him into the room and then she saw why. Mauve was with a woman! And not just any woman, a really cute one wearing a sparkly crop top and snug stretch jeans. The words bubbled from her throat as tears burst from her eyes.

"I'm so sorry, Mauve! I didn't know!" She hastily dropped her offerings at his feet and bolted away, alternately panting and blubbering as she went. Cassandra had never in her life humbled herself before a man, which was probably wise. It hurt like the dickens!

Mauve dashed out the door and raced after her. "Cassandra! Wait!"

She turned with a wail, her eyes running wildly. *"What?"*

His eyes were all red and his hair looked a mess. "Where are you going?"

"I...don't...know," she stammered. "Away!"

"Then why did you come over?"

"To bring you a card and... Oh, Mauve, what's the point? You've already got a new girlfriend."

"Girlfriend?" He glanced at the house, then back at her. "Cassandra, that's Indigo, my sister."

"Sister?" Cassandra asked weakly, her world slowly coming into focus. She pulled a tissue from her purse to wipe her eyes. "Seriously?"

"Why would I lie about that?"

Mauve took a step toward her and then another. When he saw she didn't back away, he drew closer still until he was almost right up to her. He lowered his voice and spoke quietly. "Cassandra, tell me the truth. Why are you here?"

"I came to say Happy Valentine's Day." She smiled feebly. "And bring you some flowers."

"But we're no longer going out."

"I was hoping to fix that part."

Mauve pursed his lips. "It's uncanny you showed up when you did. I was just telling my sister about you. About how I wished..."

"You were? I mean, you do?" It was her turn to close the distance between them and she did. "Mauve," she said seriously, "I have something to tell you. I got *Tempo Beat* to retract the story."

"You what?"

"I talked to the senior editor," she explained, gathering her nerve, "and told her I could no longer stand by it...given that some of my journalistic tactics were 'questionable.'"

Mauve sucked in some air and for a moment he looked like a guppy. "You mean, you admitted to breaking in?"

"Heavens no, Mauve! Do I look like I want to go to jail? Do you realize what people have to wear in there? They aren't even allowed accessories!" She showcased her pretty yellow leather bag to emphasize that point. "What I said was…" She brought her face to his and whispered, "…that I could no longer stand by the evidence; it was tainted. I also might have hinted that I made a few things up."

"You didn't! But why?"

Cassandra's lips took a downward turn. "Nothing was the same after you left. I no longer had a partner in crime." When she saw him scrutinizing her, she promptly added, "Not that I want a life of crime any longer. Frankly, I'm done with it. Except for in my imagination." Cassandra's face brightened. "Mauve, I wrote a story and it got accepted!"

"Marvelous! Where?"

"*Mystery Writers Magazine*. I know it's not much, but it's a start."

Mauve was apparently studying her with new eyes behind his horn-rimmed glasses. "I'm very proud of you, Cassandra. I never dreamed you'd make these changes."

"I no longer want to be that other person," she said. "The one you slammed the door on."

"What kind of person do you want to be?"

She stared at him with love in her eyes and hope in her heart. "The kind of girl you'd take out to dinner?"

Hunter didn't know how it had turned into February. Somehow the holidays had whizzed by in a blur because his attention had been focused on becoming re-employed. Okay, so the job hunt had consumed *most* of his focus. It had taken every ounce of fortitude Hunter had not to let himself think of Jill and the callous way she'd dismissed him at the end. If she'd only given him any indication…any sign of hope, he might have made a plea for a new beginning. Instead, she'd viewed him coolly and with apparent disdain. Naturally, she couldn't love a man like him. Not when the chips were down and all odds were against him. For a time, Hunter had believed Jill to be a different sort of woman: the kind with a caring heart. Obviously, he'd misjudged her. What was worse, he'd misjudged himself. For a fleeting instant, Hunter had actually believed himself to be falling in love.

Hunter picked up the TV remote and clicked off the television. Trying to find something to watch tonight was a bad idea. It was Valentine's Day and there was nothing on but sappy shows about *happily ever after*, with last-minute reminders from floral companies to "reward your Valentine." Right. Hunter could only imagine how Jill might have reacted if he'd dared to send her flowers. She likely would have tossed the bouquet back in his face, just as she'd done years ago with that prom corsage. If Hunter hadn't learned in high school that Jill wasn't the girl for him, he was definitely convinced of that now.

Hunter glanced around his empty apartment, the truth hitting hard. This place was depressing and lonely, and Hunter hated his life without her. But he had to put Jill behind him and find a way to move forward. He hadn't heard from her since he'd left, so there was clearly nothing left to talk about. Not the future or the past, including their ridiculously made-up marriage.

The fact was, Hunter was far better off without Jill and he knew it.

Hunter tried to think of other things, but memories of his life with Jill consumed him. From the first moment he'd seen her again at the club to that last heartbreaking good-bye in the snow, Hunter had never known a finer woman. Nor one as compelling, or as demanding of his heart. Hunter hung his head, combating the raw ache that burned through him. If he was so much better off without Jill, then why did losing her have to hurt so much?

Jill turned off her television set, thinking the shows weren't even worth watching on such a small screen. Even though she'd hated Hunter's TV at first, over time she'd come to appreciate its value. The romantic comedies she loved seemed so much brighter when presented in HDTV. It was almost like being in a movie theater. Of course, what she'd liked best was having Hunter beside her, whether or not they were eating popcorn.

Jill reached out a hand to stroke Mimi, who snoozed by her on the sofa. Fifi had curled up in a contented heap at her feet. But while they appeared peaceful now, both animals were often fretful during the day. It was like they were anticipating Hunter's return at any minute. Jill realized with a sense of absurdity that so was she.

Jill didn't know how she could dare to imagine that Hunter might really love her. Hadn't his emotions been written clearly enough in his eyes the day he'd left? If Hunter could leave her that easily, he must not have had faith in the relationship they'd shared. Perhaps the entire marriage *had been* a fake, no matter how much

Jill's silly heart had wished to make it real. She felt a
tear slide down her cheek, but still was grateful for the
things she had. Jill had been allowed to keep the
advance money from Browning, and her grandpa's
future was secure. Not only that, Morgan and Owen had
helped place her new book and it was going to press
any day. Jill's career would soon be back on track. On
the other hand, Jill wasn't as sure about her heart.

Chapter Thirty-Two

The following week, Max led Hunter into his office and shut the door behind them. Max sat at his desk and motioned for Hunter to have a seat as well. When Hunter spied the latest issue of *Tempo Beat* in front of him, he almost got up and left again. Max's secretary hadn't told Hunter why Max had arranged this meeting, but if it was to further lambast Hunter over failings from his past, Hunter wanted no part of it. He'd spent these past two months submitting his résumé and interviewing for jobs. Not everyone on the planet had heard of *Tempo Beat*, and there were other firms out there interested in Hunter's credentials. "Thank you for coming in today," Max said. Was it Hunter's imagination or did Max appear conciliatory? "I wasn't even sure if you'd return my secretary's call."

Hunter cut to the chase. "What's this about?"

Max tapped a pen against his desk blotter. After a while it began to sound like a metronome, and Hunter questioned whether Max even planned to speak at all. Finally, he said, "I'll be the first to admit that humans make mistakes. I myself am not infallible." He latched on to Hunter's gaze. "Like when I judged you so harshly, without getting all the facts."

"Mr. Abrams, I appreciate what you're trying to do. But the truth is, that's water over the dam."

"Is it?" Max leaned forward on his elbows. "Because from what I hear, you've not taken another position."

"The market is tight, but I'm looking. And making progress." Hunter started to stand. "Thanks for your time, but—"

"Hunter, wait." Max flagged both palms in his direction. "Just listen to what I have to say."

Hunter settled back in his chair, not knowing what to expect.

"The people at Kaleidoscope Kids have been asking about you. They don't like the new man on the account. He and they aren't meshing. Your work was fresh. They say it had joy in it, and that 'joy' sold product."

Hunter felt about as joyful now as a boy who'd lost his best friend, because that's exactly what had happened to him. He'd lost his best *wife* friend, Jill, and in so many ways little else mattered. But Hunter knew he had to keep going and start over somehow.

"I'm sorry I didn't read between the lines of that first article in *Tempo Beat*, because now that it's been retracted—"

"Retracted?" Hunter asked, surprised.

"Didn't you know? That gossip columnist, Cassandra what's-her-name—?"

"Evans."

"That's the one. She apparently made most of the article up."

What?

"They canned her at *Tempo Beat*," Max continued. "And now she's gone on to do other things." He waved a hand in the air. "Make trouble elsewhere, I suppose."

"But, sir, the truth is—"

"You know what I've decided?" Max asked, interrupting him. "If there's more to the truth, I don't want to hear it. Your personal life is yours to deal with, and I'm sorry that got messy for you. I really am. Because I liked Jill. I liked her a lot. I've got a hunch that you did too. But the bottom line is… We need to keep what we do here separate. I feel responsible, in part, for the pressure you put yourself under. When Kaleidoscope set their terms, I should have stood up for the company and said that's not the way we do business. We put our best people forward and stand by them. That's what our company ethics should have been, and it's what I intend to make them from here on out." Max met Hunter's eyes. "Son, I'm offering you your job back. If you'll accept this old man's failings and his apology, I'd love to have you on my team. As a full partner," he added.

Hunter carefully weighed his words before speaking. This was an enormous opportunity and one he'd never dreamed of. Yet Max had treated him so shabbily in front of everyone who worked here. How could Hunter fathom returning? "This is very sudden, Max. After everything that happened, and the way I was made to look before the staff…"

"I've spoken to the staff, Hunter. All of them. I called an office meeting when the new story broke. I publicly admitted what I just said privately to you, that I'd behaved rashly and apparently without cause. I can't tell you how sorry I am. I certainly told the entire company, and if you want to know the truth everyone was delighted by the possibility of your coming back."

"Everyone, sir?"

Max's deep laugh rumbled. "Well, all right. Fred might have looked a little sour about it. Your reinstatement would mean his getting demoted, after all. Though, confidentially, he really wasn't up to the job. Fred's previous position was a far better fit for him, and one he seemed able to handle. I think somewhere deep down he knows that. He was a nervous wreck working directly with me. Spent more than half of his time in the bathroom."

Hunter shook his head, deciding not to tell Abrams that Fred had spent more than half of his time in the bathroom while working in his previous position too. It was then that Hunter realized perhaps Max hadn't been the only one to judge people harshly. Maybe Hunter should have given Fred the benefit of the doubt as well. Fred likely wasn't a bad person, just someone who was very insecure. When Hunter was in a supervisory position, he should have noticed Fred was struggling and reached out to him. Instead, Hunter had been self-absorbed, and busy gloating over capturing Fred's coveted prize. Talk about pride going before the fall, Hunter thought soberly. "Poor Fred."

"Lucky me, I hope?" Abrams stood and held out his hand. "Say you'll come back, Hunter. Nothing here has been the same without you."

Chapter Thirty-Three

Jill didn't know how it was March already. She'd been so busy working on her book project with Morgan, the past three months had flown by. Morgan loved the revised manuscript and Owen had also given it his stamp of approval. He'd gotten it fast-tracked at a small but reputable press that was eager to build its list by adding known celebrity Jillian Jamison to its cadre of authors. Jill heard the delivery truck in the drive and raced to the door, her heart pounding. It was just what she'd been expecting! Her box of advance copies! She dragged the box into the house, but Fifi and Mimi stubbornly stayed on the porch.

They still went out there each night at six, no matter the kind of weather. Fifi would lie there listlessly, watching the road, a tennis ball positioned between her paws, while Mimi nervously paced along the railing. Jill had tried to tell them Hunter was gone for good, but they were only pets, so limited in their understanding.

The fact that Hunter hadn't tried to contact Jill clearly revealed that things were over. But if that were the case, why hadn't he formally filed for divorce? Perhaps it was for the same reason Jill hadn't: She couldn't bring herself to do it. Filing divorce papers would dredge so many things up again, many of them painful. Plus, it would take time. And time was a commodity Jill had been short on lately. She'd been working so hard on the book, she'd scarcely had the opportunity to eat well or exercise. It wasn't like in the summer and fall, when she'd had someone cooking for her. Jill tried not to remember the good times with Hunter, because that made things so much harder. It was easier to hold on to the anger and the hurt, and his horrible abandonment that had come at the end. That way, Jill could convince herself she was better off without him.

Jill grabbed a pair of scissors from the coffee table and cut into the newly delivered box. What a feeling it was to pick up *Married Love: Lessons Learned* and hold it in her hands. She ran her fingers across the glossy dust jacket, flipping it over to study her author photograph on the back. Hunter's earlier question came back to her: *A relationship expert. How's that working out for you?* "Probably a lot better than it used to," Jill said aloud. It was true and she knew it. She was a much better informed writer now, because her understanding of real relationships had deepened. It was one thing to study them from the outside, but quite another to be in the thick of one. Jill thumbed through the pages of her book, noting chapter heading after chapter heading, and it was impossible not to think of Hunter. "A recipe for love" was his idea. In a very real sense, this book never could have been written without him. No matter what Hunter thought of her now, Jill decided she ought to let him know that. It was the right thing to do, and would perhaps bring some closure between them. So Jill picked up a pen and inscribed a copy of her book. Tomorrow, she'd mail it to Hunter.

Hunter sat across from Mr. Jamison in the courtyard of Green Meadows, where spring flowers were blooming. "I've been wondering when you were going to come around," Jill's grandpa said. "I'm an old man. It's good you didn't waste any more time."

"I suppose I was embarrassed, sir." Hunter set his jaw. "But I do want to apologize."

"And well you should. You've been out of the picture forever."

"I've been working on things."

"Like what?"

"Getting back on my feet, becoming established."

"Are you still with that company?"

"I'm working as a partner there, yes."

"That's something, anyhow." Mr. Jamison surveyed him up and down. "Isn't there another reason you stopped by?"

"There is, sir." Hunter slapped his copy of *Married Love: Lessons Learned* against his knee. "This is Jill's new book. Have you read it?"

Mr. Jamison's cheeks sagged. "I'm afraid I'm not much for reading these days. Things don't seem to stay with me." He reached for the book and Hunter passed it to him. "It's a very handsome edition," Jill's grandpa said, turning it over in his hands. He thumped his index finger against Jill's author photo. "Isn't she a sight?"

"A very beautiful one," Hunter answered.

Mr. Jamison perused the book's front cover. "*Married Love: Lessons Learned*." He handed it back to Hunter. "Why don't you tell me what it's about?"

"All the things that make a successful marriage." Hunter released a deep breath. "I'd seen an earlier version, but this one's a little different."

"How so?"

"There's a section at the end on deciding whether a relationship is worth keeping."

"My goodness, that sounds clinical."

"It is written in checklist form, but things aren't that cut and dried. I'd guess they're more questions for reflection and discussion—between troubled couples."

"I see."

"The truth is, when I read it, sir . . ." Hunter hung his head. "I couldn't help but think of me and Jill, and about how good things were between us."

Mr. Jamison spoke with authority. "You and my granddaughter made a fine pair."

Hunter raised his chin. "I agree."

"Then you go and find Jill. Tell her what you just told me."

"I would, but I'm worried it might be too late."

"What do you mean?"

Hunter cracked open the book to Jill's inscription. "Jill dedicated this advance copy to me, but in a way I think she was saying she's moved on."

"Why don't you read what she wrote and I'll give my opinion?"

Hunter dropped his eyes to the page. "*Thanks for the inspiration and for the memories. It was all real to me.* Then she dated it and signed, *Jill.*"

"That sounds very nice. I don't see what's wrong with it."

"She thanked me for the 'memories,' Mr. Jamison. Jill is saying good-bye."

"Poppycock!" Jamison burst out. "That's simply woman-speak for 'Here I am, come and get me'!"

"Sir?"

"You *inspired her*. The two of you made memories together. Plus, she says it was for real. That marriage was no more fake for Jill than it was for you. Admit it, Hunter. You fell in love with my granddaughter."

"I won't lie to you, Mr. Jamison. It's true."

"Did you tell her?"

"Not in so many words."

Jamison slapped his palm against his forehead. Not once, but twice. He met Hunter's eyes with a challenge. "What are you waiting for?"

Hunter swallowed hard. "I'm not sure she'll have me."

"Well, you'll never know until you try, will you? Listen, Hunter, I might not be clear on every single detail all the time, but I know who you are. You're the man who loves my granddaughter. From the look on your face, I'd say you love her very much. From my point of view, Jill just opened a door. You're the only one who can decide if you're going to walk through it."

Hunter got to his feet, clutching Jill's book to his side. Emotion cloaked his voice as he spoke. "Thanks for taking time to see me, Mr. Jamison, and for your advice."

Jill's grandpa took his hand and shook it firmly. "I hope you'll take it."

As Hunter walked away, Mr. Jamison called after him. "And boy!"

Hunter slowly turned to face him.

"Don't make yourself a stranger around here."

Chapter Thirty-Four

Morgan sat beside Owen on a lounge chair, sipping a drink with a tiny paper umbrella poking out of it. They were under a thatch-roofed umbrella, both wearing swimsuits and sunglasses. "I'm so glad you suggested this getaway," Morgan said. "After being a publicity machine these past few months, I'm beat."

"I know," Owen said. "And now's a good time for a break: while the advance copies are out to reviewers and before Jill's book tour starts."

Morgan tried to resist a peek at her tablet, but Owen caught her gaze wandering. "Go on," he urged. "Take a look. I'll bet some reviews are in already."

"You're such a great guy," she said, fawning over him.

"I'm curious too."

Morgan set down her drink and eagerly scanned through her bookmarks. "Holy moly!" she cried. "Five stars is good!"

"Can't beat that," Owen agreed.

She excitedly covered her mouth, then pointed at the screen. "Oh, look! Here's another. *Jill Jamison speaks with passion and authority on a topic many couples will find very close to home.*"

"Excellent." Owen flagged down the waiter and motioned for him to freshen their drinks.

"And another… Married Love: Lessons Learned *is Jamison's tour de force. Never before has an author written with such insight and sensitivity on the challenging subject of marriage.* And there are more! All fabulous!"

"That's terrific so many have been posted already."

Morgan lowered her shades and stared at him. "We owe a lot of this to you."

"No, I think we owe most of it to Jill. The remaining fifteen percent," he said, making a joke about her commission rate, "is yours."

Morgan laughed and accepted the new drink the waiter brought her. "The service here is fantastic," she whispered to Owen. "Have you noticed? No one has to say anything, and a new drink appears in your hand!"

Owen shot her a rugged smile. "Just like magic."

He was so thoughtful and charming, and absolutely excellent at what he did. Plus, he was drop-dead gorgeous, making it pretty hard for Morgan to keep her hands off his rock-hard chest. But she would. At least, as long as they were in public. "I heard through the grapevine that Cassandra left *Tempo Beat*. She's now writing fiction."

"Really? How fascinating."

Owen seemed to *love* hearing all the gossipy details about Sugar Hollow. Then again, his sister had grown up there and had filled him in on most of its people.

"And," Morgan continued, "…she's got a boyfriend."

"Well, good for her. Who is it?"

"I forget. Someone named after a color."

He chuckled in surprise. "Mauve?"

"Yes, Mauve! Who would name a child that?"

Owen quirked a smile. "I hear he's got a sister named Indigo."

"Noooo."

Owen waved down a towel boy behind her, pointing above their heads. The lad instantly arrived to adjust their covering to keep them in the shade. Morgan turned her palms up in astonishment. "This place is amazing. They anticipate your every need!"

Owen smiled and lifted his drink. "Did I mention Susan's getting married?"

"To Brad!" Morgan gave a happy sigh. "At last!"

"I hope you'll consider being my date to the wedding?"

"I won't have to consider it long," she chirped. "The answer is yes."

Owen paused, then asked her, "Morgan, what do you think will become of Hunter and Jill?"

Morgan contemplated the ocean a long time and sipped through her straw. After a while, she sighed and said, "Honest to goodness, Owen? I just don't know."

Chapter Thirty-Five

Jill was busy in the kitchen when she heard Fifi barking maniacally. She raced into the living room to see what had happened, and found Mimi crazily scratching the door. He leapt repeatedly at the knob, attempting to snatch it in his claws. Fifi *woofed* again, shaking her head and crouching low, the front half of her body near the floor, her big yellow tail pointed straight toward the ceiling. It whipped back and forth and back and forth, like a gigantic wiper blade. Watching it almost made Jill dizzy. What on earth was going on?

A few seconds later, Jill heard tires crunch on the gravel drive and she peered out the window. The earth stopped turning and time stood still. *Hunter.*

Hunter stepped from his SUV, his heart pounding. In all the presentations he'd made, he'd never had this much on the line. Hunter had thought he'd wanted things before, and had been driven to achieve goals. But there was nothing more important to him at this moment than Jill Jamison remaining his wife. He'd attempted to put thoughts of her out of his mind and pour himself into his work, but he'd been unsuccessful. Each night when Hunter went to bed, he'd been bombarded by images of her sweet face: the way her pretty eyes reflected the sunlight and how her whole face lit up when she smiled. The mornings were even worse. There was no substitute for waking up beside Jill, her gentle perfume filling the air. Hunter needed her with a quiet desperation that upended his world, sending rational thoughts topsy-turvy when all he could think of was holding her in his arms. Not just for today, or for tomorrow, but for as long as their lives endured.

Jill's knees shook and her hand trembled as she opened the door. The animals shot toward Hunter like bullets, Fifi reaching him first. The dog whined and whimpered, puppy-cried and yapped, dancing in happy circles, then suddenly she found a ball and snatched it up in her mouth. She turned toward Hunter and obediently sat at his feet, dropping her offering. Hunter laughed and bent to scratch the dog behind the ears. "Well, hey there, Sport!" He grabbed the ball and threw it long as Mimi came up to greet him, mewing loudly and winding himself around Hunter's legs. "Don't worry, Mimi," he told the cat, pulling a small can of tuna from his coat pocket. "I haven't forgotten you." He opened the can and set it on the porch as Fifi retrieved the ball. Hunter took it up again and lobbed it as far as he could, clear into the neighbor's yard. When the dog took off, Hunter turned to Jill, who stood watching him in awe. "I'm sorry I didn't call or text first."

A lump welled in her throat, but she spoke past it. "Hunter, it's been—"

"Far too long," he finished for her. He motioned toward the porch with his chin. "Do you mind if we have a seat for a minute?"

Sitting sounded like a really good idea. Jill's head was spinning and her heart was beating double-time.

She had worked so hard to convince herself she was over Hunter, but there was no denying the connection she felt when his eyes met hers. Emotion welled within her, rushing like an unstoppable river, and Jill realized how desperately she'd missed him.

They sat in matching chairs just as Fifi bounded back toward them, clambering up on the porch and collapsing in a panting heap at Hunter's feet. Mimi had finished his treat and was already licking himself, preparing to claim a resting spot in the late-afternoon sunshine. "It seems the pets missed you," Jill said, glancing down at them.

"Only the pets?"

Hunter shot her a lopsided smile and heat rose in her cheeks. "It's been quiet around here," she told him. "A lot quieter, since you left."

"I know what you mean. The condo's been lonely too."

Jill flushed, sensing he'd read between the lines. Then she recalled his parting words that chilly December day, and the heart that had rapidly opened up only a few minutes ago suddenly felt coated in ice. "You left rather abruptly," she told him. "We hardly had a chance to discuss things, that first article in *Tempo Beat*."

"I apologize, Jill. That was wrong of me. I was just so…" He pursed his lips in thought. "The truth is, I was devastated by getting fired. It made me feel weak, less than a man. It was like my whole world had fallen apart, and I couldn't fathom finding a way to put it back together."

Jill was surprised to hear him speaking so frankly. "I didn't think any less of you."

"Didn't you, though?"

"No, Hunter. I swear."

He briefly turned away. When he looked at her again, his eyes brimmed with emotion. "I couldn't imagine how you could want me. How anybody could. Let's just say I had some rebuilding to do—of my heart and of my head."

She viewed him with compassion, then quietly asked, "How are they now?"

"Healing nicely. I'm back at Abrams. Have you heard?"

She nodded. "Word gets around."

"Your new book's doing well, I see. I've read some of the reviews that have come in."

"Have you?" Jill asked, finding herself pleased that Hunter had cared enough to pay attention.

"I agree with the consensus. *Married Love: Lessons Learned* is excellent. Worth each one of those five stars."

"Have you read it?"

"Every word." He hesitated. "Jill, about your inscription…?"

"Yes?"

"I wanted to tell you, in person, that everything felt real to me too. All of it, Jill, starting with the wedding and the honeymoon trip to Niagara Falls, and—"

"Ending with the heartache of you saying good-bye," she cut in hoarsely.

"Is there any way for us to get past that?" Hunter's expression was pained. "Because, you know… Your grandfather thinks there is."

"You've seen him?" Jill asked with surprise.

"I went by yesterday."

"How was he?"

"I'd say his mind was uncannily sharp." Hunter smiled, his eyes dancing. "With your permission, I'd like the chance to visit him again."

With your permission? Jill's heart sank and her spirit sagged like a deflated balloon. Now she understood why Hunter was here. He'd read her inscription and wanted to acknowledge it, and establish closure too—in part, by apologizing. Jill realized with a pang of guilt that Hunter wasn't the only one who needed to say "I'm sorry."

"Of course, Hunter. Please feel free to visit my grandpa anytime you'd like. I understand you and he developed your own relationship, and it's good for him to have visitors. Thank you for caring about him."

Hunter stared at her a long while, something telling in his eyes. "It's not only him that I care about, Jill."

Jill's pulse picked up as she absorbed his meaning and her battered heart dared to hope one more time. Was it possible that Hunter was saying what she thought he was? That he'd missed being with her, just as badly as she'd missed him? Warm breezes blew, carrying the scent of fresh flowers in from the garden, and honeybees buzzed over the lilac bushes.

"Hunter," Jill said softly. "Thanks for telling me you're sorry about how things ended, because the truth is I'm sorry too. More sorry than you know." Moisture pooled in her eyes. "I could have contacted you too, but I didn't. None of this was one-sided. I'm equally to blame."

Hunter reached for her hand. "Both of us said things we shouldn't have, and there were probably things we omitted that should have been said."

"Yes."

"Then maybe we should take a chapter from your book," he suggested, "and decide to forgive each other?"

A tear broke free from the corner of her eye. "Chapter Nine?"

"One of your best."

"One of *our* best, Hunter. I never could have written that book without you."

"To tell you the truth?" A smile lightly tickled his lips. "I would have been horribly jealous if you'd written it with anyone else."

She smiled through her tears. "There's no other husband I'd rather have."

He lightly tugged at her hand. "Why don't we go over there and sit on the swing?"

Jill nodded and wiped her cheeks as Hunter led her across the porch and they carefully sidestepped the dozing animals. Jill settled in beside him and Hunter wrapped her in his arms, just as naturally as if they'd never been apart. "You don't know how good it feels to be here," he said, holding her close. "Back here with my *wife.*" Then he asked, his voice cracking, "I hope I can stay?"

Jill held him tightly, unable to answer at first. The feelings that were overtaking her were too strong. Of course she wanted him to stay. She loved Hunter more than heaven and earth, more than the entire universe and everything beyond it. If she hadn't understood that fully before, she was totally aware of it at this moment. When he'd gone away he'd left a gaping hole in her heart, and now that he'd returned he was promising to fill it. How could she possibly say no? She pulled back in his embrace to meet his eyes. "I can't imagine a better husband than you. I don't want any other husband but you." Her voice warbled. "Please...oh please, Hunter..." She started crying again, her tears and her love knowing no bounds.

Hunter dragged a thumb down her cheek. "Does that mean yes?"

She nodded and he brushed his lips over hers. "I love you, Jill." The words were magical, mystical, strumming gently like harp music through her soul.

"I love you too," she said, kissing him back.

For a long, lovely moment, they were lost in each other and the glory of being in each other's arms. *This is what it feels like*, Jill acknowledged to herself, *really and truly being in love.* She couldn't wait to let Hunter back into her house, and into her bed. For she was his wife and he was her husband. The husband who'd finally returned to the place he belonged, right here with her.

As if knowing her thoughts, Hunter grinned. "So, what do you think? Should we have a real wedding?"

"We've already had a real wedding, as far as I'm concerned. And a fabulous honeymoon." Jill's lips tipped up in a smile. "But there is one thing we're missing."

"A reception," he said, reading her eyes.

"I have a deposit down with a caterer."

"Let's invite the whole town."

"Even Cassandra," Jill said.

"And Fred," Hunter answered.

"And friends from New York too."

Hunter chuckled warmly. "Yes, everyone."

After a long beat, Jill ventured, "Hunter, I know this sounds a little old-fashioned—"

"What? Old-fashioned, you?" he said, teasing her.

Jill's cheeks warmed as she continued, "—but I was thinking of taking your name."

"Delaney?" His arms tightened around her. "Are you sure?"

When she nodded, he said. "Why, Jill, I think that's awesome." His voice broke apart when he added, "I'd be honored." He gazed lovingly into her eyes, then asked her, "I hope you'll do me the honor of letting me buy you a ring?"

"But Hunter, you already have."

"Not a wedding band, Jill. I mean a very elegant engagement ring with a ridiculously large diamond."

Jill grinned shyly, unable to mask her delight. "You already know my ring size," she said playfully.

"Then it's settled." Hunter stunned Jill by reaching into his pocket and pulling out a small velvet-covered box. He flipped it open, exposing a gloriously glistening solitaire. Jill gasped with pleasure. "Shall we see if it fits?" he asked, pulling it from its cushion.

Jill's pulse fluttered wildly as he slid the ring onto her finger, right above the wedding band she still wore. When Hunter had gone, she'd packed her grandmother Rose's ring away, but she hadn't been able to bear removing the gold band that Hunter had given her. Now Jill noticed for the first time that Hunter still wore his gold band too. "They look lovely together," she said, admiring the rings on her finger. "Thank you, Hunter. What a wonderful surprise."

"Thank you for being my bride."

"I'm glad you're my groom."

He hugged her to him and she looked up, meeting his eyes.

"You know, I was thinking," she said lightly. "You just might inspire me to write another book."

"Yeah? What about?"

"Oh, I don't know…" she said, toying with him. "Are you still working on that account? Kaleidoscope Kids?"

Hunter grinned broadly. "Are we talking about children now? Babies?"

Jill recalled that precious image of Hunter she'd had when she'd pictured him as a little boy, and Diane's later prediction that she and Hunter would make beautiful children together.

"It doesn't have to be right away," she said. "We might have to do some *adjusting* first."

"How soon can we get started?" he asked with a sexy growl. "Adjusting?"

She smiled up at him, her heart soaring. "How about tonight?"

His eyes radiated heat and hunger. "I'm not sure I can wait that long."

Jill swooned in his embrace, needing more of him. Desiring all of him.

"I don't think I can wait either." Jill's blood pumped harder and fire tore through her veins. She was his now and he was hers. They were destined to be together. "Make me your wife, Hunter," she whispered hoarsely, "completely."

He brought his mouth down on hers with a kiss that stole her breath away. Then he rose from the swing and gently lifted her in his arms, heading toward the door.

"You won't have to ask me twice."

"That's where you're wrong," she said, flirting. "I intend to ask you every day, at least once a day, for the rest of our lives."

Hunter laughed huskily and carried her over the threshold.

"Oh, darling," he said, adoring her. "It's great to be home."

The End

A Note from the Author

Thanks for reading *My Best Friend's Bride*. I hope you enjoyed it. If you did, please help other people find this book.

1. This book is lendable, so send it to a friend you think might like it so that she (or he) can discover my work too.

2. Help other people find this book: Write a review.

3. Sign up for my newsletter so you can learn about the next book as soon as it's available. Write to GinnyBairdRomance@gmail.com with "newsletter" in the subject heading.

4. Come like my Facebook page: https://www.facebook.com/GinnyBairdRomance.

5. Connect with me on Twitter: https://twitter.com/GinnyBaird.

6. Visit my website at http://www.ginnybairdromance.com for details on other books now available at multiple outlets.

If you enjoy sweet romantic comedies, you might like my novel *The Calendar Brides*. Keep reading for an excerpt here.

Excerpt

The Calendar Brides

From **New York Times and USA Today Bestselling Author Ginny Baird**, a heartwarming story about the power of love, the dedication of family, and the realization of dreams.

Ginny Baird's **The Calendar Brides**
Twelve granddaughters share one goal, all in the name of love.

Twelve women with big hearts and slim wallets want to do something special for their grandmother. At eighty-seven, the family matriarch has reconnected with her childhood sweetheart, and wants to elope to Sicily. The catch is her intended is poor, and Mama D'Amato doesn't have the travel cash herself.

When they put their heads together, can her twelve granddaughters help their Nona achieve her dream? All it takes is a little ingenuity and a very clever plan. Meet Emma, Claire, Angie, Haley, Bev, Jane, Tiny, Zoe, Lena, Trish, Susan and Rachel, as they embark on the adventure of a lifetime—all in the name of *l'amore*.

Meet the D'Amato women and their men!

Emma is the oldest and smart mouth. She loves late-night pizza, her puppy, and Donny—whom she hated in high school.

Emma's sweet sister **Claire** reports the weather and collects seashells. Brainy Brad helps her see stars.

Stay-at-home mom **Angie** pretends to Zumba. Hot hubby Jason doesn't miss a step.

Angie's athletic twin **Haley** is a baker on the move. Mountain biker Peter grooves with her.

World traveler **Bev** craves adventure. Photojournalist Will has a passport, too.

Jane is a serious-minded thinker. Dry-witted Richard makes her laugh—and sigh.

Feisty **Tiny** has loved Jimmy for decades. Now, they're building a future together.

Tiny's artist sister **Zoe** has a secret wish. Does sexy Dillon share it?

Bev's sister **Lena** sings for her supper. Unconventional Randy digs her act.

Only child **Trish** speaks her mind. Laid-back Leo knows how to listen.

Jane's shy sister **Susan** is a lonely knitter… Then handsome Kyle smiles her way.

Rachel is the baby and a dreamer. Kindly, older Tom wants to give her the moon.

Lucia vowed to marry **Luigi** at fourteen. He still waits for her in Italy. It's never too late for love!

Chapter One

The D'Amato Women

Nona leaned forward over the photo album, pointing out another grainy picture. "And that one was Elbert, the one that got away."

Claire fanned her hand over her heart and sighed sympathetically. Her hair was feathered about her face in a feminine style, and she always wore it long. "What happened to him?"

Nona flipped her wrist. "Married a Spanish girl. Not that it matters. Men are like buses, you know."

Her granddaughters laughed, then sang in a chorus: *"When one leaves, another one comes along."* The older woman looked around the room at their cheery faces. Well, most of them were cheery. Jane still wore that perpetual scowl, and Trish set her chin. Why were those girls so serious?

"I think you're right, Nona," Rachel sweetly chimed in. "Certainly happened to me." She extended her left hand, exposing a glistening solitaire, and her cousins squealed with delight.

Nona smiled. "Congratulations! Who's the lucky groom?"

Rachel ran a hand through her curls, then proudly proclaimed, "Tom Delaney."

Across the room, Bev sucked in a gasp. She still wore that scarf she'd bought in Paris. Not that it really went with her blouse, although it did complement her angled bob and art deco earrings. "No way!"

"Way," Jane quipped from the sofa. Susan sat beside her, furiously knitting something. It looked oddly like a baby's cap, but Susan wasn't married. Susan spoke softly without looking up. "Time heals all wounds."

"Hmm, maybe," Tiny judged from nearby. She stood just over five feet and had a short, sassy haircut to match her small frame. She was also the sole granddaughter close to Nona in size, although she ate like a horse. Nona secretly feared that might catch up with her some day, but had never been rude enough to say so. She was eating now, in fact. Munching on something she kept hidden in a paper bag that looked suspiciously like fast food.

"That's awesome, Rachel!" Haley leaned into her tennis racket and grinned. Then she dipped low, flexing her knees and leg muscles. Nona had never seen a girl so fit. It was a blessing she'd found Peter, someone who could keep up with her. Haley squatted a few more times, then broke into a lunge, using her racket for leverage. "When's the wedding?"

"We haven't decided," Rachel answered.

"Might be good to take your time," Trish advised. Trish had red hair and freckles, which made her stand out among her more darkly complected cousins. Nona knew this was on account of her father marrying an Irish woman. "You'll want to build your career first."

"My job's going fine!" Rachel spouted defensively.

"I thought you watered people's plants?" Trish replied. Trish was very self-assured as an accountant, but seemed bent on summing other people up.

"Be nice," Susan warned from behind her knitting and purling.

Lena spoke gently from the corner, wispy tresses lightly framing her face. She'd had it highlighted lately with what looked like streaks of blonde. She'd said it was to *let the sunshine in,* whatever that meant. Nona had no idea. "She does have a point," she said referencing Trish. "There's nothing wrong with taking your time, Rachel. Getting settled first."

Rachel's cheeks tinged red. "I *am* settled. That's what I'm trying to tell you! Business is going great. I picked up five new clients this week!"

Trish held up her hands and shook her head.

"Leave her alone," Zoe said from the floor. She lay on her back doing some kind of yoga. Whoa! Now she was arching up skyward, stomach first. Nona wondered what it took to be that limber, and whether she was too old to achieve it. "It's not like she's seventeen anymore."

A hush fell over the room at Zoe mentioning what should have gone unspoken. Zoe collapsed to the rug, then righted herself, arms wrapped around her knees. She addressed Rachel, red-faced, straight dark hair grazing her chin. "I'm sorry. I didn't mean it."

Angie, who'd stood by silently this whole time, strode toward Rachel, her ponytail bouncing. She was Haley's twin, and the main difference between them was that Angie wore bangs. Since she'd had her first baby, Nona had never seen her in anything other than workout clothes, even though she never actually exercised. She had three kids now, each born within a year of the other. Nona supposed Angie stayed trim simply chasing after them. Angie wrapped her arm around Rachel and pulled her into a hug. "The truth is, we're *all* happy for you." She combatively eyed her cousins. "Aren't we, girls?"

"Of course… Yes… Uh-huh!" all agreed, their words overlapping.

"I'm glad to see everyone's getting along." Nona flipped shut her photo album. "Because there's more good news. *I* have something to tell you."

"Knock, knock! Where's the party?" Emma peered into the room with a happy grin. She cradled a pudgy puppy in her arms that lapped at her face with a big, wet tongue.

"I thought we were missing someone," Nona chirped.

"Emma! He's adorable," Rachel said. "Where did you get him?"

"Well, first of all he's a *she*." Emma set down the little yellow lab, who bounded toward her grandmother in happy leaps.

Nona chuckled warmly as the dog wiggled to and fro before her, wagging its whole body with its tail. She stroked the pup's head with one hand while holding her champagne flute high in the other. "Very cute, Emma! Did you buy her for Bobby?" Bobby was Emma's nephew on her husband Donny's side.

"No," Emma said with apparent surprise at the thought. "Donny bought her for me!" She adjusted a barrette in her short brown hair, then shared a glowing smile. "Anniversary gift. Can you believe?" Her eyes darted around the room, then settled on the champagne bucket on the table. Although, rather than champagne, it held a bottle of prosecco, a D'Amato family favorite. "How come nobody invited me?" she asked with a play pout.

"We *did* invite you," Claire assured.

"You know you're always invited," Jane deadpanned before Susan elbowed her.

Zoe sat on the floor with her legs in a pretzel knot. She managed to drink in that position just the same. "You've missed some big news," she said, sipping from her bubbly.

"Bigger than big," Haley reinforced from nearby.

"Well, come on! What's going on?" Emma impatiently glanced around the room.

Lena smiled, her highlights glowing in the natural light of the window. Maybe they *did* let the sunshine in. "It all started with Rachel!"

Susan set her knitting aside to cradle her champagne flute. "And, it's not over yet."

Emma turned toward her cousin with the short, springy curls. "Rachel?"

Rachel held out her hand, and Emma embraced her. "Oh, Rachel! That's wonderful!" She pulled back, meeting Rachel's gaze. "Tom?"

Bev sighed. "Did everyone know but me?"

"Not everyone," Trish responded. "Angie seemed to miss it."

"Hey!" Angie retorted, "Can I help it if Zoe called during Parent Zumba time?"

"You Zumba?" Nona asked with surprise.

Bev met Zoe's eyes. "*Et tu, Brute?*"

"No one wanted to hurt you." Tiny surreptitiously rolled up her paper bag and tucked it between the sofa cushions. "You know, given the history you had with—"

"*History's* the word, hey." Bev surveyed their faces. "I can't believe that none of you thought I could handle it."

"There's more good news!" Lena said, changing the subject.

Emma expectantly eyed her grandmother, who glowed.

"Shall we pop the second bottle?" Rachel asked.

Nona brought her hands together in a happy clap. "Let's!"

Of Nona's six sons, all had produced only daughters. World traveler Bev and singer Lena were sisters. Artsy Zoe and the insatiable Tiny were sisters, too, as were the trio Nona had dubbed *the romantics:* Emma, Claire, and Rachel. Genuinely athletic Haley and aspiring Zumba queen Angie were twins. Quick-witted Jane was shy knitter Susan's big sister, while outspoken redhead Trish was an only child. Nona smiled at them all, delighted to have them here. Their gathering once a month for Sunday Prosecco had become a tradition—whether or not anyone had anything to celebrate. The girls took turns bringing the booze and delectable chocolates. Sometimes someone baked cookies. Tiny often brought her own bag, besides. Nobody ever knew what was in there, and everyone—particularly vegetarian Zoe—was frightened to ask. So all pretended not to notice, and Nona always took care to check between the sofa cushions once all of her granddaughters had gone.

She loved them each dearly and felt blessed to have bonded with them all in different ways. While she'd doted on her sons and had tried to be a good mom to them when they were growing up, she'd never quite understood the joy of having girls. Being blessed by a plethora of granddaughters had taught her a lesson: how vastly she could love, and how deep her well of affection could run. The girls called her "Nona" after *nonna*, the Italian word for grandmother. Emma, as the oldest, had been the first to speak and write. Unfortunately, Emma had never been a very good speller. When she'd presented her Nona with that first card made in kindergarten, Nona had been charmed by her efforts and wasn't about to offer any sort of reprimand. So the grandmotherly nickname had stuck and was still used by the girls to this day.

Once Emma had settled in with her wine, Nona pointed to the photo album. Emma's puppy snoozed at her feet, exhausted from the previous attention. "Angie, be a dear and hand that over."

Angie grinned, looking perkier than normal. Perhaps she really *was* doing Zumba. "Another rundown of the men in your life?"

Nona took the book and settled it in her lap. "Did I ever tell you girls about my previous engagements?"

"All four of them," Rachel answered with a giggle. She perched on the arm of the sofa beside Jane and Susan.

"There were five, counting Grandpa," Jane corrected.

"I hardly see how that counts," Nona said with a wink. "I married him!"

The others watched as she opened the book and flipped through its glossy pages. Most of the photos were old, and in black and white.

"You really were a heartbreaker," Zoe said.

"Worldwide," Bev added.

Nona's lips took a downward turn. "Yes," she said a bit sadly. "But that's not how I planned it." For a moment she appeared wistful.

Claire reached out and gently touched her arm. "What do you mean?"

Nona's eyes brimmed at the bittersweet memory. "That's not how I planned it with Luigi."

"He was your first love," Susan commented from the sofa. She'd put down her glass and had taken to knitting again.

"Susan," Nona asked suddenly, "is someone you know having a baby?"

Susan glanced around the room with a rapid blush. "Um…no. Not really."

The others shrugged and turned their attention back on their grandmother. Susan was always knitting crazy things, like the time she made that tiny sweater for her neighbor's cat. Nona thought it was some sort of latent nesting instinct, itching to burst forward at just the right moment. But before she could nest, Susan had to find a man. It would help if she started looking.

"That's right," Tiny said, "back in Sicily. You dated when you were fifteen."

"Fourteen," Nona said.

"Wow," Trish remarked. "That's young."

Nona shared a soft smile. "It didn't feel young then."

"When your family moved to the States, you had to leave him behind," Claire said, remembering.

Nona nodded sadly. "There wasn't really any choice."

"For either of you," Claire said softly.

"No."

"Which one was he?" Haley asked, leaning over her shoulder.

Nona turned to the second page in the book. There were several old photos neatly arranged, most of them taken on a beach. While her face and figure had changed quite a bit, the girls could recognize their Nona at once from her big, dark eyes. She stood with a handsome young man, who looked about her age—maybe a little older. In a few of the pictures, they embraced.

"Looks like something out of a movie," Lena sighed.

"Who was the photographer?" Jane asked.

"My brother, Giovanni. He was Luigi's age; they were best friends."

"So Luigi was older?" Jane surmised.

"By just a year."

Claire noted the melancholy in her Nona's eyes. "Whatever became of him?"

"Of Luigi?" Nona shrugged mysteriously, and avoided her granddaughters' gazes. "Now, *that's* an intriguing question."

Jane sat up with interest and Susan dropped her knitting. "Are you saying that you've heard from him?" Rachel asked, her jaw dropping.

Nona glanced around the room with an impish grin. "The Internet is a marvelous thing."

None of them could believe it! Their Nona had been carrying on an online affair. "When did this start?" Tiny asked.

"About six months ago," Nona said. "We reconnected on Facebook."

The girls stared at each other in shock. "You're on Facebook?" Jane asked, aghast.

"Of course! Why not?"

"Why not, indeed?" Trish said, shooting Jane a look.

Angie's face brightened. "I think that's awesome!"

"Facebook or Luigi?" Haley asked.

"Both!"

Lena rearranged her tie-dyed top. "I think it's dynamite, too."

"You'll have to friend us!" Bev said brightly, until the others turned their eyes on her. "Uh, yeah… Maybe not."

"That's okay." Nona laughed lightly. "I'm not so keen on letting you in on my secrets, either."

Zoe grinned, liking the sound of this. "Oooh…our Nona has secrets."

Nona gave her a play swat in the air. "You know precisely what I'm saying. Some of what goes on there is…" She paused and sat up a little straighter. "…personal."

"Well, I think it's cool you and your old flame reconnected after all this time," Tiny said.

"Cool, and very romantic," Claire chimed in.

"Are you going to see him?" Susan wanted to know.

Nona's face fell. "If only that were possible."

While Nona wasn't poor, her granddaughters understood she wasn't rich either. She'd raised six sons mostly on her own, after her husband had died of an early heart attack at forty. She now lived on her retirement from the simple shop she'd help run at the edge of town.

"Can he come here?" Trish inquired. "For a visit?"

"Luigi is a good man, but of modest means. Always has been. That's one of the things my father didn't like about him."

"I didn't know your dad was against him," Bev said with surprise.

"Oh, yes. Both of my parents opposed the relationship."

Emma's expression was puzzled. "But I thought Luigi was Giovanni's friend?"

"He was, but he was also a fisherman's son. And fishing was what he was born to do."

Tiny frowned worriedly. "That wasn't good enough for your parents?"

"They wanted me to marry someone educated. Somebody with a future."

"Like Grandpa," Zoe said, understanding. Their granddad was a second-generation Italian American who'd been raised here. He'd finished high school, then had run the local arm of a large shipping business right here in Chandelier, their tiny seaside town. It was ironic that he and Luigi had both had maritime careers.

Claire gazed out the window, surveying the ocean cliffs and faraway horizon. "You were destined to live by the sea."

"I was destined to marry your grandfather," Nona said surely. "I believe that with all my heart. How else could I have gotten such wonderful sons, or such amazing grandbaby girls?" She set the open photo album in her lap and extended her arms, and they all wrapped their arms around her in an enormous group hug.

"We love you, Nona," Rachel said, her new diamond sparkling.

"And I love you, too," Nona said, lightly patting whoever's hands and arms were wound around her.

Jane, who stood at the back of the group, stared down through the entangled limbs to the black-and-white photo on the open page. "Yeah, but once upon a time you loved him."

"Not just once…" came Nona's muffled reply.

The girls hugged her tighter with anticipation. Zoe, who was closest to Nona's face, was the first to ask. "What does that mean?"

"I still love him, I do!"

The group hug broke apart as the girls stared at their grandmother. Nona brought both hands to her chest with a whimper. "I've never known such pain."

"Nona? Are you sick?" Tiny asked with concern.

"She's heartsick, can't you see?" Claire defended.

Nona met Claire's eyes. "You always could see things."

"Oh, no," Lena said.

"I'm sorry, Nona," Rachel added.

Susan pursed her lips in a frown. "Me, too."

"Isn't there anything we can do?" Haley asked.

"Yeah," Angie said. "To help?"

"I'm afraid there's no helping with this one." Nona sadly hung her head. "We're oceans apart."

"Oceans can be crossed," Bev said.

"Not this time, I'm afraid. I'm too old. He's too old. Neither of us has the money."

Trish met her Nona's eyes. "There has to be a way."

"There is no way, my dear. Luigi and I have discussed it. But if there were…" Emotion clouded her eyes.

"What?" Rachel prompted. "Tell us what you were going to say."

Nona looked around the group and her chin trembled. "If I *were* able to go…" She turned to Rachel sprightly. "You wouldn't be the only betrothed in town…"

Claire brought a napkin to her mouth with a gasp.

"What?" the group cried.

Nona demurred with a blush, but her eyes held the passion of a much younger woman.

"Luigi has asked me to be his bride."

"So you would go?" Lena asked first. "I mean, if it were possible? Go, and leave us behind?"

Nona studied them warmly. "You don't know how much you girls mean to me. You're my life's joy. But my heart has always been in Sicily. Ever since I was a girl. I'm not sure if you can understand."

"Of course we can," Claire said, taking her hand.

Jane nodded astutely. "It's your homeland."

"Yes. And the older I've become, I've… Well, I don't mean to put this wrong. Because I've absolutely loved America. It's given me so much opportunity. Truly, it has. But once upon a time, like Jane said, and long ago, I had a completely different life. One more tied to the soil. The land."

"Your parents were farmers," Bev said, reminding the others. "Tomatoes and olives."

"And what a delicious sauce we could make," Nona said with fond remembrance. "With shellfish." She hung her head with a blush. "Luigi used to bring us the fish."

"So you had a regular opportunity—" Haley began.

"To meet and fall in love," Angie finished with a fond smile.

"It all sounds terribly romantic," said Claire.

"We had to sneak away," Nona informed them. "Meet on the sly by the sea. Giovanni helped us. He covered for me." She dabbed her eye with a tissue. "I miss my brother so."

"I can't imagine what that was like. Having a brother," Zoe said.

"Nor can any of us!" Tiny confirmed, and they all laughed.

"At least you have each other, not just some of you as sisters, but all of you as cousins. That's something."

They all added their agreement, saying they were truly blessed.

"What sorts of things do you talk about?" Trish wondered. "You and Luigi, when you speak online?"

"Oh, you know." Nona gave a little shrug. "This and that…"

Emma lifted an eyebrow. The puppy had awakened and snuggled contentedly in her lap, as she stroked under its chin. "Now she's being coy."

"I am *not*," Nona contested. "Only private. And a woman my age…" She tittered a laugh. "…is entitled to some secrets."

"Goodness gracious, Nona," Jane said. "We weren't asking for details!"

"Oh, yes, we were," Susan said.

"The more, the better," Zoe chirped eagerly.

"Okay, I'll tell you." Nona leaned forward on her elbows and the others angled toward her. "We talk about the old days, and how things used to be. The adventures we had. And then…" Her cheeks colored dusty rose. "We speak of the adventures we'd like to have, even now. Just the two of us."

"Like?" Lena pressed.

"We'd like to picnic on the shore." Nona shared a distant smile. "With a blanket and a very large bottle of wine. In a private spot where no one else can—"

"Okay, okay." Jane flagged a palm at her grandmother. "We get it."

"What, Jane?" Susan said. "She was just getting to the good part."

"No, she wasn't," cautioned Trish. "She was headed into TMI."

Nona blinked in innocence. "What's TMI?"

Rachel giggled and hugged her warmly. After the group hug, she'd moved from the arm of the sofa to the arm of her grandmother's overstuffed chair. Rachel was their social butterfly, ever circulating, even among family. "Too much information," she said in a whisper. "I think you were embarrassing Jane."

"I don't embarrass!" Jane balked, but even so her face reddened.

"Neither do I," Trish added quickly. "I… We…" She glanced at Jane. "Just didn't want you to confess anything you'd regret later."

"Heavens!" Nona proclaimed. "I haven't had a chance to regret anything yet." Her expression was glum. "I suppose that's the problem."

Tiny studied her with admiration. "You're quite an inspiration, Nona. Oh, that we all had so much spunk at your age."

"You most certainly will," Nona said with a wink. "It's in your DNA. And I know what *those* initials mean."

"Do you think she's serious?" Rachel quietly asked the others, as they wound down the path and away from their grandmother's house. "Serious about this whole Luigi thing?"

Back on the crest of the hill, they heard wailing through the living room window.

"Oh, Luigi!" followed by a torrent of sobs.

The girls sucked in a collective breath.

"That sounded awful!" Bev whispered.

Claire choked back her tears. "Worse than awful."

"Yeah," Zoe agreed. "Totally bad."

The cousins looked at each other and nodded. Without saying a word, they'd agreed. They had to devise a plan.

"She *is* eighty-seven," Tiny offered.

Haley motioned with her racket. "Hasn't got much time left."

"That was uncalled for!" Angie cried.

"Shh…" Emma set down the pup, and clipped the leash to its collar. "She'll hear us."

All eyes turned back toward the house, which stood like a lonely beacon. A lonely widow's beacon… They were all thinking the same thing. After all this time, and everything she'd done for them, their Nona had earned some happiness.

Lena spoke next. "Whatever time she's got, she deserves to spend it how she wants. With the man she loves. *Capische?*"

Susan adjusted the knitting bag on her shoulder. "But what can we do?"

"Something, we have to do *something,*" Jane affirmed.

"Absolutely. After all, we D'Amatos aren't quitters." Trish set her chin with a determined look, and glanced back at the house. "It's in our DNA."

Ten minutes after her granddaughters had departed, Lucia pulled herself together. What was the point of it all? Weeping over a future that couldn't be. She dried her tears and inhaled deeply—recalling the sweet scent of lilacs and a faraway island blooming with wildflowers. Lucia heard a noise chirp from her computer and turned toward the adjoining room where she'd left it on the dining room table. The music sounded again, and Lucia's heart bounded. That had to be Luigi keeping their appointment for a video chat.

She pushed out of her wing chair and practically skipped toward the table with spry steps. *Luigi! My love is calling...* Lucia felt fire in her cheeks to imagine a woman her age would think of someone—anyone—as her *love*. But that's how she thought of him. *Il mio amore.* The computer chimed again and Lucia skirted toward it, first taking care to check her reflection in the mirror hanging over the sideboard. Her gray hair was tousled, and her eyes still a little red from crying. She hoped Luigi wouldn't notice.

"Ciao, bella!" came his enthusiastic greeting once she was seated and had accepted his call. He was as dashing as ever, with sea-blue eyes and deeply tanned skin that spoke of the sun. By contrast, Lucia was fair, having spent these sheltered years indoors.

"Luigi," she said in their native tongue, "this *is* a surprise!"

His laugh rumbled. "Don't tell me you'd forgotten our date, *cara mia?*" But, by the way his eyes sparkled, she knew he understood she'd been teasing.

"I would never forget you, Luigi."

"Hmm. Yes. This is why you ran away from home to marry another man?"

"That's so unfair!"

He stroked his chin and she saw that it was stubbled. It occurred to her he'd look handsome in a beard. She put it on her agenda to suggest he grow one.

"Si, si." His look was conciliatory. "You have a point. I made a slip and married, too."

"I thought you said you loved Teresa."

"Adored her. Just as I know you adored your husband. Yet, somewhere deep in here…" He drew a hand to his chest. "There was always a hole. As deep as the darkest cavern in the ocean… You felt it, too, *si?*"

Lucia recalled that bittersweet moment on her wedding day, seconds before she'd said *I do*. A memory had come flooding back uninvited, and it had painted a picture from her past. Just she and Luigi standing on a seaside cliff. He was dressed in a suit and she all in white. A crown of wildflowers adorned her hair. It was long and luscious then, a deep russet brown, offsetting her creamy skin and the darkness of her eyes. While they'd been too young to marry, they'd pledged themselves to each other and had taken secret vows. Though their lives, it seemed, had held other plans.

"Oh, Luigi…*si.* Yes, I did. It's a miracle we found each other."

"Un miracolo." Luigi's eyes twinkled. "But I also thank my great-grandson Paolo."

"The one who connected you to the Internet."

"He's twelve now, did I tell you?"

"No! He had a birthday?"

"Just this week."

"How was the party?"

"Splendid, but…" His face moved closer to the screen. "A little lonely without you."

"Have you told them?" she asked. "About your…communications with America?"

"Oh, yes!" he said heartily. "And they approve! Everyone wants to meet you."

Lucia sighed deeply. "And I them."

"I wish I could meet your family, too."

"You would love my granddaughters. All of them."

His face sagged. "Lucia?" he asked quietly. "Have you thought any more about it? Taken time to consider my proposal?"

"I don't have to consider. You know what my answer would be."

"Then why not say it?"

She felt her eyes mist. "What's the point in pretending?"

"Ah, yes." His words were tender, caressing. "Or in dreaming, either, *no*?"

"Tell me your dreams, Luigi. I want to hear them."

"The beautiful ones? About you and me?"

"Yes," she said softly. "And start at the very beginning."

"With a boy and a girl on the beach?"

She nodded and he laughed warmly. "Okay, *cara mia*, I will indulge you one more time. But I have to warn you about how my story ends."

Lucia held her breath and waited for him to say it. For, each time he did, it was like a symphony to her ears.

"With *happily ever after.*"

Chapter Two

The Plan

The next day the cousins held an emergency meeting to discuss the whole situation. The women met at Angie's house, since she had the largest one. What was supposed to be a living room looked more like a playroom. Toys littered the floor as two toddlers wrestled over a stack of blocks in the corner. Angie's oldest spent her mornings in preschool.

"I don't know how you can possibly Zumba in here," Haley commented.

Angie appeared a tad defensive. Today her sweats were tangerine orange. "I do it during their nap time."

Trish breezed in the door without knocking, her freckled face flushed. "Sorry," she said, out of breath. "It took a few minutes to get away."

They were gathering during an early lunch break, so as not to have any of the men in the way. Emma reined in the puppy, who had nabbed a pacifier off the carpet and was gnawing on it. She glanced around, then stealthily took it from the dog's mouth and wiped it on the side of her jeans.

"Emma!" Claire said, "What are you doing with that paci?"

Emma studied the thing, then plucked off a small yellow hair before setting it on a side table. "Just getting it off the floor."

"You'll have to sterilize that," Jane told Angie.

Angie shrugged. "That was with the first baby."

Rachel checked her watch. "Guys, I don't have much time. I've got six more houses to hit before five o'clock."

"Geez, Rachel," Trish said with a smirk. "Sounds like you're breaking and entering."

Rachel huffed, dark curls bouncing. "You know that I care for the plants."

Susan settled in on the sofa with her knitting. "Isn't that how you met Tom?"

"No, I—"

Bev stared at them with interest.

"I don't think we need to get into any of that now," Zoe added.

"Right." Bev still wore her Parisian neck scarf, only today it was knotted on the left side. She adjusted it slightly, then spoke, taking charge. "We're here to discuss Nona's predicament."

"And to devise a plan," Angie agreed.

"Sounds good." Tiny's gaze rolled toward the kitchen. "But first, do you think we could have something to eat?"

A few minutes later, Angie had brought out a bowl of trail mix made with kids' cereal, chocolate candies, goldfish crackers, pretzels, and raisins.

Jane scooped up a handful and stared at it. "Nice."

"Shut up," Angie said. "It's tasty."

"Mmm," Tiny agreed, digging in for some more. "Thanks, Angie. I was starving."

"Wish I knew how you can do that." Emma stared down at her curvy figure. "I've gained ten pounds since this morning."

"You have not," Claire said kindly.

"You look great!" Rachel affirmed.

"We'd all look great if we took time to work at it," Jane said flatly.

Haley was bending down, tightening the laces on her running shoes. She ran her own bakery in town, but could have doubled as a personal trainer. She looked up to see them all staring at her.

"Nona!" Zoe reminded the group.

"Right," Bev said. "What are we going to do?"

Susan pulled some yarn from her bag. "Help her if we can."

One of the kids in the corner hit the other over the head and Angie went to mediate.

"That would be great!" Emma said above the squalling. "If only we knew how!"

The kids yelped louder and Angie hissed from the corner. "Stop yelling, already. You're scaring them!"

Emma rolled her eyes at the others.

"Well…" Jane spoke firmly, but not in a yell. "As far as I can see, we have two options."

"Like?" Trish pressed.

"We can send her there, or bring Luigi here."

"What are you talking about, Jane?" Susan asked. "Buying plane tickets?"

"Precisely."

"But none of us has the money," Zoe objected.

"How about if we all chip in?" Claire asked.

"Yeah," Haley said. "We're all gainfully employed."

Trish glanced at Rachel. "In a manner of speaking."

Rachel refused to acknowledge Trish and turned toward the group. Everyone knew Rachel secretly wanted to be a writer, but had never gotten up the courage to try. Except for that one time in high school when she'd chronicled her dating exploits in the high school paper. Who knew it was possible to date three boys at once and not have any of them the wiser? Until the article went to print, that was. The episode had earned Rachel the nickname *Runaround Rachel*, and also a reputation as a boyfriend stealer. To add insult to injury, she'd been reprimanded by the principal and grounded by her parents. She'd given up her literary ambitions shortly thereafter. Or so she said. She'd still majored in journalism in college. Not that she'd done anything with it. The only lasting ramification from that early ordeal appeared to be the fact that Trish still hadn't gotten over Rachel nabbing Brett. Okay, so that had left Trish without a date to homecoming. But that was *so* long ago. "How much would that cost?"

Bev pulled out her smartphone. "I'll investigate."

"What if Luigi doesn't want to come here?" Angie asked.

"He may not," Lena said. She fingered the highlights in her hair. "As I recall, the invitation went the other way."

"Well, that's asking a lot," Jane snapped. "It doesn't exactly seem fair. That he wouldn't be willing to make the same sacrifice."

"You weren't listening to Nona," Susan said kindly. "She *wants* to go."

The women studied each other a moment in silence.

After a beat, Bev looked up from her phone. "It's more than I thought." She met their questioning faces. "The tickets. Since the island is off the coast of Sicily, it seems there's no way to get there except by ferry. And you can't fly straight to Sicily from here. You have to go to Rome, and maybe Frankfurt first, via New York or Atlanta."

Zoe sucked in a breath. "Can Nona do all that?"

"Sounds like a lot of connecting," Haley conceded.

"I don't think she could manage it alone," Trish said.

"Then one of us will have to go with her," Bev added hopefully. "As a companion-slash-escort."

"So, now we have to raise money for *two tickets*?" Emma asked. "One for Nona to get there, and another round trip—for one of us to take her and come back?"

The women slowly shook their heads. "Maybe this was a silly idea," Lena said with a frown.

Tiny stopped chewing a moment. "No. It was a good idea. A great one, in fact. We just need to find a way to make it work."

Haley bent forward and rested her elbows on her knees. "How about a fundraiser?"

"What do you mean?" asked Rachel.

Lena's face brightened. "What a cool thought. We'll raise the money!"

Tiny considered this. "Sounds good, but how?"

Angie had gotten the kids occupied with a huge bucket of connecting toys by the window and now returned to join them. "What about crowdfunding?"

"You mean online?" Trish asked. "I know it can be done, but this seems a little personal."

"She's right," Jane said. "We don't want to ask complete strangers for money."

"They wouldn't have to be strangers," Claire said. "We could start with friends."

"By asking them for handouts?" Bev asked. "I don't like that idea."

Emma stroked the snoozing puppy in her lap, then spoke thoughtfully. "It's for a worthy cause."

Zoe nodded. "But Bev and Trish are right. It seems a little... I don't know..."

"Like airing our dirty laundry in public," Susan said, speaking for the first time.

"This isn't dirty!" Lena protested. "It's about love."

Bev adjusted her scarf, flipping its long end back over her shoulder. "Yeah, but how do you think Nona would like it if she knew what we were up to?"

"Maybe she'd be flattered?" Rachel said hopefully.

"And maybe she'd be embarrassed," Trish shot back. "Embarrassed if her financial state got laid bare for the whole world to see."

"She can't help it that she lost her money," Claire defended.

"She didn't lose it," Trish corrected. "She spent it."

"Yeah," Zoe said with a frown. "Most of it on us."

The women hung their heads and sighed. Everyone knew it was true. None of them came from wealthy backgrounds. Their Nona generously had helped put all of them through school. Eleven of them had graduated from colleges and Haley had attended a culinary institute. They wouldn't have made it without their Nona's help and the assistance of student loans. Now

Nona lived on social security in the big house her husband had built them on the hill. Everyone in town still thought of her as a wealthy widow. Only her granddaughters knew the truth. Nona had sworn them to secrecy over not telling their fathers about the contributions she'd given them.

Their dads were hardworking men with big hearts, but a little clueless when it came to the costs of higher education. That was likely because none of Nona's boys had been to college. She'd wanted more for her granddaughters, and had finally been in a financial position to help. When her husband died, he'd left her a tidy sum of cash, a sum that was—at this point—all but gone. If they'd known how greatly their Nona was sacrificing, they would have refused her kindly offers. But Nona had kept her financial particulars to herself until recently. She'd had some complicated tax matter and had asked Trish to straighten it out. Trish had been dismayed by how little of Nona's initial estate was left. She'd lost additional money due to investments she hadn't properly adjusted during the recession.

Susan stared down at the knitting needles in her lap, then slowly looked up. "She wouldn't be embarrassed if we were clever about it."

"What are you talking about, Susan?" Haley wanted to know.

"I mean, what if it looked like we were raising money for something else?" Susan tucked her knitting needles in her bag and gave a sneaky smile. "Something worthy?"

Bev gaped at her in shock. "Are you talking about doing something under false pretenses, Susan?"

"Not false. Veiled."

Zoe stretched her legs out in front of her on the carpet and lunged forward, gripping the soles of her feet with her hands. "Now you've lost me."

"How about…" Susan surprised them all by raising her normally soft voice. "We raise the money for charity: a historic preservation fund?"

Fine lines worried Claire's forehead. "Isn't that kind of cheating?"

Angie grinned. "Not exactly."

Lena set her chin in her hands, highlighted hair swinging forward. "Nona's historic."

"Over eighty," Haley agreed.

"We do want to preserve her," Tiny said.

"She's not like pickles, Tiny!" Rachel cried.

"No," Emma said slowly, "but what she and Luigi have definitely deserves a chance. A chance to…" The puppy squirmed awake, but she snuggled it back to sleep.

"What, Emma?" Zoe asked impatiently.

"Hang on. I'm thinking." Emma's gaze panned to the window where the kids were finally behaving, then back around the room. "How about if Nona writes a book?"

"A *book*?" the others asked with surprise.

"Sure," Susan said, apparently getting it. "Her story."

Bev's eyes lit up. "An immigrant's tale in America!"

"That one's been done," Trish said. "Many times."

"Not by Nona," Tiny said.

Zoe met Emma's eyes. "Are you suggesting that she do research? To recapture the flavor of her early days?"

Emma wore a proud grin. "I am."

"Why, Emma!" Rachel said, "that's geni—"

"Insane," Jane cut in. "Who's going to believe an eighty-something-year-old woman traveling abroad for research?"

"Anyone who knows Nona would believe it," Claire said.

"Which includes everyone in this town," Rachel agreed.

"She's got more spunk than most sixty-year-olds," Emma confirmed.

"But *Nona* write her story?" Bev asked. "You mean actually write it down?"

Zoe tucked her knees up under her arms and grimaced. "It's true. Nona isn't much of a writer. Never has been."

"She's a talker, though," offered Haley.

"That's it!" Angie beamed. "She could record it."

"Someone else could write it down." Susan gave Rachel a pointed look and all heads turned in Rachel's direction.

"Wait a minute. Why's everybody staring at me?"

"You're the writer, Rachel," Jane said.

"You mean, when she's not practicing her green thumb?" Trish asked pointedly.

Rachel blinked and her cheeks tinged pink.

"Let's get back on track," Bev suggested. "It sounds like we're getting somewhere."

"But why does there have to be a story?" Rachel questioned.

"Because," Jane said logically, "this way it all makes sense. Nona is writing her life's tale, and she's going back to her home country to fill in the details."

Susan nodded. "Recapture the essence of her youth, so to speak."

Rachel appeared unconvinced. "Who would read this book?"

"Maybe nobody but us," Angie said. "But that would be okay. Wouldn't it?"

"I'd love to have Nona's story," Claire said. "Her complete story, written down to share with my children some day." Her sisters and cousins nodded their agreement.

Bev wryly twisted her lips. "You might not want to share all of it."

The others laughed, sensing what she was getting at. The boyfriend part. With Nona, you never knew how detailed those descriptions might be.

"I've got to be honest with you," Rachel said. "I don't think we could get something like that published. Like Trish said, that kind of story's been done."

"So?" Tiny asked. "We'll publish it ourselves. Online. There are places we can do that at no cost or very cheap. It wouldn't be a moneymaker anyway. We'd be printing it as a family keepsake."

"That's all well and good," Haley said. "But you brought up a very good point. Moneymaking. We still don't know where the dollars will come from to get our Nona to Sicily."

"That's where the veil comes in," Susan said.

Angie turned to her. "Well, are you going to lift it?"

The women listened with rapt attention as Susan laid out her cunning plan. Just as they all agreed, everyone in town knew Nona had the energy of a person half her age. People wouldn't doubt an octogenarian as spry as Nona would endeavor to take on something as bold as writing her memoirs. The

townsfolk of Chandelier loved Nona for her spunk and
for her spark. She'd been a staple of this community for
as long as anyone remembered, and had given back to
the locals through her tireless efforts with several
charities. She still served at the soup kitchen and ran the
church bazaar, and no one even came close to her
organizational skills at setting up the annual fish-fry
fundraiser for the fire department.

All the girls had to do was approach their Nona
with the idea. Encourage her to write her story and say
they wanted to help her get to Italy to complete it.
Naturally, she wouldn't have to *write*-write it. They'd
arrange for her to record it. Then Rachel would
transcribe her words, neatening things up as needed for
a smooth literary flow. They'd beg her to go through
with it, say they wanted to ensure she left her legacy
behind, so they could share the history of their Nona
with future generations. Nona was bright enough to
know where they were going with this. She might
believe the bit about the biography, but she'd more
deeply understand that her granddaughters were trying
to help. Help her find her way to Sicily—and back to
Luigi.

The beauty of the memoirs cover story was that it
gave Nona an *out,* in case things didn't go as
swimmingly with Luigi as she'd imagined. She could
travel there and see for herself how things went
between them. If they weren't meant to be, Nona would
have a guaranteed return ticket, and wouldn't lose face
before the town. Nobody would have to know she'd
secretly gone to Sicily to reconnect with her long-lost
love. That part would remain between her and her
granddaughters. Including her ghostwriter, Rachel, who

would accompany her on her mission as the logical choice.

The girls would pool their efforts to raise money for Nona's "research trip." And, well, if once she'd returned to her homeland she decided to stay…that would be up to her—just as long as she finished her story. Because now that they'd discussed it, the truth was that they wanted it, each and every one of them, to save as a memento. Their main task was raising the cash. They needed to find a product, something to sell. Something that wouldn't cost too much money to make, but that would be of value to the purchaser. Something useful yet ordinary, the type of household item every family needed. To help keep them organized, all year through. From soccer games to dental appointments, school plays…yes, even the fish fry… If folks needed to know where they had to be and when, first they had to write it down. Record it so they wouldn't forget or overschedule themselves on the same day. What every well-run home needed was…

"A calendar!" Rachel gave a happy gasp. "Susan, that's brilliant!"

"Are you saying we should make one?" Emma asked.

Trish eyed them skeptically. "Who uses paper calendars anymore?"

Zoe's hand shot up, followed by Jane's. Rachel waved her arm in the air and Lena nodded. Angie pointed toward the kitchen. "Got one in there."

"Yeah," Jane said. "Bet it's filled with Zumba dates."

"Hush," Susan told her, before adding, "I keep a paper calendar as well."

Tiny said, "I got one for Christmas last year, but I've never used it."

"Aha! But you got one, didn't you?" Haley asked. She addressed Susan next. "I've got one, too. I mean I've got two of them, one in my apartment and the other at the bakery."

Claire flipped back her flirty tresses. "Of course, I keep a calendar." The others often razzed Claire about her high-maintenance hairstyle. She fired right back with self-effacing humor. "Where do you think I keep my salon appointments?"

Rachel's eyes sparkled. "I think that settles it. Almost everyone owns a paper calendar. Even in this modern age."

"How would we get one printed?" Trish asked.

"I know a place online," Zoe said. Zoe had all sorts of connections on the Internet. She sold her homemade jewelry through an artsy website. "You just upload your photos, and off you go. It's very cheap."

Heads swiveled toward Tiny, who took snapshots for the local paper. She did this as a sideline in addition to her office manager job at a construction company. "You're good with a camera," Zoe said. "Plus, you know how to Photoshop."

Tiny hesitated. "That's when I know what I'm supposed to take pictures of. Like fishermen down at the docks."

"We'll need a more interesting topic than that," Emma said.

"It would be good to make it fun," Rachel inserted.

"And personal," Claire affirmed.

"But not too personal," Bev said.

"That's it!" Angie brought her hands to her mouth with a pleased cry.

"What's it, Angie?" Haley asked her.

Angie stuck out her index finger and pointed to them one by one, working her way around the room as she counted out loud. "Don't you see? There are twelve of us. Twelve! It's almost like it was preordained!"

"Are you suggesting we each take a page?" Zoe wondered.

Emma grimaced. "I don't think I want to be Photoshopped."

"Come on, Emma," Claire cajoled.

"Seriously," Emma said. "I've put on, like, twenty pounds in the past two years."

"Who cares?" Jane admonished. "It's not all about you."

Susan blushed shyly. "I'm not sure I want my face connected to a month either."

Angie set her hands on her hips. "Look, everybody. Either we're all in, or we're not. If we can find some kind of unified theme, then it will all work together."

"A theme?" Tiny asked. "Like holidays or something?"

Jane was decisive but not derisive. "No, not holidays. Something bigger."

"Covered bridges?" Claire piped in.

Rachel smiled but nodded sadly. "There have been lots of calendars showing those."

"Rachel's right," Trish said, finally coming around. "If we're going to do this thing and do it right, we'll have to be different. We'll need something that will grab folks' attention."

Claire clutched her heart, sounding dreamy. "Get them right here."

"More like in the wallet," Trish answered.

A slow, subtle grin spread across Susan's lips. "What about brides?"

The rest of the girls stared at their typically mousy cousin. The only one of them who'd never had a boyfriend, serious or not. "Brides are popular," Susan continued. "Everybody loves brides and stories about them."

The rest of them blinked, flabbergasted. "What are you saying, Susan?" Tiny asked. "That we each should take a spot as a calendar bride?"

"But not all of us are married," Zoe said. "A few..." She avoided Susan and Bev's eyes. "Don't even have prospects."

Haley massaged the back of her neck. "It still could work. We could tell our stories."

Angie stared at her. "What stories?"

"Our love stories," Haley answered. "Say something significant about each of them."

"Those would have to be very short stories to fit onto a calendar," Rachel observed.

"That's what I was thinking," Haley answered. "A hundred and forty characters or less."

Jane's mouth hung open. "You're joking."

Haley clarified. "I wasn't suggesting we fit *everything* in a brief log line. That's only what would go on the calendar page. We could have something more extensive, like a paragraph about each of us, in the back of the calendar."

"But this is a *brides* calendar, as in weddings," Lena said. "What about those who...um...haven't found their princes yet?"

"They can put in what they're looking for," Haley answered. "A *someday my prince will come* kind of thing. Just think of it! What great advertising! Even better than MeetYourMatch.com."

The color drained from Susan's cheeks. "Maybe I should have thought this whole thing out before suggesting it. It was a bad idea."

Rachel's head bobbed with enthusiasm. "No, I think you're onto something."

"Where would we get the wedding gowns?" Jane asked practically. "Not everyone has one."

"I've still got mine, but I'm not sure it fits," Emma said.

Claire had a thought. "Maybe we can get Victor's Bridal Boutique to cooperate? It's for a good cause, and will be great promotion for their gowns if they let us borrow a few for our shoot." Victor was Emma, Claire, and Rachel's uncle on their mom's side. He was very big into supporting family, and weddings. He'd given each of the D'Amato brides deep discounts on their gowns, and would surely be willing to help.

"This is sounding really crazy," Zoe said.

"Yeah," Tiny agreed. "Crazy like it might work."

Trish's complexion glowed beneath her freckles. "We could sell the calendar for twenty bucks. Maybe even have it ready in time for the fish fry. The whole town turns out for that."

"I could set up preorders online," Zoe suggested.

Lena smiled. "That's a great idea."

"Yeah," Trish agreed, her excitement growing. "And Rachel could blog about it!"

A hush fell over the room as everyone waited.

Rachel hesitated, then spoke slowly. "I suppose I could do that. For Nona."

Emma slid the puppy off her lap. It yawned lazily and looked around. "The blog could give more information than just what's in the calendars. It could provide background on Nona, and Sicily…"

"Pique people's interest," Bev agreed.

Susan's face lit up. "Lead to lots of early buys."

Angie fanned her hand across the room and announced dramatically, "The Calendar Brides…"

"I like it," Haley said.

"Me, too," Claire agreed.

"Don't have a guy right now, but I'm in," Bev added.

"Ditto." Tiny stopped reaching for the trail mix bowl and met their gazes. "I mean, I *do* have a guy, but I'll participate."

"Same here," Zoe said.

"You gonna marry him?" Jane asked.

Tiny nearly choked on her goldfish and pretzels.

Zoe flushed. She'd been with her live-in boyfriend Dillon for three years now, but the "M" word had never come up. "We haven't exactly talked about it."

"Mind your own business, Jane!" Susan chided.

"Um, isn't this kind of my business now? Isn't it all of ours?"

Emma was playing with the puppy, who was chasing its own tail. "Sounds good to me." She looked at Jane. "How about you?"

"I thought I already said yes?" The others shook their heads. "Okay, then…" She smiled thinly, but it was evident to the others she was concealing some interest. "Yes."

"I'll do it, too," Haley said. "I still have my dress as well."

"I'm for it," Lena said.

"That just leaves…" Angie looked around the room, her eyes landing on Susan. "The one who started it all."

Susan shrugged, her cheeks burning brightly. "You guys make it pretty hard to say no." Coming from Susan, that was just as good as acceptance.

Just then, the puppy wandered over to the entertainment cabinet and started sniffing around a stack of DVDs on a lower shelf. "Misty, no!" Emma called after it, scrambling onto all fours to collect the dog. She grabbed the chubby animal around its belly and pulled it back, but not quickly enough to prevent the pup from grabbing something in its mouth. Emma shoved her fingers between the baby dog's teeth and pulled out what appeared to be a brand new DVD, still in its original shrink-wrap. "Well, what do you know…?" Emma said, waving the DVD back and forth in the air to dry it, "Beginning Zumba!"

Angie strode over and snatched it away. She primly adjusted her ponytail before addressing the others. "So girls, what do you say? Do we have a deal?"

She stared them down one at a time until they cracked smiles. Her daughters looked over from the corner and grinned, swept up in the celebratory chorus as they all shouted together. *"Deal!"* Then, with a round of high fives, hugs, and happy chatter, they sealed it.

Chapter Three

Emma

Donny peered over Emma's shoulder as she worked at the kitchen table. "'We met in algebra class, but had instant chemistry'?" he mused. "What's that mean?"

Emma dropped the pen she'd been using onto the filled legal pad. It had all sorts of scrawl going everywhere, even sideways racing toward the bottom corners of the page. "I'm trying to work, baby. All right?"

Donny met her doe eyes, the big brown ones he'd first fallen in love with. But it wasn't in algebra class. "I think you're remembering wrong. We met in history."

"Did not."

"Did so."

"It was math."

"Uh-uh."

She turned toward him, resting her elbow on the table. "What makes you so sure?"

He smiled warmly. "Do you really think I'd forget that day? You told me I took your seat."

"Because you did. In *math* class."

"Who was the teacher?" Donny challenged.

"What?"

"The teacher. What was his or her name?"

"How am I supposed to—?"

"Man or woman?"

"It was a man."

"Exactly."

Emma blew out a breath and scooted the legal pad aside. "Exactly what?"

"Our algebra teacher was female. Mrs. Penny. Don't you remember? *Penny for your thoughts?*"

"Oh, yeah!" Emma couldn't help but giggle at the memory. Mrs. Penny had been very uptight. She was also rather tight-lipped. When kids passed her in the hall and said hi, she'd ignore them. After a while, people began to speculate about what kept her mind so occupied she couldn't talk to anyone. Students started whispering one to another, *Penny for your thoughts,* when they passed her by. Emma scrunched up her lips and studied her husband of five years. He hadn't changed much since high school, apart from the way his features had matured and the few extra pounds he'd put on. Then again, Emma had put on a little weight of her own. Didn't help that they both had a penchant for late-night pizza.

"It's good to see you smiling," Donny said. "I was beginning to worry."

"About what?"

He pulled out a kitchen chair and sat at the table beside her. "This," he said, motioning to the yellow pad on the table. "All of that. Your new *project.*"

"It's a good project, Donny. It's about us. Plus, it's for Nona."

"I know, I know." He shifted in his seat. "But I really wish you wouldn't stress about it. It's only a hundred and fifty words."

"Don't forget about the tag line."

"What's that?"

"The thing that goes on my actual calendar page. The teaser."

He reached for her with both hands. "I've got a teaser for ya."

Emma laughed and pushed him away. "Stop that."

"It's after ten o'clock. Even the dog is sound asleep."

"She's a baby. She wears out early."

Donny rubbed his belly and grinned. "I'm an old dog but I can still learn new tricks."

"Donny."

He motioned toward his head. "Just scratch me behind my ear. Or maybe someplace lower."

Emma raised an eyebrow. "What makes you so frisky tonight?"

"I saw that wedding gown of yours hanging from the door of the closet and it reminded me."

"Of?"

"Our honeymoon."

"We didn't take a honeymoon."

"Oh, yes, we did. We're still on it."

Emma sat back in her chair and studied him, this man that she cherished—still, after all this time. It was easy to forget that she'd hated him for a decade. "Just give me five more minutes, okay? I've almost got the tag line down."

Donny shrugged and stood. "You're gonna have to change 'algebra' to 'history'."

Emma snatched up the legal pad to swat his behind. "Better get out of here before *you're* history."

Donny chortled a laugh and stepped back before she could whack him. "Yes, ma'am." He grabbed a beer from the fridge and started to leave, but stopped and turned in the doorway. "How come you go first?"

Emma looked up, her mind already reabsorbed in her work. "Huh?"

"The calendar," he said. "What makes you Miss January?"

Emma was glad to be going before the others. That way she wouldn't have to sit there at Victor's worrying over her turn coming up. Worrying made Emma nauseated. She couldn't stand being in suspense, and especially hated waiting. Even standing in line at the pharmacy caused her to break out in hives. Donny, on the other hand, never worried about anything. Except for maybe selecting pepperonis over anchovies. That's why she left their prescription pickups to him. "I'm the oldest," she explained with a smile.

That's how they'd worked it out. Each of them would go in sequence arranged by birth order. There was no other way to finesse it. They couldn't go by the months in which they'd married, because not all of them were hitched. They'd talked about each woman claiming her birthday month, but there were too many duplications, including—obviously—the twins. Even between Angie and Haley, someone was older. Angie was born first and she rarely let Haley forget it, especially when she wanted to win an argument. "I'm older, so I know better." "Yeah, by about four minutes," Haley would challenge back. Emma sighed, thinking of her cousins. They were all so quirky but lovable just the same. Only Emma and her two sisters, Claire and Rachel, seemed to be the normal ones. Beautiful Claire with the never-ending hair had been born just fourteen months after Emma. Their baby sister, curly-headed Rachel, had come seven years later. God had given them several cousins in the interim. Emma marveled at how they all got along. Everyone was so sweet… Okay, so Jane could get a little snarky at times. So could Trish. But even they meant well, and would move heaven and earth for the others should push come to shove.

Emma heard the TV switch on in the next room and knew Donny was watching a ball game. It was like Donny had some magical power to touch the remote and make sports appear. Even in the dead of winter. Emma swore it was a skill. She recalled the first time she'd seen Donny since graduating high school. He'd been in a sports bar shouting at the screen because his team was losing. Emma had only been there because friends had dragged her along. There was some sort of major soccer match in action. The whole world was in on it, so she should be, too. Bev had been there and insisted on that. Even in those days, she'd worn one of those silly scarves. Not that Emma would ever tell her she looked out of place wearing them in this small fisherman's town. Donny's beer tab popped, and Emma stared at her pad, knowing he was taking a swig from the can. He didn't really drink much, but when he did, he enjoyed it. Just like during that night when they'd seen each other again for the first time in years.

"Hey, your name's Emma, right?"

She stared at him as he glanced down the bar in her direction. There was a couple seated between them. It was hard to recognize him at first, but then she did. His face was thinner now, and his build a bit more athletic, but the sensible brown haircut was the same. Donny Mallory. That obnoxious guy who was always cutting up in the halls in high school. The one who'd stolen her seat in algebra class. She'd always blamed it on him that she'd failed math. Maybe if she'd situated herself closer to the front, she wouldn't have. "I remember you," she said without smiling. "It's Donny, right?"

"Yeah!" he said. "Good to see ya!" His mood had turned jovial. His team was finally winning. At least that's what Bev had told her. Emma had no clue how anyone could watch soccer for more than ten minutes. She'd fixated on it for five and had become extremely bored.

The man sitting beside Donny turned to him. "If you and your friend want to talk we can swap places?"

Nooooo…Emma screamed in her head. The last thing she wanted was to be pinned in a bar between Donny Mallory and sports on television. Oh, the horror!

"Sounds great, Mac," Donny said. "Thanks."

The word "Mac" grated like fingernails on a chalkboard, sending chills down Emma's spine. All that year she'd had to listen to his erudite comments. And each of them began with, "Ah, here's what I think, Mac…" This was his standard reply. To each question anyone asked him. He even said it to the teacher. It's a wonder he didn't fail algebra, too. But he hadn't. He'd graduated with higher marks than hers, then had gone on to take over his dad's auto business. They sold cars or fixed them, Emma couldn't recall which. And frankly, she didn't care. She'd been to college. Yo.

With a capital C. Okay, so it had been the neighboring town's community college, but at least she'd gotten through with her associate's degree. And now, here she was back in Chandelier... working at the dry cleaner. Emma frowned into her mug and Donny noticed.

"Buy you another beer?" he asked, sidling up beside her. He took his place on the stool and she caught a whiff of strong cologne. Why did the wrong guys always go for her? She hadn't liked Donny in high school, and hadn't seen anything at present to change her opinion.

Without waiting on her answer, he flagged the bartender over. "What'll it be?" he asked. "Another one of what you're drinking, or do you want something else?" The truth was she did, but Emma didn't think they served chocolate milkshakes in sports bars.

"I'm okay with this," she answered, wrapping her fingers around her mug.

"Yeah!" The crowd roared and Donny glanced briefly at the television before looking back at her. She appreciated that he acted like the game was interference at this point. In truth, he seemed a whole lot more interested in her than in soccer. Which was strange. Emma surreptitiously peered down at her blouse, trying to remember which one she was wearing. It was the pearl-colored one, the one that shimmered in dim light like it was doing now. When she raised her head Donny was staring at her. "I remember you from high school, but you were never this pretty."

"Uh, thanks."

"What I mean is... Geez, Mac. I'm mucking this all up!" His eyes rolled heavenward then settled on his beer. The bartender had just refreshed it. "What I meant to say was, I always noticed you before. But you look different now, more mature in your beauty." He met her gaze and swallowed hard. "Yeah, that."

"Are you always this good with words?" she asked him.

"Sometimes better!"

They both laughed, something oddly comfortable settling between them.

"So what have you been up to?" he asked her.

"Oh, this and that."

"I heard you were working at the cleaner's."

"Who've you been asking?"

"I haven't." His neck flushed crimson beneath his open collar. "I just heard it around."

"I'm manager now."

"That's great!"

"How about you?"

"I'm not."

"Not what?"

"Not a manager now."

Somehow this tickled Emma and she found herself laughing again. Bev, who was seated on her other side, lifted an eyebrow, but Emma ignored her. Instead, she focused her attention back on Donny. "You're funny, you know that?"

"Funny-looking, you mean?"

She nudged him with her elbow. "Come on."

He grinned. "Where we going?"

"Where do you want to go?"

"How about the Dairy Queen?"

Emma pressed her lips together to keep from squealing with joy. "You're joking," she finally said.

"No, Mac. I'm as serious as a heart attack, one I just might have after what I'm going to order." He settled his gaze on hers. "What are you up for?"

Emma didn't see any harm in revealing the truth. "Chocolate milkshake."

"That can be arranged."

She screwed up her face and scrutinized him. "Who's treating?"

"I'll do the honors." He fumbled a bit with the words. "I mean, if you don't mind. If you'll let me."

He was suddenly adorable, his big round eyes expressing hope. Maybe he *had* changed since high school. Back then, the only thing Donny had treated Emma to was a raging headache. Could be she was setting herself up for another one now. Something else happened on television and the bar roared again. That's when Emma realized she stood a greater chance of getting a migraine in here. "Just this once," she said, hopping down off her stool.

Then, without even peeking to see who was winning the sports contest of the world, Donny extended his elbow and escorted her out of the bar.

"Penny for your thoughts?" Emma felt a warm nuzzle at the back of her neck and realized Donny had kissed her. There was this sweet spot right below her hairline that he knew made her weak in the knees.

She peered over her shoulder, still in a dreamy daze. "Donny."

He wrapped his arms around her shoulders and hugged her against the chair, placing his chin on her shoulder. "Where were you just now? Daydreaming?"

"Remembering." She gave him a soft smile. "Thinking about when we first went out."

"Yeah." He grinned happily. "I took you to Friendly's for a sundae."

"It was to Dairy Queen for a—"

"No, it was to—"

"I distinctly remember."

"Hey…" He lightly jiggled her in his arms and kissed her cheek. "Does it matter?"

Emma felt herself warm from head to toe, and kicked her shoes off under the table. "Not really," she answered with a breathy sigh.

He rounded her chair to kiss her on the lips. "Come on to bed, Mac."

It was incredible that after hating the word for so long, she now found being called Mac endearing. Almost sexy.

"My photo shoot's next Friday."

"I know. That's why I've taken that day off to be right there with you."

Emma's eyes misted. "You didn't!"

"Do you think I'd miss a chance to see you wearing that dress?"

She shot him a sultry look. "I thought you'd be more interested in taking it off?"

"Oh, I will be. Just as soon as your session's over, and after…we've hit Friendly's."

"Dairy Queen."

"Any place you'd like, baby."

Then he took her by the hand and led her to bed, making Emma feel way more important than any sports game on television, even the one still raging in the next room.

~ End of Excerpt *~*

The Calendar Brides

Available at multiple outlets now!